THE PRICE YOU PAY

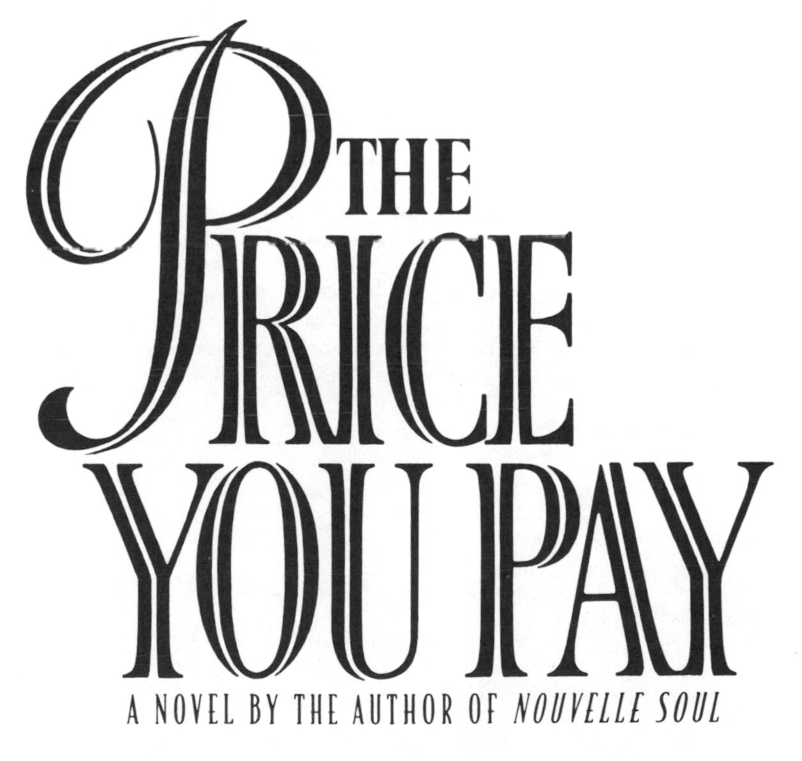

A NOVEL BY THE AUTHOR OF *NOUVELLE SOUL*

NEW YORK, NEW YORK

Amistad Press, Inc.
1271 Avenue of the Americas
New York, NY 10020

Distributed by:
Penguin USA
375 Hudson Street
New York, NY 10014

This is a work of fiction. It is not meant to depict, portray, or represent any particular gender, real persons or group of people. All the names, characters, locations, and incidents are either the product of the author's imagination or are used fictitiously. Any resemblance to actual events, locales, or persons, living or dead, is entirely coincidental.

Book designed by Gilbert Fletcher

1 2 3 4 5 6 7 8 9 10

Manufactured in the United States

First Edition Library of Congress Cataloging-in-Publication Data
Summers, Barbara, 1944-
The price you pay: a novel/by Barbara Summers.
p. cm.
ISBN 1-56743-047-3: $19.95
I. Title.
PS3569.U388P75 1993
813'.54—dc20 93-36960
CIP

For Harry

There's always room,
They say,
At the top.

"To Be Somebody" by
Langston Hughes

CHAPTER ONE

IT WAS THE first shoot of the new year and Max was glad to see things starting off with such a definite bang. One model was pouting at her reflection in the makeup mirror and scowling at everyone else because no one liked her surprising new haircut or color. Another model was holed up in the one and only bathroom for a suspiciously long and inconvenient time. And the model just walking onto the set insisted on flaunting her 36Bs in the face of any and everyone, interested or not. He for one was not.

William Maxwell, makeup artist extraordinaire, known to the world, the fashion world, that is—the only one that really counted in his eyes—as Max, was taking a break. Dressed in his winter uniform of matching cashmere turtleneck and flannel trousers, today in charcoal gray, he leaned his compact body against the doorway between the dressing room and the photographer's studio and carefully wiped loose powder off the makeup brushes that he kept holstered in the tiny canvas apron he wore on every job.

The major part of his work was done. The girls' faces were flawless. Any color changes or touch-ups could be made in minutes. If people needed him on the set or in the dressing room they had only to holler. Until then he was in his quiet observer mode, out of the direct line of fire.

He knew that fashion was famous for drama. That's what he loved.

The beauty wars. The photography shoots. The transformation of girl into goddess. After twenty years in the business, it was still magical to him. He had learned, however, to protect himself. On days like today, Thursday, Thor's day, no telling what sparks might fly. It was best to lie low.

Max liked working in this studio. It was a long, tall, pristine white space, the first floor of a renovated duplex loft. Its owner, Gianni Walker, was an up-and-coming photographer, very much in demand, who managed to combine European savvy with African-American soul. If he kept his professional life as separate from his private life as the two floors of his loft, he'd have a great future ahead of him, Max thought. If.

Humming along to Stevie Wonder's sound track from *Jungle Fever,* Max watched two women from Saks Fifth Avenue, the lingerie buyer and the associate fashion director, confer with the art director from their advertising agency. With obvious and vocal reluctance, they had decided to switch the wardrobe again for the Valentine's Day promo, a glossy full-color insert that would appear in the Sunday papers at the end of January. Tanya Forrester, the model who was supposed to wear the star outfit, had shocked everyone when she showed up minus about a foot of the romantic honey-blond hair catalogs loved her for. Now she sported a drastic, minuscule Dutch-boy cut in neon blond that made her look sexually ambiguous at best and die-hard butch at worst. For a Valentine's Day shoot? How could she do this to them?

They were forced to try the same clothes, a long, lacy gown in celadon silk with its matching peignoir, on Flicka, a dreamy-looking redhead. They had even shot a roll or two on her before admitting what they'd known from the start. The outfit simply didn't work for her. As overendowed as she was in every other department, gorgeous hair, face, shoulders, and legs, she was woefully underendowed with breasts. Nothing but hard little nipples that no amount of stuffing, pinning and reshaping could substitute for the real thing.

Finally, they did what only desperation made them do. They tried the gown on Karine Belfort, the super-hot Black model just in from Paris. She had the soft, feminine look they wanted, and the body. But a lingerie lead with a Black girl? Was Saks ready for that? Were they?

Ready or not, that's what Gianni Walker was preparing to shoot. Max was tickled. Racial progress came in so many unforeseen ways. If the head honchos hated it, they'd have to spend a minor fortune reshooting one picture. But then, even in this recession some might think that a small price to pay to keep their particular image intact.

Tanya, playing the innocent damsel, hadn't understood why everyone was so upset with her. Her hair belonged to her, didn't it? Her body belonged to her, didn't it? She could do whatever she wanted, couldn't she? Besides, her boyfriend Paolo loved it and he felt it was time to change her image. Why not? She didn't want to be stuck in the rut of one safe look, even if it did pay her over a third of a million dollars a year. Money wasn't everything. She definitely wasn't going to be one of those mega-models who worked all day every day and came home to be kissed only by a dog or a cat. She liked her new hair. Paolo liked it. And everyone else would learn to like it, too.

It was the petulant arrogance in her voice that betrayed her, Max thought. If she really believed her lines, why did she need to repeat them so emphatically?

In the dressing room the hairstylist was uncustomarily quiet as he concentrated on repairing some of the damage by curling her blunt bangs and softening the sharp sides. But later when Tanya went out on the set in her first outfit, he told Max that he felt like an undertaker working on a suicide victim. As far as he was concerned, Tanya had committed professional suicide and he was stuck with the job of cleaning her up.

It wasn't the first time Max had seen that happen, girls sabotaging their own success with misguided notions of love and style and their own importance in the business. And it wouldn't be the last time. It was a tough world. You had to be strong and resilient. Above all, models had to know the difference between who they were and what they looked like. Obviously, the smaller the divide between image and reality, the greater the chance for success. But there were plenty of exceptions to that rule. As a matter of fact, one was right over there behind the locked bathroom door. The face of a Botticelli angel and the mouth of a barroom slut.

Max wondered what was keeping Flicka in the john so long. The excessive eighties were over. Didn't we all know that by now? He'd had his fun just like everyone else. But this was 1992. Back to the basics. Of course, for Flicka diet coke, and he didn't mean the soft drink, *was* a basic. She was born to be a big, healthy country girl. She needed special help staying a size six. Most anybody almost six feet tall—and still growing—would. Nevertheless, he couldn't be the only one to notice that she'd been in there for over fifteen minutes.

What was she up to? It wasn't like her to spend time boohooing over a botched shot. And she'd only done one of her four outfits. If she knew what was good for her, she'd get her butt back to the dressing room pronto. Everybody had a job to do. That's why they were there and that's why they were paid the fabulous bucks they got.

"Max," Gianni called from the set. "Dust her off, OK?"

"You make me sound antique," Karine cooed in her ripe French accent as she draped the peignoir off one shoulder.

"We, ah, don't want Victoria's Secret here," the art director said sternly to Gianni but loudly enough for everyone, especially Karine, to hear.

Casual but efficient, Max strode across the polished hardwood floor and stepped out of his Weston loafers onto the white backdrop paper that rolled down from a long ceiling rod and out across the floor almost to the camera on its tripod. He pursed his lips in a half-smile as he whisked just the lightest touch of translucent powder across Karine's forehead and down her nose. "Naughty girl," he whispered. "You're upsetting the boss."

"And who is that, *chéri?*"

"Well, it ain't you, and don't you forget it, darlin'." He turned to the photographer. "How's that look now, Gianni?"

"A little on her collarbone, too. I like it when she gets a little . . . slinky."

Max dipped the brush again into the jar of powder and delicately flicked the excess away. Then he stroked her skin above the gown's décolletage.

"You see? *He* likes me slinky." She emphasized her words with a shake of the luxurious black hair that fell in storm-tossed waves down her back.

"Just remember, there's a time and a place for everything, doll."

Everyone knew that Gianni Walker and Karine Belfort had something going on, but no one knew exactly what it was. And in this business discretion was the better part of success, doubly so when Black folks were involved. At Gianni's signal, Max stepped off the paper and waited until they started shooting again before he returned to his post in the doorway to the dressing room.

Flashes from the strobe lights punctuated the energy flowing through the studio. When he was away too long he missed those lights. His metabolism needed them like a daily tonic, like some kind of visual vitamin. Even during the so-called holidays. True fashion junkies like him were glad to be finished with the season's fake festivities and back to the serious fantasy of work.

To his far left, at the end of the loft nearest the entrance, Max recognized a kindred spirit in Renée, Gianni's studio manager. Behind her gold-rimmed glasses she had more than an eye for talent. Renée had the foresight and the push that had helped launch several photographers into successful careers. While two hopeful models sat on a plain leather bench waiting primly to show her their portfolios, she managed to talk on the phone, sip coffee and retrieve the last of the morning's bagel from her desk, a sleek Italian number that had never known anything less than total clutter.

Max saw that she'd arranged the bouquet of lavender freesias he gave her this morning in the elegant Baccarat vase he'd given her two years ago when she first started working with Gianni. Despite the stacks of papers, black-and-white glossies, color composites, and who knows what else, she would always clear a spot for flowers. He knew that from long experience with her. Max was meticulous about remembering small, sensitive gifts to the decision makers' assistants. It was they who remembered your name when their boss was too stressed. Of course, all the genteel attentiveness in the world wouldn't help if he wasn't good at his job. No one disputed the fact that Max was better than good. He was the best. The only problem was when you were Black you had to be even better than that.

To his far right, at the shooting end of the studio, Karine was working her outfit like the superb professional she had become, leaving the clients breathless with each subtle shift in her pose. A princess, West Indian style, with hazel-green eyes, skin the color of toasted coconut and all that hair. During the past three years he'd watched her grow in the business. She had always done beautiful work in the European magazines. Editorial was great for exposure but now—in ads and catalogs—she was doing wonderful work *and* getting paid. Max was proud of her.

He turned back into the dressing room. The morning's cloudy atmosphere had lifted, shifting into the brighter, relaxed confidence that came from actually getting the job done. Tanya, her hair transformed into soft pixie curls, now sat in a nude body stocking and compared notes with the reluctant hairdresser on the latest spreads in *Vogue* and *Bazaar*. An assistant stylist from the department store was steaming last-minute wrinkles out of the outfit Tanya was to wear next, a black satin teddy trimmed in black lace.

And in a corner alone sat Flicka, at last. Bent over in an awkward angle, she rested the side of her head gingerly on folded arms. Rows of bright bulbs framing the long mirror only highlighted the obvious. The girl definitely wasn't well. Her blue eyes, normally sparkling with mischief, were red-rimmed and tired. A few bedraggled wisps of her naturally flouncy, naturally strawberry-blond hair escaped from the wide plastic rollers that helmeted her head.

"I was worried about you." Max rubbed her shoulder through the terry-cloth robe she wore. "What's the matter, kiddo?"

Only her eyes lifted to meet his. "I been puking my fuckin' guts out. First this lumpy green shit and then this thin yellow stuff and now I'm dry-heaving and still sick as a fuckin' dog. Plus looking like certain death in 3-D." She closed her eyes and let out a pitiful moan.

Max had to agree but he was not going to indulge her. As long as she could cuss she could work. Only when she stopped cussing would he really get worried. "And what tea are you taking for the fever, darlin'?" He raised his eyebrows quizzically.

"Nothing, Max. Honest. I'm not doin' shit. Shit, I wish I was. Plus, I'm dying for a cigarette."

"Well, you know there's no smoking in Gianni's studio. No smoking and certainly nothing else."

THE PRICE YOU PAY 7

"I'm telling you, Max, it's some bug I caught in the islands."

Max's expression dared her to convince him.

"It's true. I was in Martinique and Guadeloupe during the holidays. Christmas, New Year's, remember? Just yesterday? Don't look at me like that. And don't start accusing me again. You and your goddamn racial clichés."

"Did I say anything?"

"Maybe not your lips, but your eyes did. Don't worry. I'll be ready to work when they're ready for me."

Max hoped so. And really, he wasn't worried. He knew that girls like Flicka recovered the instant you placed them in front of a camera. What he knew about models could fill a book. Maybe that's what all this experience was for. When he retired he'd write his memoirs, a true gossipfest. That gave him something tasty to look forward to. The research was already there. Besides two decades' worth of magazine covers and tear sheets, he already had a shelf full of meticulous appointment books and diaries of Polaroids of the major girls he'd worked with all over the world. Maybe he should start keeping written notes now. How would he know when his memory started to fail him? When you suspected it, didn't that already mean it was too late? He'd have to think about that. In the meantime first things first.

"Come on, Miss Texas," he said to Flicka while bracing her shoulders squarely in front of the mirror. "We've got some serious road repair to do here."

Money and beauty. It was never too early for one and already far too late for the other, at least for her, she thought, and smiled to herself. She always did her best thinking early in the day.

Corky Matthews, senior booker and vice-president of MacLean Model Management, tried steaming the morning wrinkles out of her face over her coffee mug, knowing full well they'd still be there in the evening. She listened to the grandfather clock chime eight-fifteen in the empty outer office. The inner sanctum where she sat was almost as empty and even more quiet. She curled a spiral of her Irish red hair around a forefinger as she surveyed her headquarters. It had all changed so dramatically in the last ten years.

Gone were the old oak desks with each booker's paper files on the models they worked with. In their place sat the enormous octagonal computer console occupying the entire middle of the room with its eight keyboards and matching monitors and phones. Seven of them stared dull and gray-faced, waiting for their bookers to arrive and boot them to electronic life. Hers was already alive and kicking.

Corky remembered when she didn't know this vocabulary, let alone how to use these tools. The new technology had terrified her, but the stubbornness of her middle-aged ignorance had frightened her even more. She tried to convince herself that she was too old to learn. She resented being taught by instructors the same age as her own sons. But once she realized that her business was still people, that people did not change although their business could—and did, for the better—she was free of that fear. Fear of failure *and* fear of success. Now the agency was even more successful than ever, always ranked among the top three in New York. Which, of course, meant the States, which, in turn, meant the world.

Mike would be proud of her. God, how she missed that woman. Michelle MacLean, one of the great fashion models of the sixties, one of the few smart enough to see the writing on the wall expand from *I* to *Inc.,* and to read the big, big dollar signs that flashed at The End. So many changes in the business and only the dinosaurs and die-hards left to appreciate them. Corky counted herself, with pride, among their dwindling number.

The windows on the far wall looked out onto the brick and glass slabs of midtown New York. The spire of the Empire State Building was as comfortable to look at as the face of an old friend. But it, too, had changed. Or rather the world around it. She remembered when it used to be the tallest building in the world. Now others, brutally simple and massive, competed for the title.

In a closer view, she watched pigeons strutting along the edge of the agency's roof garden, its bony trees bare of everything but hope. The tiny white lights that had been hung during the Christmas festivities were gone with the old year. Settling into the new one always took some time. It was only Friday, January 3, 1992, her calendar read. No need to kick herself if her feet weren't on solid ground yet.

The coffee in her hands was fresh and friendly. From the walls, framed photos of cover girls smiled down on her in all their airbrushed perfection. This was family, this was home. Corky loved this silent time right before the phones awoke and started their rabid all-day ringing. But she could not help feeling that the daily thrill was wearing thin. How much longer would she be doing this? After thirty years she was still rousing gorgeous girls out of their beauty sleep. Why? She had lost plenty of her own and could never get it back.

Just this morning her husband complained that she was married more to her job than to him. He should talk. A cop? But that was just one of life's little trade-offs. When all was said and done she loved her work. And him. Recalling how she had proved it brought another kind of smile to her face.

The last four names glowing green on her screen snapped her back to the job at hand. It was only eight-twenty but time was money, especially in the beauty business. Corky had to make sure the girls got to work on time. Someone did. Other bookers would be coming in but she was here now, early as usual, and this is what she was here for. To check the daily job assignments, the interview and audition schedules, any last-minute changes for location shoots and weather permits: the everyday details of model bookings. It was also her job to strategize the long-term careers of girls who were made to make it big. There were contracts, endorsements and special exclusives coming up for review. But right now she had calls to make.

Before she could pick up, her phone rang. The simultaneity surprised her, but not really. Somebody lost or sick or panicking, probably. Now her day had truly begun.

"Happy New Year, Corky." It was the unmistakable, well-bred voice of Vanessa Seymour, co-owner and vice-president of Smith & Seymour, one of the hottest advertising agencies in town. It didn't surprise Corky that she was also on the job so early.

"The same to you, Vanessa. How are you?" Corky tried to sweeten her tone, although she was not a big fan of chitchat and she knew that Vanessa, the original Ice Queen, wasn't either. "Did you enjoy the holidays?"

"No broken bones, thank God, but I'm through with Aspen. It's too crowded now, too many people. Just terrible." Exasperation was a chronic condition with Vanessa. "I've got some good news for you, though."

"What's that?"

"We're down to a very short list of callbacks for the Cleo contract. You've got two girls we want to see again."

"Fabulous! Tell me who." Corky's enthusiasm was genuine.

"Nadja and Karine."

"Great! When do you want to see them?"

"Today."

"Well, I have to check their schedules. I don't even know if they're in town."

"I said today, Corky."

"I said I'd see, Vanessa."

"Very well, I expect to hear from you shortly."

"Righto," Corky answered with forced cheeriness. She'd track these girls down to the ends of the earth if she had to. And Vanessa had made it clear that she had to. It would certainly be worth it. Two and a half million to the model. With combined commissions, a half million to the agency. Not bad, not bad at all.

Corky checked their charts on her computer. Tough luck, Nadja would not be back from a location shoot in Captiva until Monday. If Smith & Seymour still wanted to see her again, great. Good, Karine was in town, but booked all day today for *Cosmo,* nine to five. No problem. She'd call her on the job first thing. Karine was a dedicated go-getter. She'd know how to make time to run by S & S at some point.

This was getting exciting. Either one of them would make a fabulous Cleo girl. Nadja was a great model, from Ethiopia, cool and elegant, with a natural, unflappable dignity. And Karine, well, she was a special case. Cured me once and for all of calling the girls pooch. Told me if I was saying she was a dog, I ought to just call her a bitch. Ouch. But still, a fabulous model. Corky laughed out loud envisioning the potential fireworks on the set between Karine Belfort and Vanessa Seymour. Those two deserved each other. In this business, though, in a karmic kind of way, they all did.

It wasn't until Corky finished with the wake-up calls that she realized neither she nor Vanessa had mentioned a word about Laura Grosvenor, the last Cleo girl. Well, girl-to-be. It was just after Thanksgiving that the big announcement had been made: the first Black model to join the roster of famous faces who had been Cleo girls. A week before the contract was to be signed, Laura was found dead of a drug overdose. Corky did not know her personally. She was an Elite girl. But she had heard rumors that the child was wild. No matter now. The tragedy sent shock waves throughout the industry. Now the search was on again, its spotlight shining closer to home.

Max could tell, as soon as Karine walked into Angelo Vassallo's studio Friday morning, that something was wrong. She was simply not the same girl who'd seduced Saks Fifth Avenue the day before with such irresistible authority. Today she looked tired or nervous or something he couldn't quite put his finger on. As Karine unloaded her Vuitton backpack and her black motorcycle jacket on the chaise longue in the spacious dressing room, Max caught her reflection in the mirror. She seemed wary, dislocated in precisely the kind of environment in which she usually thrived.

He watched her perk up to greet Angelo and the *Cosmo* editors. This shoot could be very important for her career, and she knew it. Whatever the matter was, she'd have to snap out of it doubly quick. *Cosmo* liked sultry and sexy. No pouting princess for them. And, despite the syrupy text of the magazine itself, their fashion and beauty editors were notoriously unsympathetic to the personal problems of the models they hired. Working with them was like milking the toughest titties in town.

Max waited until the hellos and air kisses subsided and everyone cleared out of the dressing room for coffee before approaching her.

"I can tell that something's on your mind," he started off seriously. "But if it's another man, I don't want to know any of the details."

"Don't worry, Max." A wan smile passed quickly over her face. "You know you're the only man in my life."

"So what's the matter? You look like you didn't sleep a wink last night."

"I didn't. Do I look that bad?" She leaned closer to the mirror, dabbing at the lines around her eyes. "Terrible," she answered herself. "The phone, it rings all night and then nobody says a word."

While Max kept his expression as neutral as possible, an unnameable fear crept up his neck. It wasn't the first time he'd heard this story. In the last few weeks several Black models he worked with had complained about the same thing. Silent phone calls at weird hours. Empty clicks on their answering machines. One girl had even shown him a note she'd received saying, "Black is *not* beautiful. Out of my magazines, bitch." Something strange was going on.

"Another thing bizarre," Karine continued, hesitating over words and feelings. "Like someone follows me. Watches me without me knowing."

"A fan, maybe?"

"A *fanatique,*" she insisted. And somehow the French sounded even more ominous.

When Max asked her if it had ever happened before, Karine shrugged her shoulders. "A few times. Last week, I thought maybe a bad connection from Haiti, you know. But it was not my family. I don't know. I tell my agent. She says not to worry. This is New York. I tell my girlfriend Nadja. She says not to worry. It happens to her, too. What do I do, Max?"

Before Max could answer, Angelo's secretary buzzed the intercom with a call for Karine.

While she was talking on the dressing room's extension, Max wondered how much he could or should tell Karine about the other girls. There was no question, however, as to *when* he would tell her. Between now and later, later was the only choice.

Preparations for the day's shoot began in earnest. Garment bags were hung up, unzipped, and emptied of today's wardrobe. Accessories were laid out in neat colorful piles on a table of their own. The clothes steamer stood like a vertical vacuum ready to dispatch unsightly wrinkles. People strolled in and out, chatting, questioning, lifting up scarves, trying on earrings. The hairdresser arranged his hot rollers and curling irons at one end of the counter while Max set about arranging the tools of his trade. He pulled open the shelves and drawers of the boxy black leather kit and selected eye, cheek and lip colors for Karine. She was the only model this morning. A second girl would come in at noon. Until then he'd get a chance to play around with a few different looks on her. Max knew he'd have Angelo on his side no matter what the *Cosmo* cubs had to say.

Angelo Vassallo was the maestro of lighting, able to sculpt faces and bodies like no one else in the business. His success afforded him a lavish lifestyle which included this town house on the Upper East Side, where he worked and lived, as well as access to society women who did not hesitate to use their immense wealth to compensate for their plain looks. He'd shot all the *Cosmo* covers for the last fifteen years, and their inside beauty spreads for even longer. None of the editors on staff, let alone in the studio today, had been with the magazine that long, except for the editor in chief herself, a perfectionist well into her seventh decade and third face-lift. She trusted Angelo completely. Angelo had told Max in confidence that if all went well today, they'd do a cover try on Karine. A cover try was the first step toward the cover itself. Karine needed to understand what was at stake. She couldn't afford to let anything deter her from a perfect shoot today.

When Karine hung up the phone, Max's fears dissolved. She wore a dazzling smile.

"Good news?" he asked, amazed at the sudden transformation.

"Fantastic! My third callback for Cleo. Corky says three is good luck."

"Brava, honey." Max applauded as Karine bowed playfully around the room. "Brava, girlfriend."

The *Cosmo* folks made a low-watt effort to be enthusiastic. But Cleo was only a distant possibility, whereas they had a definite job to do today. Max refused to let their attitude spoil her excitement. After he sat her down in an armchair in front of the mirror, he sprayed her face with Evian as he normally did before any makeup job. But then he started acting up again.

"This girl is too hot, y'all," he announced gaily to the other people in the room. "Look, steam's just rising off her face." He touched her cheek with his finger and shook it rapidly. "Ooo, just burning up! Angelo, we need some music in here. We got to start this day off right. Where is my Patti LaBelle?"

Max took his attitude out of the dressing room and into the state-of-the-art studio where he passed the news along to Angelo, who said calmly, coolly, of course, they'd do the cover try today, and then, depending, maybe the actual cover next week.

Wouldn't it be just like *Cosmo,* Max thought as he checked the CD rack, to scoop the biggest cosmetic contract of the year with the new Cleo girl on their cover. Hold on, boy, chickens ain't all hatched yet. Still, it would be simply too ironic. Every three or four years, *Cosmo*'s conscience or some minuscule vestige of such got excited to the point that they'd try a Black girl and maybe even use her on the cover. Years would pass without a Black face, even though the sisters were tearing up the runways and starring in all the other rags. Max didn't know if *Cosmo* was scared or prejudiced or some outdated combination of the two. He didn't even know who made the final decisions, although he was sure Angelo figured in there somewhere. As much as Max liked him, he would never say anything to him about all that. It wasn't his place to tell the maestro what Max was certain he already knew.

Finally, he found Patti's latest and slipped it onto the carousel. "Burnin' " was the title, sizzling was the beat. And if it was left up to him, he intended to keep the whole day moving that way.

CHAPTER TWO

THOMAS N. Thompson knew from the soft gold light slanting across his massive desk and the hands on his heavy gold Rolex that time was running short. If he hurried Tina out of here he could still miss the stubborn part of Friday evening traffic and take off on schedule for St. Martin. Then he remembered that he didn't have to hurry anymore. With his own Gulfstream IV jet, his recent Christmas present to himself, waiting near La Guardia Airport, he had all the time he needed to deal with this ball of fire blazing in his office.

Tina could not continue to talk to him this way. She had inherited determination from both her mother and himself, but the butterscotch beauty that he saw before him with the sleek French twist and sparks in her eyes was her own unique creation.

"My own father," she fumed. "How could you humiliate me like that in front of the entire executive staff?"

And how dare she raise her voice to him like that. He swung his chair around to the window, answering her with a defiantly silent back. Thomas N. Thompson had to show these young whippersnappers just who was boss around here. He was still the chairman of Aura even if his daughter did wear the titles of president and CEO. She wore clothes by Chanel and Saint Laurent, too, but those could come off just as easily as they went on. She needed to be reminded occasionally that all these fancy labels cost money. She was president only because he made her that, educated her, prepped and primed her for the position. At thirty-five, of course, she was to think for herself, but not to the point where she out and out disagreed with him. Who was she? A mere child. He was the one who had built a cosmetics empire *for* Black people *by* Black people. He was the one who had started out with less than nothing, the seventh child and only son of Mississippi sharecroppers, and risen to own one of the largest Black companies in these United States. And here she had the nerve to be telling him about modernizing, getting in tune with the times, spending money to make money. Where had she learned to think like that?

Slowly he turned his chair around and removed his tortoise-framed bifocals.

"Nobody can be right but you, is that it?" Her rage continued at full blast. "All I asked you to do was consider my plans. And what did you do? Shot both of them down without even reading the materials." She held up two black binders, one in each hand. "The Aura Woman and Aura Arts. The most dramatic advertising campaign for Black cosmetics ever seen. And the most innovative film production company ever developed. Our keys to the twenty-first century blown to bits."

Heavy gold bracelets clanked on her wrists like a warrior's armor as she slapped the folders down on his desk.

"All you want to do is spend money, Tina. You've never had to make it. Besides, we're not in the movie business. Unless you've forgotten, we make cosmetics."

Her head swung slowly, from disagreement to disbelief, before she answered in her lowest, calmest voice.

"*I* know what business we're in. And you know that *I'm* the one responsible for doubling our earnings in the last four years. Please, don't insult me any further."

"You're taking it all wrong. You're making a personal issue out of it. The truth is your figures don't hold up."

She knew this was untrue. She had spent the past month—the worst of the year with all the holiday interruptions—crunching numbers with her financial specialist to show her father, and any other doubting Thomas, that her projects could work. It was all there in the two black folders. Now was the perfect time to expand their advertising outside the Black community, to contract one fabulous model and start competing in mainstream media. Over the last forty years Aura cosmetics had gained the name recognition and brand loyalty of millions of women of color in the United States. Marketing reports proved that once they tried the products, nine out of ten women used them again.

"The perfect reason for not throwing good money after bad ideas."

That was Thomas Thompson's standard retort. In the past she'd always been able to find some way to appreciate her father's obstinacy. She understood that he had needed to be hard, even ruthless, in the old days. Back then, Black people bought Black products because they had no choice. Then, when White companies came out with something close enough and good enough, Black people switched and bought what the White folks sold. But now they were tired of supporting brands that did not support them, that did not reflect their identity unless it was in a token role. Dollars were tight. Everybody had smartened up.

Maybe not everybody. The way Thomas Thompson sat at his desk today, fingers tightly and almost piously entwined, Tina wondered if her father had gradually merged with the impenetrable oak or if he had grown out of it.

"Tina," he continued soothingly, now stroking the edge of his thick gray mustache, "if they're coming back, why should we spend a million dollars to get them to do what they're already doing?"

"Because we've got to make sure that they keep coming back to *us*. Everybody from Maybelline to Avon to Revlon to Prescriptives is coming out with a branch of Black cosmetics. Even Cleo, *without* a Black line, is contracting a Black model when they don't have to. Two point five mil to the model alone. Besides, enlarging our campaign shows respect for our customers. For our people. It shows that we're not just a little family company that happened to corner a market nobody wanted. I can see it so clearly. The Aura Woman, a radiant Black beauty on the page of every major magazine and newspaper in this country, in the world. And she'd be just as gorgeous in a full-page ad in *Vogue* as anyone Estée Lauder or Ultima or Lancôme can put up there."

"What are we doing, Tina?" His voice oozed sarcastic concern.

"Overworking you? Have you completely lost your mind? *Vogue* magazine and all those other rags didn't begin to use Black women until the revolutionaries stuck them up against the wall with an Afro. Don't talk to me about spending one red cent advertising in *Vogue* or anything that smells like it."

"That was a long time ago."

"Not that long."

"Times have changed."

"Not that much."

"It's time to move center stage."

"Backstage is where the deal goes down. That's where we stay. And as long as I'm alive, that's where we operate." His fist pounded the desk with these final words.

"Just listen to yourself. As long as you're alive. What's that supposed to mean? You're the only parent I have left and I'd like to think you'd be around for a long time to come. But there're things we need to do as a company, as an institution . . ."

"And throwing away money isn't one of them."

"Especially on private planes."

"How dare you! I'm a seventy-year-old Black man in White America. I have defied every statistic they wrote for people like me. I deserve any damn luxury I can pay for."

"That Aura customers have paid for," she countered. "And don't think I begrudge you that. As a matter of fact, I'm proud of you for thinking on a grand scale. Just don't disrespect the rest of us for trying to do the same thing."

"You're playing with fire, Tina. You don't know what you're talking about. I'm telling you once and for all, get that *Vogue* mess *and* that Hollywood garbage out of your mind."

She refused to let him dismiss her like that. When she leaned onto his desk and steadied her trembling hands against the unforgiving wood, she surprised herself. She'd forgotten that her nails were so dangerously red.

"Dad—excuse me—Mr. Thompson, I'm letting you know that there are things I intend to do. Big things. I want your OK for the ad campaign and for the arts program, but I don't need it. Some things I'm going to do anyway."

"Over my dead body." Their eyes locked in a cold challenge.

"That'll work. That'll work just fine." Tina grabbed the folders off her father's desk and, battle-ready, strode out of his office, leaving behind her just a trace of Aurora. The fragrance had been a huge success since she launched it—without his support, he remembered—less than eighteen months ago.

CHAPTER THREE

IN SANTA Monica Nicky Knight sipped from a tall glass of iced tea as she waited in Michael's restaurant for her mother to join her for lunch. She didn't know where she inherited this compulsion to be on time. Both of her parents were chronically late. She had spent her childhood rubbing the sleep from her eyes as she watched her mother rush out early in the morning to some acting job or hurry off late at night to some party. Now that Becky was directing, the roles might have changed but the pace was still the same. Her father's was the reverse of a similar story. Kayo was used to hanging out with the musicians he produced until night went to sleep and day woke up. And then, maybe, he might just come home.

Nicky checked the Ebel watch they had given her for Christmas. If she had known Becky would be this late, she would have taken her time and done more window shopping. It was so warm and lovely outside. She pitied the poor folks freezing back home in New York City. It was strange that she considered New York home now. All her life, California, and especially Santa Monica, had been home, a kind of heaven on earth. It perplexed her to find the hell of New York so much more intriguing.

Strolling through the Third Street Promenade for the past hours, she sensed how she and it had grown up in the last few months. Her first semester at NYU had been challenging. Difficult classes, new friends, tough city. But she'd come back to California for Christmas vacation with a new way of seeing things. And she was pleased by what she saw. More book shops and yogurt bars, more sidewalk cafés and movie theaters, and above all more people and more life. It was curious how banning cars on these few little streets brought so much liveliness to the neighborhood. Even the homeless people looked like props, reminders of real life somewhere else. And it was corny but also kind of fun to have the promenade guarded at both ends by ivy-covered dinosaurs spouting water through their metal jaws. Dinosaurs might be extinct but Santa Monica was thriving.

Thriving. Probably not the best word to describe her parents' marriage, though. During the ten days she'd been back, she had seen her father only twice. She had seen her parents together, in fact, only once, and that was at the beach house on Christmas Day when they seemed intent on re-creating their own little family pageant of togetherness for her. On New Year's Eve they'd gone their separate ways again. And for New Year's Day they were all supposed to rendezvous at an open house in Malibu. But, typically, they had missed each other. Nicky was confused. It certainly wasn't a new situation, but she was seeing it differently, feeling pangs of disappointment, frustration and loneliness that she had never admitted to herself before. She couldn't handle it. But then again, why should she? It was their life. She had hers to live. And for that she couldn't wait to get out of here and back home. Back to New York City.

Becky Knight breezed into the restaurant gushing apologies to Nicky as she deposited her heavy Prada tote bag and pocketbook in an empty chair next to their table. Nicky loved looking at her, her figure still graceful and elegant. She was proud that people turned their heads and stared at the beautiful, energetic woman who was her mother. Becky's coral silk pantsuit rustled and the soft hair of her pageboy swished against Nicky's cheek as she leaned over to kiss her. Swathed again in her mother's signature L'Air du Temps perfume, Nicky could not resist forgiving her for being over a half hour late. After they had ordered and laughed over Becky's update on the hilarious casting session she'd attended this morning, Nicky felt she'd finally found her opening.

"Did you call MacLean yet, Mom?" Nicky waited while Becky

sipped her Chardonnay. Behind dark glasses, her mother's eyes were avoiding her. "Did you call Corky at MacLean like you said you were going to do?"

"I've been thinking about it, darling, and it just doesn't seem like a good idea yet."

It came as no surprise to Nicky that Becky would say that. They had been arguing about Nicky's dream for months, before she'd even left for New York. Becky did not want her daughter to be a model, to be what she had been over twenty years ago. It was a hard and lonely life. She had tried to explain that to Nicky many times. Fun and glamorous, yes, but deceptive, like quicksand.

Nicky remained adamant. "I don't get it, Mom, you promised. In September you and Daddy both said what you wanted: put in that first semester at school, live in the dorm, and get good grades. You said that if I came through, then you'd help me get started on what *I* want. I did what you asked and now you're reneging on your part of the bargain. That's just not fair."

"You're only eighteen, Nicky. You have your whole life to . . ."

"Now is the time, Mom, right now. You know I'm leaving tomorrow. I have two full weeks before classes start up again. Two weeks I can use to make the rounds and start learning this business."

"But don't you see? I don't want you to learn." The vehemence in her own voice startled Becky. It took her a moment to recover her composure. "Don't you see, sweetheart? I don't want you to learn how mean people can be when they're competing for so few jobs. How vicious women can be to each other. How women and men will try to manipulate you and use you. I don't want you to learn how brainless you have to appear to be, how docile and agreeable even when people disrespect you. No one forces you in the obvious, obnoxious ways. Nasty old men aren't going to get you drunk and seduce you with their hairy hands. The men will be handsome and charming and genuinely, sincerely interested in you. And trashy White people aren't going to insult you to your face. But there'll always be something or someone who'll try to make you feel less than who you are, who'll try to cut you down to make you fit their low expectations of you. You're a beautiful Black woman in a violent world.

Don't make yourself more of a target than you are already. Please, sweetheart."

As much to reassure Nicky of her concern as to calm herself, Becky Knight covered her daughter's hand with her own. They had the same shape, long tapered fingers with large oval nails. The fruit never fell far from the tree. Becky looked closely at her and liked what she saw. A self-confident and determined young woman, tall, thin, coltish with her hair dangling in a shaggy ponytail, maybe even a little gangly, but ambitious and resolute.

Woman-to-woman she admired what she saw, but mother-to-daughter she ached for the heartbreak ahead. The beauty of her features, no longer a promise but a manifesto. The way she wore her body, between bud and full bloom, so . . . carelessly. Had Nicky heard a word of what she'd just said? Couldn't she protect her from the pain and the tears just a little while longer?

The two women retreated to the relative safety of the delicately arranged plates set before them. But neither had much appetite. Nicky scribbled around in her smoked chicken salad and Becky found her grilled tuna unusually dry and tasteless. They sat in an awkward silence, aware as never before that growing up meant leaving.

"Mom, just tell me. Was it worth it?" The question came quietly, slowly.

"If you kept your head on your shoulders and your money in the bank, maybe."

"I meant, for you, personally."

Nicky's dark amber eyes, round and wide-set, were still so trusting, Becky thought. She knew the question had been for her. Personally. It reminded her that only very young people considered life in such simple terms.

"Yes," she admitted reluctantly.

Before Becky could add "but," Nicky said, "Good. Then you understand how I feel. This is something I have to do, Mom. I have to find out for myself. Now, let's see, if it's two-fifteen here, that means it's five-fifteen in New York. You could still reach Corky at the agency."

"Don't pressure me like that, young lady."

"OK, OK, OK. But it really doesn't matter. I know that MacLean has open house every Monday morning. You can believe that I'll be the first one in line next Monday."

"You're actually going ahead with this?"

"I have to. And don't look at me like that, Mom. I'm not a child. I can take care of myself. You did."

"Times were so different. The stakes weren't so high. The competition wasn't so fierce."

"But I know there's a place for me. I can feel it. I want to show you that I can handle it. Why don't you come see me on my turf? Daddy always does. Why don't you come with him next time?"

Becky did not foresee that the door she had dreaded would open this way. But once it did, she gathered her courage and went through it. "I've got something else to talk over with you, Nicky, and I really don't know how to begin."

Nicky looked more closely at her mother now. Even through the dark glasses her eyes looked sad and tired. Suddenly Nicky felt selfish. Her mother's concern wasn't focused only on her. Something else was wrong.

As Becky cleared her throat, she twisted the gold and diamond rings on her left hand. "I've been talking with a lawyer. About a divorce."

"A divorce?" Nicky felt that kind of catastrophe happened to other people, not to them.

"Listen to me, please. Your father is a wonderful person, an adorable man, really, but things have been very difficult between us for a long while."

"What do you mean?"

"Well, you know, he's a very, shall we say, popular fellow."

"You mean, he has a girlfriend?"

"Maybe one, maybe several, I don't really know. And I guess I wouldn't mind if I felt he still cared about me. Really cared."

"He does, Mom. I know it."

"But *I* don't. No, the truth is I rarely see him and we never talk. He's always kept a place in Hollywood, up in the Hills, but now he basically lives there. And I understand it all. But I'm tired of understanding it all,

all the time. It's not like I had no idea when we first got together. I am Wife Number 3. You know about that ancient history."

"Sure . . . I just didn't know you were so unhappy."

"Well, good, because I didn't want you to know. I wanted you to get started in your own life before I started making changes in mine."

"But can't you figure something out? You don't just throw twenty years away."

"No, you don't. I never wanted this to happen to our family, believe me. You can't imagine how embarrassed I am to tell you this. How much it hurts. How much I've wanted to hurt Kayo. I was holding on to that for a long time. But I don't want that motivating me. I've got to salvage something of my own life before I'm completely over the hill. Forty-eight may be late, but it's not too late, is it?" Her lips quivered as she tried to smile.

They ordered cappuccino and sat quietly stirring the milky froth into the coffee underneath.

"I know it's hard to take, Nicky. But even if your father and I are not together I want you to know that we both love you."

"That just doesn't seem good enough, Mom. Why can't you just stick with him, stick it out?"

"Because I'm sick of having to smile when I don't feel like it. Having to swallow the insults and the loneliness and the humiliation and wipe it all away with a smile. I've been doing it for years, hoping that something would change, that my love would be enough to make him change. It didn't. And I finally saw that the only one I could change was me."

"So what are you going to do?"

"Well, believe it or not, I have a job offer and I might be coming back to New York."

"To do what?"

"We're just talking and it's all very confidential but Tina Thompson—you know, from Aura cosmetics—asked me to head up an arts organization she's trying to establish."

"What kind of arts organization?"

"A production company. She wants to expand the business into entertainment and make movies."

"Go 'head, Mom. That's a lot to think about."

"Well, Aura does nothing but print money. And I am qualified. So we shall see."

"We shall see," Nicky repeated uncertainly. No matter what happened, though, she knew she needed to keep her focus, keep her goal shining bright. "Oh boy, I don't know . . . What a load all at once. Let's get back to the house now, OK? I've got a lot to think about before I leave tomorrow."

"I hate to see you go, sweetheart."

"Mom, please, we're not going to go into that again." She shook her head and tried to lighten things up with a halfhearted smile. "Funny, huh? Here I finally manage to escape three thousand miles away from the perfect family and now my folks are splitting up and my mother's moving in with me."

"Things could be much worse."

"How?"

"We could be poor."

Satisfied, Max wiped the midnight-blue mascara off the lashes of his left eye. Without a doubt, he preferred the blue to the midnight purple on the right. It worked better against his rich espresso skin. Just sampling the latest on a quiet Sunday night. You'd have to get up really close to tell the difference. Not that he let many people do that, get close up and personal with him.

He stretched the magnifying mirror on its accordion bracket for a closer inspection. He wore his forty-two years well. The combination of his devilishly arched brows, direct eyes, and thin notched lips promised an easy wit and often delivered, he knew, an acid overdose. The people who didn't understand him called him mean and snobbish and rarely, working with him only at a client's or supermodel's insistence. Those who did understand him called him frank and refreshing and often. Very often.

"Somebody loves you," he sang along with Patti LaBelle. "It's me." His voice cracked on the high note while Patti's soared. But he didn't care. At least he wasn't one of those lazy lip-syncing wannabes.

Tilting his chin toward the light, he could see tiny white hairs in the stubble. He was hardly ready for that. Daily shaving had taken its toll on his skin as it did on most Black men, but he was careful to compensate. He took the same advice he gave. Quality skin care products and a healthful diet. About that he was as conscientious as the models he knew. Low fat, salt, and sugar. Plenty of water, fruits, and vegetables. And love.

That was a little more difficult to arrange than a diet, maybe, but Max was a resolute optimist. Love was at the top of the list of his New Year's resolutions. But where was love in his life? 1992 was already five days old and no special someone in sight as yet. His best friend, Elmo, had been right. Klaus hadn't lasted more than a few golden months before he went back to Switzerland. He couldn't blame Elmo for feeling angry and almost jilted. It still didn't give him the right to call Max a tired old queen who wouldn't appreciate the value of true friendship until it was too late.

Was it already too late? He didn't want to be one of those *folles* who lurked in strategically lit venues with a face laminated in rouge and powder and midnight-blue mascara. Well, a little black was OK. And a drop of liquid foundation was good . . . for everyone. It's not as if he wore lipstick like some people he could name who consulted him on their image and then went ahead and did whatever tackiness they wanted to do anyway. For himself he liked a fresh and natural look, manly and robust. He'd leave the girlie stuff to the real girls.

Speaking of which he'd have plenty to deal with tomorrow. *Cosmo* had decided to use Karine on the cover and they'd be shooting at Angelo's studio again. It was bound to be a challenge. He'd be prepared. Wasn't he always?

He needed to finish oiling off this mascara. Were those lines on his forehead a passing expression or the start of more permanent wrinkles? Careful, careful. We're talking serenity here. No eleven o'clock news tonight. No telling what next tragedy he'd have to hear about, absorb, and still be helpless to change. Twenty minutes on the NordicTrack and he'd be ready to hit the sack. What a chore. But he was not tall, and men who were not tall had fewer places to camouflage any excess. Thank God and good genes he didn't have to worry yet.

He wasn't like Angelo Vassallo, who'd sprouted a little mushroom of a belly in the past year. Maybe that was part of the dues you paid to have a long-term relationship. All that home cooking and staying in and conjugal bliss. Max would have to say something about it soon. He'd also have to mention that pearly pink blush that Angelo had worn New Year's Eve. Of all people, the beauty maestro should have known better. Max would be discreet about it.

The phone rang just as he was finishing the last swipe of midnight purple. It was his mother in what had become an annual plea. He didn't mind when she called him sweetheart and honey. Not even son, which made him feel two feet tall, or baby, which made him feel naked and somehow still nursing. It was when she called him Willie that his teeth began to ache. That brought on total lockjaw. She knew it and he knew she knew it. But it was only tonight that Max figured out she did it because she really wanted him to refuse what she was asking for.

"But, Willie, Reverend Gerard keeps saying there're so few positive images for young Black men these days. And Black History Month is the perfect time to come home to Cleveland and talk to them, expose them to some other careers they know so little about. I told him you'd call him . . ."

"Mama, why did you do that?"

"Well, I just thought . . ."

"Mama, please. You're overstepping the limit."

"For such a good cause, honey. It would make us so proud to see you up there in the pulpit, talking about all the famous people you work with in New York and your travels all over the world. It would make everybody so proud, Willie."

"I'm sorry, Mama, I'll be just too busy. And I don't know if I'll even be in the country next month."

"Some people make the time to give back to their community, son. That's how important family and church are to them. Regardless of how sophisticated they become or how busy. Some people . . ."

"I'm sorry, Mama, I have to go now. I have another call."

"Well, say hello to your father." Max could hear his father grumbling in the background. Neither man had much to say to the other, but his mother would always make sure they exchanged a minimum of monosyllables before she hung up. How are you? How do you feel? How's work? Fine. Fine. Good. OK. Good night. And then the awkward shuffle would be over.

One day, Max thought. One day what? One day there wouldn't be all this strain. One day they'd just leave him alone to be who he was and to love them long-distance.

He looked in the mirror again. He couldn't lie to himself. The lines in his forehead were his father's. They'd be etched there for good sooner or later. Max didn't really mind, but as long as he had a choice, he'd pick later, thank you very much.

When Nicky Knight surfaced from the subway at 34th Street her heart sank. The corner sign read Eighth Avenue and she was supposed to get out at Sixth Avenue. She was much too far away. These were long crosstown blocks and now she'd never be the first in line at the MacLean agency's open house. Fifth Avenue and 38th Street was her destination. Nine to eleven, the secretary had told her in a crisp, no-nonsense voice, and the earlier, the better.

A damp sweet-and-sour smell rose from the morning streets. Traffic inched forward through thick clouds of black exhaust and angry dia logues of blaring horns. A taxi would do her no good now. She'd have to hoof it, but the sidewalks were almost as congested as the streets. Although it was a mild day for January, puffs of her own breath reminded her that it was still winter and she was back in New York City. She zipped her rust suede anorak, pulled on her black cashmere gloves, and tightened her grip on the handles of her picture portfolio. She'd make a way for herself all by herself if necessary.

"Comin' through," a voice yelled behind her, followed by two young men, one pulling and one pushing a rolling wardrobe rack. Dozens of identical dresses in bubblegum pink swung in unison inside their plastic bags as they were wheeled along. The smell of fresh coffee and sugary pastries that people carried in small brown paper bags reminded her of the breakfast she'd been too anxious to eat back at the dorm. She caught whiffs of aftershave and perfume and last-minute cigarettes with each deep breath she took. This was New York City energy, no doubt about it, the dash for cash. Women rushed past her dressed for success above the ankles. Below, where comfort was crucial, their white socks and athletic shoes were a humorous contrast to their dark panty hose and the high heels they probably carried in sturdy shoulder bags. Nicky felt sorry for them. She liked her clunky Doctor Martens. As far as she was concerned heels were a form of torture, unnatural, uncomfortable and totally uncool.

As she walked across 38th Street she passed grimy windows and disheveled shops with "To the Trade" and "Wholesale Only" stenciled in peeling gold letters on their doors. So this was the Garment District. A potbellied man in a hooded sweatshirt unloading a huge roll of fabric from a truck parked partly on top of the curb crossed in front of her on the sidewalk. "Good luck, kid," he said, nodding his head. His grizzled smile said she could make the dreams in her big black book come true.

By the time Nicky arrived at the agency, six girls were already sitting down in the reception area and three more were lined up before her, signing in and having their Polaroid taken. And it was only ten minutes after nine. She tried not to look at the other girls, but she couldn't help it. Some were made up and dressed up. Two or three others, like her, were bare-faced and wore jeans. None of them were Black. She couldn't judge if they were pretty or not. They certainly didn't look like the flawless creatures in the portrait gallery on the wall behind the receptionist's desk. Well, that's why they were up there, she thought. Those same girls had probably started down here with the rest of us at the beginning. And now look.

She was nervous as she sat down with her Polaroid—such a corny smile, such crappy hair—and application form to fill out. There was so much she didn't know about herself. She didn't know what her measurements were. She knew she was five feet ten and a half inches tall. She put down 5′10″. She knew she weighed one hundred and thirty pounds. She put down 125. But bust, waist and hips? She wore a bra only under pressure. And she'd spent the past two years wearing baggy jeans. What did they have to do with waist and hips? She checked off the boxes in front of good hands and good legs because other people had always told her that she had them. Special skills? Swimming, tennis, skiing. Dare she put down that she was a student? She felt as if she were filling out yet another college application form. Tell us all about yourself, they always said. Well, she didn't want to tell. She wanted to show. To model. That's why she was here.

"Nicky?" the receptionist called.

On top of everything else, she had to have a common name, too?

"Nicky Knight?" came the voice again.

Nicky stood with an embarrassed smile. "I'm sorry, I didn't realize you were talking to me. I just came in and they're . . ." She pointed to the other girls waiting ahead of her.

"I know, but Corky said to send you in to her as soon as you came."

"Thank you," said Nicky, remembering her manners. And bless you, Mom. I love you, too.

"Thirteen roses, Max." Karine drew the number in the air for Max. She knew her accent was making it hard for him to understand. "The box contained not a dozen, but thirteen."

"And this is what's giving you nightmares and a complexion so pale you could pass? Karine, darlin', get a grip. Thirteen's a baker's dozen. A good-luck number. That just means someone is wishing you an extra measure of success."

"With no name, no card? No, Max, yesterday the doorman brings just a long white box with the roses inside. To me, it looks like a little coffin."

"Now just stop it. Come over here before you make yourself totally hysterical." Max helped her take her jacket off and led her to the chaise longue in Angelo Vassallo's dressing room. Then he ordered everyone else just arriving for the shoot out of the room. Karine he ordered to lie down with a cool cloth over her face for five uninterrupted minutes.

Max felt like a drill sergeant, but someone had to take control immediately. Karine had to regain her composure, not just for her sake but for everyone's. If Karine blew this shoot, it would be years before *Cosmo* tried a Black girl again. And over a problem with thirteen roses? Please. Some people didn't realize how lucky they were. Well, he wouldn't be helping much if he took that attitude. She was probably stressed to the limit. All the pressure. New to New York. New to the business on this side of the water. Big opportunities knocking on her door one right after the other. She might not be prepared to handle all the excitement. As much as she primped and preened, she had no real backup here. Her girlfriend Nadja was reliable. He knew her and they had worked together several times. But only time would tell about Gianni. And as much as Karine boasted about her family in Haiti, who knew what the real deal was there? Right here, right now, she was alone and starting to talk crazy. And he was not going to allow it to continue.

After a few minutes, Max asked her how she felt.

"I'm fine," said Karine shyly, lifting the cloth from her face. "Really, I'm OK."

"Good, I'm glad. But lie back down until I bring you some tea. Then we'll get this show on the road."

"Becky Knight's daughter?" Angelo Vassallo slapped himself on the forehead. "Corky told me you were coming, but I didn't connect you with Becky Saunders. Half a minute more and I would have figured it out, though. You look just like her. How fabulous! Oh, Max is going to die. Max! Someone get Max out here, please. Becky *Knight*. And you're Nicole?"

"They call me Nicky, Mr. Vassallo."

"Well, no one ever calls me Mr. Vassallo. Just call me Angelo. Max, look at this child. Now, don't tax your brain for whole minutes at a time. But, tell me, who does she remind you of?"

"Mind games first thing on a Monday morning, Angelo? Please . . ." Max turned the plastic pages of the black portfolio. "Mmmm, and just starting?"

"I'm between semesters at NYU and I wanted to make the rounds."

"You're stumped, admit it." Angelo laughed. "That's the only time you make small talk. She's Becky's daughter, Becky Saunders."

"Of course, how fabulous. Of course, I see it now. The lips, those cheekbones, that straight-arrow nose. But where did you get those cream-soda eyes? My favorite flavor. Your mother was divine, a classic beauty. Becky Saunders until she married that music tycoon, Kayo Knight, right? Then she abandoned civilization and moved to California, the abyss of fashion. Am I right? Too bad, I adored her." Max shut her book without further comment.

"We all did." Angelo opened the portfolio again and turned the pages more slowly. "Well, once again Corky was correct. She told me that I'd love you. But you know, Nicky, I never test."

"I understand, Mr. Vassallo." She could not disguise the disappointment in her voice.

"Oh, Angelo, come on," Max insisted. He could see something in her that her pictures missed. "Just this once. I'll do the makeup and I'll bring David for the hair."

"I hate that little queen."

"Elmo, then. You love Elmo."

"That's true. And maybe we could do something there. With the hair, I mean. Of course, the face is perfect and you wouldn't have to overexert yourself, Max. But listen, Nicky, darling, it would have to be right away because I'm going on location Friday. We're already Monday. What about Wednesday?"

"Wonderful, I can't thank you enough, both of you."

"Thank me when you're rich and famous, sweetheart. Until then, Wednesday, six-thirty, clean face and hair, white shirt, black legs. OK?"

Nicky Knight was still bubbling her thanks when she passed by the open dressing room door and saw a woman lying down with a white cloth over her face. Some star being pampered on the way to further fame and fortune. She'd be lying there one day, she just knew it.

CHAPTER FOUR

"ENOUGH," Max declared as he passed the fat powder brush in one last flourish across Karine's forehead. "You can beat a face to death, you know, even one as divine as yours. Relax, let the colors melt a bit. And show me which piece of devastation you intend to wear tonight."

Karine, in a long cream cashmere robe, stood in front of the wall of mirrored closets in her bedroom and held up two dresses: a black stretch Azzedine and a short white Saint Laurent. "Which one?" she asked him. Her indecision surprised him. She always knew what effect she wanted, and, unlike most models, she dressed carefully to achieve it.

"They're both hot," he said, sitting cross-legged on her bed's raw silk duvet, "but everybody's going to be in basic, boring black, and the white has the better neckline."

"You mean, no neckline."

"Exactly. Less is more."

She stroked the sensuous fabric as she held the dress closer to her body. Her breasts were one of her best features and this strapless top would show them off to their fullest advantage.

"But around the neck, what?" she asked again. "Diamonds by the yard? My Chanel pearls?"

"Maybe, but maybe nothing. Just ears. You're driving me crazy with these questions. Personally, if I didn't have big rocks I'd go bare. And I can't stand the thought of Cleopatra in costume jewelry."

"Still I cannot believe it, Max. They picked me for the Cleo campaign! I am dreaming . . ." She fell back onto the bed, hugging her dresses and laughing with delight.

"And celebrating tonight with one hundred of your closest friends at home on Sutton Place . . ."

She sat up briskly. "Don't make fun, it's just a sublet and you know it. But soon I will have my own place. Whatever I want, whenever I want."

"Right now I'll settle for a long hot soak in my Jacuzzi." Max hopped off the bed and started packing up his kit. "Let me get going, darlin', or I won't have time to do my own face."

A knock sounded at her door, followed by Velma Jean's heart-shaped smile. "I want you to see what we've done, Karine."

A half dozen date palms fanned out high over the room. Terra-cotta jars of papyrus and bamboo, golden mimosa, and full-blooming camelias created an exotic garden where nothing had been before but expensively empty space. Yards of white and gold lamé and sheer white silk transformed the suede sofas and wide windows into a queen's domain. Viewed from the opposite side of the room, enchantment framed the wide urban panorama encompassing the 59th Street Bridge and the East River. Glittering penthouses crowned the most glamorous high-rises in the world with the ultimate in luxury and beauty. And it was all at her fingertips.

"In another couple of hours," Velma Jean whispered, "with the lights scintillating against the dark sky, you'll feel as if you're floating along the Nile on a royal barge."

"It is perfection." Karine twirled around the room, giddy with anticipation. "Ravishing, just spectacular." Everywhere she turned, lush flowers caught her eye. "The lilies are gorgeous, and these white roses, and birds of paradise . . . divine. But not too fussy, you know. People should feel comfortable, not outdressed by the decor."

"Don't worry, your guests will feel the magic, too. The bars are all set up and the food will be here at seven. Your kitchen is fine. So all you have to do is relax and prepare to have a wonderful evening. You certainly deserve it."

"Thank you." Karine paused. "I don't know how to say this, but I want you to know I realize I owe much to women like you."

Startled by the young woman's sincerity, Velma Jean simply nodded. Maybe these new girls weren't as selfish and shortsighted as they appeared, she thought.

Alone, Karine marveled at the beautiful room. Some people simply exuded elegance and imaginative good taste in everything they did. Like Midas, their touch was automatic. In Velma Jean's case, though, whatever she touched became not hard and golden but more beautifully itself. Karine knew that before Velma Jean started her catering business, she had also been a model. That was almost thirty years ago, years before she was born, before the tides of consciousness rose, lifting everyone's vision. Black was not beautiful then. Black was not even Black. You were Negro or Colored or non-White. Or, even more likely, nonexistent. Just plain out of the picture. Now things were different. There were more Black models. More work, more respect, more money. And finally, at long last, a major-league contract. For her. She could not imagine what it was like in the old days, and she did not want to try.

"Snap out of it, Karine," Max teased. "You can't go cosmic on us yet. I'm outta here."

"Max, please, don't be late tonight. I'm nervous."

"About what? You're queen of the world now, darlin'." He made a gallant gesture of kissing her hand. "Nerves are a thing of the past. *Ciao,* kiddo."

"Ciao, Max. And thank you." As she closed the door behind him, she felt a rush of the excitement to come.

A whirlwind of congratulations kept Karine spinning around the party. Model friends and photographer friends, the ad agency people, designers and their assistants, stylists, hair and makeup artists, dozens of beautiful people who knew other beautiful people filled the room with the sheen and rustle and scent of success. Dreams were uncorked with the champagne, and laughter overflowed.

In a simple black dress and a long strand of pearls, Corky Matthews seemed like another person, charming and radiant in a way Karine had never seen before. She proudly introduced her husband, a thin-lipped police detective whose work had left its footprints on his face.

"A husband, Corky? You have a life beyond the agency?" Karine asked in mock amazement.

"It's not easy, believe me. Congratulations to you," she said as she kissed Karine on the cheek.

"And to you two." She patted Corky's arm, and both women laughed while the detective nervously adjusted his tie. He wasn't used to such displays of emotion. Or cleavage.

As she entered the room, Vanessa Seymour, vice-president of Smith & Seymour, the ad agency in charge of the Cleo campaign, smoothed back her long blond hair and cracked the shell of a smile. Karine was relieved that she had come, relieved that she was smiling. She had always gotten a frosty if professional reaction from her. Why did someone as attractive and powerful as Vanessa Seymour always appear so tense around other people? Karine watched Kyle Whitaker light her cigarette with his lighter. A gentlemanly gesture for a nonsmoker, but typical of him. Kyle, the president of Cleo and architect of the new campaign, was a smoother type, a bearded posthippie who concealed a shrewd mind and sharp claws under his cashmere blazers. Seeing the two of them together for the first time and in her own home made the campaign seem tangible and authentic. Cleo belonged to her.

Gianni Walker brought his own crowd, including JJ Knight, a couple of cute young girls, and a Latin drag queen dressed in a turquoise lamé sheath with a Cleopatra wig. She hissed at Karine when they were introduced but later she apologized, saying she was simply dying of envy. Then she miaowed at her for the rest of the evening.

Nate and Vicki came with a copy of their latest release, which had just gone platinum. Flicka, the giant redhead from Texas, wore one of Thierry Mugler's black leather creations that left little or nothing to the imagination. Carol and Coral, the twins, in copper-sequined shorts, dared people to tell them apart by feel. Tanya sat in Paolo's lap and fed him strawberries dipped in chocolate. Sarina, wearing a bronze silk bustier instead of the Calvin Klein underwear she was famous for, called everyone girlfriend and child, which was funny since she had just turned seventeen, but not laughable since she was very, very rich. Petra, back to being a blonde again, was somehow not quite as outrageous as usual. When she took her sable cape off, she was wearing only a g-string of pink marabou feathers which matched her platform mules. For a moment Karine felt sorry for her, felt she might be getting old. After all, pink? But then Carlo stripped to his tiger-striped briefs and they did a *danse sauvage* together, if you could call hair flinging, body bending, and crotch clutching, dancing. Through the hoots and hollers, the cigarette haze and the champagne daze, Karine could see that everyone was laughing and having a good time.

"Wonderful party, Karine." Gianni Walker's accent was as warm as the Mediterranean sun. "I guess I'll never get another chance to work with you now."

"Well, maybe we find other things to do beside work," Karine said with her million-dollar smile. She watched and waited. His looks were so intriguing. He was a different kind of Black man, not in color or features, although they did have, even to her, a slightly more exotic touch. It was his attitude. The way he wore the glossy, thick spirals of his jet-black hair pulled back into a ponytail said "I make my own rules and dare you to undo them." Tonight maybe she would accept his dare.

"Karine." Vanessa edged her way between them without apology. "Stunning dress, but do you really think you should be giving it all away for free? Our Cleo girl is a woman of the world, not the street."

Karine's eyes blazed with shame. She had never been so humiliated. And this was someone who was supposed to be on her side? She was speechless.

And so was everyone else, Max could tell. What was Miz Seymour's problem? Whatever it was, he wasn't waiting to find out. He grabbed the DJ's mike and jumped up onto a chair. "Ladies and gentlemen and all those in between," he announced, "we are gathered together tonight to celebrate a coronation. Karine Belfort, Queen of Cleo. Let's hear it for Karine." As he stretched out the *-een* of her name, grand applause, whistles, and assorted woofs sounded across the room. "Now, some of you pale and culturally deprived folk might not be aware of this, but no celebration in Black sassiety would be complete without—you know it!—a fashion show. That divine moment has arrived, y'all, and from here on in I want you to just kick back and relax. Make some space right there in the middle, that's right, room enough for a little catwalk. Hush up, pharaoh. Now, when I call your name, get ready to strut your stuff. We want to see those death-defying profiles and all that fierce body attitude that have made you children so famous. And so rich. Toss that weave, honey. We want to see alla y'all who've been fried, dyed, and flipped to the side. You know who you are. As for you, Carlo, either you get an instantaneous implant—and you know where—or you are totally disqualified. Everybody gets one minute. No hogging or scene stealing, although we know some of you kleptos just can't he'p yo'self. Think of me as Mad Max cracking the whip. Stop it, just stop it, S & M fans, you're drooling. Wait. Somebody, get Petra's sable so we can at least pretend to be surprised by something we've already seen too much of. Ready, DJ? Glitterati time!"

The show was amazing, unlike any Karine had ever seen during the collections. Women, men, and, as Max said, all those in between, performed for the toughest audience on the fashion planet, themselves. At Max's command, "The Rush" by Luther Vandross swept through the room. Nobody could *not* keep that beat. The alchemy sizzled. Eyes intensified, eyebrows arched, hips realigned themselves on reinvented ball joints, shoulders sliced through the air, and hands brushed through space designing a new calligraphy. Some pivoted in mechanistic double time, while others turned in languorous slow motion and all improvised from a well-worn catalog of glamorous poses.

Corky watched her husband disbelieve his eyes. He took pride in the fact that nothing could faze him. He'd seen it all before. But she knew he'd never seen anything like this. Nothing criminal, nothing life-threatening. Just some of the most original people in New York having some unadulterated fun.

After Flicka opened the middle zipper of her leather jumpsuit all the way down to the crotch, she snarled her way through the crowd flinging her mane like a lion tamer with a built-in whip. Carol and Coral looked like New Age Rockettes doing the Electric Slide, after which Nate flung little Vicki over his shoulder while she kicked her notoriously high spikes and flung her fox boa up and down like a damsel in delicious distress. Petra, in a spectacular series of her signature twirls, took everyone's breath away until she stumbled at the end, too high or too something to know how to stop. Wonder mixed with disappointment until someone caught her and everyone could start to breathe again. Then Cleocatra called out, "Zhee-von-she," snapped gold-tipped fingers in a wide arc, and proceeded down the runway in the elegantly exaggerated stride that had once made Givenchy's *cabine* so special.

"It ain't a fantasy, it's very real to me," Luther sang.

Ain't that the truth, Max thought about the drag queen. Then he looked around for Vanessa Seymour. He'd put her in the spotlight for a switch and see how she would deal. But Her Blondness was nowhere to be seen. It figured. Few who dished it out could really take it. Max knew. He was one of the few.

Max called on Karine last. From a gold and crystal vase she lifted an armful of white roses and while walking "the most elegant walk since Eve in a fig leaf," according to last fall's *New York Times,* she bestowed the delicate blossoms on her friends. They cheered her, and when the flowers were gone, she, in turn, applauded them. It was clear that she wore the crown now. And no one could take it from her.

Karine watched the foam build in the tub. Lily of the valley was one of her favorite scents, but she had to admit that the smell of success was even sweeter. When Nadja called from Jamaica to wish her a happy celebration, she'd felt a momentary twinge of envy, wishing she was on a job like that. It was still so new, so hard to believe that she no longer had to worry about the jobs she didn't get, the day-to-day business of bookings, auditions, cancellations, vouchers, and paychecks. She was guaranteed $2.5 million for the next two years for less than four weeks of work a year. Then there were the magazine covers, fashion shows, and personal appearances, the fun stuff. They'd be the after-dinner mints, tiny treats that sweetened the palate once the main meal was over.

She got undressed and put a foot in the tub before realizing she'd left the front door unlocked for Gianni. He had promised to come back and spend the night with her, and she had wanted to make things easier for him. But it was too late now. She was not in the mood. Let him dally with the date he'd brought to the party. If he begged, maybe she would open up. Maybe.

She walked through the living room, darkened and deglitzed but still etched with the shadows of palms and papyrus. She remembered, as a child in the unlit countryside, being afraid of the dark, of things that grew bigger and stronger and more dangerous in the dark. It was different now. The lights of the city danced against the night in a private command performance. And in the dark it was even more beautiful, more possessable, more completely hers.

She found the front door already locked. Reassured, she settled into the tub to truly relax for what seemed the first time in years.

"I'm sorry, sir, but there is no answer. Is she expecting you?" the doorman asked with a disdainful glance at his watch.

"Yes, of course, she's expecting me. She just had a big party . . ."

"We're quite aware, sir . . ."

"She was expecting me earlier, but . . ."

"Perhaps she's changed her mind, sir."

"Yeah, right. OK, I'll be back."

Gianni Walker hated the man's sleazy insinuations. Americans in general and recent arrivals in particular had little taste and less class. He found a pay phone on First Avenue before he realized that he did not have Karine's unlisted phone number. He started to get angry and then he started to laugh. It was three forty-five on a cold Sunday morning in January. One of the most beautiful women in the world had been waiting for him and then she changed her mind. What could be more normal? They were whimsical creatures, these models, unserious, unpredictable and totally irresponsible. He buttoned up the lapels on his black leather trench as he walked back to her apartment building.

"Look, I don't want to bother you again," he said to the doorman, "but there was no answer when I called. No answer and no answering machine. She told me specifically that Hines or Hanes . . ."

"That's me."

". . . would call up to let her know I was coming and that she'd leave the door unlocked for me."

"I find that rather strange, sir."

"So did I. I told her that. Could you at least send somebody to check to make sure that her door isn't open?"

"I see no harm in that. I'll call one of the security people. Please have a seat."

Gianni stood and looked past the circular drive out into the quiet city darkness. A few minutes later the doorman informed him that 28K was securely locked. Case closed.

He left the building with a weak smile barely concealing his humiliation. In the taxi the turbaned driver kept looking at him in the rearview mirror, wondering but not daring to ask what he was doing in this neighborhood at this hour. During the drive to his studio in TriBeCa, Gianni unbuttoned his coat and savored a few genuine chuckles trying to figure out which of several women this evening had been payback for.

Monday evening Nicky walked into the empty dorm and suddenly couldn't wait for the week that had just started to finish. It was so quiet, too quiet. Almost all of the students had gone home over the month-long Christmas break. The kids who normally gathered outside on University Place or hung around inside waiting for their friends made everything so lively. Now it felt like Desolation Row with the uniformed guard at the door, bored and always on the phone, and just a few residents beginning to trickle back a week before the start of classes. She was lonely, but she wasn't complaining, not exactly. It was her feet. She'd spent less than two weeks on vacation in California, too anxious to relax. It was her own idea to get back to New York and get her feet wet in the world of modeling. They were wet, all right, but also dog-tired.

Go-sees were not much fun, no matter how necessary, no matter what the bookers said. Trudging around all day to have photographers, magazine editors, and catalog stylists examine your teeth, your complexion, your legs, your hands and your hair was not the ideal way to spend a day as a glamorous fashion model. She had only a few black-and-white photographs in her book, dramatic shots taken by fellow students who were possibly talented but unfortunately ignorant about lighting and direction. She noticed that the more polite people said nothing and the less polite grunted when she showed the pictures. They could be more hindrance than help, Corky had told her bluntly before passing her on to Robin, the head booker on the beginners' board. They had both liked her, though, thought she had potential and were delighted when the maestro, Angelo Vassallo, agreed to test her.

But when she went back to Angelo's studio to pick up the test results late that Monday afternoon, his secretary had barely acknowledged her, and merely handed over a heavy gray envelope. There was no music, and of course no Angelo, no Max, no one to remember that she had caused such excitement only a few days before.

The crowd on the rancid subway home steamed with fatigue and damp wool. She kept the cardboard-stiffened envelope closed, afraid her pretensions would be exposed and laughed at by these grim-faced people who worked hard at ugly, anonymous jobs. But as soon as she got inside her dorm room she spread the black-and-white contact sheets across her absent roommate's bed and angled her desk lamp for more light.

Who was that? She recognized bits and pieces of herself reshaped into a totally different person. It was wild. She didn't look like that, but the proof, staring right back at her, was that she *could* look like that. Her hair was a miracle. As a young girl with thick, woolly hair, she had felt disinherited, a genetic outcast not quite good enough for her mother's and grandmother's silky tresses. Ever since elementary school she had carefully stretched, straightened and permed her hair to curl over her shoulders and blow in the breeze. Now all that madness was gone. In its place, a little chin-length bob. It could go straight, wavy or curly. It could be slicked back or tousled forward. Experimenting with Elmo in the studio and back home at the dorm had challenged her. Hair did not have to be such a ball and chain after all.

Max's makeup had started her out as a natural daytime nymph and intensified into a kohl-eyed, scarlet-lipped vamp. Angles and hollows appeared where she'd never noticed them before. She saw how tiny nuances in movement and expression altered each shot. Sometimes a smile was too toothy, too gummy. Sometimes her nose looked too long. Sometimes her eyes looked uneven or unconvinced. But sometimes everything clicked and a wonderful, beautiful face leaped off the shiny black-and-white paper. She was amazed that it could be her own self. She wanted Corky and her booker to have a look, but it was too late to call the agency now. She'd do it first thing in the morning.

Still, she wanted someone to share this vision of her new self. Maybe she should call Max. After the test he'd said to call him anytime. Maybe he could help her pick the best pictures. She'd need at least a head shot and a body shot for a beginner's composite. His sense of humor was definitely warped but she still trusted his judgment. Or maybe she could call her brother, JJ. Strictly speaking, her half brother, a term she hated. They didn't know each other all that well, separated as they were by different mothers and ten years of age. He and his girlfriend, Nadja, had been nice enough to her when she first moved to New York. But his work in the music business made him unpredictable, and she had had enough of that kind of life with the father they shared. Maybe she should just calm down, take a shower and then decide.

As she was undressing, the phone rang. It was Tina Thompson asking her to come to dinner one night this week. "Just a simple, at-home thing, to get better acquainted," she said.

Cool, Nicky thought. If someone had eyes in this business, it was Tina Thompson at Aura. Thank goodness, Mom was still on the case. Nicky would call L.A. tonight to give her an update.

CHAPTER FIVE

THE SKYCAP pushed his cart with Nadja's big Fendi suitcase and her black kid garment bag through the customs doors and into the expectant melee of the International Arrivals lobby at Kennedy Airport. She scanned the crowd for her name on a placard or the face of a familiar driver. At the tap on her shoulder she turned nervously.

"Hi, baby, welcome home." JJ kissed her surprise away and added a short, tight hug.

She looked so good, her skin a little redder than her usual nut-brown, her closely cropped hair more tightly curled from the sea and salt air. She had been gone for only a week on the location shoot in Jamaica but he'd missed her more than he had expected, more than she knew. He wanted to get home in a hurry.

The ride back to the city was unexpectedly swift. JJ drove the little BMW with egotistical skill through the early evening traffic past the exhausted neighborhoods that fronted the highway. As they crested the last hill of the Long Island Expressway preparing to enter the Midtown Tunnel, Manhattan appeared to be the stuff of legend, a landscape of lights and fairy-tale towers spread across the horizon.

"The city looks like a magic forest," Nadja said.

"Where all things are possible," added JJ.

"So why do I feel so sad? For the past week I've been working hard but feeling free, feeling so important, you know. And here on first seeing New York again all I can think of is how much I miss the sun."

"And New York? You don't miss New York?"

"I miss you."

"I like to hear that." He turned to smile at her. "You *know* I like to hear that."

They drove straight to her apartment on Horatio Street in Greenwich Village. Earlier he had brought flowers to take the edge off the emptiness in the rooms and fruit and cheese for them to snack on. The fragrance of a ripe pineapple added a familiar tropical perfume to the air.

"Baby, thanks so much," she said, leaning against the closed door. "You made things so nice for me. How can I thank you?"

"You can come here and put your arms around me and tell me again how much you missed me."

"That's easy to do," she said with a naughty grin as she sat down next to him on the ivory silk sofa and gently pushed him back into a rounded corner. They swallowed each other's kisses with wide-open lips and avid, searching tongues. Getting back together was the best part of going away. Rediscovering what had become close to routine. Appreciating what had been almost taken for granted. After they took their sweaters off they lay together with their eyes closed, fingertips outlining the hard and soft places, the smooth and hairy, the still and throbbing. Scented candles wrapped them in the soft glow of gardenias.

"I missed this," she said, stroking the deep wave of chestnut hair that fell across his forehead, "and these," smoothing the thick, glossy eyebrows that reminded her of an ancient tribal trait. "I missed this," she said, kissing the fuzzy hollow where his neck and collarbone met. "I missed this," sliding her hand down and around the muscles of his arms. "I missed this," sucking his fingers and then placing his palm over her breast. "And these," nibbling his nipples, "and this," sliding her tongue down to his navel, "and I especially missed this," she said, kissing his closed fly and squeezing the warm bulk underneath. "Let's get into bed." JJ smiled.

In the bedroom the embroidered edge of her favorite flowered sheet was turned down over the blankets and dusty-rose comforter. "You knew," she laughed, "you sex fiend. You planned it all. I don't even have to undo the bed. You knew we'd just run and jump into it." She punched him playfully on his arm.

"I don't want to be accused of being one of those insensitive, domineering males. I want to know what to do to make my woman happy." He lay down on his back and pulled her on top of him.

"You're so funny. What am I going to do with you?"

"That's what I keep asking myself."

"And what's your answer?"

"Look under the pillow."

She opened the small blue velvet box to find a diamond ring. Quietly she sat up. JJ raised himself up on an elbow beside her, watching her face as she turned the box around, tilting it to better explore the stone's brilliance in the light. Her upper lip, fuller than the lower, crept over its trembling partner, as if one part of her body had to protect itself from another. He had not yet seen her smile.

"Is it too small? You don't like this cut? Or the setting, or . . . ?"

"No, JJ, it's beautiful, absolutely perfect."

"Really, if you don't like this one, we'll get whatever you like, whatever you want. I want us to make a life together, Nadja. Will you marry me?" His question skipped like a pebble across a lake of silence.

"We've never really talked about this before, JJ. I don't know. I'm, like, in a state of shock. But I don't know if you can say that about a happy feeling. Do you know what you're asking for? I have no family, no home."

"We'll make a home together."

"My work is crazy, too. I'm a professional nomad."

"You're not going to work forever, at least not as a model."

"And you're still such a young man . . ."

"Twenty-eight's not that young."

"The business you're in takes you out a lot . . . You're bound to have a lot more experiences with other women . . . I love you so much but I don't want you on the rebound from just a week's separation."

"I want you, Nadja. I need you. We've known each other for three years. I haven't slept with another woman in two. I'm not interested in anybody else, not even looking. I told you about going to Karine's party. A roomful of the most beautiful people. And there I was, missing you—badly—the whole time."

"JJ, that's just one night, just one week."

"But I've been feeling this way for a lot longer. I just didn't know how to say it to you. I'd walk around saying to myself, I love this woman. I want to be near this woman. I want to feel her arms around me and feel her in my arms. And not just for a night over at her place or a night over at mine. We can do it, Nadja. We've got what it takes. Please say yes, baby."

She looked deep into his eyes, so dark they were almost black, and felt again the safety she had always found there.

"Yes, baby," she whispered.

And together they laughed, falling back over onto the bed, hugging and rolling and kissing. He slid the ring onto her finger but it was too loose. "Good," she laughed, "now I can grow big and fat."

"Whatever you want, just stay with me." And they eased into each other, moving slowly and then swiftly, from the shallows into warmer, deeper waters.

She woke up a little before midnight feeling as if her bones had dissolved into some heavy liquid metal. JJ was asleep, curved around her back like a long-lost piece of herself, a perfect fit. She didn't want to disturb him, but she had a dozen things to do before morning. She hadn't even checked her answering machine to see if she was booked tomorrow. The agency would have called her, though, before she left Jamaica to let her know if she was working, or when.

There was so much on her mind. There was Paris to start planning for, the tickets, more calls. She was hardly home before she was off again. Did JJ really understand that? The red light was flashing, eight recorded messages. She didn't want to play them back now and wake him up. It wasn't like she could do anything about it at this hour anyway. But there were still other things to do, unpack . . .

"Don't go anywhere," JJ mumbled.

"I thought you were asleep."

"I am, asleep and dreaming. Come here." He put his hand around her breast, circling it, caressing it, teasing the nipple. The seed of an erection started germinating toward her, the warmth of her backside encouraging it to grow. And soon they were lost to the world and found in each other.

When her phone rang just a little after eight o'clock in the morning, Nadja didn't realize it was so late.

"Hi, Corky," she said sleepily, "I was just getting ready to call you."

"Oh, sweetheart, I'm so sorry . . ."

"What's the matter? You're crying. What's wrong?"

It took Corky a moment to realize. "You don't know? Oh, my God, you don't even know. Nadja, Karine is dead."

Corky told her as best she could about trying to reach Karine all day Monday. Just yesterday, she still couldn't believe it. Velma Jean had been trying to contact her about picking up the plants and taking them back to the nursery. She had had no success, and ended up calling Corky at the agency. Corky knew Karine wasn't booked for a job and hadn't booked out for a vacation. It wasn't like her not to check in. After she decided to go over to her apartment, she discovered that none of the doormen had seen her since Saturday night. She got the manager to unlock the apartment door and that's when they found her. Drowned in her bathtub. Probably since the night of the party, the coroner said. Drowned, poor baby, dead.

Nadja heard what Corky said, but she could not believe it. If JJ hadn't been with her to listen, to ask Corky his own questions, to turn on the television news with its fast-paced footage of Karine's exclusive building, the black plastic body bag, interviews from guests at her party . . . If the factual corroboration weren't so massive, Nadja would not have believed that Karine was dead. Everything forced her to believe it was true. But no one could answer the question she cried out again and again. Why?

Nadja asked the limousine driver to turn the music off. The Mozart symphony sounded a little too jaunty, too perfectly polished for the ragged mood she was in. Taking Karine's mother and brother to the airport was one of the hardest things she'd ever had to do in her life. How do you make meaningful conversation with total strangers who have lost a loved one in such a grotesque way?

Madam Belfort had surprised her by being a dark, handsome woman whose life of hard work had toughened her spirit as well as her hands and face. She had moved through the endless formalities with a pained dignity Nadja recognized as belonging to those who understand neither language nor custom, only the weight of added trouble. The brother, it seemed, was the man of the family. It was with him that Nadja spoke in French, trying to explain what was going on so that he might translate it back into Creole for his mother. And it was through him that Nadja understood what Karine had inherited from her wealthy father: the looks, the attitude, the ambition. Everything except his name.

She was glad crazy old Max was riding with her in the limo back to town. But she wished JJ had been there, too.

The front-page article in *Adweek* carried pictures of both Laura Grosvenor and Karine Belfort. Cleo, Inc., and its advertising agency, Smith & Seymour, announced that the new campaign would definitely continue. Kyle Whitaker was quoted as saying they would "not be daunted by tragedy." In the interest of security, however, they would divulge no preliminary information on the future model chosen for the campaign. Furthermore, Cleo and Smith & Seymour were asking that the Grosvenor case be reopened and the Belfort investigation intensified. They were also offering a combined sum of $50,000 for information useful in the investigations.

Nadja wanted to throw up as she read the story aloud. The whole thing made her sad, mad, and sick to her stomach.

"These are lives gone, and all they can talk about is money?!" She folded up the paper and threw it on the opposite seat.

"At least they gave Mama Belfort a few shekels to take home with her," Max said. "Twenty-five grand ain't bad. All these years they've been lynching us for free."

"Are you saying that Laura and Karine were both murdered?" Nadja asked incredulously. "Karine, maybe, only maybe, did someone do something terrible to her. But Laura, she did it to herself."

"I'll never believe that."

"Max, everybody knows she was a special friend of yours, your protégée. But everybody also knows she was crazy. She'd done every drug on the planet. She'd try anything, do anything."

"Except kill herself. Even by accident."

"The needle was still stuck in her arm, Max."

"But I'll never believe that she was the one who put it there." Max shook his head with a dogged skepticism that Nadja was unused to seeing. "I'm dead serious. I knew that girl since she was thirteen, doing ballet with Arthur Mitchell up in Harlem. Sure, she had her spells when she would try anything. But not everything. I don't care what the cops found, and I told them that. Laura Grosvenor would never shoot up. Needles of any kind terrified her. And do you know why? Simple ghetto psychology. She lost her mother to the needle when she was just a kid and it haunted her all her life." It hurt Max to defend Laura's wild ways, but it hurt him even more that she was not here to defend herself.

"Maybe she was experimenting," Nadja suggested. "Like you said, just trying it. Maybe with someone who got scared and ran away."

"Or someone who knew what would happen. Who wanted her out of the picture, literally, quickly and with a nasty, slimy little slur after her name."

"Max, you're crazy. Who would want that?"

"The same people who didn't want the Cleo campaign in the first place. Who still don't want it. The first big-bucks beauty campaign for a Black girl. And for a full-fledged premium line, not just a minority set-aside. Only a company as long-established as Cleo could do this."

"Madam Klionsky is probably turning in her grave."

"Maybe, maybe not. Look at where she came from to get where she got. Maybe she knew a thing or two about ghettos herself."

"And now what?"

"I don't know, but if the mayor doesn't find some answers soon, I will personally doodoo on the doorstep of Gracie Mansion."

"Max, stop it. I can't laugh now."

"You've got to. You've got to look, listen, and laugh just to keep your sanity. The KKK has moved Up South and is taking names, believe me. You're on the list, too, darlin'."

"Why do you say that? They were both Cleo girls."

"But who's next? You're hot, you're big. It could be you. No one on the outside would know."

"That's absurd."

"Oh, really? A lot of the Black girls I know have told me about receiving phone calls and threatening letters. Karine told me that *you* had."

"She did?" Nadja was embarrassed to admit it. "I did, but I didn't think anything of it."

"Well, think again."

"Max, are you saying that all Black models are targets?"

"Keereck."

"But that's too wild to even consider. I'd never buy into your conspiracy theories but the trouble is nothing else comes close to making sense. I just wish I'd paid more attention to what Karine was saying. About the phone calls and something about thirteen roses. And poor Gianni. Maybe if that asshole doorman had let him in, just maybe Karine would be alive today."

"Letting him in wasn't the point," Max pointed out. "Checking on Karine's safety was. Did anybody think to knock to see if she was all right?"

"So you're saying it didn't matter if the door was locked or open? That the person was already inside at the party, hiding, just waiting?"

"Well, I who know everyone didn't know everyone *there*. It's always possible that a homicidal maniac was lurking among us. You should have seen the cast of characters. I'd say there were several, starting with that gutter creature your gorgeous boyfriend dragged in. What's her name? Cleocatra."

"Cat would never hurt anybody. All she wants is love and attention. You don't get that from a corpse."

"Spare me. I could never relate to people who confused their identity with their wardrobe. It's queers who give your decent homosexuals a bad name. She's delusional. I mean, she really thinks she could model. As a woman. That's a rather dangerous fantasy, wouldn't you say?"

"Stop it, Max, I'm getting scared. People want to *be* us, not kill us.

I never considered modeling a dangerous profession, but now I'm beginning to feel like something is closing in on us. Like someone out there doesn't like what we're doing and is going to make sure that we stop. Maybe someone inside our own world. Is that possible?"

"Now you're the one who's going too far, Nadja. That's much too big a leap. Cleo, Inc., Smith & Seymour, MacLean. You're talking White sugar here, not your usual White trash. And why? What would be the motive? These people are in the business to make money off you girls. Why would any of them want to kill the goose that lays the golden eggs?"

"Money can be made lots of ways. Maybe some of these same people just can't stand to see Black people making it."

CHAPTER SIX

CORKY closed her eyes and listened to the familiar agency bustle through her free ear. The other ear, the unlucky recipient of Jock Rosenberg's grating voice, seemed to shrivel closed in protest. Thirty-five years in the business had taught Corky that she couldn't like everybody, that she wasn't even expected to. She just had to work with people as efficiently as possible. Sometimes that required a face or a phrase or an attitude she didn't happen to have handy at the time but she did the best she could. She was only human.

Jock Rosenberg was one of those who brought out the only human in her. As much as she'd loved Mike MacLean, the brilliant founder of what was to this day one of the top modeling agencies in the world, she hated Mike's husband, Jock. He was such a tight-fisted sleazoid. Thank God, he was an absentee president. He lived in Miami and visited New York only every four to six weeks. Didn't bother to send a measly telegram of condolences to Karine's mother, the slime-bag. Grouched about paying for the little brother's ticket from Haiti, the slug. And now here he was on the phone giving her extra grief about "containing adverse publicity in the light of recent events." That had to be his lawyer's language. Jock wasn't slick enough to talk like that.

Corky held the phone away from her ear, paying him no attention and less respect. Without her he could kiss his thoroughbreds goodbye.

She waited until he ran out of breath, not words, and quickly hung up. He'd call back only if he dared.

She had other work to do. Some of her girls were leaving next week in preparation for the haute couture shows in Paris at the end of January. Only a few this time. The pret-a-porter collections in March would take more girls and many of the stars, even if they didn't know how to walk.

It was amazing to see how the runway side of the business had expanded in the eighties. And had already started to contract in the nineties. Most folks were saying, including the French wizard Yves Saint Laurent himself, that the custom-made extravaganzas of haute couture would be extinct in ten years. The European designers simply could not afford to make these luxurious clothes anymore, let alone show them to the few thousand women in the world who actually bought them. Conspicuous fantasy was out. Moderate fantasy was in.

Without the couture shows, the big ready-to-wear shows would become even bigger. More models would work doing more shows. The international circuit would become more concentrated. And the designers would include everything in their twice-yearly collections, from traditional classics to wild innovations. From racks of a thousand look-alikes to riches of only one of a kind.

As if she really cared. Personally, she had no abiding interest in clothes as such. She wore slacks to work every day, put on a skirt for her husband on Sunday to remind herself of her own femininity and stored two or three little black dresses in triple plastic bags for special agency occasions. That was the extent of her wardrobe.

Except for the pearls. Three years ago, when Mike found out she was dying, she had given Corky the long strand of big pearls that had been her trademark accessory. It didn't take long, the lung cancer. In just a few months she was gone, leaving behind one of the best agencies in New York, a jerko husband, a group of wounded friends and a portfolio of swan-necked photographs, many detailed with the artful dangle of a smoking cigarette.

About clothes Corky could care less. What she cared about was people, the young girls whose eager faces lit up the room with excitement, adventure, and sometimes that extra-special combination of looks and personality. It was one of the things her husband complained about. That she was as obsessed with *making* stars as the girls were with *becoming* stars. That she was feeding her own ego through them. Well, why not? Somebody had to do it. At least she cared about them as people, too, not just plastic mannequins with interchangeable features.

She cared about their lives, getting them into the business, seeing them grow through the ups and downs, and easing them out when the time came. She had to retire someone today. Never a pleasant task. A good girl, too, but now approaching forty and showing it. She could go to one of the other agencies that handled women with more mature looks. That was another aspect of the business that Corky had watched expand successfully. Some women could work forever if they kept themselves lean and stress-free. But who managed to live that kind of a life? A few, very few very lucky ones.

Robin stuck a yellow Post-it on her monitor. *Nicky Knight, 4pm, Angelo's pix, OK?* Corky nodded to her as her phone rang again.

Vanessa Seymour was calling all the agency heads herself, she said. She didn't want to leave this to her casting director and his assistants. The Cleo campaign was special and people needed to be personally reassured.

"Smitty and I just wanted to let you know directly, Corky, that Kyle and S & S are fully committed to a new Black Cleo girl and we're going to keep moving right along."

Corky couldn't help thinking that Vanessa's voice had all the compassion of a steamroller. "I understand, and I appreciate your call, Vanessa. But it's the girls who're scared, and you can't blame them."

"Of course, I don't, but isn't that where you come in?"

"Regardless of what *I* say," Corky insisted, "some of the girls feel that it might not be worth it, you know, for them to stick their neck out. This kind of scary stuff has never happened before."

"But neither has this opportunity. This is absolutely unique, historic. You could almost say revolutionary. Corky, I want to make sure you emphasize *first* and *only*. The first big beauty contract for a Black girl. And the only one not for a Black line."

Corky tried to keep her lid on. The woman wasn't trying to tell her how to do her job, was she? Hadn't she been in the business long enough to appreciate the uniqueness of a client actually insisting on a Black girl? The old days when people just didn't want to know they even existed weren't that far gone. Quotas, percentages, tokens. That's all Black models had been used for. She'd banged her head against too many doors, closed ones, until she got too tired of the flak from both sides. The clients, liberals and good guys mostly, thought she was a mite pushy. And the Black girls couldn't appreciate the secondhand jobs once they saw what the other girls were getting firsthand. No, Corky definitely didn't need Ms. Seymour's advice.

"Vanessa," she said, trying to keep her impatience from leaking through, "as long as everything's kept confidential like you said, I don't think there's going to be a real problem. We all need just a little time to get over the shock. I don't think that's too much to ask. Now, do you want to tell me who you're considering?"

"You know I can't do that yet, Corky. All I can say is that we're working from a very short list. But the door's always open. We want to make sure we see absolutely everyone who's out there."

"I think you've seen all our girls, over and over."

"Well, you never know who might turn the lightbulb on."

"Have you decided who's going to shoot it?"

"Corky, you know that's really more Smitty's department. All I know is that we're looking at everybody who's not already taken and one or two of the newer guys. But we really can't say until we sign our girl. The right chemistry is essential. It's a terribly intimate kind of commitment, like a marriage, you know."

"Yeah, tell me about it." The sarcasm in Corky's voice was more evident than she wished. She had always considered Vanessa such a hard-boiled career woman. What did she know about intimacy and commitment?

"Well, I meant that in the figurative sense."

"Of course, Vanessa. But if you're still aiming for a September launch, it's going to be more like a shotgun wedding, don't you think?"

"I know we can do it. Nancy and Ron made it work, didn't they?"

Corky forced a chuckle, promised they'd have lunch, sure, "21" would be fine, and hung up with relief. She'd never known Vanessa Seymour to make a joke. She hoped to postpone a repeat of the experience for as long as possible.

Vanessa Seymour leafed through the stack of European fashion magazines that her secretary had just delivered. They did such exciting layouts, provocative stuff. These girls were stranger, stronger than the homegrown American beauties, although many of them, she realized, were bicontinental now, working both in the States and in Europe.

She paused at Gianni Walker's spread in *Marie-Claire*. A Black girl from California whom she knew to be all of fifteen had copper-colored extensions swinging down to her waist. She wore a white leather bikini on a desolate beach of black sand. In another picture a pouty African-looking girl in a shiny red maillot wore a long platinum-blond wig. What is this with Black models and their hair? Vanessa wondered. It could start to look interesting, sometimes even cute. But then it got totally ridiculous.

Vanessa ran her manicured fingers through her own hair until she caught a snag, which she eased out slowly. She was proud of her hair, and wore it long, straight and perfectly trimmed. She'd been bleaching it since the summer she turned sixteen and jumped up to 5′11″. That was almost twenty-five years ago and she had been relentlessly blond and tall ever since. But it wasn't as if she invented an inappropriate shade for herself as the Black girls did. She had been angelically blond as a child, and simply decided to give Mother Nature a helping hand. People had always said that she could have been a model herself, but she'd scoffed at the idea. She wanted to belong, not to stand out. And since her youth she'd organized her life that way.

If the boys on the Main Line and in the Virginia hunt country found her attractive, they found her father's money even more so. And when she graduated from Penn in May she had a big formal wedding that June. Her husband, Doc Armstead, inherited his nickname from his grandfather and his income from the medical supplies business of his less altruistic father. And he did pretty well by both.

At her thirtieth birthday party she could congratulate herself. Her life looked like a spread in *Town and Country* with all the right things in the right places. A charming husband, a lovely home, distinguished friends, exclusive clubs. But no children and after a while, no sex. Even that had not been an insurmountable problem. She knew that many couples lived contentedly within a trusting, companionable intimacy. For all that other people could see, she and her husband led a charmed life.

Even in her own eyes it was close to perfect, until she found, not even skillfully hidden, a pile of nudie magazines under his bed. Black nudie magazines. Round, greasy women with big brown nipples and thick pubic hair, wide, waxy mouths and stiff, heavy hair.

She stood up and grabbed a cigarette from the sterling case on her desk. Even now, a decade later, she could feel a hot rush of blood inflame her face, reminding her of the confusion and shame she had felt discovering her husband's betrayal and later his chilly, so-what attitude. In his fantasy he had stumbled closer to a truth than she could ever admit. And so she left, surprising everyone, leaving it all behind in Chestnut Hill, the close-to-perfect life, with her rings and his name.

But today she was here in New York, the capital of the world, looking out on the spires of Manhattan, on top of it all. She took a final drag on her cigarette and blew the smoke out in one long, luxurious stream. Control was essential, to the basics of breathing as well as to the subtleties of success. She hadn't flaunted her considerable independent income when she first arrived in the city like some of the grosser arrivistes. She had used it prudently, along with her height, beauty, intelligence and connections, to advance herself in a world of style and business she had never paid attention to before. Advertising suited her, especially the financial end, and when she and Raleigh Smith pooled their talents a few years ago, they soon became one of the classiest acts in town.

Vanessa Seymour picked up the silver apple paperweight from her rosewood desk and rubbed it on the sleeve of her Adolfo suit. It didn't need any extra polish. Like all its glittering teammates on her meticulous desk—the bud vase, picture frames and pen holder—the apple shone with a ripe luster. Such an interesting coincidence, she thought, that the symbol for New York, the Big Apple, and the symbol of temptation should be the same. Apples were good for you. New York had been good to her. But, in unguarded moments like these, she could still feel the worm inside her, the anger and resentment that gnawed far below the surface of her success.

Her mother had suggested professional counseling. Typical, ridiculous. How could she of all people say anything? A woman groomed in secrets and silence.

No, control was the key, self-control. A few minor vices might be necessary for immediate venting. Among these she considered shopping, booze and designer drugs her private contribution to keeping the economy afloat. With the addition of an occasional lover her personal ship would keep sailing quite smoothly, she thought.

Vanessa Seymour's secretary buzzed the intercom to let her know that the casting director had finished the last Cleo auditions. "Mr. Smith is still out on a shoot," she explained. "And the crew wants to know if you'd like to see the tape on the big screen or in your office."

"Certainly not in here," Vanessa replied curtly. "Tell them I'll join them in the screening room in five minutes. And that it'd better be worth my time." Maybe they've found someone new, the next new flavor of the month. Too bad for Cleo that their tastes were so . . . uncongenial. For a long time now she'd hated any form of chocolate.

So this was the little girl Becky Knight had asked her to keep an eye on? Tina Thompson chuckled to herself and wondered why Becky had been so misleading about her daughter. As far as Tina could tell, Nicky was quite capable of holding her own. If her intelligence was as healthy as her appetite, she'd do all right in New York. She ate like a typical college student, making up for lost meals and simultaneously laying away supplies for the future. While eating she also managed to talk a mile a minute about go-sees and auditions and clothes and makeup, the things most ambitious teenage models were interested in. She was her own little cyclone, but mostly Nicky Knight was a treat.

Tina nodded discreetly to her housekeeper, Mrs. English, to leave the broccoli soufflé and the platter of grilled salmon steaks on the table. She could tell from the swift disappearance of the stuffed mushroom appetizers that one serving was not going to satisfy this child. And she admonished herself to stop thinking of Nicky as a child, just because that was the last image she had of her some six or seven years ago. Time had hardly stood still. The photographs they'd just finished looking at this evening proved that she was a spectacular young woman. She had the looks that would mature into a wonderful Aura woman. And Tina knew from her own experience with Aura ads that the camera could cheat but it couldn't really lie.

"Tell me how the folks at MacLean are treating you," Tina said as she refilled their glasses with apple cider from a cut-crystal pitcher. "I've had to deal with Corky a few times when we've used their girls. She seems a little more caring than the average agent."

"MacLean's real cool." Nicky took a healthy swallow and set her glass down. "Corky's been great, considering . . ."

"Considering she's the one who found Karine Belfort?"

"Yeah. Nobody talks about it too much." Nicky looked cautiously at Tina. "Did you know her?"

"Karine? Oh yes, we'd worked together. I was horrified to hear what happened. She wanted so much to be a star."

"Are you saying that's what killed her? Ambition?"

"No, not at all. I've heard all kinds of rumors about what might have happened. From drugs to jealousy to some kind of Tontons Macoute revenge thing. I don't know what to believe."

"I have to say that things have gotten a little strange at the agency. When I first went there Corky and Robin were totally gung-ho about me. And then a week later, after Karine, everything changed. I don't know if my mother has been talking to them again or what. I do know she doesn't want me to go into the business. But I don't lead the kind of life Karine did, that fancy jet-set stuff. None of that could possibly happen to me. I'm a nobody."

"Don't kid yourself," Tina insisted. "Anybody who looks the way you do is not a nobody. Not that anything is going to happen to you. It's just that Becky knows you need a certain kind of street smarts in New York. And as a mother she's concerned."

"So let her come and see for herself that I don't fall prey to the first drug-dealing pimp in a velvet suit that I meet in Washington Square Park."

Tina had to smile at Nicky's description. "She may be doing just that."

"Really?" Nicky was excited at the prospect of introducing her mother to her new world. "Is she coming soon?"

"I hope so. She's got her schedule to deal with and we still have some details to work out. At Aura, I mean. I want to start moving into entertainment, into movies in particular. And that's where I want your mother to come on board. But some people already on the train don't quite see it my way."

"Old fogies, huh?"

"How did you know?" Tina laughed, surprised that Nicky had understood the situation so quickly.

"Isn't that always the case?"

"Well, *I'm* probably an old fogy to you."

"Not exactly." Nicky wasn't sure how she'd stuck her foot in her mouth this time, but she knew for sure it was there. It wasn't too cool to criticize a powerful friend of the family, especially one who might be hiring your mother *and* who was feeding you your first good meal since you'd left home. Besides, Tina wasn't *old*, exactly. Just old-maidish, with her quiet classical music playing in the background and her somber housekeeper in a grim braided bun.

"I'm waiting," Tina said with a devious grin. "It wasn't that long ago that I thought anyone over thirty should just jump off a cliff. Of course, now that I'm thirty-five, I don't think anyone younger should be allowed even an opinion, let alone the right to express it."

"I'm sorry, Tina. I was out of place." Nicky blushed, embarrassed.

"I'm granting you permission this one time," Tina stated with mock severity, "on one condition."

"What's that?"

"That you tell the truth about what's on your mind."

Nicky knew that she was not going to be able to escape this without some sting. Laying her fork and knife to the side of her plate, she plunged ahead. "I'd never say this to anyone, Tina, certainly not you, if you weren't totally twisting my arm. But remember when we were looking over my pictures in the living room and you said once, 'You'd make a perfect Aura woman.' Remember?"

"Yes, go on."

"It's hard to explain. When you said that, I felt weird. Embarrassed. And this is really hard to say, insulted. Like, I want to be a model. I know that, I can feel it so deep inside me that it feels like a mission. And not one that *I* chose, but one that chose me. Now, I know that, especially at the beginning, models don't choose who they work for. But right at the moment you said that, I felt that even if you asked me, I wouldn't want to be in an Aura ad. And I don't know why, really, but they just seem so corny to me, so Colored and limited and old-fashioned. The faces look so painted and the hair never moves and the expression is totally plastic. Plus, you never see an Aura ad outside of a Black magazine. And what does that mean? That Aura's not good enough for more than Black people? That Black people aren't good enough for the world?" Nicky looked up to find Tina staring intently at her. "I'm so sorry to spoil everything. I know I must sound like the last brat."

"On the contrary, sweetheart. I just wish I'd had you put all that on tape." Out of the mouths of babes, Tina thought. Some of the things Nicky had said had been hard to take, even though they confirmed her own opinions. But she was proud of Becky's daughter. Behind that beautiful face lay another treasure just as rare, a free-thinking brain. What a provocative combination. Tina was delighted to renew acquaintance with this girl-woman who could now be a friend and possibly more, an ally.

Everybody called him Mr. Thompson, except his friends, who called him Thomas. Even his mother, rest her soul, had called him Thomas. Great people, she used to say, don't have nicknames. Did anyone ever call Napoleon Nappy? So Thomas it had always been. Until Clarice. She called him Tommy and Tom and, when she was angry, Uncle Tom and, when she was excited, like now, she called him TNT. Anything else but Thomas. He did not know what he was going to do with her.

The white ceiling fan stirred the island's gentle morning air. Long white voile curtains danced around the tall windows of the pale blue room. Through them he could see the vistas of his sun-gold paradise. The mountains were so sharp against the cloudless sky, the flowers so bright, the birds so enthusiastic in their song. And this woman so sweet in his bed.

They had known each other for years, from the early days when his wife, Ella, and he built the house, one of the first big ones for rich North American Blacks. Its spacious two stories were anchored into a hillside whose rocky core was thatched by well-tended greenery. Two broad flame trees stood sentry at the entrance to the stone drive where it branched off from the dirt road. Regal palms, their shiny green coconuts bunched under licentious leaf skirts, shadowed the polite lawns while hedges of hibiscus and bougainvillea ran riot throughout the garden. Fruit grew in edenesque quantity. Besides an enormous avocado tree and three kinds of mango trees, lemon and lime trees lived conveniently right outside the kitchen door. The pool, a turquoise jewel, had been more admired than used, until Tina was old enough to learn how to swim and embarrassed her parents into learning along with her. From a lavish structure Hill House had become a comfortable retreat, a home away from home, and the Thompsons, a well-respected family.

On their quarterly trips, they made extensive use of Clarice's services for vacation clothes, Stateside gifts and household decorating. It was Clarice who suggested the sky color of this bedroom, bringing the outside inside, taming and cooling them both. A native of Barbados, widowed and reestablished with her children in St. Martin, Clarice Brathwaite owned the best sewing shop on the French side. It had prospered as the island, with its peaceful mix of Dutch and French, developed, so that now she was a well-to-do woman.

Well-to-do, well-fed, and too old to be exciting his loins the way she did. He was seventy, for God's sake, and she'd see sixty-four on her next birthday. Reluctantly, he pulled her up to lie next to him in the middle of the pale blue percale sheets.

"Your poor little ankles don't get enough attention, Tommy. Your big bony knees either. Sometimes I hear them crying out in the middle of the night. We want Clarice, we want Clarice. Protesting, don't you know?"

"I have to leave today, Clarice, you know that."

"They're celebrating Martin Luther King's birthday all over the country but this one Black man must go to work. Yes, darling. Train's puffing at the station."

"Don't be angry with me."

"Why not?"

"I don't like to leave when you're angry with me."

"Then why go?" she asked. "The only time I'm angry with you is when you leave." She inhaled the sweet wake-up perfume that glistened on their skin after spending the night together.

"You do this every time," he objected with a soft moan as she kissed the soft wrinkles of his neck.

"It hurts me every time, Tommy. Are we ever going to be together? Or is it always going to be hello and a day or two later, goodbye?"

"Clarice, be reasonable. I have work to do. My company needs me. My daughter. The time will come . . ."

"When you won't. When I'll read in the paper, no, maybe you'll even make CNN, Thomas N. Thompson, founder of Aura Products, struck by a stroke or maybe attacked by his heart. Ten years I've waited. Ten years since you came crying into my arms. Your wife dying, that's normal grief. Can't rush that. You don't even know what you're feeling, you just keep coming back for more, coming back to good old Clarice. Then your daughter takes over, moving you out of the driver's seat. Tina's what? Thirty-five? A brilliant girl, raised up to be that way, raised up to take over, and now you can't stand the fact that she's actually doing it. Now, when you should be able to relax and let go and—how do they say it?—smell the roses, you got to rush back to the cold city on the one and only holiday for a Black man. What are you so afraid you're going to miss? The sun, no, the stock market going to rise without you?"

"Stop fussing, Clarice. Just let me hold you." He reached for her but she moved away in the bed.

"Hold what? You're hooked on power and you can't let go. And I'm hooked on you. Me, a grandmother of three. I may not fit into your lifestyle, Mr. Thompson. But I know I fit into your life. You're the one who doesn't know. Well, let me get up and save these last few shreds of my dignity."

He watched her sit heavily on the edge of the bed. Clarice was a portrait of browns and rounds and curves, carved like some prehistoric fertility figure, some antique Venus as full and caring as the planet itself. Ella had never gotten fat. She had been careful, even strict with her looks, and he had been proud to wear her like a fine-tooled ornament on his arm. Loving someone like Clarice came as a surprise. It was a surprise to hear himself think that.

"I love you, Clarice," he said softly.

"Thank you, Thomas," she said without looking at him.

Then she went into Ella's bathroom and he went into his and when he came out she was gone.

CHAPTER SEVEN

GIANNI Walker's rep was ecstatic. Smith & Seymour wanted to see his book again for the Cleo campaign.

"They like you, Gianni," Renée kept saying into the phone. In the background he could hear the clatter of the restaurant where she was just finishing a lunch-cum-schmooze session with Raleigh Smith, the president, senior art director and all-purpose genie of S & S. "I can smell it, they like you."

"You're sure that's all you smell?" Gianni teased, knowing Renée's fondness for the savory cuisine of her native Provence.

"The refreshing scent of newly minted dollar bills. Dollar bills in large denominations, *mon ami*. I'm sending a messenger for your book *tout de suite*. No, I do it myself. I want to make sure it's perfection." Her accent, crisper than usual, told him she had indulged in more than one glass of wine with the meal.

"It's perfection, Renée, you don't have to bother."

"But maybe I want to, *mon chéri*." Renee liked to play the unrequited lover. As many girlfriends as she had seen troop through Gianni's studio, she had never been treated to more than a playfully platonic, professional relationship.

"It's up to you," Gianni said in a tone that meant chat time was over. "I'm in the darkroom."

"I'm en route. *Ciao*."

Gianni hung up the wall extension and went back to work. If Renée was coming he had to get these prints of Nicky Knight out of the bath right away. He held a shiny wet black-and-white shot up in the dark. She was good. Young and fresh and willing to try anything: awkward angles, unpretty expressions, shots where her face didn't show. She had a long slim body, small high breasts, and elegant hands that she didn't pose as much as she left them for him to capture. There was something of value in her very inexperience, an instinct maybe, that excited his camera. And excited him.

He had to have her in his book before it went back to S & S. But as much as he wanted a chance at a big campaign he was not going down on his knees invoking the ancestors to get it. Working on Cleo would mean working with Vanessa Seymour and that was the next to the last thing he wanted to do. The last thing he wanted was to make love with her. Again.

He didn't know that when he first met her. He'd been in the States for only two or three years after working out of Milan and Paris. He'd met her a couple of times at professional parties and she had seen his book once or twice for jobs that never came through. Last year, though, they seemed to be running into each other more often, much more often. And after the announcement of the Cleo search in the fall, they finally met for lunch.

The China Grill was a huge gray space that could have been called cavernous except that it was always cheerfully crowded and noisy, the atmosphere effervescent with movers and shakers from the advertising, publishing, and music worlds. Even the basic art of eating took on new dimension in front of the Grill's huge servings meant for two or more to share.

It was a good place for a good time. Vanessa told him how she had discovered Europe on her junior year abroad and he flattered her on her passable French and rusty Italian. She flattered him on his mysterious good looks. And he told her about his family history: his proper Afro-American parents meeting as liberated students in Italy and living there for years before settling down as respectable Foreign Service folk in D.C.

They liked each other, especially the things in each other that they liked about themselves. Good taste, high energy, unlimited ambition. A passion for the arts, the whole of modern culture. And not just as armchair aficionados. It was the nature of their business to make moves and decisions. Feeling comfortably superior, they congratulated themselves on style being part of their work and not just their weekends. They were, proudly, two of a kind.

After lunch they browsed through the museum shop across the street from the Modern Art. Then they took a cab to SoHo to see an exhibit of photographs by Henri Cartier-Bresson taken years ago when he was in the United States. By chance they discovered some small celebrity shots by Annie Leibovitz hanging in a back room of the same gallery.

"Is a photograph important for its subject or itself?" Vanessa asked.

"I don't know. It depends. What do you mean?" Her question surprised Gianni.

"I don't know. I was just thinking. Here." She pointed to a shot of a man singing. "Is this a great picture or a picture of a great man?"

"Why can't it be both? After all, you can't hear a singer's song in a picture. So performance doesn't count. You do see his face, his hands maybe, how a lyric hits an old sore spot and makes it hurt again. So maybe there is a chance for some emotion. That's what makes for a great shot. Emotion. Even if it is a perfect stillness. I don't know. I'm just talking. My work is so different. I mean, I get paid to work with only beautiful people."

"That can't be the hardest thing to do." Her sarcasm was spicy. He liked spicy.

"Of course not. Still, it's a challenge because they're professionals. They can give it to you on cue—the feeling, the attitude—but what is it they're really giving?"

"Posture or impostor?"

"You see what I mean?" He laughed. "It's hard with them, too, the models, because they have a tendency to become more important than the picture. It's not their fault. That's what the business wants. A beautiful face, a perfect figure, it's a total seduction. But nothing an artist can arrange or simulate can compare to what Nature's already given. Sometimes I think the best photographs are of unbeautiful people, or the unconventional or unexpectedly beautiful."

"Yes, I have one like that." She spoke so softly that he did not hear her.

"That's where you can see the artist at work," he continued.

"But then, you're the artist," Vanessa said brightly, "so you're prejudiced."

"Yeah, and you're the ad exec, so you're not?"

"I wouldn't go that far."

"How far would you go?" he asked. Their conversation was taking a turn in another direction and they both felt it.

"Maybe we can find out together," Vanessa answered.

It was only a short ride to his loft on Franklin Street where he showed her some of his work, photographs that he said could never go into his commercial portfolio. From a stack of elegant folders which he kept stored in a flat file downstairs he pulled out documentaries on children, cityscapes, and Native American weavings, pictures he thought of as poems shot by the soul.

Mounted on a wide white wall upstairs in his living room were portraits taken last summer during a street festival in Bahía. From the ranks of far-eyed and work-worn women he had captured a half dozen whose huge bouffant skirts remained pristinely white as they marched through dusty streets. Their skins were wood-hued, from ebony and mahogany to teak and pine. Their head wraps soared in magnificent constructions of fabric and free will. Crossed over their bodice or draped from the neck, ropes of colored beads and amulets identified their divine patrons.

He explained to her why he kept these pictures separate from the work that paid his rent, the commercial work that comprised his real professional career. He had to keep his eyes challenged, he said. The fashion world was eccentric enough to shoot a couture gown in a jungle, asphalt or Amazon. He had to know where to go and what to do under all kinds of conditions. Daring was essential to success, he said, even if it never showed overtly in the shot.

By the time they took a cab uptown to her apartment in the Olympic Tower on 57th Street, the sun was setting and their mood, to quote Billie Holiday, which he did, was fine and mellow.

The seduction was silent, swift and mutual. She touched him first, but he reciprocated instantly, feeling through, then under her clothes to warm and secret places. They made love on her black leather couch, enjoying the sheer physicality, the tangle of sensations uncomplicated by romance. And then they made love again in a Barcelona chair with her sitting on top, swishing her blond hair across his face, making him rise, rise and finally erupt.

She was quick in the bathroom and handed him a hot washcloth as she came out, dressed in a terry robe. That's what he remembered most: her speed, the abrupt way she changed from a sexual equal, an intimate partner, to a boss. It was not as much in her voice as in her manner. While she wiped the leather clean with precise, insistent strokes, he dressed quickly and quietly. He didn't understand what had gone wrong, and he was not about to ask. There were no casual thanks, no parting kisses, no tender lies. Only a brusque send-off at the door.

"I'd appreciate it," she said in a stony voice, "if you didn't tell anyone about this last part of our afternoon together."

"Vanessa, what kind of man do you think I am?"

"The worst kind," she barked, "a Black man."

Gianni was stunned. In order to get where he wanted to go, he had always known he'd have to kiss ass and kick ass. This was the first time he wanted to do both at the same time. He felt like throwing something, a book, a bottle, a fist. But she closed the door in his face and he heard the lock click into place. "Bitch," he hissed into the empty hallway.

He had never spoken to her after that. Although she seemed to smile at him in professional encounters he made sure to stay away from her. Even at Karine's party he had only nodded and otherwise kept his distance.

If Renée wanted to take his book up to S & S, more power to her. He needed the job. Who didn't these days? But he did not crave it and he'd learned that there were certain games even he would not play to get it.

At Smith & Seymour Nicky followed the receptionist's directions to Studio C. Seated on the upholstered banquettes of the tiny waiting room were three other models. They looked up at her and one or two smiled, but a nervous silence sat guard with them while the red light burned over the heavy door that was closed on an audition already in progress.

Including herself, at least five girls were called back for the Cleo campaign. Five that she could count. She didn't know if that was a good sign or bad. On her first surprise appointment for Cleo last week she had waited outside of Studio A with eight other models. More had come by the time she was taken inside, Polaroided, interviewed, videotaped and released. The star search was back on. Robin, her booker, had said to be called back was a very good sign, especially since S & S had seen practically every Black model in New York City, L.A., Chicago and Atlanta for this campaign. Sure, it was a good sign, but she was so new to the business, she thought it was cruel to get her hopes up.

Robin reminded her that the very fact she was brand-new might work to her advantage. People liked a fresh face for a big campaign, a girl untainted by exposure in a rival's ads or the gossip columns. The test pictures she had done with Angelo Vassallo and a couple of other photographers made a fantastic difference in her book. Besides, she had nothing to lose. S & S had other accounts, not as big of course, but still good, jobs that they might book her for. Being seen and getting to know people were all to her benefit in the long run.

Nicky recognized the three girls who were in the waiting room from their pictures in fashion magazines and their ads on TV. She was awed that they looked even better in real life. Their skin was impossibly smooth, their hair calculatedly casual, their clothes chicly simple. One girl held on to a dark mink coat folded across the lap of her torn blue jeans. Another girl sat swathed in a red and black cashmere wrap over a black catsuit. The third girl wore an outfit of leather jeans in butternut tan with a silk print shirt that Nicky swore she'd seen in an Hermès ad.

But Nicky knew not to waste time feeling outclassed. She'd known her wardrobe could not compete with that of models who had worn some of the most beautiful clothes in the world. Even if the girls didn't possess such fabulous clothes themselves, they knew how to wear what they did own with style. Robin had told her to stick to the basics she felt comfortable in. Just no head-to-toe black. So Nicky had worn her basic short black skirt and black tights with a low-cut pale pink sweater. Her date sweater, she called it, except that she hadn't had a chance to wear it yet. Guys didn't exactly flock to her at school. Her roommate, who had a date every other night, had suggested that Nicky's looks intimidated them. What else was new?

As the red light over the studio door went out, a familiar face exited.

"Nadja?" Nicky asked uncertainly.

"Oh, hi," she answered absentmindedly, smiling over her shoulder, again thanking the casting director who asked for the next girl to please come in.

Nicky stood up as Nadja slipped into her shearling jacket. "It's me, Nicky," she repeated.

"Nicky? What are *you* doing here?" Nadja was clearly embarrassed but also flustered by something and signaled to Nicky to follow her out of the waiting room into the hallway.

After Nicky explained that she was called back for the Cleo campaign, Nadja congratulated her with a hug, adding, "I don't want you to miss your turn."

"No, it's OK. There're three girls ahead of me."

"I'm sorry I didn't recognize you with your new haircut. It's too cute." Nadja ran her fingers through the short waves that framed Nicky's face and stepped away to take a total look. "You look great," she said with a proud smile.

"So do you, as usual." Although Nicky had only met Nadja a couple of times with her brother, JJ, she liked seeing them together. Nadja was gracious and romantic with him, teasingly unafraid to show her affections. With Nicky she had been generous enough to refer her to the photographer Gianni Walker. He had squeezed her in after a shoot one day and she ended up with some great shots to add to her portfolio. To her, Nadja was simply a beautiful person. "But," Nicky continued, "I have to say that when you came out of the studio you had the weirdest expression on your face."

"Was it showing that much?" she asked self-consciously. "As a matter of fact, I just had the strangest audition, and my last, I'm sure of that." Nadja shook her head as if she still couldn't believe what she'd been through. "This was, like, my fourth or fifth interview with them for Cleo, right? By now the casting director, the art directors, everybody knows my book even better than I do. Then today, all of a sudden, Vanessa Seymour starts talking about my Virginia Slims ads. How the image is too conflicting. A cigarette girl couldn't possibly be a Cleo girl, she said. And the whole time she's in there she's smoking like a chimney! It was so insulting."

Nicky let Nadja blow off the steam she'd held in. "Can one person decide these things?" Nicky asked.

"No, but all it takes is one person to make you feel bad. And *look* bad. And with the tape rolling!" Nadja checked her Cartier watch. "Let me get out of here. I've got a booking in a half hour. You should call me sometime. We need to get together, just the two of us, OK?"

"I'd love to." Nicky kissed Nadja on the cheek and left traces of her lipstick there. She'd have to learn not to do that, she scolded herself on the way back to the waiting room. She'd always made fun of air kisses, but Max had explained their origin during their session at Angelo Vassallo's studio. Messing someone's makeup was like trespassing on private property. It could be dangerous.

Back inside the waiting room Nicky took a seat with the two remaining girls. Her interview over, one model left the studio, and the next was called in. Nicky was happy to see that no one was waiting after her. But she was more than a little concerned about what was to come during the audition. If a star like Nadja had been insulted, how would they treat a nobody like her?

"I told you, Mom. I told you I could do it, that there was a special place for me. But I never dreamed something this wonderful could happen," Nicky bubbled over the phone.

"It's so exciting, sweetheart, but I can't make out a word you're saying with all the screeching. Try and calm down and tell me how it happened."

"Calm down? How do I do that? A week ago I spent an eternity in the studio auditioning just like anybody else. And today, a day just like any other, I find out that I hit the jackpot. I'm the new Cleo girl. I'm zooming and you want me to calm down?"

"Ouch, Nicky! Get those feet back down on the ground and lower the volume. Talk to me, sweetheart. You can fly around later."

"OK, OK." As she recounted the scene to Becky, Nicky thought she was still in that day's dream. "First I got a wake-up call from Corky telling me to meet her at the agency at twelve-thirty sharp. No details. Just look great, she said. Then a long limo drove us to Park Avenue and we got on a private elevator that took us nonstop to the forty-eighth floor."

As Becky listened to her daughter's excited account of the announcement, she waited for an opening, some break in the rush of words where she could inject a little realism. She had no intention of dampening Nicky's enthusiasm. She was just as thrilled as Nicky was. But she wanted to tell her that there was a darker side to the shiny coin she'd just been tossed. Nicky gave her no space to interrupt as she continued gushing gaily about it all. The magnificent wood-paneled private dining room of Cleo, Inc., overlooking the bustling midday traffic all the way across to the leafless oasis of Central Park. The exquisitely laid table with impeccable linens, china and crystal glowing under a dazzling chandelier. Lavish bouquets of flowers in every corner of the room. The plush velvet carpet overlaid with Oriental rugs silencing every step. Three waiters in formal dress for six people.

"And they started off with a champagne toast. It was hilarious. Five grown-ups standing up toasting me! Kyle Whitaker, he's the president of Cleo Inc., actually apologized for having the luncheon in-house, he put it. Some house!"

"Well, Corky did explain to me that everything must be entirely hush-hush. No public announcement, no change whatsoever in your ordinary life."

"Isn't that a hoot?"

"It's an absolutely essential precaution, sweetheart, and I hope you follow their instructions to the letter. I'm so proud of you, I don't know what to do."

"Well, you can come out here and help me celebrate for one thing."

"You can be sure of that. Just as soon as we finish rehearsal."

"Just when is that?" Nicky got the slightly sour feeling she'd asked the same question many times before.

"You know how that goes. In about three weeks."

"Please, Mom." She wanted her mother to know how much this meant to her. "Make it soon. I want you to meet everyone. They're such characters. Kyle is so cool. I don't have to call him Mr. Whitaker or anything like that. They picked Gianni, yeah, Gianni Walker to shoot the campaign. He's so handsome, he should be a model himself. And who else was there? Well, you know Corky. And oh, the top guns from Smith & Seymour: Raleigh Smith and Vanessa Seymour. Smitty's got this incredible southern accent you wouldn't believe and Vanessa's straight out of central casting for the serious career woman."

"It sounds like you're in good hands, sweetheart. But I promise I'll come and see for myself as soon as I can."

"Promise?"

"Nicky, when have I ever disappointed you before?"

"Mom, let's not go into that. Just make it as soon as possible. My first job is in a couple of days and I am so nervous. I don't know how I'm going to handle this double life. I have to pretend that classes are cool when I don't care about them at all anymore. I even had to wait for my roommate to go out on a date before I could call and tell you. I feel funny practicing in the mirror when my roomie's here, and now I don't even remember what I look like."

"Well, you don't have to remember," Becky said reassuringly. "Part of being a good model is forgetting what you look like. The people looking at you know. They liked what they saw and that's why they chose you. You don't have to worry about that part."

"What do I have to worry about, then?"

"Being a target for people who *don't* like the way you look or what you stand for. Remember, other girls have been on this road before." Becky stopped abruptly. Those girls had not arrived at their destination. If Becky could have her way, Nicky would quit right now. She had proven that she could compete and succeed. If she quit, she could also be safe.

"But I'm going the distance, Mom. I can feel it. I wasn't wrong before, was I?"

"No, you weren't," Becky had to admit.

"And I'm not wrong now. The hard part was winning."

But Becky knew better. "The hard part is only just beginning, honey. Really, only just beginning."

CHAPTER EIGHT

"GREAT, perfect, right there. Now, chin down, beautiful, good. Next roll. Hair! Get somebody out here, please. Elmo, a little less hair, huh? Cut back on the wind, Steven. We want a few wisps across her face but no hurricane, OK? You've gotta tell me, Nicky, if it's too strong. We want you gently refreshed not battered," Gianni said, moving in a whirlwind of his own.

So far, so good, Nicky thought. In another half hour, they'd break for lunch. Then they could restyle her hair, wave it maybe, glamorize it a bit. They'd done indoor fresh face, were working on outdoor active, and would do a couple of luxe looks before the day was over. She was excited. All around her in the studio people were buzzing, asking her opinion on the clothes and accessories, asking how she felt, what she wanted, what she needed. She didn't want to sound goody-goody and boring, but, really, everything was more than fine.

"OK, people, clear the seamless. Let's get back to work." Gianni directed all aspects of the shoot with the confident energy of a symphony conductor. He alone set the pace, and he expected everyone to follow. "Steven, give me some Debussy, something flowing and melodic."

"How about Vollenweider?" his assistant asked.

"Perfect. OK, Nicky, think sunset at Santa Monica. Peaceful, glowing. One arm over your head, relaxed, good. Arm down, more profile, yes,

yes. Remember to give the strobe time to recycle. Yes, smaller smile, smaller, yes. The light is on inside, yes, good. Think far horizon, your man coming home. He's coming but he's not there yet. Bring him home with those eyes, yes, yes, great. Next roll."

"I want some full length of that, Gianni," said Kyle Whitaker, standing a few feet behind the camera. "I like that mood. Keep the sunshine in there, though. What do you think, Smitty?"

"Fabulous, she's just fabulous," he said. What's more, he meant it. Raleigh Smith was, despite his signature denim work shirts, not an easy man to please. In his golden brown hair, which he wore parted in the middle and which fell in smooth drapes over his forehead, could be seen the remnants of a golden and willful childhood. The only scion of Virginia aristocrats long used to indulging family eccentrics, Smitty had drawled his way through northern opposition to establish one of the hottest ad agencies in New York. His pride lay in his witty intelligence, a trait he was surprised to find most other ad folk possessed only in rare moments and reduced amounts. "She's fresh and unspoiled and credible," Smitty added, while a severely crew-cut assistant in jeans nodded earnestly at his elbow. "We do want credible."

"But I want *in*-credible," said Kyle, looking for confirmation to his assistant, a sleek young Black woman in a stylish suit.

"I know, I know. I'm just thinking with both brains at once. Full length and then real tight on the face, too, I think. We want to have lots of room to play."

Gianni let them chat behind his back. He would give them everything they wanted and more.

"Barefoot, Nicky. Jackie, lose the heels. No, no flats either. I like you standing, tiptoes, reaching for a wider view. Then we'll seat you in the chaise and tie a sweater around your neck, OK? Now, tall, good, reaching, seeking, collar up, good. Not straining, though, relaxed, OK? Close the eyes, good, relax the face, good. Bring the fill around, Steven. You can feel the sun breaking through the clouds, yes. It's coming, he's coming, yes, yes, good, great, perfect. Next roll. Wait. Nicky, break for five while we change the set a little."

Nicky stepped into her ballerines at the edge of the set and swiped a Perrier from the lunch table before heading back to the dressing room.

"Now that you've left half your mouth on the bottle you might as well take it all off." At the doorway Max handed her a tissue. "I have this lovely sheer stuff I want to try on you anyway. If they hate it, we can always change."

"I'm so glad you're the one who's here, Max. It wouldn't be the same without you," Nicky said, sitting down in front of the mirror.

"It wouldn't *be* without me, little one. How could I let an innocent babe wander into the woods with these wolves?" He let her finish drinking and then brushed her lips with a soft coral color. "What do you think?"

"I like it," said Nicky.

"Nice," Jackie, the stylist, agreed.

"Let me get at those front curls again," Elmo said, rapidly twisting a few sections of hair around his hot curling iron. "Just let them cool down and we'll loosen them up on the set. She looks beautiful, Max. You did a great job."

"Thanks, Elmo. What's with the compliment? Do you owe me money or something?"

"Doesn't it wear you out being a cynic all the time?" asked the hairdresser with the slightest hint of pity in his voice.

Kyle and Smitty entered the dressing room before Max could come up with a smart remark. And he was glad of it. This had always been his trademark attitude. Slice, dice, and stroke. Elmo's question was simply, All the time? Even though the new year was almost a month old, the new—and hopefully improved—Max had yet to appear.

"Something around the neck," Smitty was saying. "What do you have soft and floaty for around the neck, Jackie?"

"I have these two cardigans," she said, holding up the necks of their hangers, "this cream in cashmere and this dusty rose in silk. They both have pullovers to match if you want to lose the shirt." As she hung them back up she went through other garments on the rack. "Here're some blouses with a more feminine edge, a lace frill or a nice little scallop, if you like. Scarves are on the table over here. This lace fling gets a little too dressy maybe for a daytime feel, but these solid chiffons can float."

"I like the cream twin set and a chiffon float," said Smitty. "What about you, Kyle? It's your shoot."

"I like the twin set but I like tying the cardigan. Let's see how it looks on the set, you know, see if we need more breeze in the garments. I like it simple, but I don't want it to read unfinished, you know?"

"Good, good. What do you think, Nicky?" Smitty asked.

"I love it simple," she said.

When they left the dressing room, Max said, "You've just learned the cardinal rule for success in modeling, my dear."

"What's that?" asked Nicky.

"Always agree with the client." Everybody smiled. The girl was a beginner with the instincts of a pro.

Nicky took off the white linen shirt she had been wearing. Then Elmo tied a big silk scarf loosely over her hair and face, so that she could pull the sweater down over her head and not mess things up. They did last-minute repairs. Max ran the essential brushes over her face to lift her brows, smooth the eye shadow, refresh the blusher, retouch the lip color, and powder away any patches of shine. Elmo massaged her scalp and with his fingers combed her hair into the hint of a casual style.

Steven stood at the doorway. "Ready? On the set, please."

Gianni liked the outfit and helped position her in the rattan chaise.

"Feet up. Jackie, get the bottoms of those trousers, please. Relax, Nicky, more, soft, boneless. Good, hold it, I'm focusing, good. Hold it for the 'roid. Thank you. Kyle, this is great. Want a look? Smitty? Is this something of what you had in mind?"

Each one bent to look through the Hasselblad enthroned on the chrome tripod. Each one came away smiling, pleased.

After checking the Polaroid, Gianni said, "I'm going to shoot a few rolls this way and then I'm going to the Nikon, no tripod, so you'll have it covered both ways, OK?"

"Whatever you say, Gianni. It looks perfect," Kyle said.

For all the preparation and minute adjustments the actual shoot did not take long. Once freed from the stabilizing tripod, Gianni loosened up and Nicky with him, and they caught each other in a series of fleeting, flashing moments where movement, expression, and shutter wordlessly agreed. She felt silly and playful. She forgot she had makeup on, forgot she was dressed in clothes that had to be returned to a store, forgot she would appear around the world in this picture. Nothing was a responsibility. It was all carefree fun.

"We got it," Gianni said triumphantly. "Break for lunch, people."

After she had taken off her clothes but before she could eat, Nicky had to let Elmo set her hair in hot rollers. Then she slipped on her black unitard and headed for the lunch table. Although huge platters of hot and cold pasta, salads, and sliced meats and cheeses were spread out, Nicky noticed that only the armed guard from Tiffany had served himself a full plate. The others were nibbling on the tiniest portions.

"Why aren't you guys eating?" Nicky asked Jackie.

"None of us can afford to eat," she answered. "No one here but you is eighteen, sweetheart."

"Besides," said Max, "fashion people never eat in public. They wait till they get home and then out come the chips and chocolate donuts. Tell the truth, Jackie. What's your weakness?"

She hesitated, twisting one of the tiny dreads that sprouted in a neat cluster on the top of her head. "Ice cream, I confess. I admit it. I am the original Häagen Dazs-aholic. There're always two pints in the freezer. One for when I just gotta have it. The other for when I'm exercising total self-control and I manage to let the thing soften up properly before I gobble it down. It's pitiful. Me, a woman of such taste and sophistication. In Europe I'm the worst. In Italy, forget it. Point me to the gelati and I don't care what Armani and Versace are showing. What about you, Gianni?"

"Me? Are you kidding? I was born in Italy, the land of *mangia, mangia*. I eat everything and lots of everything. Plus, I have the special burden of making up for all my people who are starving. But I run every other morning, otherwise . . ."

"Don't you just hate those people?" Max cut in. "Up at the crack of dawn making you feel bad before your day's even begun because you're not out there chugging along with them? We should find some real work to put them to. You know, like maybe jumping up and down in hot asphalt to fill in all the potholes. Something useful to society, you know?"

"Careful," Smitty shhhed. "One of our clients makes running shoes."

"Oh, that's right," said Max, "the ones you have to make a down payment on, they cost so much."

"Quality, Max."

"Can you picture it? You're wearing a mortgage on your feet, and then you're going to run all over Manhattan and risk slipping in all kinds of, you know, do? Please."

"We're eating, Max," Jackie said.

"Excuse me, I forgot. I finished my little crumb so quickly."

"Feel free," said Kyle. "Have another."

"I'll wait till I get home and remove the corset, thank you. Appearances, appearances."

"Speaking of appearances," Gianni said, "after lunch, it's star time, people. Elmo, I want hair, but very different."

"I have some pieces if you want me to use them."

"No," said Kyle, "I like what she's got. I'd just like to see some more variety."

"Is she blowing or still?" Elmo asked.

"Still for the most part," said Gianni, "but I want her to be able to move if she wants to."

"Well, you can go the gamut with this cut, whatever you want. I also have the hair spray of life, responsible, I figure, for about ninety percent of the hole in the ozone layer."

"Maybe we could do without that for the time being," said Kyle.

"Thank you," said Nicky, patting her rollers. "We all thank you."

Once back in the dressing room they geared up for glamour. It was time to lay on the false lashes, the darker shadows, the deeper blushes, the vivid lips. Tension was building with each layer of makeup.

"Don't worry, Nicky," said Max. "You've still got a face underneath. A fabulous face. Remember, *you're* wearing this paint. The paint's not wearing you."

Although all the pictures were basically head shots, they had to be prepared to go full length at any time. That meant accessorizing panty hose and pumps to the dress. Nicky looked skeptical.

"You'll see," said Jackie as she handed her a pair of Manolo Blahnik sling backs. "They make you feel complete. You know you're dressed and *properly* dressed and somehow that comes through in the picture even though the shoes and hose may never show. It comes through in you."

"It's just that I never wear heels," said Nicky. "I'm not used to walking in them at all."

"Rites of passage. You'll get used to them. My favorites become my mood elevators, make me feel like I can conquer the world. Come on now, try these. If they get too uncomfortable let me know. We'll work something out."

Between Kyle and Smitty, Gianni and Jackie, they settled on wardrobe for the last two shots: a short flounce of turquoise taffeta by Oscar de la Renta with just enough ruffles around the shoulders to make a pretty frame and then a lavish red ball gown by Bill Blass with a velvet bodice trimmed in silk satin and huge satin skirt, perfect for the holiday spread.

"Gosh, it's hard to think about next Christmas when we've barely finished with this one," said Nicky.

"That's how it goes in fashion," Jackie explained. "You never live in the present. You're always three to six months ahead of everybody else. At least. That's our schedule."

"And our madness," Max added. "How can you blame fashion people for being space cadets? We're never where we look like we are."

From outside the dressing room Steven called, "How much longer till you're ready?"

"Five minutes," Jackie answered. "She's all dressed. We'll be out in five, but could we have some more coffee in here, please?"

"Coming up," he said.

"Before I put this last lip on," said Max, "are you going to have any coffee or anything?"

"No thanks, coffee makes me zoom," said Nicky.

"That's the whole point. Sometimes your energy sags and you need a pick-me-up."

"Whatever you want, we got." Jackie patted her shoulder. "We're here to make you happy so you make a fabulous picture and we all get hired again, right? OK, let's roll, comrades."

When Kyle and Smitty saw Nicky on the set, they were more

convinced than ever that they had made the right choice. She combined the looks of a princess with the spirit of the girl next door: a modern beauty both elegant and approachable.

"She's the kind of girl women will fall in love with," said Smitty, "without the fear, without the envy."

"So, you see that quality, too." Kyle stroked his beard thoughtfully. "Good, that's just what we want."

Smitty let out a panicked whisper. "Oh, God, I forgot to give Vanessa a call. I said I'd phone her during the lunch break to tell her how things are going. I'll be right back."

As he turned toward the end of the studio that belonged to Renée, he found her right behind him.

"Ms. Seymour on the phone, Mr. Smith. And not in a very good mood," she emphasized.

Smitty walked to the phone at her desk as if he were headed for punishment. "I was just getting ready to call you, Vanessa."

"I do appreciate the thought. Is it still siesta time or are you people actually working down there?"

"Vanessa . . ." he pleaded.

"Just tell me. Are you getting anywhere or have we wasted another day and God only knows how much money?" Vanessa asked. They were all used to her bark by now. Unlike the proverbial dog, it was just as bad as her bite.

"It's fabulous . . ." His drawl stretched the word to its limit.

"If I hear that expression one more time . . . Just tell me if the girl knows what she's doing."

"If you'd listen for a moment, I would." He took a deep breath. "Nicky is perfect."

"Good, that's all I wanted to hear. I don't need to tell you how much this has cost us already."

"No, you don't, Vanessa, and certainly not now."

"Well," she huffed. "Excuse me, but I have a call on another line." And with that she abruptly hung up.

Smitty walked back to the shooting area barely repressing a small grin of triumph.

"I see your head's still intact," Kyle said.

"I think she loves me." He folded his hands over his heart. "That must be it. She loves me madly but she just doesn't know how to express herself."

At that preposterous notion, Raleigh Smith and Kyle Whitaker laughed a little too loudly, forcing Gianni Walker to call out for quiet. That was a serious breach of protocol. The photographer never reprimanded his clients that way, but Kyle and Smitty understood that they were indeed at fault and they fell into an obedient silence.

"This is it, *bella,*" said Gianni to Nicky on the set. "Stand with your back to me and look around over your shoulder. I like it, I like it. Hold still for the 'roid. Thank you," he said, handing the film off to Steven before turning back to Nicky. "Now, we're at a party. I saw you when you first came in but it's taken you this long to notice me. Maybe it's your girlfriend who points me out, saying, 'Don't look now.' I want some funk, Steven, genuine. Sly and the Family, yes. Now that we've made eye contact, we move in closer. Good, good. Not quite so bold. You don't really know who I am yet. Yes, good. Hold it, I'm bracketing. Hold still for three shots. Yes, yes, yes. I like you smiling, good, but smaller smiles, yes, eye smiles only, good. Next roll, please. This girl has got it, people. A star is born today!"

They shot several more rolls in that special interplay between model and photographer, a constant, unspoken dialogue, punctuated by the crank of the camera after each shot. Nicky felt sucked into an exuberant kind of confusion, a giddy, almost sexual turmoil where trust was never in question and fidelity some kind of foreign word. Gianni was awfully cute. His hair had come undone so that a few dark tendrils fell over his forehead and around his cheeks. She wanted to touch them. Touch him. She wondered what was behind the way he moved in those baggy black pants, what lay underneath the crisp white shirt buttoned so primly at the neck. He set up these wonderful dramatic scenes that she loved improvising on. It thrilled her that he knew exactly what he was doing, how to direct her, how to challenge her and make her bring out the best in herself. She had never felt this way before. And she wondered if she was having any effect on him, anything like the effect he was having on her. He could look so closely at her, so deeply into her. When she looked back, all she saw was the round lens in the black box. Where was he? she wondered. What was he feeling?

After they finished with the turquoise dress, they prepared for the last shot, which seemed to take forever. Nicky felt the frayed ends of everyone's nerves and opted for a neutral silence. The hair was too flat, too sleek. Kyle wanted something higher and looser, he told Elmo. "You know, after the big Christmas Eve dinner, all the ornaments are finally up, but then the hairdos start to fall. Something a little more . . . accidental, you know?"

Elmo muttered around the dressing room, "You know, you know? If I knew, I'd give it to him."

Jackie liked long earrings and no necklace for the décolletage of the ruby dress. Smitty wanted what he called "small but serious sparklies" on the ears and around the neck. "I'm thinking heirloom," he kept saying. "I'm thinking family tradition. Grandmother, no, Great-grandmother is passing down a valued treasure to her favorite girl. She's seen war and calamity, migration and huge change, but she's kept the family together and now it's time to pass the torch along."

"I love the saga," said Jackie, "but I get the feeling that you're thinking about *your* grandmother, Smitty, like Christmas at Tara or something. That necklace is too complicated for Nicky. It's simply too Victorian and too heavy."

They finally settled on ear clips of diamonds and rubies and a delicate chain with a rose-shaped pendant set with more rubies and diamonds and bright green emeralds for the leaves.

"Do you feel all right, Nicky?" Max asked. "All this back-and-forth can be a little wearisome."

"I'm OK, I'm just a little tired."

"At the end of the day even the best people can wear you out," said Jackie, sipping from her permanent cup of coffee. "Let me get you some," she said, leaving the dressing room.

"There's always something else to give you a bit more of a lift," said Elmo casually.

"Keep your bad habits to yourself," Max hissed. "And don't you ever let me hear that kind of talk again. I'm responsible for this child and

I'm not going to let anything happen to her. Do you hear me, Elmo?"

"My, Mother Max is so touchy."

"Come on, you two. I want to get this over with, OK?"

"Ready on the set in five, please," Steven called.

Everyone summoned up their energy reserves for the final shot. By now Nicky was used to the waiting, focusing, relighting, scene-setting, more waiting and then action.

"You look lovely, Nicky," Gianni was cuing her on the set. "But it's not just the clothes and jewels and all the dazzle around you that make you look lovely. You're lovely because you're *in* love, OK? Everybody's gone to bed, from the old folks to the tiny tots. You and your lover are alone in front of a romantic fire. Violins, Steven. Chestnuts roasting and a crooner. Nat or Natalie. Yes. The champagne is sparkling. The tree is sparkling. Your eyes, yes, give me those eyes. Good, yes, beautiful, yes. More loving, yes, loving but still awake, sweetheart, yes, good, very good."

After seven or eight rolls Gianni said, "We got it." Everyone applauded. Relief washed over Nicky's face and left a big, numb smile. Kyle kissed her and said she was magnificent. Smitty kissed her and said she was fabulous, just fabulous. Jackie kissed her and thanked her for making her job so easy. Elmo kissed her and said to call him soon. After so much commotion she was amazed to see that the studio cleared out in less time than it took to remove the makeup from her face. The Tiffany guard left with his strongbox of jewels. All the clothes and other accessories were zippered in their garment bags ready to be picked up and returned to their showrooms tomorrow. Kyle, Smitty, and their assistants moved off in a gray stretch limousine.

As Nicky watched Gianni and Steven dismantle the set, she thought the studio seemed too big and painfully hollow. Only the Christmas tree remained intact and that would be dismantled tomorrow. Everything and everybody disappeared so quickly.

"Come on," said Max, sliding a friendly hand under Nicky's arm. "You want to have a bite somewhere or do you want to go home?"

"I don't think I can go straight home after all this." She swept her arm around the room and when she turned to look at him, he saw the seeds of tears in her eyes. "I mean, Max, is this all there is to it?"

"Funny, isn't it? The fantasyland of fashion. You can fold it all up and pack it in a box."

"The feelings, too?"

"Especially the feelings, princess. They could be hazardous to your health." As he tied a knot in the belt of his cashmere coat, he saw her eyeing Gianni Walker. "I'll go get my kit and be right back."

Nicky started to walk over to Gianni but a confused shyness stopped her. What could she really say to him? "Thank you" sounded so weak.

Gianni called over to her. "You're not leaving without saying good-bye, are you?"

"No, of course not." She wanted to say his name, but that one word seemed somehow too personal, too intimate. She walked toward him, extending her hand.

"Cara Nicole, che bella." He took her hand, placed it alongside his cheek and kissed the inside of its palm. "You were so wonderful today, perfect. My camera says that you're going to be a big star. But this is the little face I'll always love." He kissed her on both cheeks.

Her face burned where his lips had touched her. A sudden, awful yearning made her want to throw her arms around his neck and press her body into his.

"Miss Nicky," Max called from the door, "the pumpkin's waiting."

"Thanks again, Nicky," Gianni said, starting to turn back to his work. "I'll be seeing you."

"You will?"

They both heard an anxious note of desire spill over into her question. And they both knew that nothing could be done about it. Now.

"Well, you know"—Gianni hesitated—"once we get the film back and begin making our shot selection, I'm sure I'll be seeing you again."

"Oh, sure," she said, defeated. "Well, I hope it looks good."

"I know it will. You're great. *Ciao*." And he turned away.

There was nothing more to say and only one last thing to do. With the very last of her energy and the most of her courage, she walked out of the studio with a perfect smile on her face and the perfect breeze in what was a new word for her. *Ciao*. Funny that it meant hello *and* goodbye.

The black stretch limo, courtesy of Cleo, Inc., drove uptown and angled through McDonald's drive-in at 42nd Street and tenth Avenue. Nicky, Max and even the driver—at Nicky's insistence—ordered double bacon cheeseburgers, fries and shakes and then gorged on the way downtown to her dorm in Greenwich Village.

"Slumming at Micky D's," Max said, wiping his fingers on a stack of napkins. "This is the kind of stuff gossip columnists love."

"You said anything I wanted, Max. Well, that's what I want. Your basic comfort foods: grease, salt and sugar."

"Just don't blame me when it pops out on your face tomorrow."

"And why not? It is your fault. You're not a good chaperone if you allow me to do something wrong."

"I'm indulging you just this once, OK? After a hard workout in the studio, you deserve a break today. Isn't that how it goes?"

Nicky wiped a squirt of ketchup from the corner of her mouth. "How did I look, Max? Tell me the truth."

"You looked wonderful, princess."

"But they can't possibly use all the stuff they shot, can they?"

"You'd be surprised. There're so many places for pictures to go besides the magazines. You've got points-of-purchase all over the place. You know, those displays you see in department stores and on the cosmetic counters. You've got newspaper ads. They're your black-and-whites. You've got regional marketing to consider. Special gift with purchase. Personal promos. Lotsa stuff, kiddo. All part of making beauty a billion-dollar business."

"Gets a little scary when you put it like that." Nicky was starting to look a little withered.

"You did your job, my dear, so just rest easy. The next moves are up to them. You can go on back to your classes and resume life as a normal college coed. Nobody will know anything different until the fall."

"I hope."

"We all hope." After a pensive chew, Max said, "Not to change the subject, darlin', but did I see you making eyes at that gigolo after the job was over?"

"Max!" Nicky set her burger down and wiped her mouth and fingers. "What are you talking about?"

"You know what I'm talking about, and who. Now listen," Max spoke seriously, "I don't want to see you let your heart get careless about some man in a ponytail who's been telling you all day long how beautiful you are. How perfect, how great. Remember, he's paid to do that. He's paid to do whatever it takes to get the shot. That's his job. And you're paid to give him the shot. The look, the smile, the attitude. Don't get that confused with giving him your heart. Do you hear me?"

"I hear you."

"And it's not just Gianni. There're going to be lots of guys sniffing around you. People you'll work with. People who'll want to take you out and show you off. People who'll want to be your friend as long as you're paying the bill. Or be your master, since you're nothing but a brainless little mo-dell. You've got *everything* going for you. Don't sell out cheap 'cause you're feeling lonely. Or 'cause somebody looks good. Time is on your side. OK?"

"OK," Nicky said shyly.

"Good. End of sermonette." Max wiped his forehead with a pocket handkerchief. "Lord have mercy, no wonder I was exempted from parenthood."

"Too bad. You'd make a wonderful father."

"You think so?"

"Naw, a wonderful mother."

"Cruel, cruel. The child has become a wicked wench in less than twelve hours."

"God, and how long have we been sitting here? I didn't know I was home already." Nicky looked out at the dormitory and watched students, a couple of whom she knew, peering into the limo's dark windows. "The return of Cinderella," she sighed.

"Not for long, princess. Soon everyone will know exactly who you are." Max kissed her on the forehead as the chauffeur opened her door.

When JJ Knight got back to his loft that night, he was disappointed that Swayze was the only one to greet him. The Rottweiler jumped up on his chest and licked him with his own sloppy brand of affection. Nadja was still in Paris doing the haute couture shows, and he was missing her again. He had gotten used to her daily presence, the sweet surprise of finding her already at home or the anticipation of the elevator clicking up to his floor, the door opening and her beautiful face smiling at him. They'd had many talks, not to mention arguments, about keeping each other's keys. She wanted her independence. He wanted her. The new year had brought a new level of trust and unity to their relationship. Now they had each other's keys, they had their own work to do and they also had each other. It was working out fine, but he couldn't wait for her to get back.

He would chill before calling Nicky and taking her out to celebrate her first Cleo shoot.

Easing himself slowly out of the darkness, he turned the spotlights on the two Bearden collages, purchased as treats to himself for the first two platinum albums he'd produced. It was strange, the effect Romare Bearden's art had on him. There was a magical shift to another dimension beyond the paint and paper, to a familiar world he'd never lived in but which, instead, lived inside him. In one, he could hear rough-hewn, smoky blues coming from the four musicians as clearly as if there were a record attached to the picture, a 78 worn scratchy by someone's love. Same thing with the other, a patchwork vision of a woman bathing in a steel tub. Only there he heard a train in motion, just leaving the station, its long, sad whistle prolonged by the sigh of a single reed like a clarinet or a soprano sax. A different kind of composition but music nonetheless. Timeless as a heartbeat, sweet as a goodbye kiss.

He used to like this hour, the early part of what used to be late nights, the time after everyone had cleared out, when his mind could also clear out. This is when he'd stretch out on the big sectional sofa, smoke a last peaceful joint, rewind the tapes, and really listen to the sounds they'd been engineering all day. Listen and lose himself in the singer's voice, in a soaring melodic wave or a wicked kick-ass rhythm. In the total metaphysical feel of the piece. Then the phone would start to ring, he'd get dressed and hit the clubs with his posse to see what damage they could do.

That kind of action seemed like the old days now. Since falling crazy in love with Nadja, he'd cut back on the long hours, the smoke and coke, the party-hearty moves en masse. When he did hang these days it was on quality time. He liked that. He liked the respect he felt aimed at him when he and Nadja went out together. Respect, admiration, and maybe even a touch of envy. Good, served the hard-leg motherfuckers right. Besides being a famous face, she was a real woman. Now get to that. Nicky was another one with a face and a self to back it up. With the Cleo contract and everyone rooting for her to go the distance, little sister had it made in the shade.

Funny how nobody mentioned the other two, the other Cleo girls. Talk about out of sight, out of mind. He was glad for the secrecy surrounding Nicky but at the same time, he didn't trust fashion people. They were so addicted to gossip and dish in general he didn't see how it would be possible to keep anything quiet, let alone a coup like the Cleo campaign. It didn't matter if they *had* signed confidentiality agreements. You had to stuff their mouths with money, drink or drugs—and plenty of it—to truly shut them up. He vowed to be there as much as he could for her. She would need all the help she could get.

He picked up the cordless phone from the end table and pressed the button programmed with Nicky's number. "Yo, Cleo," he said when she answered. "What it is?"

"JJ," she laughed, "somehow I have a real hard time picturing you with a baseball cap on backwards."

"Well, tell me, how'd it go? How was the shoot?"

"Faaabulous," she squealed. "It was great. Great fun, but I never worked so hard in my life."

He listened as she described her day, the different moods and clothing changes and everything she'd had to deal with. And he remembered how often he would tease Nadja, saying it couldn't be that hard to smile and look pretty all day long. She had given up trying to make him understand. But some days he could see in her tired face and tense body evidence of how exhausting modeling could be, what hard work it was.

"Nick," he broke in, "save it. We can talk about this over dinner. Tell me, where do you want to go to celebrate tonight? Anyplace your heart desires."

"Listen, JJ, I really appreciate this and I do want to celebrate, but I just can't tonight. I'm pooped. All I want to do is lie down and close my eyes. I feel as if the strobe lights are still flashing, you know? Like there's still one more roll to shoot. Can we do it later? Maybe over the weekend?"

He could tell that she was still wound up. The mix of contradictory emotions, excitement, and fatigue, especially added to the brand-newness of the work, would keep her unsettled for a while. "Sure, Nick, whatever works for you."

"Cool. Maybe when Daddy gets here we can all hang out together."

"And when is that supposed to be?"

Nicky heard the hurt and skepticism in his voice.

"I'm not sure, but I got a message from him on my machine to leave tomorrow open for lunch. Do you want to come?"

"No, that's OK, just keep me posted. I'll be in the studio all day."

"Bet. Thanks for calling, JJ. Bye."

He had wanted to warn Nicky, to tell her not to hold her breath waiting for her father to come through. But he was glad he hadn't. What did he know about their relationship? Fathers and daughters had a closer thing, maybe. It's not that he wasn't close to Kayo. Being professionals in the music business taught them to respect each other in a way the father-son relationship alone had not.

Kayo was his father, but unlike Nicky, he could not remember ever calling him Daddy. Or maybe it was so long ago he had chosen to forget. What a trip. A bicoastal father, more famous than familiar. And a bilingual mother, who knew more about art and wine than her own son. He wasn't complaining, exactly. He was proud he'd made it this far with the folks he came from. But when he and Nadja had children, he was determined to never let them out of his sight. Not until they were grown. And maybe not even then.

CHAPTER NINE

"I'M SORRY to cancel at the last moment like this, kitten," Kayo Knight apologized to his daughter over the phone in his Mercedes limousine. He was tied up in a business meeting that was moving to the Four Seasons for lunch, and there was no way he could get out of it. Later on he was having drinks with an old friend at six and then dinner with an important person at eight. He didn't know how it happened but time seemed to run away from him.

Nicky wasn't surprised. Something in JJ's voice last night had prepared her for today.

"That's OK, Daddy. I understand. I should have known something was up when I got those gorgeous roses you sent. And it was so sweet to send thirteen. At first I thought the florist made a mistake. But then I figured you wanted me to have something extra-special. Well, they'll let you off the hook today, but I don't want you skipping out of town on me. Just because you don't have to support me anymore doesn't mean I don't need a father." She tried hard to keep her voice light and less demanding. "And here I had all these big plans to surprise you by picking up the tab for lunch today. Next time I'm going to make you suffer by ordering the biggest, most expensive lunch in all of New York City."

"Anything you want, honey. Whatever you say. But look, I gotta run now. I'll talk with you soon." Kayo switched off and fell immediately back into conversation with the two gentlemen riding with him.

When he checked in with his L.A. office at the end of the day, his assistant assured him that no, he hadn't wired his daughter any roses. Was he supposed to?

Men of power may sit down together to toast or roast each other, but when it comes to business they stand alone. Especially Black men. There are so few of truly serious means. They rarely do business together. They may describe, discuss, and even develop foolproof deals together, but they seldom sign on the same dotted line.

It is a matter of trust. Not in each other—which they have by instinct but have lost through experience. It is an unwanted but undeniable trust in the system. A system built to destroy them so successfully that despite their individual material fortunes, they remain afraid of being poor again one day. They have seen it happen so many times before and know that few, if any, ever truly escape.

As long as they had known each other Thomas Thompson and Kayo Knight had rarely had a drink together alone—away from the family—in over thirty years. Women and families did that to men, curtailed their socializing and shortened their life spans. While women might encourage their men to open up and "talk" to each other, they made certain—by not leaving them alone—that this could not happen often.

This evening was a novelty and the two men approached it with the high ceremony of a historic event.

It was six o'clock in the King Cole Room of the St. Regis Hotel. Well-coiffed women were draining their martinis, preparing to walk their shopping bags home. Men in expensively rumpled suits cheered each other with a raised Scotch and a handshake salty from mixed nuts. Conversations seemed as muted and intense as the mural behind the bar where the painted king sat, deep in his throne, each ear tuned to a red-suited advisor. Whatever laughter emerged rose straight to the high ceilings of the wood-paneled bar, leaving room down below for the sediment of more serious words.

"It's good to see you again, Kayo. I don't know if this is the myopia of old age, but you don't look all that different from the kid I knew taping his hands in the gym in Chicago some forty years ago."

Kayo laughed. "It's not myopia, Thomas. It's just plain blindness." But he knew what the older man meant. Thomas didn't look that much different to him either. Of course, he had less hair, soft spun silver now. Not the sleek black patent-leather dos of the old days when Thomas N. Thompson, with his booming voice and crippling handshake, made the rounds from the Hudson to the Mississippi selling his products out of a big battered case. The good old days when all the dap daddies had to have their proper jars of Aurex. Thomas had always been a hustler, but a hustler with serious style. Nothing like the dickie syndrome of the present, all front and no back. He had always been a man of substance. And with a fortune publicly estimated at $350 million, he was even more so today.

The waiter placed their drinks on top of embossed cocktail napkins. Thomas raised his Chivas Regal on ice and Kayo his Stolichnaya with lime and they drank to health, wealth and happiness in the new year.

"My eyes must be failing me, too," Kayo said. "I could swear I've seen your overcoat before."

"You're kidding me," said Thomas. He was patient when he needed to be. Kayo hadn't asked to have a drink just to chitchat.

"It's a picture I have of you in my memory, I guess, an image that's never left me. We're in the gym. I'm working the big bag. You're standing behind me but I know you've got this camel-hair draped over your shoulders and you're holding this stogie in your fingers like it could shoot darts or something bigger. And I hear you telling these Italian guys that I'm *your* boy and that if I ever have a problem, *any* problem, I'd be calling you first and you'd be the one to take care of it. You know, they never messed with me after that. I always thought it was the overcoat that did it. Those tiny stitches along the lapels. A work of art. They could see it, too."

Thomas swirled the Scotch around the ice cubes in his crystal tumbler. He took a sip and rolled it around his mouth before he swallowed. He wondered how much this was going to cost him. "Do you have a problem now, Kayo?"

"Do I look like I have a problem?"

"How much?" Thomas insisted.

"It's not money," Kayo said sharply. "Don't worry. I'm not asking for a loan or anything like that. I'm sorry if I gave that impression. Business is very good. Music is the universal language, isn't that what they say? Business is . . ."

"If business is good, then life is good. It's as simple as that." Thomas believed in cutting directly to the chase. "You're a grown man, fifty-five years old. What are you looking for? Happiness?" he asked derisively.

"Why not?" He wondered when that had become such an impossible dream. "Thomas, listen, it seems that every time I made an important decision in my life you were there. And you helped me. When the kids on my block used to beat me up for practicing my horn all day, you said to fight back. I did. When I got into boxing in a serious way, you said to go for it. I did. But when I wanted to turn professional, you said don't do it. You said I was too smart to be a fighter all my life. And how long was a fighter's life anyway? Remember? You said that people who spent all their time getting their brains beat out of their head didn't have much in there to begin with. That's when you bought me a ticket to Paris and started me back into the music life again."

"And was I wrong? Hasn't music been your life's work? Hasn't it made you who you are today? Well, answer me."

"Of course, you weren't wrong. Of course, music has made me who I am. But there's got to be something more, something beyond work and business and money."

"What?"

"Love, happiness, something that doesn't have a price tag on it. I don't know why but I thought I could talk with you about that, too."

"Listen, Kayo. Love and happiness are fine, great, wonderful. But they happen by accident. You happen to be in the right place at the right time. You meet and bang! Bliss. But business happens by design. People make money on purpose. They set about building security so that later on they can have the time to be at the right place. Then things can happen the right way."

"Maybe."

"More than likely," Thomas insisted.

"How can you be so sure about everything?" Kayo asked.

"You want to know how? Because I learned from the ground up, that's how. Don't forget I walked up north from Mississippi. Worked my way up the river, walking. I hopped a freight or hitched a ride when I got lucky. But mostly I walked. Covered an awful lot of territory. Learned a lot about what makes people friends, and enemies. Forget what the preachers say about love and all that. Money makes friends. When you were born into this world as a Black man, you automatically inherited enemies. You don't have to worry about having too many of them. But you can never have enough friends. And that's where money comes in. Imagine your life without it. You probably can't remember that far back because you have it now. You have money, Becky has money and now even your daughter has money." He savored another swallow of Scotch. "You are going to help her invest it before she spends it all on clothes, aren't you?"

"Yes, of course."

"Well, pass along a few words of wisdom to make sure she holds on to it."

"She's got a good head on her shoulders," Kayo said defensively.

"You're obliged to say that. She's your daughter. But women and money make a lethal combination."

"How can you say that? Look at your own daughter, Tina. President and CEO."

"Look at her." Thomas shook his head disparagingly. "Thirty-five years old and no man in her life. Living alone in that big old house on the West Side with just a housekeeper. No man, no family. I mean, where's the next generation going to come from? I didn't spend my entire life building a company just to pass it on to one person—and a single woman at that." Thomas coughed, then drank thirstily from a tall glass of ice water. "Now she's going completely off the deep end. Wanting to get involved in fields she knows nothing about. Tina needs to plow the ones she knows."

"Thomas, she's got some good ideas."

"How do *you* know that?"

"I read a proposal for a production company that she sent to Becky a few weeks ago. Becky's very enthusiastic, interested enough to come to New York and talk with Tina about it. As a matter of fact, I'm talking to Tina about some aspects of it myself."

"What?" Thomas set his glass down emphatically. "What is this, some kind of conspiracy behind my back?"

"Don't be foolish. Would I be telling you about it if that were the case?"

"Becky, I can't agree with but at least I can understand. She's got hands-on experience. But you? You're a music man. Tina's in the beauty business. There's no common ground."

"Except beautiful, creative Black people, Thomas. She deals with one kind of talent, I deal with another. Let's see what happens when we throw some writers and directors into the mix. You know as well as I do that we've got wonderful stories to tell, stories that will never be told unless we do them ourselves."

"You're both in over your head."

"In the old days that's how you learned to swim."

"No, I'm telling you. Now Tina's gone entirely too far. Bringing you and Becky into this madness."

"Don't insult her, Thomas. And . . . another thing I've been trying to bring up . . ." Kayo stubbed the wedge of lime in his vodka with the swizzle stick. "Becky and I . . . I mean, Becky will be coming on her own."

"What does that mean, Kayo?"

"It means we're separating. Becky wants some time to think things over."

"And you?"

"I'm OK. I've been doing OK. Whatever she wants."

"But what do *you* want?"

"That's just it. I don't know. Can you even begin to understand that?"

"Well, I'll tell you what I do understand. You and Becky are just like family to me. I've known you since hair was first growing in your armpits. And, of course, Skippy, Becky's mother, is one of my dearest friends in life. To see you split up would break what little piece of heart

I have left. Keep a hold on what you have, man. You're too old to start again. If there's another woman in the picture, I suggest you get her out of there in a hurry. Just like I bought you that ticket to Paris? You can buy her out of your life. Out, do you hear me?"

Kayo Knight heard Thomas Thompson loud and clear. But Thomas only knew part of the story. Kayo knew now that he would never be able to tell him the rest, the part that cut too close to home. It was naive of him to think he could come to Thomas in the first place with this chaotic surge of new feelings in his life. There were too many ties, a history of friendship and family spun into a web much bigger than their own individual lives. He could barely admit to himself how close he was to betrayal. How could he discuss it with someone else? He would have to find a way to deal with it. Honorably, dispassionately and on his own.

Kayo looked closely at the older man, still so authoritative in his bearing. Fine beads of sweat shone on his dark forehead and around his nose. As Thomas removed his glasses to wipe his face with a handkerchief, Kayo noticed that his fingers were trembling.

"Are you feeling all right?" he asked while Thomas gulped down the rest of his ice water.

"I'm fine." He put his glasses back on, fitting the thin curved wires around his ears. "You know that I respect you, Kayo, but some of your choices . . ."

"Some of my choices may actually have been for your benefit."

"Maybe," Thomas conceded. His wife, Ella, had always liked Kayo, had even spent time with him, but there had never been any suggestion of impropriety. And Kayo's wife, Becky, had certainly kept him closer to Skippy over the years than he might have been. "Maybe."

But Kayo was a pedigreed playboy, Thomas thought. As far as he was concerned, all this new jabber about love and happiness must mean that the other woman was some young girl. A man who played with women and toyed with words like "love" and "happiness" was still a child. A child still spoiling for a fight.

"Kayo, I'll tell you something I never thought I'd say to you."

"What's that?"

"I always hated boxing," Thomas admitted ruefully.

Kayo laughed heartily. It wasn't at all what he expected. "I don't blame you. Just be glad most of us loved the sport enough so that we didn't have to use it in real life."

"Still that boisterous, big-mouth talk. That's what I mean. I don't want my teeth knocked out. I want some money in my pocket." Thomas patted his jacket pocket where he kept his billfold.

"Well, some of us had to get our teeth knocked out in order to get some money in our pocket. Remember?"

"Yeah," Thomas nodded his head reluctantly. "I remember. Of course," he said with a self-satisfied grin, "I was always pretty good at picking winners."

"You still are." Kayo clapped him on the arm. Thomas was a good friend despite their disagreements and misunderstandings. When you knew someone as long as they'd known each other you had to expect some disappointments—to give them as well as to receive. Kayo had asked for something that Thomas did not know how to give. A perspective on life from the heart. It was the fault of neither man. But it still hurt.

Kayo checked the time, paid the bill and offered Thomas a lift home in his car.

"No thanks." Thomas smiled. "I'd get lost in that cruiser of yours and then I'd start getting grandiose ideas. My humble pickup is waiting out front, too, but for some reason I feel like walking home tonight."

"You're sure about that?" Kayo asked, helping him into his camel-hair overcoat.

"Very sure. I like the East Side. I'm glad I made the change. I don't have to worry about muggers over here. Or people asking for a handout. Besides, my driver will follow along just to make sure I don't collapse and give Tina an easy way out."

"You're cruel, Thomas," Kayo teased.

"I'm a businessman. That's how we're defined."

The two men parted under the awning of the St. Regis. As Kayo's car slowly pulled away, he watched Thomas light a long cigar and head on foot up Madison toward his apartment on Fifth Avenue.

It was a good cigar, a Davidoff. It took his mind off the troubling discussion he'd had with Kayo. He didn't like feeling this way, as if the ground could shift under his feet no matter what he said or did. At seventy life should not feel so uncertain. Especially when he had worked so hard to make it stable and secure.

Reassurance, that's what a good cigar was for. A clean line, a smooth, mellow draw, a sweet, intoxicating aroma. Nothing like . . . like what?

Memories were losing their vagueness and taking shape as Thomas Thompson walked past the grand hotels and luxury boutiques that lined Madison Avenue.

He remembered himself as a young man. A young man wearing worn denim overalls and hanging out at the King Cole Cafe, a joint on Beale Street smelling of the mighty Mississippi, reeking of tobacco smoked, chewed and spit, of whiskey no matter what else your drink was called, and of pig, from the ears to the trotters, cooking sight unseen in big cast-iron pots. He'd been all of seventeen or eighteen, making his way up to Chicago. Mama and the girls would come as soon as he found a job and a place to stay. They were saving every penny to take the train. He had only the poor man's transport, his two hard feet. But as long as he kept his hands busy and his mouth shut, he'd make it. The problem with Daddy had been just that. Couldn't keep his mouth shut, not till the crackers shut it for him, for good.

Memphis was a blues town. Country boy that he was, even he could tell that those three little tap-dancing girls were working their jazz routines in the wrong place. But they sure were fine, and the three or four times a week he saw them he clapped hard and long to let them know it. Couldn't do any more than that. He was headed up North and even friendship cost something more tangible than applause. He could tell that the girls didn't mind and maybe even liked him for acting the fool. When their set was over they'd smile and bow to everybody and then they'd smile especially for him.

One night he'd stayed late with a couple of buddies, although they all had to be down at the docks in just a few hours. They were walking home when they saw one of the girls pinned up against the wall by a big man, not so much overtall as he was extra wide. High and wide.

"Where you get them blue eyes from?" the man said, chuckling. "Pretty little blue eyes and all that wavy hair? Colonel snatch your mama behind the barn, huh?"

"Take your hands off me, mister."

"Mr. Peterson to you. And see, I like 'em hot and feisty, just like you." he laughed. "Like them blue eyes, too. Gonna snatch me some . . ."

"Let me go!"

Thomas could never remember how it happened, just that it did. He tapped the man on the shoulder. "Listen, Jack."

"My name ain't Jack."

"Oh, then it *is* asshole, like I thought."

The fight did not last long, three young ones against one big one, four, including the girl. At some point a knife flashed in and out of his huge belly. The man fell and they all ran off.

Thomas spent the rest of the night and the next day holed up in his room with the girl who had introduced herself to him as Skippy, "just Skippy, that's all." They slept some, or tried to. Skippy on the narrow mattress on the floor, while Thomas tossed on the metal webbing of the bedstead. When sleep got too uncomfortable they talked softly, trying to figure out what to do next and how, and shared what felt like death-row secrets before the last dawn. Skippy told him that the fat man was one of Boss Crump's Negroes, one of the mayor's men. And Boss Crump didn't like nobody messing with what was his, no matter what color. Couldn't hang around Memphis any longer. Under cover of night they both left town.

Skippy headed East, Thomas North. They didn't see each other again until six or seven years later in New York City. He had never forgotten her. But Skippy had a husband by then. She and Slippery Saunders were tearing up the boards from the Bronx to Brooklyn. Just like the Allies were sweeping toward the Rhine. It felt good to be home, although Thomas could only recently call New York that. When Skippy saw him, there was no hesitation in her smile or her hug. It was just like the old days on Beale Street. Except this was the Big City.

Skippy and Slippery performed everywhere and knew everybody, even people they didn't want to know. So when Thomas went into business, their name made for quick sales from New York to St. Louis. But when they tried to match him up with a beautiful woman from the entertainment world, he politely drew the line. Friends were one thing, relations another. You get too close to show business, he told them, someone was likely to get killed.

Too bad he hadn't taken his own advice. But it was much too late to think like that now. Too late in the day and definitely too late in life. He was glad the weekend was almost here. Before he flew down to St. Martin, he wanted to pick up something special for Clarice.

By the time they finished dinner and their first cognac Tina Thompson and Kayo Knight had solved most of the problems of the world. What little remained would soon be settled. The Café Carlyle did that to all dimensions of disaster. Checked it at the door. The room's gay mural of frolicking spirits evoked an eternal springtime where dogs danced, maidens rejoiced and satyrs swore off all but the least troublesome sex. People, too, came here to relax and Kayo and Tina were no exception.

"So you got a chance to see Dad at his most intractable this evening. Now you understand why it's so difficult for me to plan ahead when my father is so opposed."

"I thought we agreed to table further discussion about that tonight," Kayo said, signaling to the waiter to bring a second round of Rémy Martin.

"You're right." Tina fidgeted with her emerald bracelet. "I'm sorry. I forgot."

"How to enjoy yourself?"

"Maybe," she admitted. She did not like being under such playful scrutiny.

"Well, let me refresh your memory. First, you kick off your shoes." He smiled at her wide-eyed disbelief. "Go ahead, no one will notice."

"Men do that, too?"

"Oh, no. That's another one of the advantages women have over men."

"Another?"

"Besides possessing superior beauty, wisdom, courage and endurance. Yes, you're also able to take your shoes off at will."

She was surprised that she enjoyed him teasing her. She understood more clearly now what Becky meant when she called him an adorable man. Even with a few added pounds of success he still maintained the poised muscularity that had won him boxing championships in his early days, before she was even born. His nose also bore witness, battered flat just under the bridge before it lengthened and flared out over a thick mustache and its neat goatee. More salt than pepper, and in his hair, too. More now than she remembered from his visits years ago. California brought out the nutmeg in his skin. And the dimples in his cheeks fascinated her. For some reason she expected men to outgrow them. And for another reason she resented being so easily charmed by them.

"If you don't stop it, Kayo, soon I'll be laughing my head off and acting my color."

"And have you noticed? We *are* the only Black folks in this place."

"As usual. That's always been my case."

He raised a mocking eyebrow. "So you're probably one of those Negroes who get nervous when they see another one in the mix."

"Yes, of course." She lifted her chin to a haughty angle. "I must be the only one. *Prima donna assoluta.* Kayo, please, the way you're laughing, I don't think you understand that I'm just kidding. I'm not like that at all. I could be, but don't we already have enough insecure egomaniacs on the loose?"

"What about secure egomaniacs?" he asked with the complete assurance of one.

"Those we're still counting." She sipped her cognac. "Let me tell you what this reminds me of, though. We were shooting Aura's Christmas campaign. This must have been sometime last summer. We'd booked three models for a triple we needed. They were all gorgeous, all different, all Black, and that's just the point we were trying to make, you know. Well, one of the girls proceeded to get an attitude. I mean, right on the set. She was overdoing it, overposing, I don't know what you call it, but making herself not only stand out but stand apart from the group, right? So I got up and talked to her. Are you OK? Can I get you anything? Is there anything I can do? You know, total appeasement policy. Finally she snapped at me, 'I do no more doubles, I do no more triples.' Treeples, she said. It would have been hysterical if we hadn't needed that shot. But that scene just went click in my mind. Karine was right . . ."

"You mean, the model who was just murdered?" Kayo interrupted.

"My God, I didn't even think of it like that. That's right, Karine Belfort. She had this way about her that demanded respect, respect for her as an individual. I don't know if it came from her being West Indian or having lived in Europe or what. But she wasn't like most of our American Black models. They have to be the ultra-nice girls, you know, just to get the job. Karine was different. A *very* secure egomaniac. She wanted star treatment. She didn't want to be lumped with any group. Not as a token in a group of Whites *or* a group of Blacks. From that little blowup, suddenly I could see what she meant, what she wanted. Total, unconditional, individual, one-on-one recognition. She didn't want to be known as a top Black model. She wanted to be a top model, period."

Kayo nodded, understanding from this story a little of his own daughter's motivation to model. He had some insight into sports and music, some personal experience. There you perfected a skill, a skill you could demonstrate in harmony with or in opposition to someone else. He had never been able to understand how beauty qualified as a skill. He was attracted to beautiful women, of course. Had even married a beautiful woman. But to make a profession of it? That still mystified him.

The lights of the Café Carlyle dimmed, and with them an obscure anxiety Kayo had suddenly begun to feel. He reminded himself that this was a place for him also to relax.

As the members of the Modern Jazz Quartet arranged themselves around their instruments, they nodded and smiled genteelly at the warm applause from the audience. They began with a selection of pieces from *Porgy and Bess*. How pleasantly ironic, Tina and Kayo nodded to each other, that the first tune was "Summertime" with its unsung lyrics, ". . . your daddy's rich and your mother's good-looking."

They were a long way from Catfish Row but not so far that they had no firsthand knowledge of it. Vibraphonist Milt Jackson introduced one song by saying that in *this* neighborhood its title would probably be grammatically corrected to become "Bess, you *are* my woman now." Everybody in the audience chuckled, knowing what went unsaid.

Tina started to relax in spite of herself. Watching the musicians, she could sense Kayo watching her. Under the table his knee touched hers and then his thigh seemed to lean into hers, spreading a warmth that could be construed as casual, friendly, even familial, but which she sensed was different, more than that. She moved her leg away but his followed hers. Something was happening for which she was not prepared and yet she was not completely surprised.

Everyone knew that Kayo was a lady-killer. Knowing his reputation, she had always felt immune to any spell he could cast. Besides, he was the husband of one of her best friends. A surge of shame seared her face. Loyalty and logic were losing their force. She would have to make a clean, friendly getaway, and soon. If she allowed herself to feel any more she might not be able to.

After the musicians finished their set, they stopped by the table to shake hands with Kayo. He stood, hugged them and slapped them on the back in hearty defiance of what was called advanced age. Laughingly, they gave up trying to calculate how long it had been since the last time they'd seen each other. When they were introduced to Tina, they asked about her father, one of their most dedicated supporters during their forty years together as a group. In the updates and smiles there was the feel of a family reunion, a tradition of closeness that could be rekindled anytime, anyplace.

As the musicians left to greet other friends and fans, Tina slipped her shoes back on and prepared to leave.

"You don't have to go yet, you know." Kayo motioned to the waiter for more cognac.

"Oh, not for me, thanks. I had a marvelous evening but I do have to go." She stood up and smoothed the wrinkles out of her emerald satin jacket and black velvet skirt.

"Still," Kayo said, standing closer than need be to her, "I wish you wouldn't."

"Kayo, your leg has been chasing mine under the table all night."

"I didn't think you noticed."

She shook her head in amusement while they walked to the coat check. As he held her black velvet coat behind her, she felt the warm nearness of him magnetizing her. She managed to murmur, "Have a safe trip back to L.A."

"At least let my driver take you home, Tina."

"No thanks, I'd prefer a taxi." Her voice was ebbing with her willpower.

"As you wish."

Outside a mean breeze revived her. She welcomed the cold air and the return to sanity the next cab would bring.

Kayo smiled. "You look beautiful, all windblown and glowing."

"And you're so gallant, Mr. Knight. I have to remember that's just part of your style."

"You've got me wrong, Tina. That's part of *me*."

She could believe that was true. But she dared not put that belief to the test.

CHAPTER TEN

UNACCUSTOMED to so much wine, Nicky wanted to lean her head on something soft, to stretch her whole body out and lie down. But this was a Sunday night in Mezzogiorno, a hip spot that JJ had insisted on, which served delicious Italian food to the famous faces and beautiful bodies of SoHo. Since she was one of them, he said, or soon to be, she had to sit up straight in her teeny-weeny chair and look fetching and fabulous like everyone else.

And she did look fabulous in the little black knit Chanel dress that she had treated herself to. The one with a big gold zipper down the front and another up the back shown on the mannequin in the boutique's window on 57th Street. Only a model could wear such a revealing outfit, the saleslady had sniffed, as she reluctantly showed Nicky, wearing her baggy jeans, the way to the dressing room. Nicky had struggled to stay calm and say nothing. But then when she walked around the boutique with the dress on, looking, she claimed, for accessories, she let the perfect fit speak for itself. The fit *and* her new platinum American Express card.

JJ sat opposite her, jawing with yet another one of the fellas he was evidently accustomed to seeing here. New York looked like a big city, her brother had explained, but it was just a conglomeration of villages where like-minded souls frequented the same watering holes. Where the tribe went, he said. She was proud to be a member and proud to be related to him. But it still seemed weird that he could introduce her to the singers and rappers whose music she listened to on the radio. These people were famous, she thought, and JJ was just her brother.

She refocused on her linguine with white clam sauce. Twirling the fine pasta around on her fork and lifting it in a neat bundle to her mouth required an expertise she did not yet possess. A few strands invariably escaped, oozing olive oil and garlic, forcing her to mop her lips and chin after each overloaded bite. Her napkin was getting an intense workout. She should quit now before she disgraced herself but the food tasted much too good.

"Upgrading our taste, I see. No cheeseburgers, no fries?" Max kissed her on both cheeks while they laughed.

"Max, you're so crazy, sneaking up on me like that. What fun! You know my brother, JJ."

Max and JJ shook hands and exchanged a brief "How ya doin', man?" before continuing their separate conversations.

"So, how's it going with you, little one?" asked Max, squatting beside her.

"Oh, fine. I'm still trying to unwind. JJ demanded that we go out to celebrate and here I am. Why don't you join us?"

"Thanks, but I'm meeting someone." Max looked around the room. That someone wasn't here yet.

"Well, tell me how you're getting along without me."

"Painfully slow, chile. Life's a pure punishment until I get you in my clutches again."

"I can't wait. Just when is that supposed to be?"

"I'm not sure, in a couple of weeks, I think. I know I'm going on location to Boca Raton . . ."

"Without me? Traitor!"

"You forget, you don't need these little penny-ante jobs. A princess like you goes on *va*-cation, not *lo*-cation. But when I come back, we're supposed to shoot the first commercial."

"Which is scaring me to death."

"Why? You'll be great. But you'd better count this as your Last Supper. Film is even worse than stills for adding on extra pounds."

"You *would* remind me."

"That's what friends are for, darlin'. And speaking of friends, there's mine." Max stood up and kissed her again. "*Ciao,* sweetheart. Call me."

She watched as Max made his way through the crowded tables to Raleigh Smith. Smitty waved to her. Nicky waved back and smiled.

JJ, alone now, followed her line of sight. "Oh, Lord," he muttered.

"What's the matter?" Nicky asked, once again intent on her pasta. "Why don't you like Max?"

"Who says I don't like him? He's such an affected son-of-a-bitch. All the models love him. Nadja swears by him. He's at all the big parties. And yet I can never get a straight line out of him. It's always darlin' this and princess that."

"Of course, in the music business does a minute ever pass without a baby or m.f.?"

"You got a point. But then he always wants to call me 'JJ Knight, consort of the fair Nadja,' or some shit like that."

"He plays with everybody."

"Well, let him play with his little buddies and leave me alone." JJ drained his glass of chianti and poured more into both their glasses.

"A raging homophobe, that's what you are. Here I thought I was lucky enough to know *and* be related to the perfect man. And all the while you're in the closet . . . of the Moral Majority."

JJ pushed his chair away from the table. "Am I that bad? Dag, Nadja cracks on me the same way. I just don't get it. The brother's wearing more makeup than you."

"Like your jam master mix-a-lots don't?"

"Maybe, but only when they're working."

"Don't you get it, JJ? You can work out a rationale for anything. Max is gay."

"So maybe he can't help being gay, but he sure can help acting crazy," JJ said, sealing off that discussion with a return to his black seafood ravioli.

Nicky picked tiny clams from their tiny shells and left her slippery pasta in the bowl. The clams were chewy and salty and did not make a mess. After she finished them she decided that the wine was food enough. She gazed around the restaurant feeling warm and satisfied. The walls were paved with boxes of artwork and the tables crammed with collages of their own. She was curious to know who the people were—so glamorous and yet so casual—but she wasn't anxious enough to find out right now. Right now she was fine, relaxed for the first time since the Cleo shoot a few days ago.

JJ was right to insist on their going out. Especially after Kayo had canceled again. She hadn't allowed herself to feel a real personal kind of rejection. He was simply too busy. As usual. He had managed to drop by for a half hour to give her a dazzling pair of earrings, flawless one-carat diamond studs that she could wear every day, he said. She wasn't quite used to them, their dazzle, her wealth. She raised her hand to touch her right earlobe. The earring was still there. At least he tried to compensate.

When she showed the gift to JJ and told him about the flowers, he seemed to understand. That's how he'd gotten his first car at eighteen, he said. A Volkswagen shipped from Germany back to the States. A sort of consolation prize for a trip with the band that Kayo had promised. And canceled. She understood what he was telling her about the compromises he'd made with both his parents. He loved them but their love had taught him to keep his distance.

Nicky was on the verge of feeling sorry for him when he pointed out that she was in a similar situation. It was difficult to accept that her parents were also too busy. Not to care, but to show that they did. She liked being able to share her thoughts and feelings with JJ. At first, she didn't know if that would be possible. She feared he would resent her taking his place in his father's life or resent her mother taking his mother's place. But JJ was a man now, a fairly healthy, fairly balanced one. Resentments seemed packed away in a manageable past. And she was grateful for the space he was making in his life for her now.

She sipped more wine, cradling the belly of the glass in her palm. She was getting high. She knew it and she liked it. A soft haze outlined faces and misted their voices. She was anchored here and yet she could drift away as she chose. So this is why people drank, she thought.

She focused on a couple that seemed headed toward her table. The nonchalant tumble of strawberry-blond hair belonged to a model she seemed to recognize. And the man in dark glasses with the snow-white shirt and black trousers also seemed familiar.

"Gianni, my man!" JJ and Gianni Walker shook hands warmly.

"Bella," said Gianni as he kissed Nicky on both cheeks. He introduced her to Flicka, who smiled briefly, who already knew JJ through Nadja, of course, and who started a loud conversation about the couture shows and why she wasn't doing the grueling designer marathon this year. Not enough money for her. "Thank God and fuck the French!" she hooted, in a way that made everyone laugh with her and not at her.

Nicky tried to join in the hilarity. But seeing Gianni again and so unexpectedly excited her. She wished they would sit down at her table, that Gianni would move close enough for her to touch him. Accidentally, of course. He was with another girl. But somehow Nicky knew that Flicka did not count. She wondered if he could hear her heart pounding and her lips whispering. Come to me. Closer.

And then, out of the corner of her eye, she saw Max. He was looking dead at her, shaking his head. No, he repeated wordlessly, no.

"Good morning, Nicky." Corky Matthews sounded entirely too cheerful for a Monday morning. Nicky peeked at her clock and poked through the venetian blinds. Eight-fifteen on another dreary day. She opened her eyes wide enough to see if her roommate had left. Gone, good. Nicky closed her eyes again. She would cut class and go back to sleep after this. "Vanessa Seymour just called me to make sure you got a message she said she left for you last night."

"Ummm, I did, Corky. So strange, a message at ten-thirty on a Sunday night for a meeting at nine o'clock sharp on Monday. I was just about to call you about that. I'm not feeling so hot."

"Aw, what's the matter, bubby?" Corky was being her version of a good Jewish mother, but Nicky was in no condition to appreciate it.

"I don't know," she sighed. "Maybe a little too much wine last night?" Her question suggested that she wasn't the only one responsible.

"Well, if that's all it is, I suggest you hop in the shower pronto, fix that face, grab a cab and get up there."

"I feel nauseous, though. Really, I can barely move."

"You can't cancel Vanessa, sweetheart. Now, get going. Time's awasting. Once the meeting's over, you'll have all the time you need to sleep it off. Go on now. I'll talk to you later."

Nicky dragged herself out of bed and into the shower. She felt her insides sloshing around. Being vertical made her dizzy. She leaned against the bathroom tiles for support. The water pelting her skin felt like tiny assaults on her body. Her mouth tasted moldy. Her eyes could not stay open. How could one night out make her feel so miserable?

But then she remembered how that night had ended. How Gianni had whispered to her that he would call her. That he wanted to see her again, that he'd like to do some shots of her the way he saw her. He thrilled her and frightened her at the same time. How did he see her? What did he see that he hadn't captured already? She lathered her body with soap and watched its glistening form reveal itself.

"Juice, coffee, tea?" Vanessa offered. The handsome serving cart, which had been wheeled into her office next to the navy velour couch and armchairs where they sat, bore the essential components of a hearty breakfast. A basket of assorted muffins, croissants, and bagels. Crocks of butter, jam, and cream cheese. A fruit platter with melon slices and berries. A silver chafing dish which Nicky imagined was full of scrambled eggs. Thank God, it was covered. If the idea alone made her nauseous, the sight would surely cause an eruption.

"I'll have some tea, thanks." Tea would be safe, she hoped. Vanessa placed the cup and saucer on the coffee table, indicating the condiment tray where she would find sugar and cream or lemon. Nicky dropped three sugar cubes into the cup and stirred. The sweet aroma began to soothe her, her nerves as well as her stomach.

When Vanessa sat down, she did so with nothing but a lit cigarette. She crossed her legs at a perfect angle and kept them in a proper slant that Nicky dimly remembered from eighth-grade etiquette.

"You were ten minutes late this morning, Nicky," Vanessa began.

"I'm sorry," Nicky tried to apologize.

Vanessa waved away any possible excuse. "In our business time is money. Promptness is essential. Accuracy is indispensable. I realize that you may not agree with this, that it may even be an alien concept, but here at S & S, it is one of our guiding precepts. Do you understand me?"

"Yes," Nicky nodded humbly. She wanted this woman to accept her, even like her. She would be on her best behavior, do nothing to aggravate her. She would ask no questions. Certainly not the one uppermost in her mind: Why are you talking to me like this?

"Then let us proceed. In all the haste to start work on the fall Cleo campaign, we have never had an opportunity to discuss some of the finer points of your responsibilities. I'm not referring to the legalities now, although I assume that you and your legal counsel have thoroughly reviewed those issues. I'm speaking more about what we expect from you as a person. As the Cleo girl." Vanessa extinguished her cigarette in careful, stubbing movements and resumed her posture.

"Now, we've had a chance to look over the results of the shoot last week with Gianni Walker. Naturally, we expected to do a lot of retouching. Don't get me wrong. There are *some* good shots. But you are new to the business and I'd like to give you a little advice. Less is more. Have you ever heard that expression? The less there is of you, the more we have to work with. That means diet and exercise, paying the most scrupulous attention to your weight and body structure. We know that women of color unfortunately do tend to be heavy in the buttocks, hips and thighs. We are recommending a nutritionist and a personal trainer to help you eliminate these flaws. We also know that women of color tend to have problems with their hair. I want to make it absolutely clear that there will be no radical changes without consultation with us. There has also been some suggestion of cosmetic surgery. A nose job, perhaps. But we shall deal with that in time." She lit another cigarette and exhaled a brisk puff of smoke.

Nicky shifted uncomfortably in her chair and sat up straighter. She had never felt so . . . defective. Her legs looked too wide and soft through her olive leggings. She squeezed her buttocks tight and pressed her thighs together. She hadn't had the time to do her hair this morning, so she'd hidden most of it under a beret. She tucked the wispy bangs that she considered cute back underneath the hat. But what could she do about her nose? If she had all these things wrong with her, why had she been chosen in the first place?

Growing more uneasy, she breathed through her mouth while listening to Vanessa continue her lecure. As long as she did that she could keep the nausea down.

"Beyond your physical appearance, however, is the character you project," Vanessa was saying. "You no longer belong to yourself alone. For the next two years you are the face of an important and respected company. In public you are no longer Nicky Knight. You are Cleo. Never forget that.

"Unimpeachable morals are absolutely vital. Naturally, we realize that you are a human being with normal needs for human contact. Unfortunately, with so much invested, we cannot afford less than perfection. There are to be no public intimacies with anyone. Boyfriend, girlfriend, family, whoever. No love affairs, no marriages and it goes without saying, no pregnancies. Of course, drugs and alcohol are strictly *verboten*. All social events must be screened by us for suitability. All wardrobe for public events must be screened by us. You cannot be photographed by anyone other than our contracted photographer. And you must not put yourself in the position of being so photographed unless we arrange it.

"Now, the significance of many of these regulations will not be revealed until the campaign is actually launched in August with the publication of the September magazines. The rules pertain, nevertheless, from this day onward. I hope I've made myself clear." Vanessa let out a long stream of smoke.

Nicky could not contain herself any longer. "May I use your rest room, please?" She followed Vanessa's outstretched arm to a discreet door in the corner of her office. She had barely enough time to close it before she vomited loudly and copiously into the royal blue toilet.

Lunch with Jock Rosenberg bought her Brownie points, Corky was sure of it. It wasn't exactly like paying into a Christmas club every week. Not exactly. But she was sure that when Judgment Day came, the powers that be would score her twice-a-year lunches with Jock in the plus column. Maybe even in the extra credit column. It was crowded in "21," as usual, with lots of press and advertising people. The owners of the Ford agency waved and smiled and, knowing Jock, kept their distance. Corky knew they were chuckling at more than their chicken croquettes.

Jock had just loaded up on all the latest fashion magazines. In the *Sports Illustrated* swimsuit issue four of the models were MacLean girls. Reason enough for pride, but not for the analysis she was getting on the difference between the old broads and the tenderonis. Jock actually used words like that.

"See, Mike and her group looked like ladies in their pictures. She had class, you know. She'd been around the block once or twice and learned something from it. Looked like a lady, acted like one. But in bed? I'm telling you, a wild woman. Funny thing is somehow you could see a hint of that in the pictures. I don't know, maybe I'm reading too much into it, but these babes today look like card-carrying hookers. Like they've been around the block and they're still on it. OK, they're cute but there's no mystery to it. What's the big deal? It's like I might want to squeeze the bazooms to see if they're real, but with the cleavage hanging out for everybody to see, I don't know, I lose interest. And don't get me wrong, I'm a man who likes a little surprise. But I don't mean silicone.

"That's what kept me and Mike together. We could surprise each other. Plus, we loved to do it. You know, people think I'm a playboy, a swinger, you know. But they're wrong. Maybe I'm getting old 'cause I'm just not in-te-res-ted. You do a dame once and she thinks it's a down payment on marriage and when do we close? Who can blame her? Women don't want to be alone. If a woman's alone she's only got herself to make unhappy. A man likes to be alone. It's quiet. Nobody's accusing you of causing all the problems in the world and nobody's nagging you to fix 'em by yesterday. Shoot, let women run the world. I say, let 'em have it.

"Thirty years in real estate in New York City, you make some money but what else? You're so busy fucking people before they fuck with you, you lose your natural sex drive. You lose your friends, you lose your family, and, to top it all off, you lose your hair. You lose your hair because your brain is burning up underneath. Burning up the roots, you know? The broads want it? Let the broads have it. See how pretty they'd look coming home at the end of the day bald. I had my share. I did my duty.

"Only somebody like Mike could make it worthwhile. Too bad we were together for only a few. Who knows what woulda happened if it'd lasted a long time? If we'd had kids? The first set's OK. Clean, you know, OK, but comfy. That's what gets me, too damn comfy. Like they're so Polo it makes me wanna puke. No danger in 'em. It's not an adventure anymore, it's a damn designer safari."

As long as his monologue fascinated him, and that was usually audience enough, Corky kept the mask of fascinated listener tacked onto her face. She had to keep her hands busy with her knife and fork in order to stave off the desire to lift the mat of thin wavy hair that crossed Jock's baldness from ear to ear. Did he really think he was fooling someone? Maybe so. Even insightful people tended to lose sight when it came to looking themselves in the mirror.

"Cork, look, excuse me for a minute," Jock was saying. "There's a schmuck over there whose foot I forgot to step on the last time I was in town. I'll be right back."

Corky could feel her face relax. She wondered if everyone's hypocrisy showed as clearly as hers. If people's noses grew when they lied, like Pinocchio's, maybe they wouldn't do it as much. Or maybe there'd be even more plastic surgeons in practice than there already were.

"Corky, how convenient," said Vanessa Seymour. "Could I have a word with you?"

Corky nodded yes. What else could she do? Her mouth was full and Vanessa was already sliding into Jock's seat.

"I hope you haven't sold us some damaged merchandise," Vanessa began. She picked up Jock's crumpled napkin with the tips of two fingers and deposited it out of her way.

"I have no idea what you're talking about, Vanessa. It's not like you to make your point indirectly."

Corky watched her lift her long blond hair over one shoulder and stretch her frosted pink lips in what could have passed for a smile. "The point is this," Vanessa said emphatically. "Nicky Knight showed up late this morning. She looked terrible, she acted sullen and then she proceeded to throw up all over my bathroom. I want to know what you're going to do about all this."

Corky stirred some of the fizz out of her Perrier and sipped it.

"Accidents happen, Vanessa. What can I say? She told me this morning that she wasn't feeling well. I made her keep the appointment with you, an appointment that you did not request until ten-thirty on Sunday night, I might add. *I* made her go. Now, what more would you like me to do?"

"I would like you to talk to her and make sure that she has her head screwed on right. But then again, maybe you're not the one to do that."

"Make your point, Vanessa."

"Let's face it. People are different. And Black people . . ."

"Black people are human," Corky insisted. "And I resent any insinuation . . ."

"I'm just suggesting that even though you're doing your very best with her, you might not be able to impress upon her the full extent of her responsibilities, the huge investment we're making in her. It wouldn't be your fault."

"I'm her agent. She's one of my girls."

"One of many. You can't be expected to know what really goes on with . . . someone like her."

"Vanessa, I shouldn't have to remind you that she does not come from some hard-core welfare ghetto. Neither was she rescued from the poverty of a southern pig farm. Nicky Knight comes from a very sophisticated and successful family. And you act like she can barely understand English. I am confident that she'll do what it takes to get herself together and make a fabulous Cleo girl."

"I truly hope so. The others self-destructed before we could even get off the ground with them."

"That's what some people might say."

"That's what everybody says. Wise up, Corky. These girls just might not be qualified to handle celebrity and wealth. Maybe they can do the shows but how much does that take? They're just a momentary impersonation. But a contract is different. Our girl has to *be* Cleo. And Kyle is nothing if not persistent."

"And Kyle is right."

"Except that you know as well as I do that business isn't about wrong or right. It's about getting the job done. At this point we simply cannot afford any more losses. You know that we're scheduling the commercial shoot for two weeks from today."

"February seventeenth? Isn't that rushing things a little?"

"We've got to have that much in the can in order to get back on schedule. And Nicky has to be ready. More than ready, she has to be perfect."

"You've made your point."

"Well, then, I'll let you finish your lunch. On a diet again, I see." Vanessa backed her chair into Jock Rosenberg just as he was returning to the table. "Oh, excuse me, I'm so sorry," she said sweetly.

"No damage," he said. As Jock watched her leave the restaurant, his smile revealed a broad expanse of expensive dental work. "See, Cork, that's what I was telling you about. A woman like that, I can tell, she's got class."

Corky said nothing in response and quickly excused herself from the pleasure of Jock's company. As soon as she arrived back at the agency at three o'clock, she placed a call to Becky Knight in California. No answer, not unusual for this time of day or for a person in Becky's business. She wished she had been able to speak with Becky directly, however. It was difficult to convey a sense of urgency in a phone message without inflating it into an emergency. This wasn't an emergency. But maybe underneath all the other nonsense Vanessa Seymour had spouted, just maybe there was a grain of truth. Becky needed to get to New York soon. Nicky needed her, now. Before the hangovers became a morning routine. Before complaints about her—from anyone—became a distasteful fact of life.

CHAPTER ELEVEN

THOMAS N. Thompson asked his secretary to tell Miss Thompson's secretary that he wished to see Miss Thompson immediately.

When Tina entered her father's office he was seated behind his desk in his maroon leather chair with his back to her. Evidently his excellent view of Rockefeller Center was easier to take than she was.

"You asked to see me?" Tina could afford a deferential tone. She felt good about the meeting that had just ended.

"Ogilvy & Mather comes into my company and I am not invited?" He spoke in a careful, deliberate manner. "Not even consulted?"

"I didn't think you'd be interested," she replied evenly.

"Not interested?" He swiveled around in a sudden, ferocious gesture. "One of the largest advertising agencies in the world makes a pitch to *my* company and I'm not even allowed in the room?" His hand hit the desk like thunder.

"Now, wait a minute, Dad."

"*You* wait a minute, young lady. You had no right . . ."

"Excuse me"—she signaled *stop* with both hands—"but I think I have every right. You were invited to the last three conferences I set up for ad agencies to pitch their ideas for the Aura Woman campaign. You were invited and you did attend. But in all of those meetings you acted in such a negative and hostile manner that I was embarrassed and the agency people were embarrassed. Afterward I vowed to myself that I would never let that happen again. The last thing Aura needs is for word to get around the industry that Black folks can't get it together."

"So now *I'm* the obstacle?"

"Yes."

He removed his tortoise-framed glasses and laid them carefully on his desk. "Let me get this straight. I'm the one who founded this company, who brought Black people together in the first place. But now all of a sudden I'm the one who's keeping Black folks apart?"

"Who's keeping us from taking that next big step. We are going to revamp our image and expand our advertising, despite your resistance. We are going to contract one girl to present our best face to the world, no matter what you say. You have a choice. You don't *have* to be obstinate and disagreeable. But if you insist on being that way, you will not be allowed in our meetings. This is a choice I've made because of the choice you made, Dad. It's as simple as that."

"Well, we'll see what the board of directors has to say about all of this."

"I'm sure you'll be hearing from some of them soon. As soon as they get their copies of my proposals."

"You just don't know when to stop, do you, Tina?"

"Funny, but you're the one who taught me that stop was just a sign, not a permanent order. You stop, you make sure the coast is clear and then you go."

"Except in this case, the coast isn't clear."

Tina was tired. She had come in feeling good and now she felt terrible. Arguing with her father drained her energy. There must be some other way of getting through to him that didn't ignite so many sparks. She spoke softly, almost tenderly. "How long are you going to be like this, Dad? How long? The coast is clear for everyone else. Look at Cleo, signing Nicky Knight, a baby. Doesn't that tell you anything about the potential other people see in us? I know as well as you do that Cleo's heart might be in the right place today, but two years from now they'll be turning in their old model for a new one. Just like people used to trade in their cars.

But the Aura woman will still be there. Why can't you see it? Is it because it's my idea?" She extended her open hands to him. "Here, if it'll make you feel better, it's yours. I don't care. I don't want to own an idea. You run with it. You say how proud you are to launch a new era for Aura and for all Black women. You say it."

"I don't need to. We don't have to do what every ignorant Johnny-come-lately does. Black women know where to go to get respect. To a Black company."

"Not if that Black company doesn't *show* them respect."

"I do, I do show them respect."

"How?" She leaned menacingly on his desk. "The way you showed respect to my mother? That vast overabundance of loving respect that made her swallow an entire bottle of pills to get away from it all?"

"How dare you!"

"And let me tell you another thing. You can fire me, get rid of me, whatever you want to try. But I'm going to fight. I am not going out her way."

Tina turned on her heels and headed out of her father's office. At the door she hesitated. There was one last thing she wanted to say to him. But when she looked around, he had turned his back again. He wouldn't begin to understand what she meant if she said she was sorry.

The long day had finally come to an end and Tina was glad to turn the key in the front door of the big brownstone on West 76th Street. But before she could set her briefcase down Mrs. English came rushing over with the look of bad news on her lean mahogany face.

"Your father's been taken to the hospital. A massive heart attack, Miss Christina."

"What? Oh, my God!"

"The call came about half an hour ago. You'd already left the office and I was just getting ready to go to the hospital. Here's the note I was leaving." Mrs. English picked up a piece of notepaper from the table in the entrance hall where the daily mail was kept. A horn sounded from the street. "That must be Connors now."

The two women walked quickly down the front steps of the brownstone. Her father's driver held the door open for Tina and her housekeeper while they climbed into the backseat of the dark Town Car. In silence they drove through the dark city, through Central Park to the hospital complex on the East Side.

When Tina and Mrs. English arrived at the nurses' station outside of the cardiac care unit, Dr. Kellerman was just coming out with Lucas, her father's valet.

"He's not out of danger yet," the doctor reported, "but we're doing all we can. He's stable and seems to be resting a bit more comfortably. If he makes it through the night we've got a chance."

As Tina went through the motions of listening to Lucas recount her father's collapse and then interpreting Dr. Kellerman's intricate medical terms, she wrestled with the echo of their own harsh words spoken that afternoon. She and her father had done nothing but argue for weeks now. There seemed to be no common ground for them to stand on. He *was* an obstacle. She *would* fight him. But she certainly did not want things to end this way and she hoped it was not too late to tell him that.

It did not occur to Thomas Thompson that he was dying. It did not occur to him that he could. By the time the crashing pain in his chest made him want to die, there was barely a bargain left in him. He was on the verge of complete surrender, but he couldn't quite let go. He knew only one thing. He would give anything and everything to keep on living.

The shock numbed her. She did not want to think, let alone feel, until she was home, safe, far from the nightmare vision of her father entrapped by tubes, withered and cold.

In the car Mrs. English sat wrapped in her habitual silence. Once or twice she actually reached over where Tina sat, staring fixedly into the empty streets, and patted her gloved hands. It was not comfort that Tina felt. Just a dry, hesitant reminder that she was not totally alone.

A light rain spotted the windows and Connors turned on the windshield wipers. Their movement was swift and automatic, hypnotic. Suddenly a memory awoke from a deep sleep, stretching its arms and legs until all the parts came alive. It was the last time Tina remembered hearing a doctor use those same words: "If he makes it through the night."

It was nighttime then also. But a South Carolina summer night, hot and sticky, dark, with thick folds in the blackness. The kind of blackness where some things stood solid and for certain and other things crawled by and made you wonder. She had also been in a car, but not like this one, which even with its leather upholstery and chauffeur was still a rather modest limousine for the nineties.

Back then the car was a valiantly battered station wagon emblazoned with campaign signs, bumper stickers, and pictures of Jesse Jackson. Its suspension had seen better days long before 1984. Yet it managed to summon a kind of mechanical courage, carrying them for many miles over roads considered lucky to have seen a steamroller. Asphalt was still a controlled substance in South Carolina. Politically controlled. Jesse was running for the Democratic presidential nomination. And they were on a mission, running behind him to get out the vote.

Carter Washington came from the area although Tina did not know what that meant and did not even know him until the campaign fund-raiser in the spring of '84 at her father's house. After her mother's death she rarely went back to the big West Side brownstone. Working around her father, or rather Mr. Thompson, as she called him on the job, was difficult enough. But when he let drop that Jesse Jackson would be at the house in person, she knew she had to go.

It was the kind of occasion full of sophisticated glad-handing and boisterous back-slapping made especially for Thomas Thompson. His success was tangible and even inspirational to younger people who had that special entrepreneurial spirit. They were a dynamic breed that could never be content with just a job. Their goal was a business of their own. Despite the loneliness she'd suffered as a child, Tina was glad, proud of her father for stepping out of the pack and for encouraging her to do the same.

Like all political gatherings, this one was the scene of many dramas large and small. Polite cocktails and genteel hors d'oeuvres could not camouflage the tensions. Behind their clipped mustaches and careful ties, the establishment pols were nervous, caught between Jesse's overwhelming popularity with ordinary people and their own allegiance to the traditional party machine. The numerous small fish swimming with them included independent idealists, rhetorical ramblers and intellectual sharpshooters all too ready with inflammatory sound bites. Responsible, mature adults who confessed they'd be voting for the first time—and only because of Jesse—turned out in enthusiastic numbers. Some even contributed money. Tina knew her father gave, but he never said how much. When people were asked to announce their donations she pledged a week's salary, a substantial amount in the low four figures that surprised most people. They'd forgotten how truly wealthy the Thompsons were.

It was at the party that Carter introduced himself, correctly, respectfully, as befitted a new Columbia Law School graduate. Besides an alma mater, they also shared ideas in common. Carter wasn't an idealist, he said, he was a pragmatist. And he considered Jesse's campaign the latest next step in organizing Black people for national political power. It wasn't a question of whether Jesse was more powerful as substance or symbol, if he could really win or if he was simply reformulating the message of the sixties to fit the eighties. In these leaderless times, Carter said, Black people needed all the help they could get. It all made sense to her.

Tina Thompson and Carter Washington got to know each other better that spring. She visited with him and his mother uptown at their Harlem apartment in Lenox Terrace, one of the middle-class enclaves in what her father always called, with some affection, the Bottom. In turn Carter visited with her at her apartment downtown on exclusive Gramercy Park. Differences mattered less than similarities. So when Carter announced that he was taking off from job-hunting to work full-time on the campaign down South until the convention, she realized how attached she had grown to him in such a short time. They both realized that the feeling was mutual. But they also recognized that to separate personal passion from the political had become impossible. She decided to go on the road with him.

"Don't you know the sixties are dead?" her father raged when she told him she was taking a short leave of absence from the company. "Dead and burned-out just like the inner cities. Just like the Black neighborhoods that used to be thriving, productive communities. Stick to what you know, Tina. You know the law, you know business. You don't know the South and you don't know a thing about backwoods campaigning. Traipsing around behind some Ivy League radical who's forgotten how to speak to the people, if he ever knew. The whole thing is ridiculous. Your mother and I didn't raise you up to delight in the squish of mud between your toes. If you want to get so all-fired involved, raise funds right here in New York. Work on voter registration right here. There's more than enough dirt right here at home to play in. Nothing good can come from your going down there, trust me. Nothing good."

She had listened because she was obliged to. But she already knew what she was going to do. Her father had never once said that he needed her, that he feared for her, that he loved her. If he had, maybe she would have left with some reluctance. As it was, she was glad to go.

It was a heady time to be in love. Everything seemed possible. The energy and optimism of Jesse's campaign revived a vocabulary unused since the early seventies. Brotherhood, rainbow, change, and peace. A new, emphatic tone of voice delivered those words. A man had come along with a message. And though neither one was perfect, together they helped keep some eyes open while others slumbered during morning in America.

The South *was* different. The stagnant heat, the slow drawl, the endless, oversweet iced tea. Many Black people were still scared and still shockingly poor. But they opened their tattered screen doors to the fast-talking young folks who were somehow connected to Jesse. They could see he was a special one. He had the looks of a ladies' man combined with the strength of a man's man. And that singular charisma made all kinds of people sign on to vote for him. To vote for Jesse and to vote for change.

The night she was remembering, Carter's cousin John Lee was driving. Carter was up front while Tina was in the backseat trying to keep the posters and flyers and stickers and everything else from overflowing their boxes. They had just dropped Junior Woolsey off outside of Orangeburg and were headed back to Sumter. Despite the late hour the air was warm and thick with insects that splattered loudly against the windshield. She wanted to feel a real breeze but she knew better than to ask. John Lee drove with the air-conditioning on high like all the other southerners she'd been with.

"That pickup's been on our tail for a while now," she heard him say to Carter.

"You think they're headed for the base?" The Air Force base in Sumter was home to a crew of young hotshots who considered driving merely low-level flying.

"We'll soon find out. Got some cousins you might not remember right out here near Jamison. Might have to give them a little surprise visit. What you say?"

"I'm with you," Carter replied.

They turned off the main road, which was neat and clean and might have been called a highway by some. The road they took was paved and wide enough for two-way traffic but that was about it. There were no lights and the few houses there were sat far off the road behind tall cornfields. A couple of cars passed going in the opposite direction.

"They still there, ain't they?"

"Yeah."

"Well, reach under the seat and get the shotgun ready. We got a minute to go before our next turn and I don't want no one-way target practice."

As John Lee turned sharply onto a hard-packed dirt road the pickup started bumping them in the rear. He accelerated but the truck sat higher and could maneuver better. John Lee did what he could to maintain control of the car but the pickup kept punching the station wagon with metal-crunching, bone-jarring blows until the final impact sent them hurtling through the air into a steep roadside ditch. When Tina came to, the truck was gone. There was darkness and the loud scratch of crickets all around. She heard other breathing beside her own, but she could not see who or where. Paper flyers were scattered bright white against the black ground.

She cried "Help" long after help had come. Old Claude Poinsette thought he heard something and came down the road with his two yellow dogs to have a look. What he saw brought out the tenderness he had stopped showing to people years before and bestowed only on the prize-winning tenants of his greenhouse. The station wagon's banners, stickers and pictures were ripped and sprayed over with big white Ks. Its nose was ground into the ditch, its doors blown wide-open. John Lee was crushed behind the steering wheel. Carter lay crumpled at the edge of the cornfield and Tina huddled in a pool of mud. It was only when the police and the ambulance arrived with their lights and sirens that Tina began to see, to realize what had actually happened. John Lee was dead. She had a broken leg. Carter was critical. When they got to the hospital in Orangeburg she overheard a doctor tell the police, "If he makes it through the night, he's got a chance." Carter Washington did not make it through the night. And, despite all the hope and newly registered voters, Jesse Jackson did not win the nomination.

CHAPTER TWELVE

"MAX, IT'S me, Becky Knight." She stood in the doorway to his Central Park West apartment and watched him fit the startled pieces of his face back together.

"Becky! Girl, you've got me time-traveling. Come on in. And give me these gorgeous skins. The doorman said Ms. Knight. I didn't think . . . Where's Nicky?"

"She was running late at school, so we decided that since you're so rarely at home to do makeovers we wouldn't waste this opportunity and I'd keep her appointment."

"How fabulous. You look wonderful, I just can't get over it. Scared me to death, though."

"Well, thanks, that always makes a woman feel good."

"Stop it. I meant, it was like déjà vu or *This Is Your Life,* only standing right on your doorstep without all the lights and cameras. It was wild. But it's so good to see you. Your gorgeous daughter told me you might be coming into town but she didn't say when."

"She didn't know until the last minute. And I've got a million things to do in just a few days, including a kind of job interview."

"Acting? Or what is it now, directing or producing?" He took her coat to hang it in the foyer closet.

"Nothing's for sure, but it's something that has to do with them all."

"Well, great. We need your kind of taste in this town again."

"There's nothing like New York schmooze. And you were always so good at it. I love it, and I love seeing you again."

"Stop, you know I can't handle excessive praise."

They walked into his living room, a square white space landscaped with islands of overstuffed sofas and chairs in the palest gray tweed. The room gave Becky the relaxing impression of being decorated by air and clouds. Max had always seemed such a hyper character. To find him in such a serene environment surprised her, pleasantly.

"Please," Max continued. "Make yourself comfortable and tell me what you'd like to drink. Soft, hard, spring water, champagne?"

"A glass of champagne would be wonderful."

"Indeed, just what we need to celebrate."

"But I hope you wouldn't be offering my daughter this."

"Becky, I'm insulted. You know she couldn't be in safer hands than mine."

"The same old reprobate, huh?"

"I'm scandalized. Here the plague has wiped a whole generation off the planet. But we're still alive and some of us are still kicking. Don't we deserve some recognition? Thank you," he answered, and applauded the two of them. Becky joined in and smiled.

While Max was in the kitchen she looked around. A bouquet of giant cala lilies leaned their stark white trumpets out from a tall silver column. Tables in flawless smoky lacquer held arrangements of geometric figurines in crystal, but were otherwise clear of books, magazines and, Becky realized, color.

She watched herself in the mirrored wall and silently mourned her lack of style. The silk pantsuits that she liked to wear in California seemed too soft for New York City. She wanted shoulder pads and sharp lapels and clothes with neat, crisp edges. Tomorrow she had to go shopping.

When Max returned, he carried a silver ice bucket with a bottle of Dom Perignon and two crystal flutes. After he popped the cork, they drank to both survival and success. Neither one had been guaranteed and they appreciated being here to talk about it.

And talk they did. Hours spent with each other in dressing rooms—even many years ago—made it easier to shed the inhibitions of the present. They reminisced over old times spent together and recounted major forks in the road taken separately.

"But Max, nobody'd ever done that before. Jumped from *Vogue* to *Bazaar* and back to *Vogue* and lived to tell the tale. Models couldn't do it. You were either in the Vogue and Condé Nast Club or you were out."

"See how those old editorial dolls had everyone so intimidated? But then you learn that they don't respect you if you kowtow to them. Eventually they love you for breaking their own rules."

"Love you?" She raised a skeptical eyebrow.

"Well, at least, respect you. And then there're the golden people like you, darlin', who play by the rules and actually win. You end up confirming the fairy tale. Which, of course, makes it all that much harder for the girls who don't manage to latch onto a White knight or a Black one, for that matter. Tell me, though, wasn't it still a little hard to quit? There weren't that many of us in the business in *any* capacity that we could afford to leave."

"When I *first* started, you're right. I remember people being absolutely tongue-tied when I showed up on go-sees. As if a Black model was a basic contradiction in terms. The men didn't know what to say and the women weren't any better with their petty, envious attitudes and their snide remarks. Where do *you* come from? Remember, Max? As if I couldn't possibly be from *this* planet."

They laughed together in joint recognition of the many times they'd had to bite their tongue and suffer. She hadn't thought about these things in a long while. The old life she knew with Max was so far away but being with him now made it not only easier to remember but also worthwhile.

"Sure, it was hard to quit," Becky admitted. "But by the time I did, more Black girls and more different kinds of Black girls had come onto the scene. Light-skinned, dark-skinned. Girls with straight hair and girls with Afros. Girls with high drama and girls who lived next door. I was glad to get out when I did."

"You make it sound entirely too easy, though," Max chided her. "You can't tell me that you didn't miss all the madness."

"I confess," Becky threw her hands up with a laugh. "I did miss it. I was used to being the center of attention, used to people catering to me. That sounds spoiled, doesn't it? Of course, I worked hard and played hard, too. But then all of a sudden there was this big fine man who wanted me to work and play just for him."

"What they call marriage, right?"

"Right. A one-woman show for an audience of one. Except there was no telling how many others would be invited to the performance . . . You know how musicians are. I had to be the gracious hostess at all hours. Food and drink and lots of it, on the spur of the moment. And I had to look like there was no place on earth I would have rather been. That's where all the training came in handy. One pose after another. But with no guaranteed rate, no double overtime for lingerie, no money of my own. And me, a longtime working girl."

He laughed. "What torture! Somewhere it had to be worth it, though."

"Sure. I wasn't alone anymore. I wasn't hungry for love and desperate for attention and scared I'd lose my looks before I landed a husband. All that fear was gone. Kayo was fascinated by me, and I was intrigued by him. We were a perfect match. After all the ups and downs in the business, marriage was like a special lifetime booking. There were still surprises, but the basic fact was that I knew I had a regular client. But enough about me. Look at you, still going strong."

"While everyone else is counting T-cells instead of T-bills?" Anger unalloyed by his usual sarcastic humor seeped out of Max's voice.

"I didn't mean that . . ."

"The whole business, completely changed. What we knew as Forever Fabulous is a thing of the past. Way, André, Victor, Piero, Willi, Perry, Halston, Patrick, Antonio, Isaia. And on and on and on." He pressed the cold glass of champagne against the side of his head and closed his eyes. "I hate talking about it. It's like, tick-tock, time to update the obituaries."

"I'm sorry, I didn't mean it like that, Max," Becky repeated.

Max exhaled loudly and opened his eyes to the serenity of his home and his beautiful friend still in it. "I know *you* didn't. But there're just so many people who come to New York, who pass through on their little antiseptic, automatic sidewalks or whatever, who gape at us like the last Tasmanians on exhibit. It tends to make my blood boil."

"Well, cool down. All I meant was that it's amazing to me that you've been able to stay in the business for so long. Makeup artists, even healthy ones, have about the same longevity as models."

"It's no secret. You have to leave and give them a chance to forget you. Give them a chance to miss you and need you again. Over and over I've watched people make the mistake of staying around, wining and dining everyone in sight, working nonstop with all the top people and so on. Then those very same people get tired of you. It's not that they don't like you. They're just bored with you. You're too much there. As fabulous as we are we do tend to forget that no one is indispensable."

Max refilled their flutes with champagne and continued. "In my case," he said, "every couple of years I'd go away and stay. And then come back with all these unique and wonderful products that nobody else would have for at least six months. Paris, London and Milano. Tokyo, do you believe? I even spent a year in Rio, honey. And you know as much as I love my furs it was absolutely wonderful to do without. And then once Jon A. opened his L.A. salon, every now and then I'd spend a week out there doing those poor tired faces."

"Is that why you never called me?" Becky asked with a mix of accusation and regret. "Because you thought my face would be too old and hard to work on?"

"Still supersensitive Becky. I don't think so. Honestly, I think I was just too busy. So many canceled appointments and reschedulings and ego trips. I love to go there but once I get there I can't wait to get out. All the vitamins they take for the body, it's a shame they take nothing but drugs for the mind. Whatever happened to original ideas? I always get the feeling everything that's important has already happened there, so life is just a series of endless reruns. What can I say? I try to make my work fun, Becky. That's the secret."

"It makes sense, but it still sounds awfully Peter Pannish to me. Don't you ever want to settle down with somebody, have a nice quiet country house and a subscription to the Opera?"

"I don't know. I used to. But half my friends are dead and the other half are trying so hard to reform they might as well be. Sometimes I do get these decorating pangs—what a dreadful cliché. Maybe have my own business. But ownership is such a noose. And that's what love's really about, too, isn't it? Having someone? Well, I have my apartment, I have my car. And I have my friends who have houses and yachts and their own little pew at Carnegie Hall. Let them pay. Let them worry. Being a guest is so much more entertaining than being a host. You don't have to clean up afterward."

"In my house you do," Becky insisted.

"I would tend to doubt it, darlin'. From what I know about Kayo Knight, the Immigration Service probably just camps out on your doorstep waiting for the new Marias to arrive."

"Max," she sputtered, insulted and amused, "that's gross."

"But is it untrue?"

"I don't think Kayo's been poor since he was twelve years old and that's over forty years ago."

"And is your life with him what you want it to be?"

Becky stood up from her chair and walked uneasily over to the broad windows facing Central Park. The unexpected tenderness in his voice touched her. She turned and faced him.

"It was . . ." she admitted. "Some things have been wonderful. Like Nicky. I can't imagine life without her. And finding myself in good work again. Acting and directing might have shortened my life, but they saved it, too. Made me remember who *I* was. Other things . . . I don't know. Maybe I should take your advice about leaving and making people miss me . . ."

"Well, maybe that's what New York is going to do. Wake you and Prince Charming up. I'd go after him myself if I didn't have so much respect for Big Missus and Lil Missus."

"Oh, Max, you're too crazy." She laughed softly.

"Crazy and Colored and that's only the Cs. Now come on, let's get you started. I do have a four o'clock after you."

"I'm disappointed." She feigned a pout. "I thought I'd have you all to myself."

"But you do have me. For now."

In the mirrored dressing room off his stark gray and white bedroom, Max had Becky change into a thick white terry robe. He covered her pageboy with a matching turban. Then, scowling, he sent her into the bathroom to wash her face. She could hear him puttering around the living room, half muttering to himself, half scolding her.

"You dolls know you're coming for a facial and a makeover and what do you do? Beat that face to death before you even get here. I want it all off. Everything. I want that skin squeaky clean. Do you hear me?"

She laughed. It was rather silly but she was so used to wearing some makeup, she hadn't given it a second thought. Getting a new face was fun. She looked forward to wearing it out to dinner tonight with Nicky and JJ. What fantastic young people they both were. Nicky had been an instant, unpredictable success. And JJ, he was certainly moving ahead in the world, too. Of course, Kayo's name had given him a leg up, but he had proven he could stand on his own two feet. Too bad the same couldn't be said for his mother. She had never remarried and seemed to be drinking herself to a slow death in a big old house on the North Shore of Long Island. Why? Divorce wasn't death. At least, it didn't have to be, Becky thought. But then again, maybe she felt this way because she was the one who wanted the change. Maybe if she didn't want it, if Kayo did, and it came as a surprise . . . She closed that drawer of thoughts and presented her freshly scrubbed face to Max in his living room.

"Beautiful," Max declared. "I want you on this chaise right over here." He swung a gray leather lounge of Scandinavian design around to face the windows, warm from the early afternoon light. She began to relax as Max's fingers gently massaged her face.

"Your view of the park is wonderful," Becky enthused. "California's made me so green and New York is so . . . drab."

"You're not turning into one of those boring snobettes, are you? Full of causes and wearing combat boots twenty-four hours a day," he groaned.

"You are so funny."

"And your laugh is so lovely. I finally figured out what the problem is—you haven't changed enough. I don't feel like you're twenty years older since the last time I worked on that gorgeous face of yours. I see you haven't tortured yourself in all that naked California sunlight."

"I did, at first, but then it got boring. It didn't take long to realize that I wasn't on vacation. I was actually living there."

"I know what you mean but enough chitchat for now. You need quiet to relax. First, we're going to steam clean these big old pores and then we're going to shrink them smooth. They say smooth as a baby's bottom but I don't have enough experience to know about that. I call it a little nonsurgical face-lift. I want you to keep your eyes closed. But remember to smile inside. Happy thoughts always help the complexion, don't you think?"

He adjusted a hot cloth pack stuffed with herbs over her face. They smelled good enough to eat or drink. The champagne, the talk and now this soft sweet dumpling covering her in healing darkness made her drowsy. She could feel little muscles relaxing, and not just in her face. Knots in her shoulders, hands and legs seemed ready to dissolve if she could only reach them and rub them away. She would order a massage at the hotel for tomorrow. For the moment she was content to float in Max's care.

"How are you feeling?" His voice almost startled her.

"I think I was starting to fall asleep."

"Good. Is the pack still warm?"

"It's delicious."

"Fine, let me turn it over and give you ten more minutes. After that we'll let you cool down and breathe. Then I have a wonderful masque for you."

"I don't remember going through all this when I was younger."

"You didn't need to, darlin'. *Then.* Now we have to take serious care of ourselves."

"Max, do you think Nicky can?"

"Can what?"

"Take care of herself in this business. Tell me the truth, because I'm . . . concerned. One of the reasons I'm here is to spend a little time with her before all this Cleo business goes to her head and spins it around. She's still so young and vulnerable."

Max understood that Becky was speaking as a mother now, not as a model. There would be too many conflicts if she tried to combine the two. The urge to protect and the love of freedom just did not mix.

"I'll tell you, Becky. The first time I met her, I could see that she was special. Now, you were good, very good, but Nicky is great. Working with her just confirms it. I try to keep tabs on her, quietly of course. She's learning to handle the pressure. I think her head's on straight. It's her heart that might not be so . . . dependable."

"Max, what are you saying?" Becky removed the pack from her face and sat upright in the lounge. "There's a boyfriend in the picture already?"

"My goodness, Mama, relax and lie down. Now, to answer your question, I'd say no. I don't think there's a boyfriend on the scene yet. But remember the loneliness and desperation you mentioned before?"

"Sure, occupational hazards."

"Well, just imagine how it's compounded for her. Her peers, her college pals, can't know what she really does. And to her they must seem retarded compared to the men she has to work with."

"Men?"

"Men. Becky, face it. She sees herself as a woman. And so do they."

"But . . ."

"But nothing. And don't start getting all square on me. You and I go too far back together."

"Still, a man, the wrong kind of man, could break her heart or lead her in the wrong direction. To drinking and drugs . . . Like those other Cleo girls, poor things."

"Don't believe everything you hear."

"What do you mean by that?"

"I don't know. I guess I'm just getting paranoid in my old age. Forget it. Now, look at you," Max chastised her. "The herb pack is cooling off too quickly because you've been jabbering all this time. Let me get a hot towel out of the steamer and cover you all up again."

Max left for the kitchen and returned with a towel whose penetrating heat reactivated the herbs. Soothed and quieted by the dark warmth of the treatment, Becky dozed off. She never heard the intercom and when the doorbell rang it jarred her.

"Max, what was that?" she asked sleepily.

"Leave that pack on and stay right where you are, Becky. I'll get the door."

She heard him flirting with the delivery man.

"What's a fine brother like you doing delivering flowers?" Max could be so outrageous. And then she heard him tell the man to wait, "wait just a minute, I have something for you," while he went back to his bedroom. Then she heard footsteps and then she heard nothing.

When Max returned to the empty doorway, he was surprised that the guy hadn't waited for his tip. People just weren't as hard up as they seemed, he thought, while he untied the ribbons around the long white box.

"Oh, Becky, look. Roses, beautiful long-stemmed roses. And so fragrant. Now where's the card in all this? Hellooo. Do you believe it? Just how am I supposed to figure out who sent these? Becky, Becky . . . ?"

The telling took no time. Over and over again Max told the story: the Black delivery man, the wait for the tip, the flowers with no note, Becky's face covered, her neck opened, her life gushing away. Everything happened so quickly, it and the telling of it. He didn't understand. It didn't seem fair that something so important, so absolutely final, could take so very little time.

Police Detective Richard Matthews asked him to repeat what he had seen. Stone-gray two-piece uniform, Knicks cap, mirrored glasses, black mustache but otherwise clean-shaven, smooth complexion, Honey Glow.

"What's honey glow?" the detective asked.

"His skin color."

"What's that, like a tan color?"

"Well, yes, but you asked for specifics. That's what I would use on him."

"For what?"

"For foundation, for the makeup base to match his skin tone."

"How would you know that?" Matthews asked.

"What do you think I do? Kindergarten finger painting? This is my business. I've been a makeup artist for twenty-two years. It's my business to know all the different skin colors. My business." Max found himself shouting and immediately applied the brakes. "Listen," he said quietly, "I can't do this anymore. I just can't go through it again."

"If you could just try," Matthews insisted. "Every little thing is important. And I know this is hard to believe now, but it's going to be OK, Max. You're going to be OK."

"Listen, I am not OK, Dick, and I don't expect to be OK ever again in this life. Now, will you please just leave me the fuck alone?" It was then that Max knew he was really out of control. He never, ever, used profanity.

The Saturday afternoon service at the Frank Campbell Funeral Chapel was restricted to family, as if only blood relations could measure and regenerate what had been lost with Becky.

Nicky stood up and walked over to the coffin. She had to take a last look at her mother's face. But this was a face she had never seen before, some grotesquely discolored substitute. Some terrible mistake had been made, she thought, none of the features were the same. And for a heartbeat Nicky hoped for a miracle. But the hair was proof that the horror was only too real. Only her hair, in the lovely classic pageboy her mother always wore, felt soft and familiar enough to bring back the tears.

"Why, Daddy? Why?" she cried again and again as Kayo put his arm around her and led her back to a front-row seat. The minister made his consoling remarks about life and death and God and Divine Purpose. But she knew that no one there had the real answer. They were all asking the same question themselves.

As she sat listening to the eulogy, her mind wandered, searching for some plausible explanation. It wasn't a robbery. No money was taken. A random killing with her mother an accidental victim? But why?

Her father had suggested that whoever did it wanted to punish beautiful women. Maybe the guy had been spying on Max's place for a long time, watching models come in and out, watching Max be friendly with women he could never know. There were crazy, bitter people in the world who would destroy what they couldn't have.

Max thought it was a racial thing. The Klan or someone who

thought like they did. Someone who hated to see Black people becoming successful just like everyone else. Max had told her that other Black models had gotten threats, letters and calls, for a few months now. Even roses. Maybe it was connected to the other Cleo girls who never made it.

Nicky's mind was spinning with all the possibilities. It was too much to handle. All she knew was that she was the one who had the appointment with Max. She was supposed to be sitting in the chair. It could have been her. Maybe it was *supposed* to be her.

Before heading downtown to JJ's loft where a larger reception would be held, Kayo decided to walk with Nicky and JJ the few blocks back to his suite at the Carlyle. Everybody needed to calm down. He had ordered private security guards and from certain bulky overcoats he knew that they were close around them on the busy sidewalks. At the end of a winter working day Madison Avenue looked as prosperous and unconcerned as ever.

"I always liked New York," Kayo said, "the feeling you get that something great is about to happen. But I don't care if I ever set foot in this hellhole again. I want you out of here, Nicky. I want you back home." Anger made him more adamant than ever.

"Don't make me have to say no, Daddy."

"As a matter of fact, Kayo, I think you should plan to spend more time out here," JJ added. "Then we'd all be closer together."

"Once a month is enough."

"Yeah, but I never see you. You're always on another line, you know what I'm saying?"

Kayo scrutinized his son. JJ was taller, leaner than he'd been at his age. It shocked him to see his son as a man now. They continued walking without speaking. The air had a metallic sharpness to it, making it dangerous to breathe. Nicky raised the hood on her anorak over her beret. The cold outside was an intruder seeking to flash-freeze her bone marrow. The cold inside had stunned everything else. When they arrived at the hotel with its familiar, unhurried demeanor, everyone was relieved. But the major question still swung in heavy silence between them. They ordered coffee from room service and tried to relax in the soft floral armchairs of Kayo's living room, until JJ finally asked, "What are we going to do now?"

"First off, we have to cooperate with the police as much as possible."

"That's taken for granted, Kayo," JJ said dismissively. "But they're into the lone lunatic mode and with everything we know now Max's story makes a lot more sense."

"Nicky, you know him. Do you believe Max?"

"I don't know. He was the only one who knew that I was supposed to be at his place, not Mom."

"The *only* one to know?" JJ asked.

"I mean, my roommate knew. And I told the agency I was going for a treatment after class. I guess I don't know who else knew. Everything's so twisted. Just like the roses that came to the dorm. I still don't understand why you didn't come right out and tell me that you hadn't sent them, Daddy."

"I'm sorry, sweetheart. I just couldn't. I felt too guilty about breaking our date."

"If only I had known."

"But what could you have done?" JJ asked.

"Maybe nothing, but I would have been more aware. That was a warning right there."

Kayo shook his head in despair. "Three beautiful Black women murdered in a matter of weeks. I don't know. That's wild."

JJ felt that was a fact of life that everyone should know by now. "It's a jungle out here, man."

"But I don't want my family eaten up by it. You both have got to protect yourselves more."

"I'm not a pretty woman, I don't have to worry."

"Well, your sister is. She needs protection. If she refuses to come home . . ."

"I'm right here, Daddy. You don't have to talk about me as if I'm not here or not capable of taking care of myself." As tears threatened to sabotage her confidence, she pushed her dark glasses higher up on her nose.

"I'm sorry, Nicky. I'm sorry. I just want to see you settled in a secure environment. Out of that dorm, for one."

"And into the loft with Nadja and me."

"With you, JJ? No way," said Kayo. "I've got enough nightmares already without thinking about her hanging out with you hotheads."

"Why d'you want to call us hopheads? We're musicians, artists. Why do you old folks want to call all young people drug addicts and stuff?"

"I said *hot*heads. And who are you calling old?"

"Will you guys cut it out?" Nicky pleaded. "Aren't things bad enough already without the two of you at each other's throat? Listen, if I still have to find some other place to live, why can't I just get my own apartment? I've got a couple of friends, *girl*friends, who'd just love to share a place."

"That still doesn't deal with the security aspect, though, does it?" JJ asked. "I'm telling you the loft is the jam. There's a receptionist downstairs until six and there's the TV intercom. And there's no way to get out of the elevator if my floor is locked. There're alarms on the windows and codes for the doors, and best of all, my main man Swayze is on the premises twenty-four hours a day."

"That beast."

"Every beauty needs one, little sis."

At JJ's loft Tina Thompson kissed Mother Saunders again and left her to some old friends who'd known her long enough and well enough to still call her Skippy. Skippy Saunders, queen of the sepia tap dancers. Thomas Thompson had been one of her many admirers, from the thirties and forties. They both liked to joke that maybe it had been a little bit more than admiration that had kept them lifelong friends. They included their families in the friendship, though, and Tina had always looked up to Becky like the big sister she never had, like the mother she had and lost. She was proud to see Mother Saunders holding up so well, considering. The muted turquoise of her eyes, glowing in the weathered dunes of her face, had seen so much. She was an old trouper whose bedrock sense of survival always left her something to stand on.

Tina leaned against a column, unsure of her footing. Her grief weighed too heavily, tottering on the edge of control, especially in this crowd with hundreds of people paying condolences but still talking, drinking, happy to see each other, laughingly alive. How dare they? How could they do it? With her father still in the hospital and now this, she felt overwhelmed by an unrelenting wave of bad news.

She took angry little sips of Saratoga water, hoping not to bite through the glass, swallowing slowly so as not to scream. Too many funerals, too many memorial services. They were becoming regular social occasions. AIDS, cancers, heart attacks, murders. Didn't anybody just die of old age anymore?

Tina forced yet another smile and this time a buss on the cheek for two still-stylish women, one whose hair seemed blonder every year, and another, her faithful but less flamboyant sidekick, in a mink cloche. They had been belles of the ball in the fifties, a decade before Becky's time, some of the first Aura models photographed for the Black magazines. Now, slightly broader in the hips and softer at the jawline, they wore the delicate smiles and nostalgic grace of aging party girls. Loyalty to one of their own, one of the model clan, brought them out. And Tina saw how glad they were to be remembered. There'd been so many changes.

Tina had overestimated herself. Exhausted, she watched Nadja move around the room helping people with refreshments, easing their reason for being here with a gentle smile. JJ was a lucky man. She could never do all that. In the past hour she had commiserated with as many people as she could endure. She would have to leave now before a nasty mood settled in. As she headed for the door a familiar voice made her turn around.

"You weren't leaving without saying goodbye, were you?" Kayo Knight carried that same note of positive authority in his voice that her father did. It was part of their charm. "Becky was so happy coming to see you, Tina. You know how much she loved you."

His words were too much to bear. Tears slipped out of Tina's eyes and her nose started to run. She felt childish, trying all at once to find a handkerchief in her pocketbook, hold on to her glass and keep her nose from dripping. Kayo handed her a neat linen square, still warm from his pants pocket. What an odd reversal of roles that he was comforting her when she should be trying to comfort him.

"Thanks, I'm sorry, I guess I'm not doing too well," she said. "How are *you* holding up, Kayo?"

"So-so. Just trying to take care of business. How's your father?"

"Improving. Mother Saunders said she stopped in to see him at the hospital today. She didn't mention anything about Becky."

"Of course not. I admire her so much. She and Thomas go back a long way."

"I know. Kayo, I'm so sorry about Becky. I feel so responsible."

"It's not your fault."

"But she wouldn't have come to New York if I hadn't asked her."

"Tina, that's not true. You know she came to see Nicky too. She also wanted to see Thomas and other old friends. And sometimes I think Becky was looking for something else, something more. Maybe even a way to leave."

"And you were just letting her go?"

"It wasn't quite that simple, Tina."

"Well, I am sorry, for everything. Is there any way, anything I can do to help?"

"I don't know. Maybe keep an eye on Nicky. She refuses to come back to California. And I just don't like the idea of her continuing to live in the dorm."

"What about staying with me? She could have the third floor. Mrs. English would love to have someone else to fuss over," Tina added.

"I think maybe you'd better think about it some more. It would be wonderful for me but that's a selfish daddy talking."

"Let's all think about it, then. It would give me something positive to do, make me feel useful."

"You shouldn't ever have to worry about that, Tina. And please don't feel that you have to atone for some guilt either. We've got enough baggage to carry without taking on someone else's. I'll be in touch." And he moved back into the crowd of mourners who couldn't help but greet him with a smile.

While the reception was still going strong, in a book-lined alcove of JJ's loft Nicky was hunched over the phone trying to keep as much of the noise out as possible. It was Max. He was scared, his voice hushed and conspiratorial, as if he were present but whispering in her ear.

"I've been trying to reach you."

"I've been staying with my father at the hotel for the past couple of days."

"Nicky, listen. I know everybody's calling me paranoid but I smell something that doesn't love Black people."

"Who is it, Max? What is it?"

"I don't know, princess. But I do know that you have to be extremely careful. Keep your eyes and ears open. Someone's doing more than just scaring us to death. This madness isn't over yet. You've got to protect yourself."

"It's so hard to believe, Max. Why me?" she cried.

"Because you're Black and beautiful and that's the price you pay."

"But I'm not the only one."

"No, but you're the next. Someone has a thing against you Cleo girls. Don't you see?"

"And what am I supposed to do, quit? You know I can't, Max. You know it's what I've always wanted. If I quit, it means they win."

"But you live. Think about it, please. Look, I've got to go. Please be careful."

"I will, Max. You take care."

She sat up and wiped her eyes, but the tears kept coming. Swayze lay across her feet as if she were his prize possession. The Rottweiler's smooth black hair and warm weight obliged her to be still for a moment. With so much going on she didn't want to disturb his claim to peace. At least someone had found a bit of it somewhere.

She was swollen with sadness. She had spent the past couple of days in a kind of numb, automatic mode. Ever since Corky and the police had first brought the bad news to her, she had heard people speaking and felt their hands touching her. But that all happened on a surface she hadn't known existed. She had always been so open and eager, so California. Now she felt a steel plate lying just below her skin, protecting her real self.

And she was angry. Not just sad and confused, but venomously angry. Angry at the killer and at the world for letting such evil exist. Angry at her father for not loving strongly enough to protect everyone. Angry at her mother for dying without knowing, without seeing, without leaving anything special behind for her. And angry at herself for surviving the trick, and now for having to view it all through the prism of racism.

But no one was going to make her back down from her dream. No one. The crying was over. She tilted her head back, willing the last renegade tears to slide back into their little drains.

Finally, gently disengaging her feet from the dog, she stood up and braced herself against the wall. She took a deep breath and moved cautiously out of the peaceful little alcove and into the noisy wide-open living room. People with handsome, time-tested faces, famous people whom she knew she knew, patted her shoulder or her cheek. She felt uneasy under their scrutiny, as if they were searching for some surviving trace of her mother. She could not tell whether they found it or not. They seemed to struggle for a moment with their own combination of grief and relief and then they moved away in mute sadness.

She looked around, above the many people who had come to pay their respects to her mother, above their colors and gestures and cigarette smoke. There were so many nooks and crannies to this place. She could like living here. She could brush up on her old piano lessons on the baby grand. SoHo was just a few blocks away from Washington Square Park and the NYU campus where she still took classes. JJ and Nadja would have lots of cool friends around.

It reminded her of the days when her parents used to entertain at the house on the beach in Santa Monica. When did she notice—or did she ever?—that the live music stopped playing and the CDs took over and then they, too, quieted down and all she could hear were her parents' cars coming and going, often at the same time but rarely in the same direction?

There'd be people here all the time, though, all kinds of unknown people. Max had said to be careful. How could she do that, go to school, model and live here, too?

"Oh, there you are, baby. I've been looking all over for you."

"I was on the phone, Grandma."

Skippy Saunders sat down on an empty love seat next to her granddaughter, the spitting image of her own only daughter. The same glossy copper skin, pointed nose and high-angled cheekbones. The same passion in the eyes. The same eagerness to feel, as if feeling were the surest route to knowing.

"I wish I had some words of wisdom for you, Nicky," she said, taking her hand. "But I'm stuck. I don't know what to say."

"You don't have to say anything."

"Maybe you're right. Maybe that's best. But I keep thinking, what am I going to tell your grandfather?"

"How's he doing?"

"He's fine, as fine as he can be."

"When you go see him does he recognize you? Does he know you at all?"

"He doesn't know who I am or who he is or where he is or anything. Well, no, sometimes he thinks I'm his mama and he wants to go home, just like a child."

"So maybe that's a protection," Nicky suggested. "Maybe that's part of Alzheimer's that helps people. It takes them back to a safe place."

"I just get so angry sometimes, Nicky. I know it's not right, I know it's not his fault. But he's gone from me and at the same time he's still here to remind me of what it used to be."

"I wish I could remember him better. JJ played me some tapes he has of you all dancing. You were fabulous. I am so proud to come from you."

"That's a sweet thing to say, Nicky. We had the time of our lives together, I'm telling you. People just don't seem to know how to do that anymore. Work and live together and still love each other. Still love. It was so hard. I can almost laugh now but sometimes we would fight every day, it seemed like. My steps would get in the way of his steps or I was being too cute or he was being too cute or the money wasn't right or something. There was always something wrong. But then we had to dance together almost every night, you know? We had to touch each other and put our arms around each other and smile. You're just acting for the audience, pretending, and then sure enough, the bad mood leaves and you're back together again for real. See, we were partners in everything, the good times and the bad. So how can Becky be gone and he not know it?"

"It's OK, Grandma, don't cry."

"I'm all right. It's not the crying that hurts . . . Now tell me about yourself, what your plans are. Your father says you're determined to stay in the city."

"I have to, Grandma. I just have to decide where I'm going to live."

"Well then, I hope to see more of you. We're only a couple of hours upstate. You've got no excuse not to make your face more familiar."

"I know. I'll be seeing you more."

"I hope so, baby. People say they want to live a long time, but when they get old, the only people left are young. And, you know, young people don't want to be bothered."

"I'm not like that, Grandma."

"Good, 'cause I still got a few steps to teach you."

Grandmother and granddaughter hugged each other warmly, bridging their loss with love.

When Kayo first gave Nicky her mother's mink coat, she refused it, even felt insulted that he would do such a thing. The coat was too gruesome a reminder. And it was too old for her, too rich, too unlike her own desires. Her grandmother was the one who convinced her to take it. You can't control your inheritance, she'd said. You give thanks and make it your own.

She had it on now as she stood by the dark window of the dark hotel room in her father's suite. She pulled back the heavy drapes and sheer curtains. The glass was cold, although she was not. Not on the outside, at least. The coat's heavy silk lining was warm against her bare skin. She had brought a decent nightgown and robe to wear in her father's presence, cuddly pink-and-blue-flowered nightclothes that Becky had chosen for her. Nothing like the battered T-shirts she slept in in the dorm. But she had taken them off when she woke up about two-thirty, restless, angry still, crying again. And then she'd put the coat on, slippery cold at first, but fragrant with her mother's cherished L'Air du Temps perfume. And something similar to calm came over her as she stroked the fur, easing her fingers through the silky hair, smoothing softness into jagged feelings.

The city was black with sleep. Except for the lit rooftops of New York landmarks, there were only a few lights that looked as if they might belong to real people. Someone working late on an inspired idea. Or someone eating a forbidden postmidnight snack. Or maybe some couple who refused to go to bed angry at each other and decided to stay up all night and fight it out. They all had a place to be, someplace called home. Where was her place?

JJ wanted her at his loft. Tina asked her to stay at her house. Each had advantages. JJ and Nadja meant fun but Tina meant security. Max—and everyone—had said to be very careful. So that left no choice. The move would be to Tina's.

She had decisions to make. She would not fall apart. She couldn't afford to now.

Corky said that she'd pleaded with S & S to reschedule the Cleo TV shoot. But there was no way anything could be changed. Arrangements had already been made for the director, the camera crew, the equipment and most important, the location, for February 17, a Monday. That was the only day of the week that the Metropolitan Museum of Art closed its doors to the public.

Nicky had all of one week to pull herself together. She could do it. She had to. Vanessa Seymour had made it crystal clear that she didn't belong to herself anymore. She belonged to Cleo. Well, Nicky would show her and anybody else who needed to know. Nicky Knight was still her own person.

She pulled Becky's coat more closely around her, glad now to have some tangible reminder of her mother. But regret continued to sting. Why hadn't they been closer when they'd had the chance?

CHAPTER THIRTEEN

WHEN Thomas N. Thompson did not return to Hill House the second weekend in February—and did not call—Clarice Brathwaite began to wonder and then to worry. He always phoned if he wasn't coming. Feeling awkward, she called the house to see if he was expected. It was then that Wilson, the housekeeper, told her in a few discreetly sympathetic words that Mr. Thompson had suffered a serious heart attack the week before.

She hadn't expected to get the news like that, quietly, personally, in the same lilting island voice she had. She'd always thought bad news would come in the square-cornered accent of northern people and that somehow their crisp, cool words would make it easier to take. Serious, but still alive, he'd said, oh, yes. She would take no more chances. She immediately called New York and asked Lucas for more information. They were used to talking, not that a once- or twice-yearly hello was exactly a conversation, but they knew who they were and what place they occupied in Mr. Thomas N. Thompson's life. There was a bridge of respect between them, enough so that when she asked him to prepare a room for her, he did not question her authority and asked only her flight information in order for Connors to meet her at the airport.

Clarice had been to New York many years before. She knew what cold was like, how it hurt to inhale such air, how the skin tightened up and how one's insides squeezed together for warmth. She knew about heavy coats and thick stockings and waterproof boots. As far as wardrobe was concerned, it was clear that she was not at all prepared. But, unlike another kind of woman, she would not waste time wringing her hands and wailing, "What am I going to wear?" Once she made her reservation to leave, she had two of her shop assistants run up a loose cashmere coat in navy, two wool skirts and two pairs of wool trousers, one each in navy and gray. She already had a couple of sweaters on hand and she would buy whatever else she needed once she got there. Getting there was the main priority.

Her first stop on arrival was the hospital. As they traveled in the car from the airport Connors explained the bypass operation to her using the careful, impersonal language of one uncomfortably close to a dangerous chasm of feeling. How the surgeons had to cut through the rib cage to open up the chest; how they took clear-flowing arteries from the leg to replace the clogged arteries in the heart; how they had used a respirator for two days until he was strong enough to breathe on his own again. He was now out of the cardiac care unit and in a private room.

"He's past the crisis and getting better," said Connors, his glasses glinting at her in the rearview mirror, "but we should not expect too much."

Despite his attempt at delicacy, Clarice did not like Connors' tone or his attitude. She supposed it was his way of preparing her for the worst. That seemed so contrary to what Thomas would want. He always expected the world from everyone. And he expected no less from himself. Of course, the heart attack was a setback. Naturally, the operation was extremely serious. But he was a heroic man used to confronting heroic challenges. She would expect him to recover fully. If it meant a return to his old demanding ways, so be it. It would be nice if he softened up a bit, but that was the only area where she might be expecting too much.

At the nurses' station Clarice was asked if she was family. The question unhinged her and she had no time to lie. "Almost," she said quietly. The nurse told her gently that all visitors were restricted to five minutes at a time, and Clarice nodded that she understood.

When she walked into the room Thomas' eyes were closed. He looked so still and vulnerable, smaller and far less heroic than she had ever seen him. Standing at the foot of his bed, she felt suddenly overwhelmed by helplessness. The mysterious monitors with their jagged, mountain-climbing script, all the tubes and tape, the metal and plastic . . . All these artificial things were attached to him in more meaningful ways than she was. She could not even put her arms around him and hold him to her own strong heart, tied as he was to the machines. There was no place, no space for her. It hurt and yet she was too astonished to cry. Anger burned her pity away. How could he let this happen to him? How could he be here without her, without letting her know? How could he do this to himself? And to her? And what could she possibly do for him now?

She felt like a fool, a sad, old, unfamily fool. Bringing herself all this way when nobody had asked her. Assuming she had some special right to take care of him just because she loved him. Who knew? Maybe some other woman was sitting outside right now, waiting for her to leave in order to come in to see him. Some other woman who also loved him and wanted to do for him. She sighed loudly and shook the threat of tears away.

His eyes opened slowly, unsteadily, uneasily. Then he finally focused and saw her. And smiled.

"Clarice," he whispered.

She went to the side of the bed and held his hand. It was hot, swollen and weak.

"I need you," he said. A lone tear slid out of the corner of his eye. "Stay with me."

"I will, Thomas. I'm staying right here." And she took off her new winter coat and sat down.

"Is Mrs. English always going to call me Miss Nicole? I mean, is she *always* like that?" asked Nicky one night not long after she had moved in with Tina Thompson. They sprawled on the honey silk sofas in Tina's second-floor sitting room, drinking herb tea after dinner. Framed family pictures covered one entire wall, a teak bookcase another.

"Always like what?" Tina smiled at Nicky's lack of pretension.

"You know, so stiff and formal all the time."

"Basically, yes. And I don't know all the reasons why. I'll just tell you what she used to tell me. Most people don't know her first name, don't know she even has a first name. It's Mona and her maiden name was Connors. She'd been married to Robert English for only six months when he died of a cerebral hemorrhage and left her three months pregnant. She always said that her baby died in the womb when he did. When she left Calhoun County, she was eighteen. No husband, no child and no possibility of having another. She came North and moved in with relatives here in the city, uptown on Sugar Hill. And like most Black women, she worked as a domestic. She did day's work for several families until she was hired as a full-time maid for my family. She liked us, she used to tell me, not because we were the first Colored family she worked for, which we were not, but because my parents called her by her married name, Mrs. English. As a matter of fact, they never called any of their help by their first name. When she succeeded Mrs. Brewster as housekeeper, a long time ago when I was just a little girl, the only change she made was to move from the ground-floor room to the very top of the house. Nobody had lived there since housemaids didn't live in anymore. We thought it was too far to trek, but I think it gave her a sense of dominion, authority, you know.

"She knew our habits and we knew hers. My father is a very proud man, and she is, too. You can see that. I never heard either of my parents gush, like White people used to do, that she was just like a member of the family. They had more respect for her than that, I think.

"To this day I'm sure that I'm the only Thompson she's ever called by the first name. And she'll almost never call me Tina. It's always Christina and in front of company, always Miss Christina. It used to drive me crazy. But she was always teaching me something. She'd talk about history—herstory, she called it. She'd stand up straight as if she were talking to thousands of people and tell me that in 1964 in Atlantic City one southern Negro woman introduced herself to a convention hall full of White politicians, old White men who weren't good enough to shine her shoes but who were running the country. And this one southern Negro woman said, 'My name is *Mrs.* Fannie Lou Hamer.' That's what she said and that's how she felt. I always thought it was some etiquette thing, you know, doing things the right way, the White folks' way. But for her it was always about total respect. White folks had never called Black people by their complete and rightful name. Never admitted that we had families of our own and names that belonged to us. *Mrs.* English meant that she came from family, from love and care and support. That's why she calls you Miss Nicole. She wants you to know that she respects you and expects you to respect yourself.

"She has a good heart but I can count the times on one hand when she's spoken my name with the same feeling that I know she has about me. Like when I first got my period and I thought that meant I was dying and going to heaven. You know what I mean? My mother wasn't home, as usual, so Mrs. English was the one I told. And she's the one who told me what was going on so that I understood. She loves me, I know that. I love her. But tenderness and softness, she just can't let them come out in words.

"The hardest part came the morning after my mother died when Mrs. English wouldn't let me into her bedroom. She kept saying, 'You don't want to see, Miss Christina, you don't want to see.' I mean, I was twenty-five years old then. I had graduated from Columbia Law. I had just passed the New York Bar. I was bad, I was fearless. And who was she to refuse me? She stood right there across the hall, stood right in the doorway and refused to let me pass until I finally screamed at her, 'Don't tell me what I don't want to see.'

"And she said, 'You don't want to see this, baby.' 'Baby' she called me.

"And it was true. I didn't want to see it, but I had to. She was my mother. I owed her that last courtesy, to see her, fully. Mother, my mother, lay in a blue satin nightgown, her body contorted on the floor, smelling of vomit and feces. And Shalimar. She'd left a bottle open. She knew what it would be like. Her face, always so beautifully made up and so carefully composed, was twisted in pain. Horrible, the whole thing was just horrible. She left two notes. The one for my father read, 'Loving you was my sorrow.' The one for me, 'Loving you was my joy.' That's all she had to say.

"I screamed for hours. I remember crying for days. I couldn't bear to look at my father. I hated him. I couldn't stand being in the same house with him and with what she had done. I moved out. I had to. Stayed away for five years. Then when he moved to the East Side a few years ago, I moved back in. Mrs. English has remained here all that time, perched up in her crow's nest, watching."

CHAPTER FOURTEEN

"JEAN-JACQUES, *enfin. Et la belle Nadja.* How good to see you!" Sophie LeClerc took turns hugging them on the porch, kissing each on both cheeks over and over again. "It takes a leap year for you to make an appearance, eh? You," she said, clapping JJ on the chest, "I don't mind missing. I know you. But this one is new to me, so beautiful and with short hair, too. Some things about your old *maman* you cannot forget despite your best intentions, eh?" She fingered the wavy gray hair of her own pixie cut.

"Sophie," JJ pleaded, "please."

"You see, I annoy him already. Typical. But let's go inside. The breeze here can lift you up and carry you soaring across the harbor like a Chagall."

Nadja felt that it could have been true. The tall gray and white Victorian sat on the third tier of a steep and windy hill overlooking Northport harbor, which bristled with insolent little waves. Inside the house, the air was warm and fragrant. Sophie moved with surprisingly delicate grace, her solid squat shape clad in faded charcoal corduroys and a light gray turtleneck sweater. She led them through the first two salons which were the heart of the gallery to a large all-purpose room at the back of the house. A fieldstone fireplace did its duty at one end while at the other an open kitchen served up rich smells from a huge Garland stove.

A braid of garlic and bunches of dried herbs hung along a wall. In front of the bay window, a large easel faced a terraced garden just beginning to show signs of spring green and yellow. Nadja studied the canvas with its patches of thick paint. It seemed that a section of the world outside had been carefully peeled off and pasted on inside. Up close she could see minute strokes of bright, unexpected color. A few steps back, however, the vivid reds, oranges and blues disappeared into tentative neutrals.

"It's lovely, and so sad," she said.

"*Winter Garden,*" Sophie explained. "The grays make it sad, no? The light, so flat, so little of it. But that is part of the cycle. Everything that grows needs to rest at some time and winter is the time to rest. Even dying is just resting, you know? Come sit down by the fire and have some wine, some good red wine." She smiled up at the tall brown girl whose own sunshine seemed to break through and then cloud over so quickly.

JJ and Nadja sat on a worn velour sofa, while Sophie sat on thickly textured pillows next to a low weathered wooden table. A slab of pâté, small ceramic dishes with mixed olives, radishes and celery, and a long loaf of French bread in a checkered napkin were spread out next to two bottles of Nuits St.-Georges, one of which she emptied into a glass carafe.

"I will pour the first glass of wine, but then, please, you serve yourself. I don't know about you, Nadja, but I was not the serving kind of woman. And I think Jean-Jacques must have suffered for it, having a mother like me and a father like . . ."

"Sophie, please, we didn't come here to talk about old things, really. Nadja wanted to meet you. We're going to get married in a few months."

"Very good, *very* good. But all the more reason to talk about old things, Jean-Jacques. So we are not afraid of what is past, what we don't want to remember. So we don't stay afraid. If you give these old bones a minute, I want to show you something." She got up from the pillows and went up the stairway off the kitchen.

JJ poured the wine while she was gone and they toasted each other with a kiss. He needed the reassurance. "I told you she's a character. I don't think this was a good idea at all. She can get very weird."

"I like her, JJ. I need to see her and get to know her. With all that's happening around us, we can take nothing for granted. I'm glad I made you call and she asked us to come. I like her. I like that she is an artist. Her house is beautiful and so are the paintings. All that comes from her, from inside her."

"What's inside her is not always so beautiful, baby, that's all I'm saying. And I can say that because I know her."

"So then she is imperfect, like the rest of us? Is that what's so hard to take? Your mother being imperfect? Do you ever stop to think how lucky you are to have her, JJ? How very lucky?"

Nadja did not need to remind him of the past couple of weeks. She had returned to New York from the couture collections in Paris to find the loft dark and deserted, so unlike the way JJ typically welcomed her home. While she struggled with her luggage Swayze had grumbled at her until she took him out for a walk. When she returned, JJ was there. What a blessed relief. She had shed a few selfish tears before JJ even had a chance to tell her what had happened to Nicky's mother that very day. And then she had truly come undone. Being with Nicky, hostessing the reception, helping anyone else in pain always seemed to ease her own.

Sophie returned carrying an old-fashioned family album, heavy with thick black pages and fragile black-and-white photographs.

"Don't worry, Jean-Jacques, I will not torture you with all these ghosts from the past. I just want to show Nadja the picture of Kayo and me when we got married." She withdrew from little triangular tabs a glossy picture of a tall Black man in a beret and blazer, standing with his arm around the shoulder of a short White woman with short dark hair and dark lipstick in a light suit. "*Voilà,* complete with the Eiffel Tower in the background. *Amusant, non?* One of the rare times I ever wore a skirt. I almost put one on today but I said, my own son, he would not recognize me without my pants. He would know that I was masquerading and while he might like me more for the present, for the pretense I mean, he would end up respecting me less. So here I am.

"And here I am in Paris, 1960, the new wife of Meester Kenneth Knight, better known as Kayo, ex-boxer and now trumpet player extraordinaire in exile. What a prize for a struggling student at Beaux Arts. It was such a wonderful time, the late fifties, the sixties. We had survived the war, you know, and nothing could stop us. There was such marvelous energy in the air. Ideas were percolating everywhere. In music, literature, painting, everywhere. My friends and I would go to all the jazz clubs, the Mars Club, Birdland, *le Caméléon, le Chat qui pêche*. We'd sit for hours, feasting on the music. From these cold and smoky little caves would come pure treasure. Pleasure and treasure, I like that rhyme in English, don't you? We had so little money, but no one else had much more. Three of us would puff on one Gauloise, like this you know, taking turns, trying to look sophisticated. All the big names would be there and we would be there, too, rolling in the magic. I didn't know Kayo ever noticed me until one night he asked me to wait for him at the end of his last set. And *voilà,* that's how it all started. Like Cendrillon, you know."

"Cinderella," JJ explained to Nadja.

"Now, tell me about yourself, my dear," said Sophie, carefully replacing the photograph in its brackets.

"But wait, what about the rest of the story? If it started out like Cinderella, what happened? How did it end?"

"I've already told you about that, Nadja," said JJ.

"But I'm asking your mother."

"Call me Sophie, please. My son already does. When a child calls a parent by the first name it shows a lack of fear, no? Some people might say even a lack of respect. I don't know. I'm not sure. Before Jean-Jacques was even a teenager he was calling me Sophie, and somehow I did not mind. Not too much. He was a fearless child and I had to face the fact that I probably was not the best *maman,* so why should he call me that?" She closed the album, touching the cover with the briefest caress.

"You were a good mother, Sophie."

"You did not always think that." It was a statement, not an accusation.

"I did not always know it."

"And what makes for this change?"

"Life. Nadja. Us getting married. The idea of being a father myself, Nadja being a mother."

"And you don't want to repeat what your father and I went through?"

"Yes, something like that." JJ busied himself spreading a chunk of pâté on bread. She never seemed to give him a break. Let her concentrate on Nadja for a while.

"You see, Nadja," Sophie said, "Kayo had been married before, when he was very young, still a boxer in Chicago, living a very rough life. He always said that his wife was young and liked a very gay life, liked to run around. He said he found her with another man and he almost killed the guy and then almost killed her. He said he left town after that, left boxing, and put all of his energy into music. His hands just couldn't do both, he said."

"Sophie," asked JJ, annoyed, "why do you keep saying, 'he said'?"

"Because there is always more than one, how do you say, side to the story. Always. I never knew his wife, of course. I did not know the States until 1961 when we moved to New York. By then Kayo was doing more writing and arranging and organizing bands, you know. They would travel, playing all over the country, while I stayed in the city.

"I understood, I mean, I hated it, but I knew about the States. The racism and fear and hatred. The war with Algeria was tearing France apart. So I knew that it was not only America. No one wanted to see a Black man with a White woman. Well, not many. But we thought we were going to revolutionize the world with love. We would show them. Artists were too crazy to care and lots of musicians already lived that way. We lived in a tiny flat in the Village, for us, paradise on earth. I worked in an art gallery on 57th Street. *Quel prestige,* me with my little French accent. But one day when Kayo came to pick me up, the people there said to have him meet me elsewhere. That was the first time I remembered hearing that word, 'elsewhere.' Have my husband meet me elsewhere if I wanted to keep my job. Which I did. We needed the money. I needed the experience. When you are young you are so convinced of your own truth that you laugh at compromise. You say 'fuck you' with a smile and they never know. And that is all part of the fun. But it was hard and then it was even harder once Jean-Jacques was born. Freedom summer, 1964, you know, a very dangerous, very exciting time. Total revolution.

"I never knew about the other women. In a way, I did not want to know. But when Kayo started seeing Becky Saunders, I knew that something different was going on. Still, there was nothing I could do. She was beautiful, her pictures made her famous, she had money. And she was Black. I guess they fell in love. What could I do? I swallowed all my feelings, all the hurt for the first couple of years, because I had a small child. But when Jean-Jacques got to be five and six and started asking me where was his daddy, I had to confront Kayo. It was the last thing I wanted to do. If it had been just me I probably would have stayed ignorant and scared and maybe even married forever. But that man, who was just a little boy then, he wanted the truth and someone had to give it to him. Married in '60, divorced in '70. A neat little box of time. You say tidy, no? It was very difficult. I kept the apartment in the Village and I continued to work at the gallery. But I gave also French lessons, painting lessons, even cooking lessons, anything to keep mother and child together. Then a few years later Kayo started making money, as they say, big money, and he could afford to send Jean-Jacques to private school, and then to boarding school and Yale and out into the world. But I never took a penny from him. And he offered more than pennies, believe me." She held her glass up, admired the wine's color and took a hearty swallow.

"And you never went back to France?" Nadja asked.

"Not until Jean-Jacques was much older. I was too ashamed, you know. Already my family was not too pleased when I married a Black man. Then they were less pleased when we moved to America. I could not go back until I had fortified myself, until I could look at myself in the mirror and not see what they would see: a complete failure. It took a long time."

"But you have no regrets?"

"How easy that would be, Nadja. Of course, I have many, many regrets. I wish many things were different. But maybe that is why I am an artist. I compensate for my regrets by painting the world the way I want to see it. The irony, of course, is that the way it is, is still the most fascinating—and the most difficult—to re-create. But *assez,* enough of this painful past. You can see for yourself that I am not quite the drunken ogre they all make me out to be."

"Sophie!"

"Stop it, JJ." Nadja placed her hand on his arm and turned to Sophie. "I want to know why they think of you like that."

"Ask Jean-Jacques, ask Kayo. I don't know the answer." Sophie spit an olive pit into her hand and threw it into the fire. Sometimes she did not like herself much either. There was a nonchalance in her own voice that aggravated JJ, intrigued Nadja and—despite her best intentions to honesty—misrepresented how she truly felt.

"Why, JJ?" Nadja turned to him.

He shook his arm free from her and stood behind the sofa, away from them. He would not be taunted or pacified. "Do you really want to know why? Because she sits up here and contents herself with her bottles of wine and a hick town gallery when she could be doing great things in great places. Because she hangs on to her bitterness and spins more and more of it around her. Because, when it comes down to it, she cannot forgive and forget."

"This is true," Sophie conceded. "I cannot forgive and forget. I cannot forgive the cowardice, the way the great, dashing Kayo Knight would lie to me and avoid me and treat me as if I had less value than a fly. But not just me, me and my son, a little boy who cried and cried because his father said, of course, he would be coming back and he never came. That I cannot forgive and I cannot forget. I cannot forget that I birthed you and that he bought you. You shake your head no. He did, he used his money to win you back to him, to paper over all the holes where the tears had burned through. I cannot forgive that. And then I saw something else. I could see you becoming ashamed of me, a brown boy wanting so hard to be a Black man, burdened with the shame of having a White mother. Did you ever once stand up for me? I was not beautiful or rich or anything you or he could explain to those who wanted to know why. Of all women, why me? I was the wrong class and the wrong color, doubly inconvenient. How do you say now? Politically incorrect.

"And then I understood that it was not just about a dead love or a wrong color. I saw it with my own eyes the last time I saw him, at your graduation almost seven years ago. There we were at Yale, so beautiful and majestic. Everyone feeling imperial and dynastic. And there was Becky. Beautiful Becky, now a mother herself, so alone, so far from the joy, stranded on some bright little island, smiling too hard. I felt sorry for her. I could see that he was doing to her what he'd done to me. Maybe not in the details, but in general. And now Becky, too, is gone. All the talent and beauty, gone. And Kayo? The miracle, still here. He pretends to care but he cares only about himself. He is a very sad man, arrogant, ignorant of himself and dangerous to women. I cannot forgive that.

"So I live here. You can see, it is not complete isolation. I am not a hermit. I do have regular human contact and yet there is still the wildness of the wind and water at my front door. I do not wallow in the past. I don't stick pins in voodoo dolls. I haven't spoken this much about Kayo in seven years. I bother no one. A few people like my work and the work of the other artists I show and I make enough to live well."

"And die young."

"Who would care about that? Not you, my son. Certainly not your father. And certainly not me."

"I care," said Nadja.

"Bless you, *ma grande*. I need that."

When Sophic got up to chcck on the coq au vin in the oven, JJ reached for Nadja's hand and kissed it. He was reeling from his mother's words. He had never known the depth of her pain and his responsibility in it. And he would never have delved into it without this woman whom he loved so much.

"We have some time yet," Sophie said from the stove. "Why don't you two get a little fresh air before dinner? JJ, maybe Nadja would enjoy our *corniche,* the walk along the harbor."

"Are you putting us out already, Sophie?" Nadja tried to lighten the mood.

"*Au contraire*. Please understand, Nadja," she said, coming back to the fireplace, "words are not easy for me. I am not good with the polish and the perfect tone. I would like to get to know you but I want you to stay because you want to, not because you think you must. And if you want to go, I don't mind eating my own cooking."

"Well, I would like to go for a little walk, but I'm afraid I'll insist on coming back."

"Wonderful. You can find your way out. In about a half hour, then?"

"Is there anything we can bring back?" asked JJ bashfully.

"Yes."

"What's that?"

"More of whatever you brought in the first place. *A tout de suite.*"

Nadja and JJ held onto the iron railing as they walked down the steep stone staircase to the road. Directly across lay the park with its white gazebo and trim walkways and then the port itself, small and snug, where dozens of empty boats waited impatiently for the open water. The wind was strong and cold, its salt smell invigorating. JJ held Nadja's hand in the pocket of his parka as they braced themselves against unpredictable gusts of air. The afternoon sky was layered with thin dark clouds and the fading flames of a setting sun. They passed a man throwing bread to honking seagulls. A few hardy folk were strolling. When they sat down on a bench, JJ asked Nadja if she was cold.

"Not really. I like to feel this kind of air on my face, free air. I'm very glad we came, JJ. I've learned so much today about you."

"About me?"

"Yes, of course. Where all that burnt sugar comes from."

"Women."

"I like your mother, JJ. She's courageous, she's a survivor. I used to wonder, well, I still do, really, about your family and me. Where would I fit in? What would I bring? I mean, besides the looks and the phony snob appeal of modeling and all that. What would I bring that belongs to me? You know that since I was a child I've had no mother and father to love and fight against. My other relatives have been good to me because that is our tradition, not because they know me. With my country in ruins they had to send me away to school in England. And, well, you know what happened. I grew up very fast, and mostly by myself. Fashion was my finishing school. Modeling was my university. But it's a hard and lonely life I've had for six years, except for you. I feel tired at twenty-six, and that can't be right, can it?"

"You've worked hard, Nadja, you have a right to be and feel whatever you want. But one of the reasons I'm here is to take some of that weight off you. Give you a chance to feel that it's not just you alone against the world."

"But what do I give back to you?"

"Peace, baby, strength, the courage to be here and find out more about myself. You give me perspective. Purpose. Joy. Everything I always wanted."

"And I don't even know how to cook."

"Sophie would love that. To teach you would be her dream come true."

"And yours?"

"I don't know. I think that's the kind of stuff that drives men to hang out in corner bars. Mother and wife doing that joint hen-pecking patrol. Now that I think about it, don't learn. I'd rather eat out."

"Not every night."

"Then I'll do the cooking. You like my cooking."

"It's Swayze who likes it. I just eat it."

"I'm crushed."

"No, you're not, you're JJ. But I'm starving. Ready to head back?"

They walked briskly, this time helped by the wind pushing behind them.

"JJ, will you tell her you love her?"

"What if I don't?"

"Tell her or love her?" Nadja asked.

"Love her. Look how bitter she still is. She doesn't really love herself."

"But look how much you hurt her. You, not your father. You with your own rejection. Please, baby. We have no time left for anything but forgiveness."

"I'll tell her," JJ said simply.

Back at Sophie's they sat in the kitchen at the long plank table over big plates of chicken stew.

"This is so good," said Nadja.

"It's the wine that does it," said JJ. "The French are always drinking, even when they're only eating."

"It's the culture," Sophie shrugged. "They invite you out to eat, but that is just pretext. What they really want to do is talk and argue and get excited. But just to make sure they never run out of things to say, they feed you, so at least, you can argue about the food."

"Sounds very civilized." Nadja laughed. "Maybe that's why I love Paris."

"Is that right? Tell me what you like, where you like to go."

JJ left the two women to the sweet hum of their conversation and went to stretch out on the couch in front of the fire. There he rested, thankfully, in his weird mother's house for the first time in many years.

CHAPTER FIFTEEN

CLARICE knocked softly on the door to Thomas N. Thompson's bedroom. His nurse told her to come in and then left with a pile of yet unread magazines.

"I thought you might want the lovely tulips Mrs. Rowman brought here in your room where you can see them." She placed the pot of frilly peach blooms on the little tea table in front of the wide windows.

"Thank you."

"It's been so busy since you've come home. You have many kind friends."

"Too bad you die to find that out." He spoke slowly, breathing heavily after every few words.

"She's very attractive, Mrs. Rowman. And so is the lady who stopped by yesterday."

"Jealous?"

"Maybe a bit."

"Been thinking," said Thomas. "I want to give you something, something you always wanted but never had. Think big, not long. I want to know today."

"Why must you know today, Tommy?"

"Because spring is coming, life is sweet and I have a second chance to see all that. No time to waste."

Thomas closed his eyes. Talking was less strenuous now, but it still required effort. Walking was excruciatingly difficult, but his nurse and his pride made him get up every day and try. He had never been a humble man and he was paying the price. Walkers and weakness, they were for old folks, not people like him. He watched Clarice standing in front of the windows. He felt good being home, felt good having her here at home with him. She deserved whatever she wanted.

Clarice looked across Fifth Avenue into the budding greens of Central Park. Brave crocuses and daffodils poked their yellows through metallic rock and dead soil. She had not known the names of these plants whose beauty needed the cold to rebel against. Clouds scudded through the afternoon sun's tentative shine, changing the light from warm to cool in minutes and back to warm again. This island, she thought, was so different from her own, where heat and blue skies were daily constants. It was a changeable place, this city. No matter how high the stone palaces, no matter how wide the busy streets, they filled up and emptied out as quickly as the weather shifted. The city felt exciting, dangerously alive, as if it were a ship on a mission and had gathered together all these people at this one time to help it reach its goal.

She was part of the crew now. The first two days had exhausted her. It was not so much the physical care that Tommy had required in the hospital. In the beginning he had spent most of his time sedated, resting in bed. The energy drain on her came more from the continuous attention, the constant praying, willing him back to health, to strength, to life. She envied his visitors, women mostly, who were skilled at entertaining chitchat. She was not. She envied their ability to float a story in a sparkling voice and lift his spirits with it. She had done little more than hold his hand, especially on those many days when he was in severe pain or depressed. She could tell, not so much from his words, which were few, as from his eyes, downcast and teary. The heart was more than a pump, she knew. And now she could tell that he knew it, too.

Weeks of recuperation lay ahead of him. But at least he was in his own home. She had to smile at him. As flat on his back as he was, he was still the businessman, trying to negotiate, trying to repay her love as if it were part of some deal. That was his element, she had to admit. She knew a bit about that herself. And she knew that he was not cheap. He already provided a comfortable annuity for her. Her home had long been paid for, her grandchildren's education secured. She did not want a boat. She had no need of a bigger house at this age. Maybe a pool or a better building for the shop or a Range Rover. Or a cruise around the world. There were several things she could list that he would probably be delighted to supply.

And she was proud of herself for thinking like that. It had taken so long to realize that she was allowed to dream beyond subsistence, so long to give herself permission to want things beyond basic necessities. They said that living on an island shrank your mind, gave you a limited view of the world and low aspirations. Perhaps. It certainly depended on the island. For her, priorities were more important than geography, personal priorities. She found that raising two children by herself had deprived her mostly of time, not imagination. And it was the lack of time that had stolen her dreams. When she had gotten around to retrieving her self and her vision, she was a gray-haired woman, beyond all foolishness, except that she had tripped and fallen in love with an old friend.

Her face felt hot. She had to laugh at this childish folly. As she pressed her cheek to the cool windowpane, she watched Tommy napping in his huge, gilt-encrusted bed. She would never be able to tell him what she really wanted. It was not on his practical kind of list. Besides, if he didn't already want it himself, she knew better than to try to sell him on it.

"Come here. Tell me why the smile," he said softly, patting the right side of the bed, without fully opening his eyes. "Come here."

As she went to sit down, he lifted the cashmere blankets up. "Here. Shoes off. I want you here," he said. "Now tell me what you were thinking."

"And all along I thought you were asleep. What's Nurse going to say or Lucas if they find me in bed with you?"

"Nothing, if they have the good sense I pay them for. Now tell me."

Clarice removed her shoes and sat against the antique headboard. She held his hand in the lap of her pants and stroked it while she talked. "It's no mystery, Tommy. I was thinking about you."

"What about me?"

"You and me."

"What about you and me?"

"You and me together."

"Together, like this?"

"In a way, but in other ways, too."

"I see, I see, said the blind man."

"Is that right?"

"An old expression."

"Oh."

"Disappointed?"

"Oh, no. How do you feel?"

"Not too bad. Funny how things don't hurt so much when you're next to me." His hand eased into the softness between her legs.

"Take it easy. My goodness, Tommy. I thought this medication was supposed to, you know, slow you down."

"That's what you do to me, Clarice. That's your medicine."

"Well, we don't want any more heart attacks here, my goodness. Nitroglycerine and TNT, you are some combination."

"We're some combination."

"You think so?"

"I know so. Stay with me, Clarice."

"You want me to take a nap with you now?"

"I want you to stay. Period. Understand?"

"Let's talk about it when you get up."

"No, now. I never know. I might not wake up again. Clarice, I haven't had a wife in many years and I may not have been the best husband to the one I had. But I want to try again with you." The proposal had exhausted him, but he would stay alert until she gave her answer.

She slid down into the bed and looked at him closely. She would be no good at describing his face. His eyes reminded her of roasted coffee beans, but what would she call the color of his hair? Silver and smoke. What texture? Soft and springy did not say nearly enough. And how could she put into words the way she felt about his mustache filling so perfectly the space between his nose and lips? And what about those lips?

The illness had dried them out, split their softness into something she was trying to heal with more than salve. She would never be able to say what she saw in him. All she knew was that he had the dearest face in the world.

"Tommy, a minute ago you asked me to tell you what I wanted, some gift you wanted to give me. I'll tell you. I want nothing more than to share the rest of my life with you, to be a part of your life. But now's not the time to decide that. You might be asking me out of a sense of obligation or some temporary surge of affection. You have to get back on your feet before you start making decisions like that."

"That will help me get back on my feet, knowing that you are with me."

"I am with you."

"That you will stay with me."

"I will stay with you."

"Forever."

"Forever, sweetheart."

CHAPTER SIXTEEN

"CUT!" Joel Saxe's voice filled the Sackler Wing of the Metropolitan Museum of Art with steel-edged impatience. "Look, Nicky," he said, striding angrily toward her. "Nicky, *honey,* you've got to hit your mark and pivot on that mark. Otherwise we lose you, you're out of focus, and we miss the whole point of the shot. Let's rehearse it without the camera, OK?" He signaled to the camera crew to take five.

"Now, listen. You're supposed to be the queen. The queen, honey! You're *supposed* to be here, not tiptoeing around like you're afraid you're trespassing or something. You belong here. OK? OK. From the top. You've just come off the royal barge to pay a private visit to the Temple of Dendur. You've passed through the gateway. You're walking up the wharf about to enter the temple. Now you turn. We see that beautiful face between the columns, then you go. OK, now do it on your own. Ready? Stand by and action."

Nicky repeated the steps, picked up the soft ivory silk of her one-shouldered tunic before she turned on the black tape, faced the camera for a split second and then turned away.

"Your movement is better but your expression is still way off," said Joel from the video monitor. "Let's try it again. And action."

Again, Nicky walked toward the columns, pivoted, completed the turn and walked on.

"Better, you're getting there. Now shake it out, relax the face, get the feel of the movement so you don't look like you're concentrating so hard. Just go with the feel. OK, last run-through. And action."

She felt lighter, somehow warmer, more confident. What seemed like a heavy stride up the slope just a few moments ago was now an easy glide, a kind of ascension. She felt as if she could smile, and she did.

"Yes!" Joel cried. "I knew you could do it. Now give it to me just like that on camera, please."

All the camera crew and technicians moved into place, readying for a take. The assistant director yelled, "Quiet on the set!" When the clapboard sounded and Joel called "Action!" Nicky was transformed. She was a young Cleopatra, in the spring of her power and beauty, preparing to enter history. They shot several more takes. One with faster pacing, one with a mysterious smile, one with a more startled look into the camera, one with a hand up to the face. All tiny variations on the basic image.

Next they shot close-ups. Her feet in golden sandals with straps that crisscrossed high on her tan legs. Then her hands, encircled by simple gold bracelets, sweeping up the liquid fabric of her gown. After several takes Joel called for a break to set up for the next scene. Nicky retired gratefully to the dressing area, a tiny corner of the huge area partitioned off by folding rattan screens.

"You looked fabulous, darlin'," said Max, back on the scene if not quite at his best. "You are going to knock everybody out."

"Gorgeous," added Elmo. "I am truly impressed."

"You all are just giving her a complex," said Jackie, sipping coffee. "She's going to walk out of here with a swelled head and . . ."

"And she will deserve it," insisted Max. "After all she's been through?"

Nicky listened to their sympathetic murmuring without really paying attention. She was relieved to be off the set. The cross of black tape on the floor had made her panic. An X-marks-the-spot, not for focus but for death. As she was leaving Tina's house at six-thirty this morning, she found one of her composites on the floor between the two entry doors. Someone had slipped it through the mail slot. Someone had also crossed her face out with a big black X.

In the limo that the agency had sent for her she'd had to deep-breathe and calm her nerves all the way across town until they got to the museum. She would tell someone as soon as she could, but she certainly couldn't do that just yet. She had a job to do. A very big job.

She didn't know it would be like this. As much as she'd tried to prepare her role from the storyboard S & S had sent her, she had not expected to feel so tiny and insignificant, while everything else—the camera rig, the lights, the miles of thick cables—felt oversized and absolutely necessary. And to be surrounded by so many people, dozens of different faces, it seemed, people whose names she would never know while they all knew hers. They were people with specific tasks to do correctly, not even well. And they had all watched her make a fool of herself.

All these people and no one to inspire her, to talk her into the feeling. Joel Saxe was nothing like Gianni Walker. Joel could tell her where to go but not what to feel. Kyle and Smitty had assured her that Joel had worked in fashion photography for many years and knew how to deal with models. Neither one had mentioned that his way of dealing with models was to put them down.

Maybe that was his way of making himself look good, Nicky thought. He was a tall gruff man with graying blond hair and a voice with few modulations beyond barking orders. The tiny black-haired woman always at his side shared the same gruff and distant attitude, only on her it was laughable. While Sukie looked like a kitten, Joel Saxe fit the picture, exactly, of the big blond bear. And she would just have to deal with that.

And then the room itself. A sacred spot of living history that was also a part of her heritage. She had to remember to drop a coin in the moat that surrounded the temple. She had so many wishes to make. This shoot meant so much more than a perfume commercial.

"How're you doing, Nicky?" called Kyle from outside the partition. "Are you decent?"

"Absolutely not. Wait a minute," she said as she slipped into a cotton kimono. "OK, you can come in now."

"We just wanted to say that you looked great out there," Kyle raved. "How are you feeling?"

"I'm OK, I guess." She tied a belt around her robe. "It just took me a little while, you know, to get into the swing of things. But I'll be fine, really." She hoped she sounded convincing.

"Don't worry about it." Smitty patted her on the shoulder. "Stage fright is natural. It'd be natural for anybody." Quickly changing his direction, he added, "I'm telling you, this spot is going to be superb, absolutely fabulous. And to think, in the old days we would have gone all the way to Egypt to shoot on location, right, Kyle?"

"Probably. In the good old days, when everyone had money to burn."

"But this is equally authentic," said Smitty. "I think this gives us all the clues and signals, all of the ambience with none of the Third World headaches. So maybe it does pay to buy American. Jackie"—he pointed to the clothes rack as his voice rose nervously—"are *those* the silk shorts we loved?"

"These are the beige, a tad darker. I thought we loved the cream."

"That's right. Whew, boy, yes, everything creamy, ivory, pale."

"We're panic-proof, remember?" Jackie smiled and poked him jokingly on the arm. "I brought these others along just in case. You never know what happens with the light and what Joel will see in the camera. Gotta have backup."

"The best. See, Kyle? That's why she's the best. I know Sukie wanted her own girl, but this girl is the best and she's all mine."

"You flatter me, Smitty. I haven't been called a girl since my mother threw me out of the house for being a bad one."

"Her loss, my gain. And the hats? What do we like?"

"See for yourself," said Jackie, twisting one of her dreadlets.

Nicky tried on half a dozen straw hats. They all agreed on one with a small rolled brim which would not cast a shadow over her face.

Elmo moaned, "You know any hat is going to mash all her hair down."

"Well, before we write it in stone, let's show Joel and see what he thinks," said Smitty.

"He can't hate it if I love it," Kyle said. "And I love it. It's already in the storyboard. He knows what's coming. We whirl from the ancient to the modern, and back again, back and forth. The same girl, the same beauty, even some of the same clothes and accessories. That's where we get our tag line, timeless. But some things have got to read ancient and some things have got to say today. This hat says today."

"We know all that, Kyle, but it doesn't hurt to tenderize him. If Joel plays bully in the playground, that's only because all the other kids are too scared to get to know him. Inside he's really a cream puff. No, that's too gourmet. A Devil Dog. Come on, Nicky, let's go tame the beast."

"Wait," said Jackie, "you might as well give him the whole look. Why don't you guys step outside and hold your horses, OK? Keep the sandals on, Nicky. And here, just slip into these shorts, good. Drop that tank over her head, will you, Max? And here's your blazer. Clean and simple, ideal for strolling along the Nile."

As Nicky, Kyle and Smitty walked across the room, she whispered, "You didn't tell me Joel was mean."

"I couldn't," said Smitty. "So beat me."

"And he never smiles."

"They defanged him at puberty and he doesn't want anyone to know. Now stop whining. Why do you think we pay you so much money? To hang out with nice guys like us? Time to feed the lions, sweetie."

Joel liked the hat and asked Nicky onto the set for a light reading. Adjustments could be made, he said, no problem. Kyle and Smitty were relieved and sent Nicky back to the dressing area.

"OK, doll face, off with it," said Jackie. "Can't wrinkle the merch. Anybody want coffee?" Before anyone could answer she left for the buffet table where the huge coffee dispenser sat among the colorful remains of breakfast.

"You want something, Nicky?" asked Max.

"No, I'm fine."

"Are you sure, princess? I know it's not easy for you to do this." He squeezed her shoulder.

"Or easy for you. I'm glad you came back."

"I had to be here. I owe it to you . . . and to Becky." Nicky nodded silent thanks to him in the mirror. He was the one she would talk to later.

"Now then," Max said, "let's see if we can do some repairs on this pretty face. The name of this game is hurry up and wait, but we do like to be ready, don't we, Elmo?"

"Can't be in this business on CP time," Elmo stated flatly. "And no attitudes either. Like during show season? Total revenge of the divas. You need to see that, girlfriend. I've seen Kyle Whitaker and his wife at the collections. Maybe you ought to go to Paris, too, Nicky."

"What does she need the shows for?" Max asked. "Nothing but glorified mud-wrestling."

"Don't believe him, Nicky. It's fun, too. At least there you get to holler back, thank you very much. Here, well . . ." He nodded toward the director and the crew. "You're doing just fine, Nicky, don't worry about a thing."

"How're you making out with these two maniacs, Nicky?" Jackie blew across her cup of coffee.

"I'm fine. I just never understood why it took so long for a makeup artist to make it look like you didn't have any makeup on."

"Ooo, she's a smart one, Max, smart and rich," said Jackie.

"May she live long and prosper," he said, anointing Nicky with the fat powder brush.

"Man, I could spot you in a blackout," Gianni said, laughing and shaking JJ's hand. JJ stood at the bar of the China Grill in a curry-colored blazer, royal-blue shirt buttoned at the neck with no tie and maroon slacks. Gianni was in his traditional black and white.

"Corporate city, what can I say?" JJ ran his thumbs under the lapels of his jacket. "The suits get you on their turf and just 'cause you don't dress like them, they think they've won. Surprise, motherfucker."

"Rich rebels are the worst. You kill me. Here I have to come all the way midtown to see your downtown behind."

"Gianni, man, you said you were going to be in the area anyway."

"Peddling wares, boss. Word is spreading about the Cleo campaign, and some of the other agencies decided they wanted to see me again."

"That must make you feel good."

"Yeah, but it's like, 'Just who is that Colored fellow?' Like, 'Who is that masked man?' But I'm not complaining." Gianni wanted to make that fact perfectly clear.

The waitress led them to their table in the raised section near the front of the restaurant. They ordered dumplings and a calamari salad to share.

"So how's it going with Nicky?" Gianni asked. "Has she been able to, you know, deal with everything?"

"She's coming around. I wished she'd decided to live with Nadja and me but maybe staying with Tina Thompson is better for her. School and work have pretty much kept her together. She's shooting the perfume spot today, you know."

"So soon?"

"That's what *I* said. But you know how it goes, a contract is a contract. Except maybe in music where a contract is a rip-off."

"So tell me something new. I see you're still on your mission."

"Damn straight. I'm sorry, man, the shit burns me up. But I'm cool."

They laughed and in that laughter said many things. They were glad to see each other, to be with each other, to be part of the next great leap forward. Talent, ambition, hard work and good luck had gotten them this far. Now they were both getting ready to break through to another level. In music, in photography and, in the not-too-distant future, they hoped, in film and video. They were eager to collaborate, applying their skills and their friendship to what was sure to be the major business of the twenty-first century: art and entertainment.

But they both knew that the plantation system was still in effect, especially when it came to music. JJ's specialty was an eclectic blend of rap and R & B. But it wasn't the name tag that mattered to him. His heart—and his business head—followed a certain indefinable beat, a rhythm that crossed label barriers.

JJ told Gianni about being in the studio recording a couple of the older bluesmen, in their seventies now. About listening to them tell stories of the old days when they sold the rights to their music for a few dollars—they didn't know, they were hungry—and then the record companies went on to sell hundreds of thousands of copies. And the kicker?

The companies still claimed that the musicians owe them money.

"I'll tell you, man, overworked and underpaid is not just a line from a song," he said. "It's a way of life. And to see these old brothers be laughing about it? It just tore my heart out. I got to be a part of changing that. I just have to. Our music is traveling around the entire world. But you've got to search high and low to find a brother—let alone a sister—who can sign a serious check. It's got to change. You know what I'm saying?"

Gianni did indeed understand.

Their egos were healthy and they were not afraid. Black men in White America were not supposed to survive, let alone thrive. But they had come this far. And despite the statistics, they knew that they were not alone, that there was a generation who had their back and two or three trusted comrades by their side. Young men, they talked with the ease of old soldiers recounting battles won and lost, lying when it was called for and laughing out loud when they got caught in the lie.

"Oh, man, she was a total bowwow," said JJ.

"Not true," Gianni said in self-defense. "You just had to see her . . . in a certain light."

"Like pitch-dark, you mean. Let's face it, she was a slut."

"How can you say that about a *Vogue* cover girl?" Gianni asked with mock indignation. "Maybe she wasn't to everyone's taste . . ."

"Uh-huh, the fashion food chain. How does it go? The public eats the client. The client eats the ad agencies. The agencies eat the photographers. The photographers eat the models. And the models . . ."

"Eat everyone in sight," Gianni finished for JJ.

"Just don't forget who you're talking to. Future husband of a star, brother of a future star."

"And two of the few exceptions to the rule. You know it. You've run through enough yourself."

"My sordid past took place long ago." JJ made the sign of the cross and bowed his head in penance.

"Angelic JJ. And now Nadja's spoiled you, dulled your senses."

"That's not what my senses say."

"Can't get you out of the house. Never see you around anymore."

"Give me a break, man, we're just settling in. It's different when you're really living with someone. You've got to finesse the thing and it takes serious, quality time. I don't want to blow this, Gianni. She's my soulmate."

"Look, Nadja's beautiful people. I can't say anything against her. I love her. But I see what happens to men when they get all cuddled up and pacified. They don't have that bite, that anger and that drive anymore. We've got a lot to do still and you risk getting lazy. Chillin' 'cause you're getting paid and getting laid."

"Check out ol' homeboy Gianni. What is this? Some kind of street wisdom all of a sudden? Listen to you."

"Yeah, listen to me. I'm serious. Just because the price is higher today doesn't mean we still can't be bought and sold."

"Look, I hear you. But what I'm trying to tell you is that Nadja is my partner. She's not blinding me to what's happening. It's just the opposite. She's got different eyes than mine. That doubles my vision and we help each other to see even more. I don't know how to explain it, man. It's just real."

"I don't mean to put you on the defensive. I just want you to stay aware. Plus, I might be a little jealous," Gianni admitted.

"All those beautiful women you have parading through your studio? It's not like you don't have the opportunity."

"It just hasn't happened yet. Maybe I'm not ready for it to happen, I don't know."

"Poor brother." JJ offered no sympathy. "Suffering from too much of a good thing. Can we get a tear over here? Skirts blowing up in his face everywhere he looks. Pussy galore. Now I understand. Misery loves company and you want me to be miserable right along with you and all the girlies you're just not quite ready for. Better be careful out there. Especially today. Pussies scratch and bowwows bite back."

"Maybe what I need is somebody like Nicky. Keep it all in the family."

JJ leaned back from the table. "Hands off, man. That can't even be a joke."

"No joke. I like her. I think she likes me. We have worked together, you know. It would be perfectly natural for me to take her out."

"If I haven't made my point clear, Gianni, let me do it now. There is no motherfucking way in the world I'd let you take my sister out."

"Maybe it's not up to you."

"I don't believe this shit."

"And I don't believe it either. What am I all of a sudden? Some kind of killer rapist? Check yourself, man. You're not her father and she's not a little girl."

JJ did know that, although the distance between knowing and accepting was larger than he would concede. He looked at Gianni again. Could it be that Gianni really wasn't his friend? Friends didn't betray each other over cheap thrills. Friends didn't take advantage of vulnerabilities. Sure, he had seen Nicky salivating over Gianni when they'd had dinner in Mezzogiorno a couple of weeks ago celebrating her first Cleo job. But he'd racked that up to the shoot syndrome, where model and photographer fell in love with each other through the lens. It happened all the time, Nadja used to tell him. She said that it was actually part of what made a good picture. But Nicky would have gotten over all that by now. So much had happened since then.

"Just forget it," Gianni insisted. "I can see you're taking this way too far out. While you've been torturing yourself, I changed my mind."

"Really now."

"Mm-hmm. I decided I need a nice little country girl."

"Oh, yeah?"

"That's right. Healthy, uncomplicated . . ."

"Uh-huh, like that big blonde who's been staring at us for the last how long? Either she's trying to read the label in my clothes or she's getting even more personal." Gianni turned around to see the woman JJ was talking about. He turned back again quickly. "Oh shit, that is the original bitch from hell."

"Why'd you smile at her, then?"

"She pays the bills, brother."

"And just who was accusing whom of selling out?" JJ reminded him.

"That's Vanessa Seymour. As in Smith & Seymour?"

"Tell her I'm already taken."

"And be glad. I had a little roll in the hay with her last year and she was lucky to get out alive."

"So that's how you got the Cleo campaign."

"You must be crazy." Gianni was insulted. "I never wanted to see her again, period, for anything, regardless. If it wasn't for Renée taking my book and making her pitch again and again, I'd still be doing editorial. It had nothing to do with the casting couch. I'm telling you, her sushi's not wrapped too tight."

"Well, chill, G, she's on her way over."

Vanessa Seymour detoured away from her luncheon companions and stopped at Gianni and JJ's table. Gianni's greeting was only professionally lukewarm, but Vanessa's was positively sizzling.

"How wonderful to meet you, JJ. And what a marvelous coincidence. I'm on my way right now to the Met to catch the last of the Cleo shoot. You know Joel Saxe, don't you, Gianni? Joel's doing the perfume spot over at the Temple of Dendur. Isn't that fabulous? Why don't you all come along with me? Your sister is just divine. We all love her at S & S. All the Cleo people adore her. Come and see your sister in action."

"Sorry, I can't," said JJ, nodding to the waiter, who had returned with his credit card. "I have an appointment upstairs at Columbia."

"Then you come with me, Gianni. You've been so scarce recently. Everywhere I go people are talking about your work. How does it feel to be the hot new kid on the block? Pretty soon your old friends will be left in the dust, saying 'I remember when.' Right, JJ?"

"I doubt it, I seriously doubt that. But look, man, I do have to go," JJ said, getting up from the table. He shook Vanessa's hand. "A pleasure to meet you." He and Gianni shook hands.

"You're a rat, man," Gianni whispered to him.

"Sinking ship," countered JJ. "Check you later, peace."

"Yeah, thanks," said Gianni glumly. *"Ciao."*

Except for the Haitian cabdriver who proudly informed them that the Metropolitan was closed on Mondays, and except for the frosty moment when Gianni had to remove Vanessa's hand from his knee, the short ride to the museum was uneventful. The walk through the quiet, people-free halls made Gianni feel eerily vulnerable, especially in the close Egyptian rooms with their massive stone sarcophagi, open, empty, waiting.

Just as Gianni and Vanessa entered the Sackler Wing they heard the snap of the clapboard and Joel Saxe's voice call, "Action!"

In a short, white, one-shouldered party dress and strappy high heels, Nicky strode between the two parts of the stone monument, turned, smiled and waved, and walked on. Joel Saxe ordered, "Cut," and went to confer with his cameraman. Smitty motioned Vanessa and Gianni over to the video monitor where he and Kyle were seated. They shook hands quietly with proud smiles and thumbs-up of accomplishment.

It was going very well. And Smitty was glad to have Vanessa here to see for herself. She was such a strange creature, he thought. All height and angles and polish. Like a giraffe but with the mind-set of an eagle. No mild-mannered leaf-chewing for this one. He sensed something in her that liked to wrangle with fresh meat. He liked that quality when it came to business. When it came to life he had reservations. But the television shoot today was strictly business. And sooner or later, she would have to admit that he was right.

Vanessa had disagreed totally with Cleo's plan to go ethnic, to break with its fifty-year tradition of the Cleo girl and high gloss for a White elite. S & S had only had the account for a couple of years before and she was satisfied with their customary campaigns. But then came the summer of 1990 and the plane crash that took the lives of most of Madam Klionsky's descendants. The youngest daughter, Esmé, and her husband, Kyle Whitaker, assumed control of the company. When they did, Smitty recognized that other changes would be coming. Vanessa did not.

Esmé Klionsky and Kyle Whitaker brought a new attitude to Cleo. And they wanted new faces. Every few years a new modern goddess, White, but also Black, Yellow, Red and all the indefinable mixtures that constitute the human race. Beauty was global, and so was their business. And they were prepared to bank their money on that concept.

Smitty was not prepared for Vanessa's reaction: the adamant protests, the endlessly gloomy financial projections, the hard-boiled tensions between them. The Cleo account was a coup for a small shop like Smith & Seymour. They could not afford to lose it.

If it was true that seeing was believing, then Vanessa would have to believe now. She could see how beautiful Nicky Knight looked in person and through the camera. The main reason the shoot was going so well was Nicky. But Smitty would let Vanessa judge for herself.

The intensity on the set was palpable. Joel Saxe called for another take. Everyone moved cautiously, careful not to disturb the director or distract the talent. The day was winding down. There remained only this last dolly shot and the final close-ups. Then the "Timeless" spot would be in the can.

Joel kept the energy high and concentrated, calling for hair and makeup retouches on the set, not letting the momentum wane. This last push inspired Nicky to go beyond modeling, beyond acting and pretending. She seemed to become the breeze, the river, the queen, the goddess. There was no distance in time, no separation of culture, no audience for a performance. She could smell the jasmine wafting through the evening air. She was making it happen, live and for real.

Max stood at his post near the edge of the set. He was so proud of Nicky. She was performing like a champ. If he'd had any doubts at the beginning of the day, he didn't have any now. Her ability to rebound from tragedy had inspired even him. He who'd never needed anyone's help, and, worse, tended to pride himself on that.

Nicky was a quick study, subtle in her gestures on the set and reserved in her dealings with Joel Saxe. For that alone she deserved a halo. His manner could be so harsh. Experienced actors respected him because he always came through with a quality product, but there was none of the affection that some directors encouraged. How Nicky had figured out the best MO for dealing with him was a mystery. However she did what she did, Max saw that it was working very well.

He would talk about it with her later that evening. Nicky had suggested that they go out and celebrate, as they'd done after the photo shoot with Gianni Walker. Max had the distinct feeling it would not be about McDonald's tonight. He felt confident that Kyle Whitaker could get them into Le Cirque even at this late date.

"Makeup!" the assistant director called to Max. "Powder, please," he specified as Max hastened in his stocking feet to the focus position where Nicky stood.

"Not much longer now, princess," Max told her. He took a tiny triangular sponge and swabbed under her eyes and around her nose. "These lights are enough to make the Sphinx sweat. Try saying that fast twenty times." She tried it and giggled. "And no laughing either," he said, wielding his big powder brush, "or this powder will fall into all those wrinkles on your face and presto! Darlin' Dorian Gray." With the last swipe he declared, "Perfect. Now knock that camera out."

And she did. They covered each scene simply at first. Then Joel would suggest a tiny variation—in a facial expression or a hand movement—and they would reshoot. Nicky gave him what he wanted, sometimes slightly less, sometimes slightly more. And as she did, she discovered a creative freedom within the narrow margins he'd set up, a space where unpredictable but beautiful things could happen. She could tell that he was surprised and also very pleased. The takes went quickly and well. Then Joel asked for his signature shot, a kiss directly to the camera, and he finally cried, "Cut! It's a wrap." Everyone—director, camera crew, agency people, fashion staff and talent—applauded. The long day was over.

Nicky stepped down from the stone platform and sat on the edge, where she took off her high heels. Her throbbing feet recoiled from the cold stone floor but they brought her back instantly to the here and now. Soon she could begin to relax.

Joel lumbered over to her, shook her hand and said curtly, "Congratulations. Great job." Turning to Kyle and Smitty, he nodded his head and added, "Anytime."

"That's a smile," Smitty bubbled to Kyle.

"But his lips were turned down."

"They moved, didn't they? From him it's a smile."

A chorus of "Fabulous" and "Wonderful" followed Nicky to the dressing area where Gianni Walker stood outside the screens. Suddenly exhilarated, she ran up to him and threw her arms around his neck. The sight of him could make her forget about everything and everyone else.

"I'm so glad to see you!" She kissed him on the cheek and leaned back in his arms, laughing. "What are you doing here? How long have you been here?"

"Long enough. Long enough to see you do some great stuff. *Che bella.*"

"Thank you." She leaned in closer, "No offense, but Joel Saxe wasn't you."

"I don't know how to take that, Nicky."

She could see that he was smiling, though. He was taking it the right way. "We can talk about it later," she said. "Let me change, then we can go celebrate."

"Your wish is my command."

"I'm going to take you up on that." She laughed and disappeared behind the screens.

"So am I," said Vanessa, coming up quietly behind him, sliding an arm around his waist. "What about *my* wish being your command?"

"I don't think so," answered Gianni, moving her arm aside as politely as he could.

"We'll just see about that." She turned with a smile and walked away. Joel Saxe deserved her personal congratulations. His lighting was the work of genius. It had done such wonders for Nicky Knight.

Inside the dressing area everyone was packing up. Jackie waited for Nicky to take off her last dress before zipping up the final garment bag on the wardrobe rack. Elmo was wiping down his curling irons, checking that they were cool enough to store with his other tools in the tan leather duffle he carried. Max stacked pots of paint and powder in his kit and neatened up the trays enough to close. He'd give it a thorough cleaning tomorrow.

"Where're we going to celebrate, princess?" he asked. "The coach is at your disposal and I am at your service."

"Oh, Max, I'm sorry." She wriggled into her brand new raspberry wool jumpsuit by Ralph Lauren. "Can we do it some other time? Gianni's here."

"And I'm not?" His bitterness stopped her cold.

"Please, please don't be angry with me. I had no idea he was coming." She finished with the buttons and buckled a crocodile belt around her waist.

"Nicky, I've talked to you before about this guy. He may be the Avedon of our era, but I don't like him and I don't trust him."

"Max, you're just jealous," she said, laughing and stepping into her Gucci loafers.

"As long as I've been around, I'm not just anything, little darlin'. But if I were you, I'd try to remember who my real friends are. This guy spells trouble, you hear me? Trouble with a capital *T*."

Nicky decided that she would deal with Max's attitude tomorrow. Right now she wanted to reap the rewards of this long and grueling day. What fun that it came wrapped up in the delightful package called Gianni Walker. "I gotta go," she told Max without looking at him. "So long, guys." She blew kisses to Jackie and Elmo. "Thanks for your help."

Outside the dressing area, as Gianni helped her into her mink coat, Kyle and Smitty repeated how wonderful she'd looked on-screen. "Well, then, let's get together and do this again sometime," she said with a straight face. "And next time, tell Joel to put some film in the camera."

They all shared a good laugh. Nicky hoped that Vanessa was somewhere joining in the joke. She thought she'd spotted her long blond mane earlier. After hearing all the praise, what would Vanessa have to say about a nose job now?

Nicky sipped red wine while she watched Gianni toss the pesto into a bowl of steaming-hot angel hair. The basil and garlic sauce smelled delicious. She was starved and for the first time in weeks she would eat as much as she liked. The Cleo girl would just have to be fat for a day.

She was glad they'd decided to come to his loft to relax after shooting the commercial in the museum. In the limo he had suggested a number of smart restaurants around town, even some that were not far from Tina's house in case she got tired earlier than she wanted to. But she had explained all the stipulations about public appearances that Vanessa Seymour had spelled out to her two weeks ago. No social occasions without the permission of S & S. No private relationships in public without the permission of S & S. Basically, no life at all without the permission of S & S. Gianni had laughed at the fact that the sole alternative was one that S & S would hardly permit, if they could even conceive of it. And so they told the driver to take them to Franklin Street. It's not that he had anything fancy to offer her but he always kept pasta on hand.

Gianni's living space upstairs had the same clean, white spaciousness as the photography studio downstairs. The living room and kitchen were defined by chairs and tables, not walls. From Nicky's seat at the round white marble table she could look in one direction and see gleaming stainless-steel pans hanging on the wall in the kitchen. If she looked in the opposite direction she could see photographs lining the wall of the living room. Soft solo guitar music was playing in the background. The whole place was comfortable. It certainly didn't feel like Bluebeard's castle.

And Gianni didn't act like a monster either. What was Max's problem? And why did Tina sound so unenthusiastic when Nicky called her to say that she was having dinner with Gianni? Her "Have a good time" had all the charm of a lock closing on a chastity belt.

"For you, *signorina*." Gianni placed a bowl of pasta in front of her with a flourish that made her giggle and the candle flames waver.

"Thank you. But don't laugh at me, Gianni, if I end up with pasta all over my face. I'm not too good with this fork and spoon business."

"Use your fingers, I don't care." He smiled as he sat down to his own dish.

The phone interrupted their peace. After four rings it stopped. "Excuse me." He stood up from the table. "I'm going to make sure the answering machine is on. We don't want any more intrusions."

Intrusions on what? Nicky wondered with mounting excitement as she listened to him walking down the stairs and through the studio to Renee's desk. She would love for him to sweep her off her feet into a passionate embrace. She could feel his lips pressing hers, feel his hands caressing her body, transforming her into the woman she wanted to be with him.

If he was headed in that direction, he certainly was taking his time. She liked that, the slow drawn-out tease. He wasn't some wolfish gigolo. He was torturously considerate.

Much to Nicky's dismay, she watched the evening slowly pass in that same considerate mood. After they finished eating, they took their wineglasses into the living room, where they continued to talk. Where Gianni continued to talk. About the business. His early start in Milan, then the move to Paris and finally the ultimate success in New York. He impressed her with an endless stream of anecdotes about famous people and interesting places. But most of all he impressed her with his drive, his ambition and his desire to be at the right place at the right time.

She had so much to learn. She would never know all that he knew. And she felt that somehow he was trying to show her this. She was disappointed that he might consider her just a young and inexperienced kid. Somebody not worthy of his love. The wine also helped to sadden her, lowering her defenses against the intrusion of her own painful memories. She missed her mother, wished she could talk with her.

Nicky felt melancholy and lonely and hoped that soon Gianni would put his arms around her to comfort her. Would she have to come right out and say it? When she had unbuttoned the top of her jumpsuit and asked him why it was so hot in here, he had jumped up to open a window. Hardly the response she expected. What had happened to the man who'd directed her in the photo shoot with such sensitivity that he seemed to read her innermost feelings? Why were they sitting so far away from each other on the same sofa and why were they still just talking? She felt foolish.

The phone rang several more annoying times so that she felt as if she was just borrowing him and his time. His real life probably lay with all the people calling him. People who wanted to hang out in noisy, glamorous places and be seen by others like themselves. That could not be her, the must-be-perfect Cleo girl.

It was almost midnight, time to leave. Her driver would still be on duty downstairs. She knew that the agency had instructed him to pick her up at home in the morning and return her to her door at night. Just how romantic could you be with someone waiting, keeping an invisible watch over your shoulder like that?

"You look tired, *cara*."

"I am, Gianni, I'd better go."

"Look, Nicky." He hesitated, clearly uneasy with what he was thinking. "I want you to understand something about me and this evening. You're the sister of a friend of mine. You're an important public figure in your own right. There are certain things I might have wanted to do, certain ways I might have wanted to express myself, that I had to refrain from. And I did that just to prove to you that I'm not the terrible person some people think I am. The downside is that I haven't really been myself. I haven't shown you that I care about you. And I do."

She could not look at him. So that was it, she thought. All this nice friendly distance was really a performance, to protect her? But how could she be sure that this confession wasn't just another act, another way to let her down easy? She was tired and confused. And hurt. He had read her desire all along but chose to ignore it. All in the name of chivalry. What a joke. No private life in public and no private life in private either.

"I'm glad you explained, Gianni," she finally said. She stood up unsteadily.

"Are you OK?" He stood up and straightened her shoulders.

"Who, me? Sure, I'm just fine." She twisted away from him and headed down the stairs to get her coat.

"I'm sorry, Nicky." He followed her, tried to help her with her coat, and when she refused, he put on his own jacket.

She stopped him at the door. "I can make it by myself. You don't have to come with me."

"I want to. You're upset. You're leaving with some kind of misunderstanding and that's the last thing I wanted to happen."

"Don't worry. I . . ." The ringing phone cut her short. "Forget it. I'll see you around." And she left, alone. When she got downstairs to the limousine, she knocked on the driver's window to wake him up. That's what this evening had been for her. A wake-up knock. What fun.

The smooth ride uptown lulled her to the edge of sleep. After a full day's excitement that's exactly what she needed, she thought, the deep forgetfulness of a good night's sleep. Maybe she'd have another glass of wine once she got back to Tina's. It would help her to relax. She was beginning to like wine, the way it rounded off the sharp edges of things. No wonder wine was a sign of sophistication. No wonder it was as old as water.

When the driver opened the car door Nicky was grateful that the show was over at last. She was home. The brass lanterns cast a soft golden glow on the impressive stone stairway that rose to meet the front door, stalwart in its solid, wooden simplicity. Two flights above it was her own room with her own sweet little balcony. A prop for Romeo and Juliet, she thought when she first saw it. A faint light escaped the drapes. Tina had left a lamp on for her. A cold wind off Riverside Drive swept up the block. She clutched her fur coat at the collar, thanked the driver and climbed the steps. Once inside the front door, but before she stepped through the glass door to the foyer, she noticed a flyer on the floor. She picked it up. Oh, God, not again. It was another one of her composites. This time her face was X'ed out in red. And a sickly scrawl had written: "Quit, Black bitch, or you're next."

A monstrous fear gripped her. "Tina!" she cried from the foot of the stairwell. The house was quiet and dark. Instantly she forgot the code for the alarm between floors. She could not climb another step. "Tina! Help me!"

By the time Kayo returned Tina's frantic call, Nicky was deep into a Valium sleep. Tina explained what had happened, how Nicky had found the two disfigured composites slipped through the front door's mail slot, one when she left to shoot the commercial early in the morning and one at midnight when she came home. Tina spoke with him from the phone in Nicky's room as if keeping her in sight would somehow reassure them both that she was safe. It was not a long conversation. Kayo would start making phone calls tonight and leave Los Angeles for New York the next day to make arrangements for their security. The police would have to do something and so would Cleo. But since these outside forces did not seem to be enough, he would take matters into his own hands. They had to be able to protect themselves from the inside.

CHAPTER SEVENTEEN

"MY SKIN is tingling," said Vanessa Seymour.

"That's the aloe tightening up those pores," said Max. "But your face needs your mouth to be quiet so the masque can work. Close your eyes and use this time to relax and rejuvenate. Think peaceful, happy thoughts and you'll wake up to a brand-new you."

Max put on the CD of "Spring" from Vivaldi's *Four Seasons*. He needed some sunshine. All this February rain was depressing. Another month and spring would be here, hallelujah. Things were finally looking up after the darkest days of a deadly winter. He was surprised, most pleasantly surprised, that Vanessa Seymour had called him a couple of days after the Cleo commercial to reschedule a private appointment for Friday. A new face was a good way to start the weekend, he thought. Of course, his regular salon customers had rallied around him after the Knight affair, but special people, or those he would like to be special, had become exceedingly creative in canceling their at-home appointments with him. He couldn't blame them. A facial was one thing. A bloodbath, something else entirely.

There was no doubt about it: Miss V was a catch. And she certainly had enough clout within the shiny set to restore him to favor. Of course, his constant magazine work earned him fabulous credentials. But real people had a lot of problems with models, with photography, with the whole notion of beauty fabricated in a germ-free environment. Real women had to walk down real streets. No one taught them how to use cosmetics, just how to buy them. They couldn't help it if they looked as if their skin were encased in biscuit dough and their eyes colored in with Crayola. And, of course, real women were not beautiful and they knew it. Despite the feminists and the ego-boosters and the self-esteem raisers, women had as many subtle evaluations of looks as Black people had skin shades. More, probably.

To rate Vanessa Seymour, you could say that she was your basic so-called good-looking blonde. But Max was skilled at noticing details and flaws. After all, much of his business was about correcting them. In Vanessa's case he thought her blue eyes were a little too close together, which made her intense instead of alluring. Her nose was a little too long and fleshy on the end, even for her stature. And her chin slid a little too quickly into her neck for true grace. But beyond the physical features, some opaque unhappiness blocked her real beauty from shining through.

She made the most of what she did have, however, and that's where the benefits could be seen. Her money paid for the professional consultations which kept her looking contemporary and chicly dressed. She was a working woman, though. Not to put her down for that. *Au contraire,* that was part of being modern. Too bad that power played such a nasty trick on women. If power was an aphrodisiac for men, turning even the most physically repulsive into irresistible sex objects, it had quite the opposite effect for women. He had seen it too often to deny. Power seemed to harden or at least diminish a woman's beauty. It seemed to undermine and call into question both the nature of beauty and the substance of power. As if a woman couldn't have them both.

The fair sex had it rough, Max had to admit. But he had seen enough to know that some things were changing, and for the better. Look how long he'd been in the business. He could remember when a Black makeup artist would have been quarantined to Black women only. When someone like a Vanessa Seymour would never have allowed someone like him to touch her, let alone make suggestions to improve her look. Thank goodness for the crazy models of yesteryear with their secret Black boyfriends and their not-so-secret desire to swing out of that stultifying

White Only thing. Not that they were going to stop being White. Give up that privilege? Never. They'd give up some of the visible power, since it didn't appear to work for them anyway, and make sure to retain the privilege. The entitlement. The automatic me-firstness. It was a pretty good deal. Let the men worry about the money and let the women wear it.

Of course, Black women didn't have much choice. They had to work and do it all, poor things. Show me a Black woman who didn't *have* to work and I'll show you a sister passing for White, he thought. Worked so hard for so long, wouldn't even know what to do without it. Fall apart without working. And working most often just to maintain. Can't see far enough ahead to stretch, create and truly excel. Well, maybe this new breed. Camille, Oprah, Tina Thompson. Maybe if they hitched some vision to their dollars, they could change things for us. How many times had he heard that Black women's burden was to bear the conscience of the entire planet. And their reward? Fewer wrinkles and a slower aging process. Mercy. Well, at least it was something.

"How do you feel, Vanessa?" Max asked, fingering the edges of the masque to see if it was properly dry.

"I'm fine, but my face feels like it's wearing a girdle."

"Well, we're going to peel it off right now. Just lean back and I'll roll it up from the chin. See? Now, isn't that nice and smooth? Smooth as a baby's bottom, they say, but I wouldn't know about that."

"About babies or about bottoms?"

"My, aren't we getting personal?"

"Max, you're the one peering into my pores."

"But not your private life, darlin'."

"I'm sorry. I didn't realize you were so sensitive."

"Just don't call me uppity."

"You are funny."

"Born *that* way, too." Carefully, he peeled the rubbery masque off her face.

"Seriously now," Vanessa said, "don't you just hate it?"

"Hate what?"

"Don't you hate being Black?" Her blue eyes caught his surprised brown ones. "Don't you really wish you weren't?"

Some divas never quit, he thought. The nerve. "Miss V, I hate to disappoint you but I love being all of who I am. Now, let's do something with this face right here so you can say the same thing about yourself."

The patient layering required for a flawless finish took about three-quarters of an hour. Max worked with small sponges for under-eye concealer and foundation, with tiny brushes for brow enhancer and eye shadow, with a thin curved brush for mascara, with large round brushes for contour and blush and with a big brush the size of an orange for the final all-over dusting of translucent powder. Instead of using lipstick from one of the dozens of tubes in his kit, he pulled out a miniature paint box which held rows of stamp-sized samples of color. After outlining her mouth with a colored pencil, he used yet another fine brush to fill in her lips with a mix of three shades, blotting and reapplying to make the blend last longer.

"Now, that is a fresh spring face," he announced triumphantly. "Come over here and look in the mirror and tell me what you think."

"I've been sitting for so long, my circulation's stalled," she said, easing out of the chair. "And how can you stand having an entire mirrored wall? I'd hate to be so aware of myself all the time."

"Too bad. I like to look at myself, darlin', and you would, too, if you looked like this every day. Try to get used to the shock and if there's something about what I did that you don't like, let me know. Not that I'll change it, but maybe I'll explain it. Now, how about a little more cranberry juice?"

"Yes, thanks."

"You'll see that I've given you more stain on your lips than wax, so there will still be color left after your important luncheons. Don't you just hate it when you find you've eaten all your gorgeous lipstick off and the men are sitting there, incredibly handsome and apparently au naturel, wondering just what it is about you that's faded away? Be right back."

When Max left for the kitchen, Vanessa approached the mirror, stepped back and then stepped closer. She wasn't used to this face. The eyes were darker, the lips were warmer, the skin more polished. She liked it, of course. Still, it was hard to accept that Max could read her face better than she could. She'd had doubts but the proof was staring her right back in the subtly smoke-smudged eyes. It was all in the details. She knew what she had to do. She just didn't see how she could ever do such a perfect makeup job herself. The time alone was an inconceivable luxury.

"Your juice, *madame,*" Max said on his return. "Well?"

"Well, it is different, but I need to get dressed to see the total picture." From his dressing room, she asked, "How can I do this myself?"

"If I told you, then I'd be out of business, now wouldn't I? But generosity compels me to make a list of all the products I used on you so you'll have some starting point. I'm sure you're smart enough to figure it out. But I do want to see you three months from now so we can give you a nice new summer face. You are careful of the sun, aren't you?"

"God, yes. Maximum sunblock, minimum exposure. Unfortunately. I used to love to tan. I could get almost as dark as you. I mean, really, really black."

Max froze. What had taken him so long? Why hadn't he seen it before? He was hopeless with names but he never forgot a face. This face. With a Honey Glow foundation . . .

"What's the matter, Max?" Vanessa asked as she came back into the living room. "Oh, God, did I say something offensive again?"

"Don't worry, I'll survive." This face and a mustache you could just glue on.

"Max, don't look at me like that. I didn't mean it. Really, it just slipped out."

"No problem." He was staring at a nightmare. "Excuse me, Vanessa, but I've got to clean up before my next session. I'll send the bill to your office. Fair enough?"

"That's fine. Thanks so much. I hope to see you soon."

"Oh, yes, very soon." He closed the door and bolted it, leaning against it in relief.

The knock panicked him. "Max, it's me." Vanessa spoke through the door. "I forgot something."

"I'm sorry, Vanessa. Can't it wait?"

"It's my umbrella, right by the door."

He saw a large Burberry umbrella drying in the stand nearby. It was raining. He opened the door to give it to her. She thanked him again and then she pulled the door closed.

As Madison Avenue was emptying out and dimming its shop lights at the end of the day, the Polo Lounge at the Westbury Hotel was beginning to fill up. As it did, it changed mood from a private English club with hushed tones, dark velours and even darker paneling to that of a commuter car clacking its way home to modern neighborhoods where families still had children, noise and color. Rich leather briefcases, sturdy with work that would never get done at home, stood obediently near the candlelit cocktail tables. Men and women crossed their legs in flirtatiously sophisticated poses, silently admiring their good taste in hosiery, fine footwear and thick carpeting. New York was mean on the feet. Oases like these were mandatory in some neighborhoods. Madison and 69th was one of them.

While waiting for Kyle Whitaker, Smitty sipped his second Dewar's, and Vanessa, second martini already in hand, stubbed out her cigarette, shaking her head at the retreating back of a wraith of woman in an extravagantly ragged-edged fur coat. Everything about her was so overdone: the clothes, the jewelry, the makeup. Especially that phosphorescent eye shadow. Exactly the opposite of the muted tones Max had used on her own face earlier.

"Lina was always such a rebel," she clucked. "Even at school where it was almost part of the program. Lina Cranshaw. . . Forrest Astor Baylor." She counted three husbands' names on her fingers. "No, I think I'm missing one or two. She likes to get married."

"And you? You could have any man you want."

She was flattered. "Except you."

"Except me. Nothing personal, just a twist of nature."

"Still, there are marriages like that."

"Plenty."

"They even have children."

"Often. Perpetuating the name or the bloodline or some such. Look at Esmé Klionsky and Kyle."

"You mean Kyle Whitaker?" Her astonishment told Smitty something did not compute.

"No, Kyle's straight as a Princeton part. But he's such a mogul wannabe, he has Jewish envy."

"And with real WASPs dying out . . . Maybe we should try it, Smitty. Two fine old families . . ."

"Two tired old lines. I'd say it was time to reinvigorate what's left of this gene pool. In the old days it was different. A little racial mixing was good for the family stock."

"How can you say that?" she objected. Vanessa found Smitty's gleeful nonchalance about race upsetting. He was so demanding in the office, but outside he changed completely.

"I'm from Virginia, remember? When we say our servants are like family, it's because we don't want to admit that they *are* family."

"Smitty, that's terrible, that's a shameful thing to say."

"That's just what my parents said when I came out." He crunched an ice cube with his teeth, a sound that made Vanessa's skin crawl.

"But you can't help being gay, now, can you?"

"Not any more than I can help being what color I am."

"That's ridiculous. You're a White man."

"All in the eyes of the beholder," he said. He liked to provoke her, tease her out of that starched character she wore like a uniform. "Modern America is a mixed country. The secret is out. We even have clients—like Cleo—who understand that. Get a grip, Vanessa."

But she could not and she would not. Something down-shifted in her liking for Smitty. She lit another cigarette and exhaled carefully away from him. Smitty hated smoking, even more so since quitting a year ago and converting to self-righteousness. He was becoming obnoxiously liberal and correct. And she was becoming seriously annoyed.

"I wish Kyle would hurry up and get here," he said, checking his Piaget. It was a few minutes past seven. "I'm meeting someone at eight. Philadelphia's playing at Carnegie Hall. I have the tickets and he hates to be late."

Smitty rambled on about the concert. Vanessa finished her martini in larger swallows than usual and ordered a third. The room was getting warm and crowded. A trio of Japanese men in charcoal suits and wire-rimmed glasses sat in a squad of armchairs under a corona of cigarette smoke. A Japanese woman in a white round-collared blouse and flat shoes sat next to them but apart, smiling and nodding, although no one addressed her.

A couple of real estate lawyers that Vanessa knew had signaled briskly to her when they first came in. She had twiddled her fingers hello. Looking at them now, she figured them to be younger than she was, although their hair was thinning and lifeless, which made them seem older. Some men, no matter how much money they had, would not age well.

A Black couple entered and sat on the banquette next to Vanessa and Smitty. Vanessa handed her umbrella and its matching Burberry bag to Smitty to make more room.

He groaned as he hefted the plaid pouch. "You could kill somebody with this thing."

The woman apologized as she shrugged out of a huge silver-fox coat, gathering it and her quilted Chanel satchel close to her. Vanessa watched as they ordered cognac.

"Rémy Martin," the man said, in a jauntily exaggerated French accent. His silver hair was receding but he cut a dashing figure in a navy double-breasted suit. The woman was obviously not his wife. She wore a gold signet ring on one pinkie and Cartier rolling rings studded with diamonds on the other. As they talked with their heads close together, they seemed to share a joyous secret. After a few minutes the woman excused herself to go to the ladies' room. When she returned, stepping carefully around the tables and settling comfortably onto her coat, she smelled of a fresh dab of Boucheron perfume.

Vanessa recognized the sienna silk gabardine coatdress and spoke before she realized what she was saying. The third martini was kicking in. "A lovely dress," she slurred. "Armani, isn't it? Where'd you get it?"

The woman turned cool espresso eyes to her and lifted the corners of closed bronze lips.

Vanessa kept on insistently. "I know it wasn't on sale at Bergdorf's. When I got mine they said this style never goes on sale."

The woman turned away and moved closer to her companion. As Smitty pulled Vanessa toward him, she caught fragments of the woman's serene voice of dismissal: "Some people" and "no class" and throaty, confident chuckles.

"And Chanel bags never go on sale, never," Vanessa continued, but now to Smitty. "The suits and the shirts and the shoes, maybe. But the bags, the good bags, never."

"It's OK," Smitty said. "That's enough."

"I want another drink."

"I don't think so. You've had enough."

"Who are you to tell me what's enough?" she whispered angrily. "I am sitting in the Polo Lounge with a bunch of niggers and Japs and Jews, for Chrissakes! Do you believe it? I mean, just who do they think they are?"

"Have you gone crazy?" Smitty was quietly fuming at her sudden loss of control. "We're getting out of here right now." He signaled the waiter for their check.

"You're goddamn right. Not a White person in the fucking place. Nobody but me. Not even you, Smitty." She poked him in the chest.

"Shut up, Vanessa," he hissed. "You're making a fool of yourself. I'm very sorry," Smitty apologized to the Black couple, as he struggled to get Vanessa out of her seat and into her shearling coat. She was heavy and leaned unsteadily at awkward angles. One glass fell to the carpet, then another. "I'm so sorry. Please, have another drink on me," he continued to apologize.

The Black man waved his hand disdainfully at Smitty's offer and acted as if they were both beneath contempt. The four Japanese sat silently, not daring to look at each other's flushed faces. The room settled into an embarrassed hush as two waiters escorted Vanessa and Smitty to the exit.

Kyle Whitaker opened the heavy glass door to the Lounge just as Smitty and Vanessa were heading out. "Sorry to be so late," he said with a contrite smile. "You're not leaving, are you?"

"We've got to," Smitty said as he rushed her to a cab at the curb. "Vanessa's sick. I'll call you first thing tomorrow, OK?"

Kyle stood perplexed for a moment. He had never seen Vanessa Seymour so . . . untogether. And he could swear she was babbling something about Chanel never going on sale.

"Mr. Maxwell, please, 15F." JJ would have forgotten again if Nicky hadn't reminded him to drop this packet off to Max before heading farther uptown to Tina's for Sunday dinner. An old *Harper's Bazaar* from 1972. One of Becky Knight's last big shoots. Photography by Vassallo. Makeup by Max. Nicky had found it in her mother's valise on her last trip to New York.

When the concierge indicated no answer, JJ felt relieved. He wasn't up to dealing with Max and his mannerisms right now. He sealed the manila envelope and wrote Max's name and apartment number on the outside. Nicky had already jotted a note for him inside. She was a sweet kid, remembering stuff like that in circumstances like these.

Back in the car he drove west on 72nd Street toward Riverside Drive, then north to 76th. Everyone had thought she'd be safer uptown. But with this latest incident of the defaced cards, the threat on her life was still very real. Kayo had called for a family meeting to explain the changes he was making. Private twenty-four-hour surveillance, in-house security. Of course, Tina already had someone on the lookout even more ferocious than Swayze. Mrs. English must have trained at Sing Sing and then learned to cook on the side. Heavy-duty. Well, that's what the situation called for now. Red-alert, heavy-duty protection.

When he arrived at the house, Mrs. English buzzed him through the first door. He knew she had identified him from the outdoor camera. With a cautious look that eased into something like a smile, she opened the inner glass door and let him into the foyer. Then she slid open the tall doors to the parlor where Tina and Nicky were stretching out on parallel sofas in front of the fire. A fireplace in Manhattan, that always knocked him out. And all the doors. He had forgotten about them after living in what was basically one huge room.

"JJ." Tina hugged him. "It's good to see you."

"Hi, JJ, how're you doing?" Nicky asked.

"I'm fine, but how are you?" He went over and kissed her on the cheek.

"Slowly freaking out." Nicky sounded exhausted. "Did you see Max?"

"No, he wasn't in, so I just left the package with the doorman."

"Well, thanks for trying anyway," she said glumly.

"Come on, kid, snap out of it. What's the big deal?"

"Nothing really. I just didn't want Max to be mad at me. And I've been trying to reach him all weekend."

"He's probably just out of town. By the way, Nadja sends you both her best."

"From sunny . . . ?" Tina asked.

"Cancún," JJ answered.

"How wonderful. That gives me an idea. We need to get away, too. Nicky, what do you say to next weekend in St. Martin?"

"Sure, it's fine with me." But everyone could hear the lack of enthusiasm in her voice.

"I'm sure this cloud will lift as soon as your father gets here, Nicky. Shouldn't be long now. JJ, what can I get you?" Tina pointed to the beverage trolley.

"Don't bother, I can fix it myself." He poured a bottle of Rolling Rock beer into a glass mug. "The place looks so nice, Tina. Before Nicky moved in I couldn't remember the last time I was here. You've changed it around a lot."

"I had to, had to modernize. And I wanted to make it more my own, you know?"

Pillows of batik, mud cloth and Senoufo designs were plumped against the back of the white leather sofas. Clean lines characterized all the furnishings from the chairs and luggage-tan chaise to the huge Deco mirror over the fireplace.

"It's beautiful, really, I like it. It feels comfortable," he said, sinking into a chair.

"I keep telling Nicky that I want her to feel at home here. To feel that she can bring her friends over and have her privacy. I mean, I'm not a parent yet but I remember what it was like. Even in the best of circumstances it can be stifling when you want to be more on your own."

"Little Mother Tina," said Nicky.

"I don't think so. At least not yet. Mrs. English thinks she still runs my life the way she did when I was in school. And she's not even my parent."

"Don't parents *ever* let you grow up?" asked Nicky.

"Not till they're forced to, believe me." Tina smiled.

"You can say that again. It's going to be deep on Tuesday, being with Dad at the Grammys with one of his groups nominated and one of mine." He saw no need to squelch his pride.

"It should be fun watching you two."

"You're going to be there, Tina?" asked JJ.

"Yes. Didn't Kayo tell you that he invited me?"

"No, but that's cool." JJ fidgeted with his beer mug. "I mean, cool."

"See what I mean about being a parent?" Tina added self-consciously. "He probably feels sorry for me with my father so ill and everything."

"And how is he doing?"

"As well as can be expected. The bypass surgery was successful, they tell me. He might have been living in pain for a long time, telling no one about it. I don't know how he did it. His girlfriend came up from St. Martin."

"His *girl*friend?"

"That's not quite fair, JJ, his lady friend. She's wonderful. I've known her all my life. Very down-to-earth. We've been talking a lot since she's been here."

"She's staying *here*?"

"Calm down, JJ, now *you're* beginning to sound like a parent," said Nicky.

"No, as a matter of fact, she's staying at his place. It's much closer to the hospital and all. But mostly because it's their business. I want to respect their privacy, too. But I'll tell you one thing, love is the cure. She's done wonders for him. Done wonders *with* him."

"So how are you taking it?"

"I don't know. The best way I can, I guess. Everything is wide-open to change. He's like this huge boulder I've been pushing against all my life and suddenly he's no longer there. Then I catch myself. What am I pushing so hard for? And it turns out that the boulder is not really him but all kinds of fears and fantasies I had about him. About myself. About growing up to be like him or not like him. And it also turns out that I wasn't pushing against him all the time like I thought. Sometimes I was leaning, too, you know? Just leaning on that strength."

They settled back into a thoughtful silence broken by sparks from the fire and the steaming hiss of something liquid burning up inside the wood.

When the doorbell rang, Mrs. English showed Kayo and a powerfully built young man into the living room. After settling in, Kayo introduced Derek Connors to everyone and explained his new role as Nicky's bodyguard. An ex-marine and veteran of the Gulf War, Derek was also the nephew of Mrs. English, and the son of Mr. Thompson's chauffeur. He was chosen for this extremely sensitive position because he was superbly qualified in security work and also because he was a member of a trusted family whose ties to the Thompson family, and by extension, to the Knight family were in existence even before Nicky and Derek were born. They were a family in crisis. And they needed to pull together as a family.

When Mrs. English announced that dinner was served, they all prepared to move into the dining room. Hanging back slightly, Kayo asked Tina if she would mind inviting Mrs. English to eat with them.

"All these changes are totally upsetting to her, Kayo." Tina spoke softly, confidentially. "You know how she feels about *her* house. She's permitting Derek to eat with us this one night only. She would never sit down with us."

"May I just ask her?"

"Of course, but she's liable to shoot you for trespassing in her kitchen."

When Kayo pushed through the swinging door into the service kitchen, Mrs. English wore a look that could only be described as flabbergasted. If she had been carrying the soup tureen instead of merely filling it, she would most certainly have dropped it.

"May I help you, sir?" she managed to ask.

"Mrs. English, I was wondering if you would mind joining us at the table tonight. It would mean a great deal to me to have everyone who is actively caring for my daughter sit down with us."

"I appreciate your thoughtfulness, Mr. Knight. But I could not possibly do that. I would not be able to discharge my duties in the proper manner." She emphasized "proper" as if there were only two choices: proper and unthinkable. "Now, if you'll excuse me, sir, I would like to serve this lobster bisque."

Kayo moved out of her way and accepted defeat. The old hen had an admirable stubbornness to her. But he should have known better from the talk he'd had with her when Nicky first moved in. He had made the mistake of offering to increase her salary or at least give her a sizable bonus for the extra work Nicky would cause. And she had practically pecked his eyes out. She could accommodate only so many changes, she'd said. But a child in need had no cash value. She would protect this home—and all who lived in it—as she had done for the past thirty years.

CHAPTER EIGHTEEN

NICKY poured herself another glass of wine and tried to reach Max one last time. Over the past few days she'd left several messages on his answering machine inviting him to watch the Grammys with her at Tina's house tonight. And no return call. He must be on location. He couldn't be nursing a grudge against her for this long, over a week since the TV shoot. She had managed to talk with him once to explain what had happened with Gianni. Which was absolutely positively nothing. But he'd sounded rushed or irritated or something that cut short any real conversation. Still, he didn't seem to be unforgiving. And he had promised to get back to her. So, he wasn't that angry. He was just probably out of town, the lucky stiff.

She sipped more of the red wine while she surveyed her bedroom. The twin beds were covered in a yellow and green floral print, so spiffy and cheery. The ruffled bed skirts, the overstuffed armchairs, the vanity with its mirrored tray of perfumes, so lovely and comfortable. The yellow-and-white-striped bathroom, so sunny. She was grateful to Tina. But—and she could never say this to anyone—she felt as if she were locked up in a luxurious prison cell. She had everything a person could want, except freedom.

After her father and Tina had left for the music awards at Rockefeller Center, she felt lonely, almost abandoned. She didn't feel like eating dinner, sitting at the big teak table alone. There was no one to talk to, no one to be with. Since he'd moved in a couple of days ago Derek was careful to keep his distance. Except for their daily outings to the gym, she barely knew he was around. Her father and Mrs. English must have given him very specific instructions about his behavior. She did learn that he was all of twenty-one and yet his silence and size made him seem much older.

How long could this tension last? How long would she have to be isolated and protected? She hated that feeling. She wasn't afraid anymore. The cards that had been slipped through the mail slot had shocked her more than they'd actually frightened her. If somebody wanted to do something to her why didn't he just come out with it? She could deal.

A knock sounded at her door. She quickly hid the wine bottle and her glass under the skirts of a bedside table. "Miss Nicole?" It was Mrs. English.

"Yes, come in." Nicky sat back up on the bed and zapped the TV channels looking for the one that would carry the Grammys.

Mrs. English stood in the doorway. "I just wanted to know if there was anything I could get for you before I retire for the evening. A sandwich maybe, or a salad?"

"No thanks, I'm not hungry."

"Well, I know you models have to watch your weight but eating nothing is not a very good idea."

"Mrs. English, I am simply not hungry. Is that clear?"

"Yes, miss." Mrs. English closed the door. The child was obviously upset but that was no excuse for rude behavior. Something else was going on, going wrong. Miss Nicole had kept her eyes focused on the television the whole time she was talking. That was not like her to be hiding something. Ever since that awful night last week when she had stood paralyzed at the bottom of the stairs, crying over that wretched picture, she had seemed more open. Weakness did that to you, pried you wide-open. Then when you got strong again, you closed down, forgetting that people have seen your tender insides. It was not her place to tattle, but she would have to mention this to Miss Christina tomorrow.

She walked across the hallway to Derek's room. He was watching an action film and lifting hand weights in what he called curls. "How about a snack for you, Derek? Something to drink?"

"Sure, Aunt Mona, a nice cold beer would be great." They both chuckled at his joke. Until this crisis was over he was on twenty-four-hour duty. No alcohol allowed. "What about an iced tea with a sandwich on the side?"

"Very well. I won't be long." Mrs. English liked young people who ate properly. As she understood it, food was a form of love.

In front of the little kitchen TV in her apartment Corky Matthews mashed low-calorie mayonnaise, pickle relish and onion flakes into the bowl of canned tuna, and then spooned it onto crackers. Not even a real sandwich. She was too beat.

The meat loaf and macaroni and cheese baking in the oven would be for Richard's dinner. One of her New Year's resolutions had been to cook for him more. To be home in quiet Riverdale, out of the city and away from the agency early enough and often enough to cook for him. She'd listened to him complain for too long. He wanted to retire but he didn't want to live in an empty apartment, he said. Now that their sons were grown and gone, he wanted their life back. He wanted a meal that wasn't eaten out or taken out. He'd seen enough paper and plastic and tinfoil containers to last a lifetime. And if the microwave died tomorrow, he'd be one happy man.

Now she was making the homiest of home-cooked meals and he was nowhere in sight. No telling when he would eat it or when he would even get home, for that matter. Since the 20th Precinct was put in charge of the so-called Cleo case, she saw him less than ever.

Today she knew he was in a mean mood. Who wouldn't be after the letter he received, hand-delivered by Mr. Knight's chauffeur, with copies to his captain *and* the commissioner *and* the mayor? Jesus. He'd faxed a copy to her after calling the office to let her know it would be for her eyes only. She remembered the feel of the slippery fax paper in her hand as she was reading it. "Inadequate response to the death of three prominent individuals of African-American descent." "Lack of appropriate anger and action." "Nearly two months of murderous anxiety." "My wife already a victim and my daughter potentially the next."

What could she say? It was a torturous situation. You had to sympathize with the man. But it wasn't as if it were all Richard's fault. He was doing the most and the best he could do. Life wasn't like this TV where the music let you know when the bad guys were near and every crime was neatly solved in under sixty minutes. What about the fifty percent that weren't? Cops—and their families—had to live with failure as much as with success.

And then the punch below the belt. "What if the victims were White?" Knight had written. "Wouldn't the entire city be in an uproar?" It was unfair, grossly, outrageously, undeniably unfair. Except that, Corky had to admit, it was blatantly true.

It wasn't just her experience of being in the beauty business, where she'd had plenty of time to see the two-tier treatment at work. Where, sure, all beautiful faces were equal but White beauty was more equal than Black beauty, or at least earned more. More money and respect. No, it wasn't just this business. It was a simple social, racial reality. Everybody knew it. Every ambitious Black girl she'd ever seen had reached that glass ceiling. Some broke their wings and their spirit trying to break through. Others calmly positioned themselves in another career and continued to fly high. Most just wrapped up the fancy memories when the good times were over and lived out modest lives as real people. But still they kept coming, the Black girls as star-struck as the White ones. They kept coming and kept hoping and kept pushing that ceiling farther and farther away. Until now. Someone had actually broken through. The Cleo contract put little Nicky Knight in the same league with the other mega-models.

A brand-new kid with stardust in her eyes out of nowhere. Well, nowhere wasn't exactly accurate. Corky remembered Becky Saunders from the old days, even though she had been with Eileen Ford and not MacLean. Eileen had worked hard for her and Becky had done well, very well. She did even better by marrying a music mogul. Everyone should retire so gracefully. And here comes the kid, cute as a button, with that California ease that says I'm here, I'm golden, aren't we lucky? But with a little bit more, too. The beginning of depth, maybe? The understanding that the whole world didn't live the way she and her family did. And now this series of shocks. Only six months in New York City and already Nicky was a motherless child.

But let's not confuse the situation. The city was to blame, not Richard Matthews. The whole United States of America was to blame, not one individual police officer with twenty-five years on the force, twenty with a gold shield, and now this. He wasn't a racist. They weren't racists. They hadn't taught their kids that they were better than other people because they were White. They were better because they were their kids, the sons of Carolyn and Richard Matthews, parents who loved them and expected them to be great people, period.

She hated this month of February with its Black History lessons. Not that she'd ever say it out loud, to anyone. No, never. But she had to admit the ambivalence she felt. How could the country ever get beyond the terrible things that had happened in the past if they were unearthed every year on prime time? It was so corny, this little moral set-aside. Such a painful reminder, this annual national reenslavement to a bitter history. The same heartbreaking speeches excerpted every hour on the hour. The same TV miniseries with their martyrs and madness.

Repetition without resolution just trivialized the real struggle. The struggle that she had been a part of in her own quiet way as much as protesters who shouted in the streets. Enough already with the pointing fingers and the pointed hats. She was not an enemy of Black people. Far from it. And she would not accept her husband being chastised for something that was the whole society's fault.

This was a city where kids not old enough to have facial hair killed each other over sneakers. Where turf wars could direct a stray bullet to enter an apartment window and explode the brain of an innocent little girl. Where some people's weapon of choice was a machete and others' an AK-47. The city was at fault, not one man.

Violence was just as random as beauty. Just as far-fetched and outrageous and unpredictable. Hadn't she seen it a hundred times? A thousand? Who could tell which girl would make it big and which one would fade? Who could tell which kid would be the gangster and which one the teacher? Who would win and who would lose?

Even these silly endless Grammy awards. How could you tell which group would win? Which song? And Whoopi Goldberg, the mistress of ceremonies, a woman, for a change, saying she was too sexy for this show. It took some nerve to be Black and *not* beautiful and make fun of it all. Corky had to hand it to her. If you couldn't laugh, it became too sickening. There just didn't seem to be an answer. The only thing she knew for sure was that it wasn't all her husband's fault.

After Mrs. English carried a tray up to Derek, she wished him good night and climbed another flight of stairs to her rooms on the top floor. She wouldn't mind a little television while she worked on her knitting. What a big splash they made, the 34th Annual Grammy Awards. All the fancy-looking people in the audience, Miss Christina somewhere among them. All the wild musicians and loud music on stage. And the mistress of ceremonies with those long woolly dreadlocks scaring people and making them laugh at the same time.

Mrs. English had never felt that she was getting old. Sixty-five was no spring chicken but it was nowhere near old. She had seen too many styles cycle in and out of popularity—and back in again—to feel that there was one point in time where things and people—and her own self—would be classified, once and for all, as old. But when she listened to what the young people called music, she felt that the time had come for her to be old. And she didn't mind. It was their loss. People of her generation had grown up with real music, songs with beautiful melodies and lyrics to them with feeling *and* good grammar.

She smiled to herself that "Unforgettable," a song over forty years old, could win Song of the Year in 1992. Just goes to show that quality is timeless. And so are memories. She had never forgotten the shock of her early years. Burying Robert English's body in a small sandy cemetery down South, along with the dreams of the child she had carried. She had never forgotten the facts, but she had lost some of the feeling, and in that way she had recovered.

At eighteen she thought that love had died with everything else, but the older folks, who knew how long life was, told her differently, said that dark and sweet as she was, for sure she'd find another man. But Mona

English was too hurt to stay around and wait for him to appear. Then once she made the move, she was too busy learning new ways up North to even think about a man. She went to work six days a week, to school five nights a week and to church twice on weekends for five years. It seemed that every minute of her life belonged to somebody else. Maybe that's why she didn't realize what she had missed with Macon Bernard until it was too late.

Learning the best shops along 125th Street had taken time. But once Aunt Mayme showed her who sold the freshest collard, mustard and turnip greens, who not only sold the best fish but cleaned it for you properly, which pork store cut the thickest chops and changed the sawdust on the floor most often and who sold the freshest chickens if you didn't want them live from the butcher on Amsterdam Avenue, Mona English felt proud of herself. Proud enough to treat herself on Saturdays to a grilled cheese sandwich and an ice cream soda at Thomforde's before catching the bus to go back up to Sugar Hill.

The record shop right behind the bus stop near Thomforde's corner had intimidated her for the longest. Not the shop itself but the groups of young men hanging around, jiving on the sidewalk, especially in the summer when people seemed to practically dance in the street. How could our people be so crude? she thought. Didn't they have jobs or anything better to do? Her straight back would get a little stiffer, her narrow lips a little thinner and her bright eyes a little harder, the longer she waited for that bus to come.

Until she went inside the shop one day. It was 1951 and she wanted "Unforgettable" by Nat "King" Cole. Uncle Gene always bought the records for the house, heavy 78s for 35 cents a piece or, when he was splurging, three for a dollar. But his newest record player could play all three speeds, 78, 33 1/3 and 45. The 33s were ten inches or tweleve inches wide and cost $2.98 and $3.98, far beyond their budget on a regular basis. But the new little 45s cost only 69 cents. That day she skipped her treat at Thomforde's to buy a 45 of "Unforgettable." And that's when she met Macon Bernard, standing behind the counter, singing along with Nat, working his jaw and his lips the same way the King did his. But his voice was crisp and clear where Nat's was soft and powdery. Macon had a pretty voice, she later overheard people say, a voice fit for a pretty man.

Mona English was not one to truck with men, let alone pretty men. But when Macon Bernard asked her what church she went to and she said Convent Baptist, he said what a nice coincidence it was that he was part of the guest choir from Canaan Baptist scheduled to sing there tomorrow. He hoped, he said, that they could meet again. And they did. She took to making small economies so she could buy a record a week. He began inventing instant sales as soon as she walked in the door. Uncle Gene, who was in real estate, knew Macon's father, who owned the shop, so that helped. And Aunt Mayme knew his mother from the Coal Club, so that helped, too. In the beginning.

Despite his being pretty, Macon was a good man, ambitious in business and sincere in his feelings for her. She could not believe her luck. All her life people had called her a good person, praised her good manners and good cooking, patted her hair that wasn't straight enough to be called good but was still considered better than bad. All her life. Even Robert English had married her because she would make a good wife. But Macon was different. He was a pretty man who felt relieved that, for once, a woman was not competing with him in looks. He was intrigued by the books she brought him from Micheaux's, and more than that, inspired by their vision of a wider world. Using books and records, Macon and Mona took the time to talk, to reach past the obvious to see who they really were inside. And after a year he started hinting to his parents that they wanted to get married. Although he grieved that he and Mona would not be able to make their own babies, he was convinced that adoption was a blessed alternative. His family and friends were not. The more serious their love grew, the more determined grew the opposition. Aunt Mayme and Uncle Gene were made to understand that Mona English was damaged goods, a good girl, and none of it her fault, but perhaps she was setting her sights too high, aiming for someone like Macon.

Then came Korea. She was the one who decided to wait until he came back from the war. He never did, not dead or alive. The fighting exploded his body into too many pieces to reclaim. So he stayed over there in some place she could not even pronounce and she stayed in easy-talking Harlem, shattered, frozen, jinxed, commanding God every day to make her die, imploring Him for answers that came only in the grudging step of one foot placed in front of the other.

For He did not obey her. Instead she lived through other wars and in other families, surviving long enough to see the magic of modern technology present Natalie Cole live, dressed in a long white gown with black beads, singing "Unforgettable" in a duet with her smoothly coiffed father on a black-and-white video screen. Nat "King" Cole had been dead for twenty-five years. But when she blew a kiss to him at the end, that incredible fact seemed the most minor technicality.

"You don't have to apologize," said Tina as she climbed into Kayo Knight's limousine.

"But I am sorry," he repeated as he settled in beside her. "I thought I could handle it and I just couldn't." After he lowered the window separating them from his driver, he said, "Littlejohn, drive through the park for a while, please." And the long Mercedes headed north on Sixth Avenue into Central Park.

Kayo had suggested they make an appearance. "Just an appearance," he said. Time Warner had reserved all the restaurants and cafes around the skating rink at Rockefeller Center, blocking off the underground passageways so that audience guests from Radio City Music Hall could make their way to the grand postawards parties unmolested by any New York surprises. The nasty weather outside was bad enough.

But after JJ and Nadja had gone off with their crowd and Kayo and Tina headed toward the festivities, he found that he could not suppress the powerful feelings that churned inside him. Not about the Grammys. Neither he nor JJ had won in their respective categories. But that was not important. He had won before. He might win again. And JJ had a brilliant future ahead of him. There was no cause to worry there.

Something else was eating away at him. Anger, sadness, frustration, fear and still something else. He found the parade of sequins and glitter and wild, fantasy hairdos irrelevant, ridiculous, even insulting. And he'd stopped all of a sudden in the middle of the arcade and told Tina that he could not go on. Without asking or even knowing why, she felt she understood. And he appreciated her for that.

The ride was smooth and quiet. The heavy rain outside made them feel even more secure and protected within.

"Would you like some music?" he asked.

"No thanks, I think I've had enough for one evening. Kayo, you know, you don't have to entertain me. You don't have to explain anything or do anything . . ."

He took her arm and fit it under and around his own. He could not trust himself to talk just yet but he needed her to ground him, to keep him attached to the saner realms of the real world. Otherwise, he would take off, howling and punching, hacking his way through the pack of confident smiles and the sparkling perks of success until he reached whatever he needed to stop him. A tank maybe, a tall brick wall. Or maybe it wasn't something hard and cold at all. Maybe it was something soft and warm. He covered her hand with his.

"Kayo, I don't want this to seem out of place but Becky told me a lot about you."

"Women talk too much."

"And men don't talk enough." She smiled but removed her arm and moved slightly away from him.

"Becky." He pronounced her name as if he had not dared to speak it aloud in a long time. "Becky thought I was a demon."

"She also loved you very much."

"I guess that's something I'll just never understand about women." He shook his head, bewildered. "How women can care so deeply and carry so many conflicting emotions around inside of them. And then talk about it with their girlfriends. It's a complete mystery to me."

"I'm insulted, Kayo." She smiled. "You make us sound like an alien species."

"Tina, look," he spoke seriously, "all my life I've tried to do what I thought a man was supposed to do. Take care of his woman and his children. Take care of business. I know I haven't always succeeded. I learned that you have to sacrifice. You know that yourself. And this is not to excuse myself, but sometimes I wanted something just for me, a feeling that wasn't on the program, maybe even somebody to take care of *me*."

"And did you ever find it? Did you ever find her?"

"Let's put it this way: I'm still looking." But he was not looking far. That's what had him so perplexed. "Come and keep me company for a little while."

"It's getting late."

"Your home is secure. Your business is not going to close down if you're not there in person to open up at nine o'clock in the morning. Nobody in this town is going to be doing any business before noon tomorrow anyway, believe me. Come on up, just for a little while."

"Kayo, you're old enough to be my father."

"You're right about the age but wrong about the relationship. Come on, I don't eat young virgins alive."

"And old ones?"

"I don't know about that, but you shouldn't be giving me any extra ideas."

She was not a virgin and had not been one for quite some time, but when he kissed her, it felt like something new and not dangerous at all. Later, in the soft rose bedroom light of his hotel suite, she was surprised to find herself enjoying the way they moved and fit together. After he had taken off his tie, she carefully removed each gold and onyx stud from his tuxedo shirt, kissing his chest as she went along. He was softer and rounder than the younger men she had been intimate with. But she was also softer and rounder than her younger self. She felt her breasts swelling under his caress.

"I can feel you smiling," he said, nibbling on her neck. "What's the joke?"

"No joke," she said half-indignantly, pulling her unbuttoned jacket closed. "I'm just feeling nice. I have to admit something, though."

"All right, out with it."

"I'm almost afraid you'll call me by someone else's name." She leaned on one elbow and looked closely into his face.

"Someone in particular?"

"Well, no, just someone not me."

"So, are you disappointed that I haven't?" He grinned, proud of himself.

"Maybe just a little bit."

"But why on earth would you want me to do that, Tina?"

"So there would be some rationale, you know, some logical mix-up for us being here together. As if you have this overwhelming need and I'm just a convenient stand-in, helping to fulfill it. That it isn't about you really caring for me."

"Or you really caring for me?"

"Precisely." She nodded curtly.

"We could call it some kind of feel-good mission, just a generous hand extended in charity."

"See, you understand me exactly."

"I do more than understand you, Tina." He stroked her cheek. "I care for you and I'm not going to let you get away with this fake Florence Nightingale act. You care for me, too. I can feel that. We don't have to be afraid."

"*You* don't," she insisted.

"Neither one of us. We're both grown."

"Being grown means you're no longer afraid?"

"It means you can discriminate between a light fright and the truly terrifying." He twirled a lock of hair that had come undone from her French twist. "What's the worst thing that could happen between you and me?"

"Well," she said with a frown, "we could hate each other."

"You're right. Now you've got me scared. Come here and tell me it's going to be all right."

"It's going to be . . ."

"Uh-unh, you've got to say it like you mean it."

She lowered her voice. "Don't worry, it's . . ."

"You've got to put your arms around me and . . ."

"Like this?"

"More."

"Like this?"

And his wordless answer embraced her body and soul.

Derek Connors returned to the third floor after his midnight check on the lower floors' doors and windows. The ground floor with the big kitchen and laundry. The garage with its spanking new Mercedes 500SL. The first floor with the parlor, dining room and service kitchen. The second floor, Miss Thompson's suite with her sitting room, bedroom and dressing room. Everything was in place.

He was resetting the codes to the security system between the floors when he heard a loud thump. Something heavy had fallen. In Nicky's room. Her light was on. He could see it under her door. Her television was on. Some talk show. He knocked. No answer. He went in. He did not see her at first. She had fallen off the far side of the bed. Dead drunk. Naked under a fur coat. An empty wine bottle lay near her and another had spilled. He lifted her up, put her back in the bed, removed the coat and covered her with quilts. She was breathing OK, snoring. He checked the windows onto her balcony. Then turned off the lights and left. He would make his report in the morning.

Vanessa Seymour shook her head in disbelief. "Max?" First the whisper was a question. With repetition it became a total impossibility. "Max, shot?"

Detective Matthews looked away, giving her a moment to compose herself. Her office was postered with ad campaigns and slogans which even he, who was too busy to read a magazine or watch TV, recognized. He was impressed.

"How can I help you?" Vanessa asked.

"We understand that you had an appointment with him last Friday."

"Yes, I did. I still can't believe it. Today I just spent a fortune at lunchtime buying all the things he used on me." She pointed to the clutch of shiny little shopping bags on her office couch. "Didn't have time to eat a thing. Please excuse me. I'm famished and I also have a very important client meeting in exactly fifteen minutes."

He watched her spread a cloth napkin on her desk and then unhinge the plastic top from the deli salad that was her lunch. From a drawer she pulled out a fork and knife and wiped them to a meticulous shine.

"I'll be as brief as I can. What time was your appointment with Mr. Maxwell?" he asked.

"Four-thirty. I guess I must have left about six o'clock. I went to have a drink with my partner. Smitty is going to be in a complete state of shock. We all loved him here. And poor Nicky Knight, she's going to be devastated. We have some serious damage control to do here. When do you think it happened?"

"We can't tell for certain yet. His maid found the body right in the doorway when she went in today. Wednesday's her regular day, she says. But people have been trying to reach him at least since Monday when he didn't show up for work. There are messages on his answering machine for several days. You might have been the last person to see him alive."

"My goodness, if I were, he'd still *be* alive, Sergeant."

"Lieutenant."

"Whatever. I'm a businesswoman. That's as dangerous as I get." She chewed a forkful of salad thoughtfully and swallowed. "Did you talk with his next appointment?"

"Who was that?"

"I don't know his name. He came in just as I was leaving."

"It was a man?"

"As quiet as it's kept, you guys are getting facials and everything else these days."

"Can you tell me what he looked like?"

"A Black man, about my height."

"Anything else about him?"

"Well, Max didn't exactly introduce us. I mean, I'd have to think about it. I wasn't really looking, you know. We literally passed each other in the doorway."

"Anything you can remember will be helpful, Miss Seymour. What was he wearing? A hat? Glasses? A raincoat?"

"Just give me time, I'll remember something. The thing is, you have to forgive me here. I guess I didn't really look at him, I mean, on purpose."

"What are you trying to say?"

"I'm a woman. You know how it is with two gay guys."

"You're certain that Mr. Maxwell was homosexual?"

"Detective, that can't come as a surprise. Everybody knows that."

"And the man who came to see him was gay, too?"

"I know that's a sensitive issue, but that's the impression I got."

After a few more questions Richard Matthews left his card with Vanessa Seymour, saying that he would be speaking with her very soon. They would probably need to go to Mr. Maxwell's apartment together. Oh, no, she'd said. She couldn't stand the sight of blood. Women, go figure. Some would burst into a storm of tears just watching the daily disasters on the news. Others wouldn't miss a beat no matter what happened to whom. They'd keep right on stepping. Vanessa Seymour was as dry as the bread sticks she crunched with her lunch. He wondered if she was always so detached. Or maybe she was just overattached to herself and the business at hand.

The fact remained: there'd been two homicides in the same luxury apartment in a matter of weeks. The first one, a beautiful woman with her throat cut. And now this one, a gay guy, well-known, well-to-do, shot twice in the head. If lightning struck twice that would be an accident. What was going on here was part of a definite plan.

CHAPTER NINETEEN

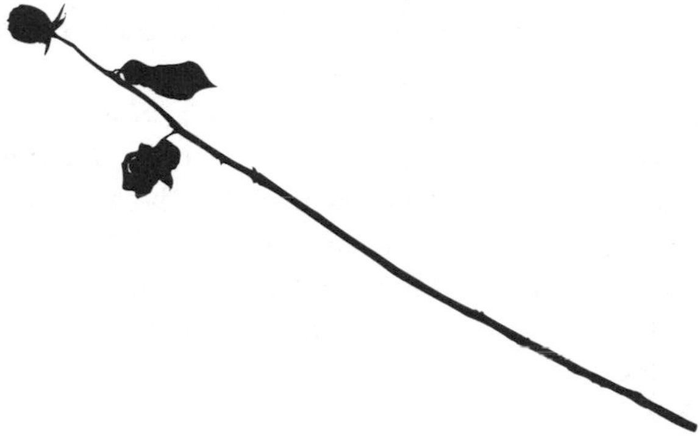

TINA lay back and floated, letting the mild water of the pool caress her under the hot St. Martin sun. She had forgotten such simple pleasures, but now more than ever she needed to remember them. The past three days—like the past three weeks—had been agonizing for them all. But, she thought, especially for Nicky. Her brave exterior had crumbled. She had spent Wednesday recovering from a nasty hangover only to find out the next day that her friend Max had been killed. Corky, again the reluctant bearer of bad news, had called Tina at her office. No one was saying how or when. Just that his cleaning lady had discovered the body when she came in on her regular workday.

Thank goodness they had already planned to get away and spend the weekend at Hill House, leaving Derek to hold down the fort in New York. She had made surprisingly easy arrangements with her father to use his private plane. She sensed how delighted he was that she had asked him for something that he could give, for a change, without argument. Tina had invited JJ and Nadja to come along but JJ had to stay in town for work and Nadja was too brokenhearted about Max to leave. Tina had also invited Clarice Brathwaite since she hadn't been home in several weeks. But Clarice sweetly refused her invitation, letting Tina know without saying the words that she considered her place to be by Tommy's side.

Nicky was simply not talking. She had barely had a dry moment since the morning after the Grammys when she'd cried so pitifully in Tina's arms, ashamed and embarrassed about her own behavior. She had promised Tina that she would never get drunk again. She had learned her lesson. And she had begged Tina not to tell Kayo. He would make her return to California for sure if he knew that she'd been drinking to the point of passing out. Tina did not commit herself to telling or withholding, saying only that she would wait until a better time to say anything. And so Kayo had left Wednesday afternoon none the wiser about his daughter, or Max.

That better time couldn't get here soon enough, Tina thought. Someone was getting away with murder. She had to get out of the pool. Relaxing was starting to drive her crazy.

Mrs. English walked down from the veranda as Tina was toweling herself dry. "Wilson is driving me down to Marigot before it gets too hot," she explained, "to pick up a few things for Mrs. Brathwaite. Is there anything you'd like me to bring back for you?" She held up a large straw basket to indicate that there was plenty of room.

"Thanks," Tina replied. "But I can't think of anything right now." She turned to Nicky and asked if she wanted something.

"No, nothing," she grumbled, not bothering to turn over from her facedown position on the chaise longue.

Tina shook her head in exasperation and said to Mrs. English, "Well, check and make sure we have enough popcorn and Raisinets and all the other stuff she's been eating since she won't eat real food."

"She knows she's not supposed to be doing that. But maybe if the junk food wasn't here, she would eat the healthy kind. One day or another she's got to . . ."

Nicky sat up suddenly. "Will you both please stop talking about me as if I weren't here? As if I weren't even alive? I just can't take it anymore!" She snatched her towel from the lounge and, sobbing, ran up the steps, past the veranda and into the house.

The two women stared at her in helpless silence. They never knew what to expect. Volcanic tears erupted out of silence. Moods swung from bad to worse and back to bad again. No one could take it anymore. But what was the alternative? Kayo would be coming in from L.A. tonight. The traveling must be exhausting for him, Tina thought, but Nicky needed his presence. He was the one who'd said last week that they needed to pull together. That was even more true today than before.

"You go on, Mrs. English, I'll take care of her." Tina wrapped a short terry kimono over her wet bathing suit and headed toward the house.

"Poor baby. I'm so afraid she'll do something foolish in the midst of all this upset."

"She'll be all right. I'll see you later."

But Tina knew there was no guarantee that Nicky would be all right. One shock after another was enough to unhinge even the strongest of souls.

In the living room Nicky was nursing a tall lemonade.

"I'm sorry, Nicky," Tina said. "We were rude. I know how you must feel . . ."

"Do you, Tina?" she cried. "Max was my first friend in the business. My best friend. And I never got to tell him how much he meant to me. He was the one who was always telling me to be careful. And now look. I don't know what to do. I'm so sick and tired of crying all the time."

"There's nothing wrong with that. You've got to let it out." Tina tried to console her but the words rang hollow in her own ears. People had told her the same thing after her mother died. But how could they understand? And how could she understand Nicky's feelings?

"But I've got to do something *more*," she protested. "I turn all of nineteen soon, but sometimes I don't feel like I'm going to get a chance to get there, let alone grow all the way up. I get such a creepy feeling. Someone is out there killing off everyone that I care for, trying to get to me. Whoever he is, I wish he'd just come on and get it over with. I'd rather be dead than crying and crazy all the time."

Tina put her arms around Nicky as the young woman continued to sob. "But you've got to see that it's not just you that he's after. He won't stop with you. If I understand what you told me about what Max believed, this killer is after anyone who crosses the racial divide. Any Black woman who dares stand up to the world and say I am and I am beautiful. You've got to stay strong, Nicky. Don't do his dirty work for him."

The two women sat in silence for a while longer looking out into the bright colors of the Caribbean morning. Mother Nature was doing her utmost to heal them. And as they left the cool living room for the already hot outdoors, they were grateful to put themselves in her hands.

"I forgot how beautiful it is here," said Kayo, walking through the garden beyond the pool. A hedge of white hibiscus, its blossoms closed to the night, angled around the gazebo where he and Tina finally sat, out of view from the house. The lights in distant Marigot harbor were the only reminder of the rest of the world. "It smells so good. The sky is so clear and there are so many stars. You forget that in L.A. You see one or two through the haze and you count yourself lucky. Here, it's like being a kid again. There's so much out there to wonder about."

"How is Nicky now?" Tina asked.

"Better, I think. We had a long talk. That's not exactly my specialty, you know, long talks with women. She's got a lot of woman in her, but she's still a kid, too. She still believes in justice and fair play."

"You sound as if you don't, Kayo."

"How can I? I know the world. She's just getting her feet wet."

"And maybe more than you think." Tina told Kayo about Derek having heard Nicky fall out of her bed drunk. He was stunned at first, then angry at Nicky and furious that no one had told him. Tina did not know what else to do but listen as he stumbled through a thicket of feelings. In a way, she wished she could put her arms around him to calm him down as a parent would a child. But that gesture was sure to be misunderstood. It was hard enough to remember that they were making love while Nicky was drinking herself blind. Fingers of accusation seemed pointed at her from so many directions. Becky's death, her father's heart attack, Nicky's binge. Her good intentions seemed to produce precisely the opposite effects.

"I'm sorry to rail at you like this," Kayo said after a while. "You look as if you're carrying the weight of the world on your shoulders."

"Right now, that's about how I feel."

"Well, I don't want to be another burden. I want to be part of the solution, not part of the problem." He took her hand and cupped it to his cheek. She let it stay there until he started to kiss her palm. Then she snatched it away.

"Don't," she whispered.

"I want to hold you in my arms right now, Tina."

"No, Kayo. It's not right, certainly not with Nicky around."

"She's sleeping now. She was worn out, said she'd been having nightmares."

"Don't you think that the thought of you and me together would be another nightmare for her?"

"Maybe. But she doesn't have to know."

"I can't live with lies, Kayo."

"And as hard as I try, Tina, I swear, sometimes I feel that I can't live without you. Don't laugh. Do you think this is so easy for me? Looking and sounding like a ridiculous kid. Why do you think I leave New York so quickly? It's not easy to be around you and not tell you how I really feel."

"I'm a woman, Kayo, not a one-night stand. If we want to get to know each other, there'll be plenty of time for that later."

"When, Tina? We all think that and then later turns out to be too late." He pulled her to him and kissed her, stroking the resistance out of her back and shoulders, pressing her to agree with his desire.

"I'm sorry, I have to go." She twisted away.

"Where, baby? You're already home. Where're you going to run to this time?"

She did not know. She had nowhere to go but away from him, away from his embrace, from the sweet dampness of his neck and the heat rising from his groin. But even under the shower she could not run away from her own desire for him. When she curled up underneath the cool sheets of her bed, the hot tears were gone but not the frustration that yielded them. Later, much later, when he came into her arms, she cried through their kisses, softly, quietly and then silently, accepting him and giving herself, just this once, this one last time.

She was late. Hot and sweaty from trying to get there on time, but she was still late. Maybe she smelled bad, too. She wanted to apologize to all the people on the set but no one paid any attention to her. The clothes hanging on the rack were hideous but, even worse, they didn't fit. They were too tight or too long or had holes in the wrong places. Tense but ready to work, she sat in front of the makeup mirror waiting for the hairstylist and the makeup artist. She could see her own face but the mirror chopped everyone else's head off. They were just a mass of bodies milling around behind her, moving, finally converging, coming closer to her, coming after her . . .

Nicky bolted upright in the bed, startled by the darkness in her room and by the vision so near, right on the other side of her eyelids. She didn't dare close them. The horror was still there.

She threw the tangled sheets off her bed. They were soaking wet. Although the air was soft and mild, she was chilly. And scared.

Outside, night creatures croaked and sang. Inside, the dark seemed to dampen live sounds, leaving only faintly motorized vibrations humming in her ears. She put on a long, dry T-shirt, opened her door and stepped into the hall, a broad tiled mezzanine that overlooked the open living room below. Through the double-height windows she watched the crests of palms swaying in the breeze. The pool lights projected eerie shadows into the house. If she moved she felt something would grab her and slide her forever into the night. She squinted down the corridor. There were five bedrooms on this level. All the doors were closed against her, but she was grateful to find a sliver of faint light at the end under Tina's door. She walked quickly now, shedding her panic with each cooling footstep, willing herself to safety. As she knocked, she entered.

Shock crashed through on several waves. A tall naked brown back. Languid undulations. "Baby." Whispering voices. Pale soles of feet wrapped around his neck. "Baby." As Tina's eyes opened, Kayo's head whipped around. They both stared at Nicky in mute astonishment.

"Oh, my God," she cried, and dashed through the dark down the stairs.

"Nicky, wait," Kayo called as he grabbed his robe and ran out after her. He heard the doors slide open and then a splash of water in the pool.

He walked alongside as she did noisy, furious laps. At times her white shirt ballooned out of the water, at others it clasped her body like a second but imperfect skin. "Please come out. Let's talk, Nicky, please.

Talk to me, Nicole. Don't shut me out like this. Please."

She continued to beat the water in long, loud strokes. Each kick was an accusation, each breath a curse. It was useless. He sat in a padded chair to wait. He didn't know what he would say to her. How could he make her understand? And what was Tina feeling now? A minute ago he had been inside her, not in lust, not in some quick and easy rush to discharge himself, but in peace, in a kind of homecoming, in the comfort of her soft, strong arms. He wanted to be with this woman who made him think, who talked back to him, who could share and disagree and still rock him so sweetly. How could he ever tell Nicky that? How could he even tell Tina?

The sky overhead was the same clear, magnificent infinity he had marveled at just a few hours before. Below, the world was crazy, dangerous and unpredictable. Broad shiny leaves glowed with an eerie yellow blood in their veins. The air's sweet perfume nauseated him, but there was no escape from breathing it. Here he was, a man, one of the masters of the universe, yet he felt dirty and broken, a foolish Humpty-Dumpty helplessly watching his child swim off her rage toward him.

He saw Tina walking barefoot down the stone steps toward them. Her turquoise peignoir, the same color as the pool under its night lights, fluttered in soft waves around her legs. Shiny tears streaked her face. Carrying towels, she said nothing, simply left the things on the table and returned to the house. The rest was up to him.

Why did his heart feel as if it were being wrenched out of his chest? He was losing something, some of his old assurance, that effervescent urge to seduce. Watching Nicky in the pool made his eyes ache with nostalgia. He hadn't always been such a bad guy, had he? Where did his daughter get all that temper from? Not from him and certainly not from her mother. Nothing could really ruffle Becky's feathers. At least, not that he ever saw.

Becky had been a good woman. And a good woman was a good thing. He had never wanted to *be* with anyone else. He just liked to *visit* other women occasionally, to recharge his batteries, to keep things from getting stale. Something in him always balked at the idea that hers was the last love he would ever get in life. Of course, she punished him in those silent sexual ways women had, withholding until he learned his lesson.

But did he ever really learn? He would swallow the punishment while deep inside, he continued to swagger, I am who I am. So they traveled on parallel rails of pride. He always went back and she always took him back. She liked being good: the noble forgiver, the understanding wife. And now if there was anything more to learn about her, it was too late. He would never know.

He watched a tiny green lizard dart along the white stone edge of the pool. It looked like an ancient monster reduced to a tiny scale. He knew nothing about evolution or anatomy. The science of visible things. He knew even less about the things you couldn't see, feelings. And until that instant he thought he was safe in not knowing. But when his tears started to creep out, he knew he was wrong. Not knowing was no protection. There was no place to hide, not in past romances, not in Tina's arms nor in dreams for the future. He had no future if it just repeated the past.

For the first time, he missed Becky, really missed her, knowing now that she was never coming back to forgive him, to hold him and reinvest in him. Cool, beautiful Becky. He had driven her away as surely as anyone. And he was sorry, so very, very sorry.

Under the soft night sky, he cried for forgiveness from those he had wronged. They made a long list, starting with his own child right here, swimming in a pool of pain. From a hollow space where his heart should be, tears flowed in a hot and starry stream.

The soft curtains billowed over Nicky as she lay across the foot of the bed. In and out, the warm daylit breeze sucked them flat against the jalousied screens and then blew them back into the room, like a dancer in a gossamer skirt. When they fluttered over her, full and for that moment still, she stroked the inside of the sheer white fabric, as fragile as a bubble. Air moved in mysterious ways. No, it was God, not air. But God was air and everything. And for the soft still moment, tearless and safe, she felt on the inside of God.

With the knock on her door she sat up, annoyed.

Mrs. English entered carrying a tray with a bowl of fruit salad and a platter of cheese and crackers.

"It's not good for you to stay cooped up in the room like this, Miss

Nicole. You've missed a perfectly beautiful day that you will surely regret when we get back to New York tonight. Come and have a little something to eat before we have to leave. Things can't be that bad."

"Mrs. English, how can you be like this? Do you know what happened? They betrayed me, my father and my mother's dear friend. Fucking . . ."

"I will not permit you to use that word!"

"Fucking behind my back. Excuse me for being so real. I just don't know what else to call it."

"Maybe because you don't know what else it could be." Mrs. English, contrary to her notions of what was proper, sat at the foot of Nicky's bed. "If you'd only give someone a chance to explain . . ."

"I don't want an explanation!"

"What do you want?" she asked softly.

"I want everything to be just like it was," Nicky cried.

"I know . . ."

"How can you? How can *you* know?" Nicky sobbed bitterly.

"You don't have a monopoly on grief, Miss Nicole. You may look at me now and see just a tired old woman. But I was young like you once. I was eighteen, too. And when I was eighteen I thought I had lost everything I could lose. My husband. My baby. My womb. I even thought I was going to lose my mind. But I didn't. Some small part of me I didn't even know was there wouldn't let me go all the way. Some people might call it God. I don't know. I was so angry at Him for so long. I used to spend a lot of time in church just so I could get within better shouting range. He must have liked me, though. Gifted me with even more pain."

"But I'm not like you, Mrs. English. I can't just sit back and accept it and go to church. I don't know what I'm going to do. But I know I can't do that."

"Well, just remember that not everything is up to us. You were blessed and for that blessing maybe you have to give something back."

"How much? For how long?"

"I can't answer that. I've been asking those same questions all my life."

CHAPTER TWENTY

"I DIDN'T want to upset your weekend, Tina, so forgive me for not calling you at Hill House."

It was Monday morning, New York City. Clarice sat by the hospital bed stroking Thomas' hand. His eyes were closed and the oxygen tubes were resting on top of his mustache. "Here, you hold his hand," she said, getting up from the chair. "He told me that he feels it somehow, if I'm touching him, even when he's asleep."

"No, no. You do it. It means more from you."

Clarice looked at Tina. When had that note of polite competition crept in?

"The doctors say that he's fine," Clarice continued. "They just wanted him in for a few tests. This shortness of breath, they don't seem to think it's all that serious, but they preferred monitoring him here."

"They're right, of course."

"Of course. But you know your father. That made him more upset than anything, having to return to hospital. He took it as a step backward, spitting thunder the whole time. He should be waking up in a few minutes. He'll be so glad to see you. Here, Tina, hold his hand. He will know it was you."

"No, that's all right."

"I see that it's upsetting you. You don't like to see your father sick."

"No, that's not it," she said, shaking her head, but unwilling to say more. "You take good care of him and I'll call you from the office."

Tina walked through the colorless hallways. Of course, she didn't like seeing her father sick. But that wasn't the real problem. She kept waiting for some rush of affection, some loving spark to light the fire and warm her heart toward him. It was not coming. She was so glad for Clarice. Let Clarice love him, let her stroke his hand and communicate all the tender concern he needed.

Tina could not. She rummaged around in feelings and came up numb and void. Maybe that was the safest way for the time being. Connors drove her to the office. She had a lot to catch up on before the day was over.

"What a surprise! Kayo, what are you doing here?"

"Aren't you going to ask me in, Sophie?"

"Of course, excuse me, please, come in." She led him through the gallery where two assistants were hanging paintings. "We are preparing a new show, so everything is upside down. I'm afraid you'll have to sit in the kitchen."

"That's fine, it doesn't matter."

Kayo sat tentatively at the head of the long plank table. At the other end a rectangular vase, like a large glass brick, held a bright abundance of daffodils, daisies and yellow tulips. Sophie picked up the last few flowers from the florist's paper and finished arranging them in the vase.

"I am so ready for spring," she said. "How nice it is to snatch a little bit of it before it gets here. I talk nonsense. I make you a coffee, no? Or what would you like to drink? You surprise me and I completely forget my good manners."

"Coffee is fine, thanks."

The preparations gave her something specific and tranquilizing to do. Her back turned to him in busywork gave him time to look around. Both needed to find their bearings. It was the first time Kayo had been to Northport, Long Island, to Sophie's home, to the gallery. It was the first time they had seen each other in many years. And alone, in years too many to count. She finally sat down.

"Oh," she said, hopping up again, "a little cognac *avec?*"

"Non, merci." He watched as she poured a glass for herself.

"I was very sorry to hear about Becky."

"Thank you." Even before she had opened the door he had not known what he was going to say. Just that he needed to see her. For some wild reason he felt that she might need to see him also.

"What brings you to Northport, Kayo?"

"I should know the answer to that, Sophie, but I don't. I was on my way to the airport, going back to L.A., and I told my driver to stay on the highway, to keep going. All of a sudden I wanted to see you."

"All of a sudden? We haven't seen each other in almost seven years."

"I know."

"JJ came out with Nadja last week. I see him about as often as I see you. That's a joke, Kayo. It doesn't really matter."

"What doesn't?"

"How often people see each other. Not at this point in our lives. Only the care matters."

"You always sounded so philosophical."

"The French like to believe they have a monopoly on philosophy. Part of our national ego. So you are here, but you don't know *why* you are here. The great existential dilemma, *n'est-ce pas?*"

"And I thought it was just me." He tried to smile at her, this gray-haired, coveralled bohemian he once knew as a daring young woman. Her body had thickened and her face had deep lines curving around her mouth. But her eyes had brightened since he'd last seen her, brightened and sharpened.

"Come, come, spit it out. Your lips are moving but I can't hear the words."

"Don't make fun of me, Sophie. It's hard enough as it is."

She was losing patience, she could feel it. Anger was rising in its place, longing to spew out all the hurt and hate in the foulest words of the language she had learned in his country. Did he think he could just stroll back into her life again and take his time with what he had to say? Steal her hard-earned peace away and maybe not even listen to what she might have to say after all these years? She poured the cognac from her snifter into the coffee cup. Holding it in both hands, she opened her lips carefully, sipping, savoring.

"That's a beautiful piece," he said finally, pointing to a large pastel hanging on the wall. "Somehow it looks familiar."

"The entrance to Beaux Arts, that big double door. Of course, you would find it familiar. We met there so many times. I tried to recapture the feeling when I was in Paris last year. That kind of dark green lacquer they use on the doors. Almost black, but richer. The wrought iron. And then the light once you enter. It was my doorway, my passage. So long ago. And still useful, that's what was so beautiful to see. The same students, the same smells, the same dreams."

"You made yours come true."

"And you?"

"I don't know. I mean, some of them, yes, sure. My work, that's exciting, you know, rewarding."

"You are a rich man now."

"Yeah." Regret bent his smile downward at the corners. "We had some tough times back then, didn't we? I wish you would let me help you, Sophie."

"But, Kayo, I don't need your help. You can see for yourself. I don't need it and I don't want it."

"But I feel like . . ."

"Like what? Like you owe me something?"

"Yes."

"You do, but it has nothing to do with money, nothing at all."

"What is it, then?"

"You know what it is. Whatever it is brought you here. Grow up and spit it out, for God's sake. You're still waiting for someone to squeeze your cheeks and force you to let go. That's not me. Furthermore, I have no time to sit here and wait."

"Sophie, please, don't get angry with me. Listen to me, please. Last night I was in the Caribbean. It was warm and beautiful and I was sitting under a brilliant night sky in total agony. It was the strangest feeling, to suddenly see things more clearly by the light of darkness. Things I've ignored for years. Please, can't you see how hard it is for me?"

"No, I can't. I'm sorry."

"You are so unforgiving."

"Jean-Jacques accused me of the very same thing. I do not disagree. But is that what you want? Forgiveness?"

"Yes."

"Then you have got to say it."

"I wish you would forgive me, Sophie."

"For what?"

"For everything."

"Oh no, no, no." She laughed and waved one hand in the air, discharging the seriousness of his appeal. "You understand nothing if I forgive everything."

"You want a list?"

"You need specifics."

"Please, Sophie," he said. But when she continued to ignore his self-pity, he straightened up and spoke. "Forgive me for lying, Sophie, for leaving you alone, and for not loving you anymore."

She was surprised at the freshness of her own pain. It was so old, it should have died by now. But it hadn't. It took all her strength to stay calm. "I forgive you, Kayo, for lying. And I forgive you for leaving me the way you did. If that is what you came for, you can go on your way. You are who you are. I am who I am. That principle does not seem to change."

"You still have such a low opinion of me, Sophie?"

"In a few years you will be a man of sixty years. I am only one year younger than you. Yet I feel like an adult and you seem still a child. Maybe it is a lucky protection around you. Something that shields you from pain, from the real pain that compels change. Who am I to say? Maybe you were old when you were still so young and then you reversed, and you grew the other way. I don't know. Maybe I underestimate you. Perhaps this visit is a signal of something new in you. I wish you good luck. You owed me nothing more than this, this meeting face-to-face. A chance to be as honest with each other sitting in the daylight as we were thirty years ago lying together in the dark. It is over. You are free."

"Can you forgive me for not loving you anymore?"

She sipped the cold coffee. The cognac gave it another kind of warmth. She saw a man carrying well-dressed weight, aging but confident, perhaps even arrogant. He seemed to be a man wrestling with a new astronomy, conceding the infinity of the universe; some things beyond his control, but still retaining for himself the sun center of the solar system. Forgive him for no longer shining on her, no longer loving her?

"I'm sorry, Kayo, that is not in my power. We have no control over love. You cannot help who you love. So how can I forgive it?"

"I hope we can be friends, Sophie, if only for the sake of our son."

"Life has many surprises, *n'est-ce pas?* So many things to look forward to." She smiled at the yellow flowers in the vase. Soon these colors would bloom in her garden again.

CHAPTER TWENTY-ONE

"CORKY, good, I'm glad I caught you."

"Nicky! I was just about to lock up. I'm so glad you called. I've been waiting to hear from you for a week. Where are you?"

"At the airport."

"Oh." Corky's voice dropped an octave. "You decided to go back to California?"

"No way. I'm going to Paris."

"What? When did you decide that? What are you . . ."

"Slow down, take it easy. Everything's OK, it's just that I'll be certifiable if I stay cooped up for another minute. Listen, Corky, I want to work. Is it too late for the collections? Do you think I can still get booked?"

Corky took a deep breath. She tried to explain that it wasn't a question of Nicky being booked by the designers in Paris. She was already under exclusive contract to Cleo. She couldn't just run away to Europe and shuck her obligations at home.

Nicky insisted that she knew all that and that she would take full responsibility. But she had nothing scheduled for Cleo for the next two weeks. It couldn't hurt her image to do the shows, she said. On the contrary, all the top girls—including girls with contracts—did the collections. Even music stars like Madonna and Diana Ross. Why couldn't she?

Because, because, Corky found herself stuttering, things just weren't done like that. "You don't seem to understand that you're not just Nicky Knight now. You're the Cleo girl."

"Except that when I freak out, Corky, I freak out as little Nicky Knight. Alone. The Cleo girl doesn't freak out with me. I'm telling you, as Nicky Knight, I need to get out of this place before I'm the next headline."

The kid had a point. Corky decided to take a chance. "OK, this is totally off the record but here's what you do. I'll arrange to have a driver meet you at the airport and he'll take you to a decent hotel. Things are always crazy and crowded with the shows but our travel agent should be able to find something somewhere for you. Now, by the time you check in, the Star agency will be open. I want you to call Monique over there as soon as you can, first thing, very first thing in the morning. I'm going to fax her now so when she gets to the agency tomorrow she'll know you're coming and she can take things from there. Wow, you sure are crazy, kid. What's your dad going to say?"

"He'll blow his stack the same way everyone else will. That's why no one will know until I'm gone."

"Well, I don't know anything. And I won't know anything until I hear from you officially tomorrow, naughty girl."

"Yeah, but aren't they the ones who have all the fun? I've got to run. Thanks for everything. *Ciao.*"

It wasn't until they were actually in the air that Nicky could believe what was happening. She had never done anything like this on her own. Derek had been his cool and quiet self, as usual. No questions asked when she told him to bring along his passport although they were just supposed to be spending the day at museums. No questions asked when she took him shopping at the Gap for clothes and a duffel bag. The first time he asked a question was after they had gotten in a cab and she told the driver to go to Kennedy Airport.

"Who are we going to pick up?"

"Nobody that I know of," Nicky answered.

"So what's this all about?" The day had been long and busy and he didn't feel like playing games.

"We're going to go to Paris."

"Paris, you and me, just as simple as that. Are you out of your mind, Nicky? Do your folks know about this?"

"What folks, Derek? Get real, I'm on my own."

"Except that I'm here with you, and wherever I go my nine-millimeter goes with me. Problem is airports don't really like seeing me and my metal together."

"Shoot, I forgot all about that."

"Well, good, so let's forget all about Paris, too."

"You know, for a moment you sounded just like Mrs. E. Please don't go square on me, Derek." She knocked on the Lucite partition and asked the driver where she could check some luggage and leave it for a few days. He told her that the lost-and-found at Grand Central would hold things for as long as you wanted for two dollars a day. They made a short detour at the railroad station, where they bought a small satchel and stuffed it with books, magazines, newspapers and the gun. After depositing it with the clerk, they headed unarmed for the Midtown Tunnel and Kennedy.

Now their bags lay snugly in the overhead bin of the 747 and Nicky had unlaced her Doc Martens. When they woke up, they'd be in Paris. She told Derek they'd have to hit the ground running. Well, he said, he was used to maneuvers, and, to tell the truth, he liked them better without the uniform.

When the stewardess came around with champagne, Nicky took two glasses for herself and proposed a toast, "To flights of fancy."

Derek clenched his jaw, reminding himself that he was still on duty even at 35,000 feet in the air. Somebody had to keep a cool head. Maybe the champagne would help her relax. She couldn't overdo it as long as he kept her in sight. And he fully intended to keep her there. It seemed to him that the only person she needed to be protected from right now was herself.

Nicky tried to control her squirming but the upholstered swivel chair was too much of a temptation after sitting still on the plane for so long. On the other side of her paper-cluttered desk Monique, the head booker at the Star agency, kept smoking and talking animatedly on the phone. But after almost fifteen minutes Monique had yet to say more than a cursory *bonjour* to her.

What was Nicky, invisible? What could she do? Star was MacLean's sister agency in Paris. She couldn't exactly stomp out, which is exactly what she felt like doing. She'd have to wait it out.

Five white round-faced clocks lined up across the wall nearest the other bookers' desks gave the time in Los Angeles, New York, London, Paris and Tokyo. It was 9:55 A.M. in Paris and only 3:55 A.M. in New York. She felt grouchy and jet-lagged, barely able to understand what Monique was saying when she finally did start talking to her. Maybe it was not such a smart move to come to Paris at the last minute like this, she was saying.

Drawing heavily on her cigarette, Monique pushed back in her chair, removed her dark glasses and looked intently at Nicky. *"S'il vous plaît,* walk for me."

She knew Monique meant something more than putting one foot in front of the other and not falling down. But she didn't know what. Her jeans suddenly felt too tight, her turtleneck too funky, her jacket too wrinkled. But Nicky managed to walk across the room toward Derek and back. The look on Monique's face told her that she'd failed that test.

"You have done the shows before?" Monique asked.

"Not really."

"Not really or not at all?" Monique insisted.

"Not at all," Nicky conceded.

"How convenient that Corky says nothing about that in her fax," she muttered, and lit another cigarette. "*Encore, chérie,* do it again, the walk. This time you take your blazer off halfway, OK?"

Nicky tried. She tried to put more bounce in her step, more glide in her stride, but the more she did that, the more ridiculous she knew she looked. Then she tried to take off the jacket, removing each arm in careful slow motion from each sleeve. But something snagged in the lining and one sleeve of the jacket turned inside out and trailed along the bright black floor while she struggled with the other one. It was a complete fiasco. Everybody saw. Derek, the other bookers, plus a couple of models who were just checking in. Everyone saw and no one said a word.

Nicky sat down with tears of frustration burning in her eyes. Monique ran both hands through her short hennaed hair before she spoke. "*Chérie,* it is only one week before the collections." Her voice weighed heavy with discouragement. "All the shows are already booked, of course. You are late and also not, ah . . . prepared. But we cannot say no to MacLean." She went on to explain all the little accidents that could happen that might work on Nicky's behalf. After all, this was not the couture where the clothes are made to fit a specific model. Prêt-à-porter meant just that: ready-to-wear by anyone of a standard size. But, she had to speak frankly, being a Black model had its limitations. Some designers loved to use Black girls but others were not so . . . enthusiastic. She hoped Nicky would understand. Nevertheless, she would send Nicky to see all the designers on the Chambre *syndicale's* list and also to all the magazines. Even if she didn't do a lot of shows, she might win some good editorial and that would mean even better mileage. But, Monique insisted, Nicky would have to help herself. "This is Paris, Nicky, the capital of fashion. You must always look your best, your clothes and makeup. Pretty is not enough. You must also have style. Learn to walk, *chérie*. And always be on your best behavior. Control yourself. I make no promises. But you do your best for me and I do my best for you, *d'accord?*"

Nicky nodded. She had so much to learn.

"I can't believe you're actually here!" Nadja hugged Nicky in the doorway. "Let me look at you." Just then the stairwell light went out.

"What's happening?" Derek asked, ever on the alert.

"Don't worry, that's just the system," said Nadja. "Look." She pointed to a button glowing in the wall. "You just push a little switch to turn the hall light on, then it's timed to go off automatically. Generally, it gives you enough time to get up the stairs and inside your apartment. But this is a steep climb. Sorry about the six flights. The main thing is you're here. Come on in."

She introduced her roommate, Valerie, whose dramatic eyebrows and full, sexy lips Nicky recognized from the fashion magazines. Contrary to the painfully thin brows now in fashion, Valerie insisted on keeping hers naturally thick, glossy and insolently arched. Nicky liked that attitude and liked her right away. She introduced Derek as they took seats in the cozy living room. Exposed wooden beams crossed the low ceiling and pastel silk scarves muted the lamplight, making them feel as if they were in another century.

"It's just what I pictured, Nadja. Just what I thought it would be."

"You're such a romantic, Nicky. I'm glad you like it, but please, make yourselves at home. Aren't you absolutely exhausted? Tell me what you'd like to drink: juice, water, Coke, or are you ready to be terribly French and have some wine? Tell me quickly," she said, heading out of the living room toward the kitchen, "because I want to hear all about how your first day went." When Nicky and Derek both decided on spring water, Nadja returned with tall glasses, a liter of Evian and a plate of tiny hot quiches.

"I don't know where to start. The hotel is very nice."

"I love it! She calls the Plaza-Athénée very nice, Val. It's only one of the grander places on the planet."

"I know. I feel like I have to get all dressed up just to sit on my own toilet. OK, it's great, I admit it."

"Well, please excuse the dire poverty of two working girls in Paris," said Val with a smile.

"Who just happen to keep a place in Paris all year 'round 'cause they're booked every season for as many shows as they can handle. Dire poverty, my behind," Nicky snorted. "To have your very own apartment with a terrace and a view of the Arch of Triumph! I'd trade places with you any day."

"Any day?" Val teased.

"OK, except for the next ten." They all laughed, easily, knowingly.

"OK, next," Nadja said, "the agency?"

"A horror show. I totally flunked. Imagine, I get to the agency, I've got no makeup on, she's suffocating me with cigarette smoke and then she tells me to walk. A complete disaster, but Monique set up all these, what do you call them here? Castings. Starting tomorrow. You know I can't say a word about the Cleo campaign."

"You can't, but don't worry, everybody who needs to know will find out. For work, I mean. For the rest . . ."

"You know something, Nadja? I'm not afraid like I was before. As soon as I decided to *do* something, I felt good. And as soon as I left New York, I felt even better."

"I'm glad about that, but you've still got to be careful." Nadja was never far from a serious note. "Paris is no kind of paradise for Black people. Or even Black models, no matter what the fashion propaganda says. And you're such a special case. If *you* can hop a plane, so can . . ."

"Don't talk to me about it anymore, OK?" Nicky cried out. "Don't you think I torture myself enough? If this, if that? Can't I get through one day, just one day?"

Everyone was astonished at Nicky's outburst. No matter what she'd said so confidently about feeling better and not feeling afraid, it was clear that she was fragile and emotionally unstable. Her fears and nightmares had traveled with her.

"I'm sorry, Nadja. Gosh, Val, you must think I'm crazy. I don't know what happens to me sometimes. It just pours out."

They all hastened to reassure her that it was nothing to apologize for.

"I thought I'd already lost as much of my mind as I could. But after Max, I just couldn't sit around and wait for something else to happen. That's why I'm here and that's why I brought daredevil Derek along, right?" Nicky tried to smile the mood away.

Derek had never heard himself described as a daredevil before, but he liked it and nodded in agreement.

"Is it your first time here?" Nadja asked him, trying to keep the conversation light.

"Very first."

"And it might as well be my first time," Nicky added. "My mother brought me here a few years ago but I wasn't really paying attention. She spoke French and knew everything and I just sorta tagged along behind her." Her voice shifted to a quieter register. "I miss her so much. I never thought I'd be able to say that without breaking down."

"It gets easier," Nadja said softly. "Not really better, but a little easier."

Val helped to change the mood again and keep Nicky focused on the future. They chatted about places to go, landmarks to visit, exhibits to see. And shopping, which was according to her the best therapy in the world.

"Listen," Nicky asked, "is it just my imagination or does every department store in the world sell cosmetics on the ground floor?"

"It's not your imagination, just good business," said Nadja. "It also happens to be the one you're in, remember?"

"Just another brainless mo-dell, what can I say? But we did go to the Galeries Lafayette."

"What'd you buy?"

"This long tight black skirt that I don't know how to walk in. I'm so used to short stuff. Some fabulous black leather jeans. A half a dozen pairs of panty hose and two pairs of heels, you know, regular grown-up lady shoes. Monique said I'd better practice. I could read jungle bunny flashing in her eyes."

"She's right but don't let it scare you," said Val.

"There's so much to see everywhere. It blows me away."

"Well, it's supposed to. Make the rounds now, because after the madness of castings and fittings and shows, I guarantee that all you'll want to do is slip into your baggiest clothes and go pig out somewhere. Speaking of eating, aren't you hungry? I thought we'd have dinner right in the neighborhood. Nothing fancy, just your typical five-thousand-calorie French meal."

"I can't gain an ounce, Nadja. I'm scared I won't fit into any of the clothes."

"I'm just teasing. I'm the one who's over twenty-five, I'm the one who has to worry. You haven't even finished growing yet."

"That's just what I'm afraid of."

"We should all be so frightened, *ma belle.*"

"Ma Bell, I forgot, I should call home. What time is it?"

"It's almost eight here, so that means it's two in the afternoon in New York and eleven in the morning in L.A."

"Oh, boy, which dragon should I try first, the East Coast or the West?"

"Leave us out of this one. Come on, Derek, let me show you the view. Give my love to everyone."

"No fair, you're abandoning me in my hour of need."

Nadja laughed and handed Nicky the phone. She decided to call Kyle Whitaker first. Somewhere she thought she remembered hearing that he attended the collections. Although he had a pretty easygoing sense of humor, he might not appreciate bumping into her over here. Like, Hi, Kyle, fancy meeting you here. She didn't think that would work at all.

Spring came sooner in Paris than in New York. It was only the second week in March and the air was already mild enough for cotton clothes during the day. The sight of young green leaves made Nicky ache for her mother. She felt foolish for having wasted the time she and Becky spent together a few years ago in Paris. That time could never be repeated. And Becky would never see springtime again. Nicky wanted to soak up as much as she could of the city, let nothing slip by her this time.

The night was cool, though, and damp, as Nicky and Derek walked from Nadja's apartment on the Rue de l'Etoile down the gentle slope of the Champs-Elysées. The city's scale was so changeable. They passed from tiny dark streets through which one small car could barely squeeze to the wide-open space of the Champs-Elysées, with its three lanes of traffic speeding in opposite directions and cars and motorcycles creeping up even onto the sidewalks.

The Elysian Fields. Broadway in New York City was so typically American, Nicky thought, a practical name for a big, busy street. But to name a street after a neighborhood in paradise? That took either tremendous pride or a love of poetry, and probably a crazy combination of both. It was glorious, though, this boulevard, and since they had walked it twice in their first day, she felt as if they knew it, as if it was starting to belong to them.

Not that they wanted to own it. Some of the shops were downright tacky, although a few of them were nice. Still they were nothing compared to those on the elegant side streets. It was not Nicky's desire to possess things. It was the experience which she wanted to absorb.

Everything was so breathtakingly new. When they turned around in the middle of a traffic island and looked back at the Arc de Triomphe, glowing majestically alone against the midnight sky, all they could do was stop and stare. Like hayseed tourists. That's the feeling she wanted to swallow and digest. She wanted things to settle down.

From the Champs-Elysées they passed shops glittering like pirate chests with expensive clothes and jewels. Walking past ornate apartment buildings they gazed on lavish chandeliers sparkling from regal ceilings. If the streets were not paved with gold, the buildings lining them seemed to be. Extravagant privilege spread before them like a magic carpet.

The walk was also a decent stretch of exercise, almost enough to shake them out of dinner's red wine daze. Not nearly enough to make Nicky feel less guilty about the basket of crusty bread chunks she had wolfed down with her pâté and veal cutlet. The restaurant was wonderful, good food, good service without the sissified put-on or the snobbish put-down she'd somehow come to expect from the French. This was turning out to be a very different trip.

Nicky slipped her arm through Derek's. "How're you doing?"

"I'm OK. How're you doing?"

"I'm OK, but I meant, what were you really thinking about?"

"Nothing."

"Please don't do that to me, Derek. Talk to me, I know you're thinking something."

"OK, I'm just wondering how this is going to go. I mean, your father hired me to protect you, not to be your friend."

"Is it so hard to be my friend?"

"No, but I can do my job for you without it. I don't have a problem being a hired gun. I do have a problem being a hired friend. This world you live in, I don't know, I would never meet people like you. And you would never meet someone like me. I mean, I feel like I need bank clearance just to walk on these sidewalks. This level of luxury is just plain new to me. It's a lot for me to handle."

"Maybe you're getting a little too analytical about the whole thing. I think it's all going to work out just fine." She stumbled against him. "Excuse me, maybe I had a little too much to drink."

"Is that, uh, getting to be a habit?"

"What do you mean, Derek?" She straightened up quickly.

"The wine, the Valium."

"The doctor prescribed them," she said defensively. "I need them in order to sleep. I need them."

"And the wine?"

"*You* might not know it, but wine is a sign of sophistication."

"Like falling out of bed drunk? Is that a sign of sophistication, too?

"I don't have to listen to this." She walked quickly ahead of him.

He caught up and stood in front of her, blocking her way. "That's right, you don't have to listen, because you already know it. Deep inside you're still scared of what's going on. And you ought to be, Nicky. All I'm saying is don't you make the job any easier for the lunatic who's out there. I can't do it all. You have to help take care of yourself, too."

"I'm trying, Derek. I'm trying so hard." And hot little tears burned tracks down her face as they walked into the quiet crystal majesty of the Plaza-Athénée's lobby.

Upstairs the two connecting rooms appeared slightly less enormous than they had earlier in the day. Familiarity had rearranged expectations so that what had been too grand before now seemed somehow appropriate. Antique lamps filled the luxurious space with the charm of candlelight. The covers had been turned down to reveal fine linen sheets. Fresh fruit in a crystal bowl and tiny chocolates in a dish sat on the marble-topped chests next to each bed.

"I'm exhausted," Nicky said, flopping immediately onto the bed in her room. By the time Derek came out of his bathroom with his shirt off she had thrown her clothes on an armchair and was snuggling under the covers.

"Aren't you going to check your messages?" Derek asked, pointing to the phone's blinking light.

"You do it."

"Don't you want to wash up?"

She shook her head lazily. "I can't move another step."

"Come on, I'll help you. You'll feel better with a little cold water on your face."

"You have a nice chest, Derek. I bet you have a lot of nice things about you."

He went into her bathroom and returned with a thick, hot facecloth and hand towel. "Here," he said sternly, "at least wipe your face with this. And you'd better stop talking like that. I lay a finger on you and my ass is grass and you know it."

"Look, but don't touch. I'm lonely, Derek."

"And I'm sorry. But that's not part of my job."

He sat down at the desk in her room and called the hotel operator, who gave him three messages, one each from Corky, Tina and Kayo. Nicky insisted that she did not want to talk to anyone again tonight. When she'd called everyone earlier she told them that she was fine. Well, she was still fine, but now she was also exhausted.

Derek was, too. His good night to her got no response beyond a heavy liquid breathing. He removed the key from the mini-bar in her room, turned out the lights and locked the door between their rooms. He did not know if he could trust her, but he knew for certain that he could not trust himself. As he got into bed the smooth, cool sheets shocked him but his erection returned in seconds. In the luxury of darkness, solitude and silence, he could not deny what he felt. He wanted to press against her, press into her warmth, deep into the damp warmth of her lips and beyond. Instead his hand became hers, became her, and he came and shrank and came again and was glad all the while that she could not hear what she was doing to him.

It was a good thing she had practiced in those god-awful high heels. You had to be able to walk in any and everything and do it all on a runway that stretched a block, it seemed to Nicky, in front of hundreds of powerful invisible people and bleachers full of TV cameras, and dozens of still photographers, lapping at the edge of the catwalk like eager piglets, panting and oinking whenever it looked like a tit would fall out of a décolletage or a jacket would fail to glide off easily or something else wild and unpredictable would happen.

She was new and all she wanted to do was a good job. She wasn't at the point where she could cause a ruckus like the model Monique told her about. Last season a top girl had stepped clear out of her spikes, right on the runway, and carried them on the tips of her fingers along with an insouciant smile while she paraded in an impeccable black satin dinner suit. Many of the buyers and press in the audience had laughed sympathetically. They knew that pain firsthand. But word had it that the model, as hot as she was, worked only in Milan now. Her boyfriend lived there, so it was not total exile. But the message was clearly sent and clearly received. A model could always make fun of herself, but never of a designer.

Nicky knew better than that. She was determined to make the outfits she wore look great to the audience steaming in the darkness. Her first show for Yohji had been easy. Flat shoes and boots, loose clothes, the most fun in black one could possibly have even though smiles were not allowed. Little rag dolls sewn onto long dresses and coats, soft, strangely cut-and-tied bohemian garb. His fans showed appreciation in their eager applause. She felt at home. It was easy and fun.

She liked being around so many other models. There were dozens of girls as tall as or taller than she was. Lean and quiet or lean and loud, telling dirty jokes in the nude in several languages at once, or merely laughing at them while smoking and drinking and catching up on the latest. The Cleo shoots had been so lonely. She was the only star. Here the camaraderie was instantaneous. Even if the girls didn't know each other as individuals, they knew they all had to be stars just to get here, to be seen in this privileged light. And not just in front of one rather small crew. The collections took place in multimedia Sensurround with a cast and crew of thousands and an eventual audience of millions.

She was thrilled when she got booked to do Chanel. It was the hot ticket in town and she was a newcomer unused to the company of the established queens. But one of them had gotten sick and Karl Lagerfeld had liked her enough to take a major chance, Monique explained. The fitting was suspenseful. Would she fit the clothes? Could she walk in them? The way Mr. Lagerfeld wanted it done? The session was less intimidating than she feared. He liked her. He liked what she did to the clothes. She would be brilliant, he said.

She had five outfits: two tweedy day suits with the classic jacket, one coat, one day dress and one evening dress. Numbered in order of their appearance, they hung from a tubular rack on wheels with a shopping bag containing shoes, hose, scads of jewelry and other accessories attached to each outfit's hanger. Each of the three dozen or so models had her own clothes rack, labeled with her name, a dresser to help her change quickly in and out of the clothes, a plastic chair to sit on in front of maybe three square feet of table space—for makeup and hair tools—leading up to however much mirror space you could grab. She quickly got her bearings. For some things you had to sit down, but for others you had to stand up for yourself and stake out your territory.

Nicky reveled in the backstage chaos of people and clothes and tempers and, above all, dreams. But nothing about behind-the-scenes was fantasy. Nothing was plush. Not even out front. When Monique had told her that the shows took place at the Louvre, for some reason she imagined elegant runways in marble hallways among masterful works of art. Nobody had mentioned anything about tents. That's where the shows actually took place, inside one of three huge canvas tents erected in a cobblestoned courtyard of the Louvre Palace, blocks from the actual museum. Each tent had a runway and viewing stands, and, in the back, a large communal dressing room. Nicky found the contrast between the fancy clothes and the drab environment astounding. No wonder models were so blasé. They saw the topside and the underside of the dream and made it all appear seamless.

Two hours before the show tension was already building. Some girls, she knew, would be running in late, coiffed and painted, panting from other shows just ending in nearby tents. They would have to be redone according to Chanel's specifications. Others, like Nicky, were already half-dressed and dabbling in more makeup, prepping for the first outfit, checking the accessories, or smoking and joking around.

She didn't realize that White girls needed so much time to work on their hair. Wasn't it already straight? Wasn't that the battle? Now she saw that was only half of it. The other half required time and energy to blow it out with powerful hair dryers wielded like trick firearms. Time and patience to set it on plastic rollers as big as beer cans. Time and dexterity to tease, muss and spray it. And pray that it stayed shiny, gorgeous and, to the outside world, naturally carefree. Compared to all that, her short wavy do was a breeze.

As the time wound down a kind of calm settled in. This was it. No retakes, no retouching, no one last roll. This was all the way live. They were dressed now. Her high heel workouts had come in handy and so did practice in her long skirt. Skirts were all up and down the leg this season and walking in the long ones took some getting used to. As did the platform shoes. But she was ready. Anxiety was under control. The lineup was numbered and orderly. As the show was about to begin, she saw that she had winners before her and winners after her. That meant she had to be one herself.

Then the music blared, a hip Euro-techno beat, and the lights came up, and the girls started peeling off, like parachutists into a gorgeous sky. Mr. Lagerfeld was the last one to check her. Behind dark glasses his eyes were unseen. But after he loosened the brace of gold chains and pearl necklaces she wore and after he pulled a spit curl farther down on her forehead, he tapped her on the shoulder with his fan, said *"Bella"* and sent her off.

And there she was. Out front, onstage, in a bad-ass, drop-dead group of four, variations on a theme, moving it, working it, loving that stretch, then that smooth flowing turn and then that singular moment when she was the only one to capture the fat black lenses at the end of the runway. At the end—or maybe the beginning—of the rainbow.

After the first dive, the rest was easy. Out there on her own, then down the long and glorious road to the pulse now of a funky James Brown tune, to the click and whir of cameras, and the silent thoughts of those in the dark watching, counting, never blinking. She had to take the blue jacket off. She managed. Her moves were not perfect, but she was not embarrassed. Attitude was crucial. Easy, elegant, confident. Not the grotesque bitcheries that made some models caricatures of women. The flapping wrists and the side-slit eyes. The cold-shoulder roll of the girl who passed just a little too close to her right in front of the cameras. Nicky's aloof determination said none of this can faze me. And none of it did.

She was untouchable, in the rhythm now, throwing her hips forward, defying gravity, exaggerating the slink, especially in the strapless black leather evening dress which she wore at the finale. There the girls lined up on the runway in their last, most dazzling outfits and smiling, finally, applauded the designer in unison with the cheering audience. Karl

Lagerfeld bounced out with a nervous grin on his face, his sleek gray ponytail slightly disheveled, his fan open and fluttering and oddly appropriate. It was all fabulous fun.

And then it was over. Backstage was instantly mobbed by well-wishers speaking in a dozen languages. The models changed back into their jeans or, if they were regulars, into their own Chanel ensembles. A head taller than everyone else, they stalked with impassive arrogance through the crowd, which drank champagne and bubbled with congratulations down below. This job was over. On to the next.

Nicky had no next, but she didn't feel deprived. Although she'd done only two shows, during that same time she'd also shot two editorial spreads, one for French *Vogue* and one for American *Elle*. She'd get a few decent tear sheets when they came out in a few months. Not that she really needed them, she thought, except to establish her credentials to herself as a working model, not just a lucky kid.

But a feeling of panic suddenly seized her. Whenever something too wonderful had happened to her, some horrible disaster soon followed. She would never get a chance to relax and really enjoy her success. Not even here in Paris where she had grown to feel more secure. Trembling, she searched the different compartments of her makeup case for a Valium. She breathed a sigh of relief when she found a dusty pill at the bottom. Within minutes she was starting to feel calm again.

With Derek at her side she left the Louvre feeling the euphoric relief of an opening night without the pressure of a repeat performance. Outside in the rocky courtyard students besieged their favorite models for autographs. She wondered if that would ever happen to her. A tap on the shoulder startled her.

"Fabulous, but I still think we should sue."

"Kyle!" She turned and laughed. "What a wonderful surprise."

"My wife, Esmé." They shook hands, genuinely pleased to meet each other.

"You've been a bad girl, Nicky," Kyle said, shaking his finger in her face. "Vanessa Seymour wants your head on a platter. And I must admit, she wasn't the only one. If you hadn't called me first she would have come over here to collect it personally."

"I'm sorry, Kyle. I've been trying to explain this to everyone.

Things were just getting to be too much for me."

"Well, you have your biggest fan in Esmé. She's the one who really helped me understand. She's seen it all."

Nicky looked more closely at Kyle's wife. She was tiny, with a cap of curly brown hair and eyes so pale gray they seemed disturbingly transparent. Nicky knew the story of the plane crash and she sensed that behind her frail appearance lay a tenacious strength. "Thank you," she said humbly.

Kyle continued, "You have enough experience with Vanessa, though, to know that excuses won't work with her. She will make you pay."

"She's already doing that. She calls me every day at the agency *and* the hotel. Why, Kyle? What terrible thing did I do to tarnish the image of the Cleo girl?"

"That's not the point. You disobeyed orders."

"And I should be punished for maybe saving my life? I just don't get it."

"Well, don't worry about it while you're here. Which is how long, by the way?"

"Another couple of days."

"I'll round up Smitty and Corky and keep the bucket brigade going long enough to squelch any fires until you get back. But once you're back, don't say I didn't warn you. Don't worry, Nicky. *We* still love you. But business is business."

CHAPTER TWENTY-TWO

HE WAS only supposed to be in for observation. That's what the medical personnel kept telling him. The fluid in the lungs was not really anything to worry about. They wanted to adjust his medications in a controlled environment. Nothing unusual, Mr. Thompson, the surgeons said. And the nurses and the assistants and the aides. Just routine checks to make sure that everything was all right. It was the casual way they spoke that irked him. The prostate scare he'd had five years ago shocked him into annual physicals and closer ties to his doctors. But it had been just a scare and he'd emerged more convinced than ever that he was invincible. After a lifetime of never being sick he saw no reason to start now. Death would just snatch him by surprise one day, conk him over the head as casually as he might crush an ant underfoot on the sidewalk. Crunch, and it would all be over. None of this prolonged deterioration for him. If he'd known the pain of recovery would be so intense he might not have bargained with God to save him. Now he had to fight in ways he was not used to. Delegating authority to assistants and secretaries could do nothing to help him here. Here he was on his own.

Except for Clarice. She was his anchor and his inspiration, the one who kept him rooted in reality and yet ready to dream at inspiration's cue. She soothed and challenged him, broke the old rules and wrote new ones. He'd watched her charm his daughter and his friends, his staff and even

Mrs. English, whom she insisted on calling Mona, as if they could be equals. She had reconciled him with a younger part of himself that had never grown old. It was an unexpected combination and an unexpected time of his life to be feeling these urgent flashes of desire for living.

She should be here by now. The heavy Rolex sliding around his wrist said it was past nine-thirty. He was being released this morning. Finally. He wheeled his chair over to the window. Where was she? Nothing could happen to her. Not now. He was finally getting the priorities of his life back in order and he wanted to spend what time he had left with her.

How different she was. A self-made woman who chose to devote herself to him. Not like Ella, who had wanted to give herself to the world in general, but not to him as her husband, as a man.

Back in the dark old days, he remembered, before Black women were allowed to be salesclerks behind the counters in department stores, Skippy had told him about "the most adorable little Colored girl" who ran an elevator at Macy's. One summer day he had ridden up and down in her elevator half a dozen times before they were alone together and he could talk. When he picked her up from work a few evenings later, he was pleasantly surprised to learn that she had just graduated from Hunter College at age twenty. That pleasure was short-lived, though, when she confided that she really wanted to sing.

"That's no life for a beautiful, intelligent girl. You've got an education. You could teach," he said, struggling to keep his eyes off her and on the late-afternoon traffic which all seemed headed, as they were, toward the oasis of City Island and its seafood restaurants. "You could find a nice secure position for yourself. Then you wouldn't be like most of our girls, sitting around looking pretty and waiting to be rescued."

"I don't want to be rescued," Ella stated firmly. "I want to be discovered."

She was not kidding. Neither was she unprepared. She had her teacher's license and a school assignment in September, but she was counting on her summer job at Macy's to make other things happen. "Somebody's going to take one look at me and my whole life will change. Don't laugh," she insisted. "I know it can happen. Wasn't Paul Laurence

Dunbar discovered on an elevator in Dayton, Ohio? And he might have been a wonderful poet, maybe even the greatest poet of our race, but he sure wasn't easy to look at. And see what happened to him!" And when she threw that radiant smile at him all he could do was be happy to catch it.

The truth was, unlike Paul Laurence Dunbar, Ella McKinley was extremely easy to look at. What she couldn't do was sing. Thomas Thompson tried, against his own experienced instinct, to help her in the business, to get his friends to help her. But they were too professional to lie, even to him, especially once they saw that he really cared about her. She was an attractive woman, Skippy said, and everyone agreed, attractive with a sweet voice, but a voice without a shred of originality, distinction or conviction.

What she lacked in talent, however, she more than made up for in determination. "What does Lena Horne have that I don't have? What does Josephine Baker have that I don't have? I have what it takes. I know it. I just need somebody to believe in me, Thomas, and then I can do it all," she told him with complete confidence.

It surprised him that while he didn't exactly believe in her, he did want to protect and support her. And so he married her, bought her new clothes and one-night appearances at his friends' clubs uptown. Even bought her a ticket to Los Angeles to visit her sister who did extra work in the movies. "So I can see for myself. If Evelyn can do it, I mean she's cute and all, but . . ." And Ella let it be understood that there could be as little comparison between their looks as there could be between their eventual success.

He even took her to Paris and left her there for two months on her own, at her insistence and the couturiers', to see what she could do in the café society over there. But when she came home to New York she was different. A kind of fire in her had been doused and with it some private dream. Not exactly eager but at least apparently willing to put all that performing business behind her, she settled down with a tart-tongued practical grace to accept her fate of being the wife of one of the wealthiest Black men in the country. With her air of dimpled innocence, she eked out recriminations in quiet little jokes. And a Scotch-slurred litany of what-ifs curdled, but never completely ruined, more than one perfect dinner party.

"What if I were brown-skinned with kinky hair?" she'd asked one evening. "Then people wouldn't have been so intent on criticizing me for every little thing. They say, If you're light, you're all right. I say light is a fight day and night."

She took to scathing social commentary like a newborn politician, and claimed that if she was poor and downtrodden and knew nothing but honky-tonk songs, she would have had more success. Just another big-butt 'Bama with a bawdy-house style. People didn't believe a Colored woman could sing a love song without grunting all the way through it, she complained. Sadly, she was not the one to show them any better alternative.

It was always someone else's fault that she had not become a star. One night as they applauded a performance by Sarah Vaughan, Ella had asked their table of friends, "What if I'd found a man who wanted me to shine, not someone who wanted to keep me locked up and quiet and all to himself? I could have been like Sarah. I could have been somebody with somebody else."

She was the kind of woman who lived for an audience, even if it was not a star turn. Alone with Thomas, she said little. He learned more about her in her public confessions than through the shared intimacies he had expected. She told stories in public whose anguish wounded him deeply the first time he heard them. But once he understood her habits and learned the stories by heart, he saw that if no one else would cast her, she would cast herself in a perpetually beautiful and tragic role.

"Tell them, Kayo," she had said at a party celebrating one of his concert successes, "tell them what you said about me when you were starving in Paris. You won't believe this, Becky, really, it's just too funny. You know, I had Diors, I had Balenciagas, I had gorgeous gowns to the floor, exquisite things. At first they didn't even want to sell me their clothes. But once I had them on, what could they do? They saw it as plain as the nose on their face. I was just a little Colored woman to them, but once I put their outfits on, something happened. My style elevated theirs. I made them look even better. But what did the people say about me behind my back? White people who didn't know any better *and* Black people who should have. The best-dressed Colored woman in Paris and they said I had style but no soul. A Black woman with no soul. Isn't that the funniest thing you ever heard? I mean, there's no such animal. It just doesn't exist. How the hell could they know anything about my soul? Any of them?"

And when she laughed her poignant, bitter laugh, their friends were kind enough not to let her laugh alone.

Thomas had been resilient. A marriage was a deal. And a deal was a deal. The only part that pained him was the private. A man used to living in public did not examine painful issues out there. Or anywhere, really. It was a matter of swallowing the bitter with the sweet. Getting your priorities straight. No one was perfect and love did not last forever. It hurt, but it was nothing to cry over.

It hurt that after that first trip to Paris never again did her legs spring open at his touch, did her arms grasp him tightly, her lips whisper God and his name in the same breath. Each time he had to winch her open. Afterward, she would clamp shut with a dutiful sigh, and sometimes a dutiful smile until the next time he wanted her. She never really refused him, but she never invited him in either. When their daughter, Christina, came, the child bound them together as a family and separated them completely as individuals. Yet to the outside world they were the perfect couple for thirty years.

In his drive to succeed in business Thomas N. Thompson had forgotten what it was like to be wanted, to be passionately desired, to be stroked to a panting hardness. Clarice had retuned him to forgotten melodies. Now it was his turn to sing. Not in public, seeking others' applause. But for himself, out of the happiness of loving and being loved again. He was more than ready when she came bringing her smile of springtime into the winter of his life.

"Hello, darling, I'm sorry to be late." Clarice was still breathing heavily from rushing through the hospital corridors. She knew how he hated to wait. Lucas followed close behind her. "The traffic to Harlem and back was just terrible. Are you ready?"

"I am. And you?" She nodded yes. "Where's the good reverend?"

"Waiting in the car."

"Well, Lucas, don't expect me to leap out of here in a single bound. Get me and this daggone wheelchair to the car and get me home."

Although Tina could not bring herself to say that she loved him, she did admit that she admired her father. Even if Thomas N. Thompson were not her father, she would still admire him. His dignity, his pride, his disciplined old-fashioned standards. Three days after being released from the hospital, he'd asked her to come over. To take care of some business, he said.

Here he was, thinner, but still formal, dressed in navy silk pajamas and a maroon dressing gown with a dark paisley ascot tucked between quilted satin lapels. His dusty silver hair, freshly trimmed in a close schoolboy cut, made him look curiously youthful. He insisted on receiving her in the library of his apartment where he was already seated behind the leather-topped writing table which he always claimed belonged to Frederick Douglass when he edited *The North Star* in Rochester over a century ago. Outside the door sat a wheelchair, a polished reminder of how some things had changed.

Inside, still other changes were taking place. The fireplace warmed the weathered oak timbers of his face and hands while he read. His voice was low, slow and steady. When he finished, he laid the two white sheets of paper down on the desk and said, "It's all yours." He had resigned as chairman of Aura.

"Thank you." Tina got up from her chair and hugged him gently. "Thank you for trusting me, Dad. You won't regret it."

"Of course I won't," he said, patting her on the back. "The thought of the old man charging back to stick his finger in the dike will be enough to . . ."

"To what?"

"To make you do exceedingly well. I'm not going to worry about the business anymore. I can't."

"I'm glad to hear you say it."

"Well, you saw what it took. I might have gone on forever. I don't quite mean forever, but I could have lived the rest of my life in a comfortable, well-padded rut. I'm so glad I got a chance to get out. Alive.

I want you to think about that, too, Tina. We all have our ruts. Paved with the best intentions in the world. Don't let Aura hypnotize you into thinking that work is life. Work is only a part of life. Don't neglect the other parts like I did. Don't wait too long for happiness. Your heart's happiness. That's the only thing that makes hard work worthwhile."

Tina was amazed to hear her father talking this way. Money had always been his only measure of success. If business was good, life was good, he liked to say. What also amazed her was her own heavy investment in that equation. Personal happiness seemed so complicatd to her, as if it required special skills beyond the executive abilities she had worked so hard to perfect. She listened to her father preach. She didn't mind. He had a right to. He'd been to the mountaintop while she was still climbing.

One day she would risk bringing up the old sore subject. But today was not that day. It was time for a truce, for healing and looking toward the future.

"It's been like a constant interrogation in my own home, Smitty. I don't understand it. I'm the one who gets the damn flower delivery and yet I'm the one who's got to do all the explaining."

Raleigh Smith leaned against the rounded edge of Vanessa Seymour's rosewood desk as she continued to describe the police investigations into what was now being called the Cleo case. Three days ago a box of thirteen red roses was waiting for her at her apartment building along with a card that read, "You're next, nigger lover."

"Question, questions and still more questions. The same thing over and over again. The craziest details. Family and friends and personal stuff which is none of their damn business!" She leaned back in her navy leather armchair and blew a stream of smoke into the air before she crushed her cigarette out.

In a strangely objective way, Smitty sympathized with her, but he was not about to hold her hand, which is what her newly peevish tone suggested. Just the opposite, in fact. That morning he'd begun planning ways to approach telling her that she needed to take some time off. Her nerves were shot, and understandably so. She was in a state of shock and unable to concentrate on her work the way she needed to. A break from the pressure would do wonders for her. As much time as she needed, two weeks, two months, whatever. He had carefully rehearsed a polite presentation, one that was sensitive and suggestive, but also one that gave her no real choice.

But when he told her, she exploded.

"You can't do this to me. You can't just take me off these accounts."

"If you're jeopardizing the relationship with our clients, you'd better believe I can," he insisted. "Something's happening to you . . ."

"Damn right, something's happening to me."

"I'm trying to help you, Vanessa. Now is not the time to be belligerent."

"I don't mean to be, Smitty." Her voice was panicking, breaking on the verge of tears. "I just want you to understand what's really happening to me. Please. That note? Don't you see, Smitty? It's all these Black people. They're too many, too much trouble. I always told you it wouldn't work. You've got to call the campaign off . . ."

"That's absolutely out of the question. You don't know what you're saying, Vanessa."

"I *do* know. Nigger lover? I have that in my own family. Things no one ever talked about. You're a southerner. You know what color means."

"Color means nothing to me, Vanessa," he said coolly.

"Oh, you're so liberal, you're so evolved. You can say that now. But you know very well what I mean. You know." She reached over her desk and picked up the sterling bud vase that held a single spray of waxy white orchids. She replaced it carefully in its original spot. "It's not so easy being White, when Black is just a generation or two away. When you've been taught all your life that Black is everything that's poor and pitiful and ugly. And you stumble on a photograph that nobody says anything about. And you learn that you've got sides to your family that don't talk to each other, that *can't* talk because somebody on one side lynched somebody on the other. And an old picture—black and white, now faded to brown—is all that's left of someone from the other side and that someone is your mother's mother. It's not so easy when you've been brought up in complete safety and complete silence. Can you feel what I feel, Smitty? Nobody ever told. Can you see how some things could really tear me up inside?"

Poor Vanessa, he thought. She was tortured by ghosts of the past, but she was still feeding them, still keeping them alive. "I can see. And I'm sorry to hear it. But you need help, Vanessa, more than I thought. Do the police know any of this?"

"Bits and pieces."

"What did they say?"

"The same thing you did. That I need help."

"That's all?"

"Well, that detective said I'd better get a doctor *and* a lawyer."

Smitty had no idea of what to say. Was this some sort of confession? Was Vanessa the one who'd been terrorizing the Cleo campaign to the point of madness and murder? He could not believe it. But something that was straining between them had finally snapped. To Vanessa he extended his hand and an offer of assistance which he hoped she would be tactful enough not to accept. And then he was out of her gloomy web.

If she was going down, she was not taking the business with her. She was still fighting battles that had been lost long ago. Who cared about race anymore? Brainpower, not brute power, was the name of the game now.

Walking through the hallway back to his own office, he started toying with a new name for the shop. Instead of Smith & Seymour, how about Smith & Company? No, they were already on 44th Street. Smith Unlimited? Yuck. Raleigh Smith? Tony but egocentric. Smith, Inc.? Nice. He didn't want to be overly premature, but he thought it sounded modern and snappy, easy to remember and far less complicated.

CHAPTER TWENTY-THREE

IT WAS not by accident that Jezebel's catered to the fashion crowd during the Paris collections. The slim and chicly dressed were known to be big spenders and little eaters.

While they were thoroughly international, many were often homesick enough to appreciate the pleasurable irony of down-home corn bread in the middle of gourmet Paris. And only the rich could afford to order and *not* eat the pricy, smallish servings of what generations had copiously served up as soul food. Fried chicken, barbecued ribs, jambalaya, black-eyed peas, greens and peach cobbler challenged even the most assiduous anorexics. Even those souls relentlessly modern and scornful of the past felt somehow obliged to reminisce. Taste buds activated fond memories, real and imagined.

At Jezebel's food was love, the unconditional love of the ideal grandmother, who existed somewhere in your personal history if you were lucky, and if you were not, eventually turned up on-screen in late-night movies. Nostalgia reigned, not only in the cuisine but also in the decor. Delicate laces, fringed shawls and hand-embroidered silks hung gracefully from the restaurant's ceiling, making customers feel as if they were sitting on the floor of a huge closet organized by a madly romantic wardrobe mistress. It was a happy-days plantation esthetic transplanted to a narrow Left Bank street off St.-Germain-des-Prés. And why not?

Many others besides Americans not only shared the fantasy of a sunny Southland but were more than willing to pay for it in crisp currency or neat plastic credit cards.

Nicky was entranced. She loved feeling part of the in crowd whose talk was so fast and furiously opinionated. Around Nadja's table sat Val and another model, Alexis. All three had done Saint Laurent that morning, always the last show of the season. There was also Pippo, the male model from Guadeloupe who was sweeping through all the Italian magazines; Andrew, an American assistant designer who lived in Paris with his French lover, Jean-Claude; Elmo; and Derek.

"I thought I saw you in the Chanel show, that black leather strapless at the end, right? I said, Go on, girlfriend."

"No, you didn't, Elmo. You said, I hope girlfriend doesn't fall and break her face."

"After what we've been through, Nicky? I have complete confidence in you."

"That's a lot more than I have."

"You don't have to have it," said Nadja. "If Karl has it, that's enough for the rest of the fashion world."

"Amen," said Andrew. "Kaiser Karl's had the Midas touch these past few seasons."

"So expect to work your butt off in October," Elmo said. "Where Midas leads, the minors are sure to follow."

"Oooo, you're calling Saint Laurent a minor," said Nadja.

"Never, never. He's been too good to me. It's just that now he's beyond competition. He's in a class by himself."

"But, Elmo, that sounds suspiciously like what they say when someone is over the hill."

"Semantics, Val. You're just picking on me because of the hair spray at Mugler." Val stuck her tongue out at him and shook her auburn hair loose to show that no permanent damage had been done, thank God.

"Good point, though," added Nadja. "What does it mean to be at the top? Who's there and how long do you stay?"

"And how do you get to first place in the first place?" asked Andrew.

"I'd say Saint Laurent is still number one," said Elmo, "because he paid his dues with Dior, because he's stuck it out for twenty-five years with Bergé and because he's never denied who or what he is. He also has the impeccably good taste to hire me."

"But I'd say Karl is number one," Val challenged.

"He's German," said Alexis with disdain.

"And so? He's disqualified?" Val asked.

"Come on, you know as well as I do. The French rule the image of fashion. They'll never crown a German king. Especially one that's *not* a tall, blond, swaggering Prussian who forces them to their knees."

"Alex, you've been hanging out in the leather bars too long," said Elmo.

"Talent is what counts," Val insisted, "and Karl's got the talent. He's not German, he's global. He's versatile enough to portion his genius out to several different lines—Chanel, Fendi, and his own label—and *still* take the shots for his perfume ads."

"Which are great?" Pippo asked. "No, please, somebody tell him the truth. No. I think there is such a thing as doing too much, being too many places. How do you say in English? Spreading too wide."

"Spreading yourself too thin," Val corrected him.

"Oh, that's right, too thin. You must concentrate. And then I think number one is in the head, in your own belief. I am number one male model."

"Until?" asked Elmo.

"Until I get scared and forget to believe."

"Until someone younger, cuter and better comes along," said Alexis. "You want to be number one while you're struggling on the way up. Once you get there you just want to survive."

"And to survive means you must evolve," Andrew said. "What gets you to number one is not what keeps you there. You constantly reinvent yourself, restyle yourself. I think change is the key to staying on top."

"Change on the outside, maybe, but not the inside," said Nadja. "You can change country and language and hairstyle. . ."

"And bust size," added Elmo, smiling at Alexis.

"And sexual preference," said Alexis back to Elmo.

"And bank account," added Pippo.

"All of that. But as long as the inside stays strong and honest you'll be number one no matter what anyone else thinks. What do you think, Jean-Claude? We need to hear from the civilians."

"I don't know what to say, Nadja. I am a businessman. Without Andrew I would not even know these names. Because of him I pay some attention and I learn to dress better. But these names, they are only a label. People are not so stupid as to think they are buying the maximum creative genius when they are only buying a dress. These guys could be dinosaurs, extinct, but because the business must go on, the labels get sewn in and they are propped up to sell them. Don't ask me. I am a big cynic. I look at Andrew, who has a grand talent. But backers? They run the other way even when you test negative. Maybe I am too old to be optimistic. Maybe fashion is only for young people. I don't know. Nicky, what do you think?"

Too much was coming at her too fast. Opinions, challenges, information, discussion. She felt a red buzzer going off in her brain: overload. "I think I'd better quit while I'm ahead. What if I'm just a has-been by the time I'm twenty-one?"

"We'll beat your ass up and down Fifth Avenue and the Champs-Elysées," said Elmo. "You can't get out of it that easily. As long as it took to get you, we intend to keep you around for a good old while."

"I wish everybody felt that way."

"Who doesn't?" asked Andrew.

Nobody answered. Instead they ordered more corn bread, poured more wine and waited for the notoriously slow service to provide their main courses. Meanwhile, friends, acquaintances and other fashionalities making the rounds stopped by their table to say a quick hello. Kyle Whitaker and Esmé Klionsky were hosts at a long table of friends. When Esmé went to use the ladies' room she stopped to give Nicky an encouraging pat on the shoulder. Toni Fleming, the novelist, waved across the room to Elmo, who had styled her dreads for the jacket of her latest best-seller. Buster Wilson was having a bite with some of the boys in the band before a late gig at the New Morning jazz club. Pearl Ashton, the psychiatrist in residence at the American Embassy, chided Andrew for missing his last two appointments.

"Pearl, it was collection week. What can I say?"

"You can say you're bringing me a four-ply cashmere twin set instead of the two-ply you usually try to bribe me with."

"See, this is who we wrack our nerves for, trying to create for the modern working woman. And what do we get in return? Beaucoup de grief and very specific instructions."

"Hi, Val, hi, Nadja. Elmo? Hiii. I thought they ran you out of town after last season."

"They tried, Pearl, they tried."

"You know, I heard about Max. I was devastated. I'm so sorry, I know you guys were real close."

"Once upon a time."

"I'm still sorry. He was a unique kind of gentleman."

"And one who preferred blonds."

"Well, let me take my last foot out if I can. Hi, everybody," she continued. "Don't worry, this is just our regular run-of-the-mill conversation."

"Not true," said Andrew. "Our regular conversation is me whining about why am I so different from everybody else. And then Dr. Pearl takes off her extra-strength trifocals and says, 'Well, let's see.'"

"But, Andrew, it's obvious that I couldn't cure you even if I knew how to. I mean, if you stopped asking me questions like that, what would happen to my wardrobe? Just think of everything I'd have to buy, and *retail.*"

"I'm finally out of the closet and what do I get? A slave to fashion for a shrink."

"So, sit, Pearl," said Elmo, "and have a drink with us."

"So sorry, Stevie's already shooting poison darts my way. Some other time when I don't have the wife to contend with. *Ciao,* folks."

They all smiled as Pearl made her way slowly, deliberately stopping to chat with friends, before reaching her partner's table.

"Stephanie Marzotta," said Andrew, "rich bitch extraordinaire and now just a fool for love."

"See, that's another thing you have to be careful of if you want to stay on top," said Pippo.

"What's that?" Nicky asked.

"Love. The whole idea. *Tomber amoureux.* To fall in love. Just the words show you you're headed down."

"But who would want to be on top and be all alone? Not me," said Nadja.

"Me neither," said Nicky.

"Well, Pip, I guess that leaves all the fun to you swelled heads," said Elmo.

"OK, *d'accord.* How do the Americans say? Die hard."

"X-rated, no, Z-rated, you guys," said Val. "Men are all the same."

"Says the virginal voice of experience."

"Nadja, I thought you were on my side. That's a low blow."

"I like that, too," said Pippo. "Low blow, this is the English I like."

To Nicky the laughter, chatter and wine were intoxicating. She felt far away from any danger. Behind her smile she could coast in and out of the conversation, not saying much, not hearing details, but still feeling part of a secure family of friends. A model, a brown-skinned Asian girl with black hair to her waist, came up to their table followed by a man she felt she knew from another life. Her stomach shrank into tiny knots. She kept both hands on her wineglass. And she felt her lips tremble as Gianni Walker kissed her hello. He and his companion went around the table greeting everyone, laughing at the latest gossip, quizzing about the next. Paris seemed a kind of pit stop where everyone checked in but no one stayed. She had not expected to see him here. And after the frustrated evening they had spent together she was surprised at such a nervous reaction.

When Gianni and his friend left, Nadja asked Nicky if she was feeling all right.

"I think so, yeah." Nicky took a long drink.

"Good, because for a minute there, you looked as if you'd seen a ghost," Nadja said.

"I did." She took another swallow. "I was in love with that guy once."

"With Gianni?" She smiled. "Oh, everyone has been."

"And believe me, honey, everyone," Elmo added with exaggerated dismay.

The circle changed mood again, revved up by a sudden cry of outrage at a neighboring table.

A woman dressed in black leather from slouchy hat to pointed toe was screaming through the molten tracks of her black mascara as friends huddled her out of the restaurant. "I am sick and tired, *vraiment, énervée,* by these Americans who come to Europe and try to tell us what to do. *Espèce de cons,* go back to the States. Solve your problems over there. We can never be *racistes* like you. We love Black people. *Vraiment, ça m'enerve.*"

"Jean-Pierre's *première,*" Andrew said. "She gets it every year for using too many Black models in his show."

"Every year," agreed Val as they all turned to witness her spectacular exit.

"I'm ready to go home now," Nicky said quietly to Derek, seated beside her.

"OK, but you know, it's not really late."

"I mean, home home."

"I hear you. Whenever you want. We can leave tomorrow. Is that what you want?"

"The sooner the better."

CHAPTER TWENTY-FOUR

THE SQUINCH lines were returning. Corky watched the creases bunch up between Richard's dark eyebrows. His eyelids constricted, his lips tensed shut in the midst of chewing and the whole center of his face seemed to collapse into one solid, sour wrinkle. After many years of marriage she knew better than to panic over every little facial expression. But still. She looked down at his plate. Half-eaten. Baked pork chops and sweet potatoes, Waldorf salad. She was trying in the kitchen again. Maybe she was trying too hard.

"Something wrong?" she asked.

"It's just not making sense," he said, releasing his frown. He finished chewing, set his silverware down, wiped his mouth and staked his elbows on the kitchen table. "Linking all these Cleo cases together. I don't know. I think it's a big mistake. Too many different motives, different MOs. Something's not clicking . . . The Knight kid is back safe and sound, you say?"

"I don't know if that's what she'd say, but she is back."

"Things might be heating up again. Since our man has moved on to making late-night phone calls to the Thompson house, he just might want to try a house call. And then we'll have a nice little surprise waiting."

"Just when I was getting used to having you around."

"I'm not going anywhere."

"Until the next call." She reached over and kissed his frowning lips. "So are any parts of the case coming together?"

"Yeah, I hope so."

"You don't sound like it."

"It's just the motives are bugging me."

"You always told me motives were the lawyer's business. All you had to worry about was the evidence."

"Yeah, thanks for reminding me."

"Well, are you closing in on anyone?"

"I don't know. The only other person besides you who kept such close tabs on Nicky was Seymour. But she fell apart once she was threatened."

"And I thought she would always be in complete control."

"This last incident really hit a nerve, I think. Didn't you say that she wasn't overly enthusiastic about this new Cleo campaign?"

"She never made any bones about it. But she's in charge of it. Or at least, was. And with Vanessa business always comes first. You know the type. She's a shark, not a killer."

"I thought sharks *were* killers." He sawed the meat carefully into several small pieces and then cut each one even smaller. He wasn't usually so fastidious. Then he started eating again. "This is good, hon. But maybe not so long in the oven next time."

Corky nodded. She'd keep trying. He was eating it *now*, though, wasn't he?

Tina watched as Kayo examined the family pictures that covered the wall of her second-floor sitting room. Her smiling parents in splendid formal wedding attire surrounded by troops of bridesmaids and groomsmen. An ornate silver frame holding a dour Grandmother Thompson in a severe black hat with seven solemn children standing around her. Ella and her parents strolling along Riverside Drive with an imported baby carriage and Ella's precious jewel inside. There were aunts and uncles and cousins whom she knew only from these photographs, lives that had certainly metamorphosed from these isolated moments, lives that had ended for many by now.

Tina and Kayo tried in their own way to relax. This evening's welcome-home dinner for Nicky had been a disaster, ending in an angry standoff between father and daughter. Tina found that Nicky had changed dramatically in less than two weeks, but the change could have been brewing for a long time. She looked more mature. She called Kayo Dad. She wasn't her old affectionate self with Tina but she wasn't as hostile as she had been when she felt so betrayed in St. Martin. She was clearly intent on living in her own place. No one disagreed with her except on the timing. Now was impossible. With threatening notes and silent calls harassing them, she would simply have to wait until the time was right, until she was safe.

Tina felt exhausted by all the tension and hoped that she could find some peace somewhere soon. The music of Shirley Horn, especially her wise way with a lyric, was a step in the right direction. Tina swirled her cognac, glistening like liquid topaz, in the belly of its crystal snifter.

Nicky's running away had forced Tina and Kayo back into conversation. They were still edgy around each other. But out of the wreckage of St. Martin they had salvaged a genuine core of respect to build on. What form a relationship would take was not clear. At least, at best, they were talking.

"She was so beautiful. Ella," he said, pointing to a glamorous picture of Tina's mother in a beaded gown. "Thomas was so proud of her. His possession."

"How could he be proud of owning someone, someone who didn't own herself? My parents always mystified me."

"Is that why you never married?"

"Oh, I see you've crowned me the Queen of Old Maids, too." She smiled.

"No, no, I just wonder . . ."

"I haven't found anyone, haven't had the time to find anyone. And after Carter . . . It's been hard."

"Not too hard to try again."

"No, of course not."

"With me."

"Kayo, please."

"Please, what?"

"Please, let's not go into that again."

"And let's hope it goes away? Let's pretend we have no special feeling for each other? Let's just have a quiet little cognac and call it quits? I'm not going to do it. My eighteen-year-old daughter is showing me what spunk means. I don't agree with her, but I have to respect her and I almost even admire her. I have to say what I feel. Try me, Tina. I care for you. I'm good for you. Give us a chance."

"Maybe when this is all over. When we're not under so much pressure with Nicky and with Dad. Nicky's taught me a lot, too. There're some things I'd like to get straight with my own father, but he's got to get better before I can really talk to him."

"Business?"

"No, family, about my mother. Why he drove her to kill herself."

"You can't be accusing Thomas."

"Why not? He never believed in her, never believed in her talent."

"You can't go on thinking that way, Tina. There're things you've got to understand about your folks. I just don't think I'm the right one to tell you."

"You're here now."

"You sound so brave."

"Tell me, Kayo. Tell me that I'm wrong."

"Well, in a way I can't because you are right. Thomas never did believe in Ella's talent because, well, Ella had no talent. I don't mean that. I don't mean, *no* talent. Listen, your mother was a stunning woman who wanted to be a singer during the era of some of the greatest singers this country will ever know. It wasn't her fault she didn't have more to work with than she did. She tried. I mean, she knew what it was supposed to look like on the outside, but she just didn't have it to give from the inside. Her ambition was much greater than her talent. That's not necessarily a negative. In fact, it's rather common these days. But she also had the notion that somehow the world owed her something. That distorted her vision. I don't know if a true artist ever feels that way.

"Do you know when she first came to Paris, Thomas let her stay a couple of months on her own to try to get it together. I was there, too, so naturally he asked me to keep an eye on her. But it's not as if we moved in the same circles. I had a room at La Louisiane with a one-ring hot plate and a shower to share while she was living in a hotel on the Right Bank with maid service and milk baths. Still, we'd bump into each other once in a while 'cause the music was happening all over town. She even borrowed a couple of boys from the band to back her once or twice. But everybody knew what the deal was. She was paying them, not the club owner, 'cause he was barely paying her. Then the fellas would tell me, it wasn't any big secret, but she just didn't know how to swing. She used to put down the blues, put down jazz and bop and what the old-timers used to call race music. But what she didn't see was that the style didn't matter. It was about something in your soul.

"She took me to lunch one day, I'll never forget. Oysters, steak, wine, I mean it was fabulous. And then she propositioned me."

"My mother?"

"Your gorgeous, sophisticated, ambitious and very lonely mother. Said she'd support me, with Thomas' money, of course, if I would work strictly for her, coach her, arrange songs for her and . . ."

"And?"

"And . . . Well, a lot of people think that talent sort of rubs off and if you can get close enough to it . . ."

"My mother wanted to sleep with you?"

"With anyone who could help her."

"And did you?"

"Of course not. *I* didn't but . . ."

"Wait a minute, Kayo. You're calling my mother a . . . ?"

"I'm not calling your mother anything. All I'm saying is that Ella tried everything she knew. Everything. And when none of it worked, she came back to New York and settled down."

"Settled down . . . To make life miserable for my father?"

"I don't think Thomas would say that at all. Remember, he loved her. He knew all about her and still he loved her, although she didn't know it. She didn't *want* to know it, even when she got sick."

"What do you mean, sick?"

"With the cancer, breast cancer. Didn't you know? That's why she killed herself. She wanted it to be over with right away. We used to talk a lot. She'd call out to California late at night and I knew it was even later here. She was drinking, couldn't get to sleep. She was so miserable. I tried to get her to talk to Becky, you know, thinking that another woman could help, but somehow that never clicked. I don't know if it was some kind of rivalry or envy or what. But I never thought she'd take it as far as she did. She didn't feel Thomas would want her if she was less than perfect and she never gave herself the chance to find out. She didn't want him or you or anyone really, but especially him, to see her waste away and become somebody else. She thought she had already failed him, you know. And you, well, she was so proud of you and who you were becoming on your own. And yet she still felt some kind of competition. It's weird. She couldn't stand losing, not even to people who loved her. *Especially* to people who loved her. I thought you knew, Tina. Please don't cry. I'm so sorry. I always thought you knew that part."

In her bed, in the safest part of her world, Tina scolded herself. She wasn't crying. She wasn't going to cry ever again. Whatever the amount of water allocated for tears was left in her body would have to stay there. Forever. How could she have lived a life so completely misunderstanding her mother, her father and everything?

The phone on her night table rang softly, its red light blinking in the dark beside her private line. No one but family had this number. Now the killer had it, too? She would have to answer. She dreaded the deadly silence on the other end, but she would have to pick up the phone just to stop it from ringing. She didn't bother to turn on the lamp. It would be an obscenely late hour. She knew that would be part of the torture. She would lift the receiver and hold it to her ear. If he said nothing, she would say nothing. Two mutes could play this game. She picked up the phone.

"Tina? Tina, are you there? I know it's late . . . Are you awake? Tina, it's Clarice. Tina, Tommy's gone."

"Clarice, what did you say?"

"I said your father's passed away. He died in his sleep about an hour ago."

His dying woke her up. Clarice thought it was her dream. She'd been watching her son Roland, a grown man with his own son now, but always still a little boy in her dreams. In this dream he was anxious, hopping barefoot on the beach, waving tearfully for her to come in from the deep water. She didn't want him to cry. The water was not too deep for her. In fact, it was rather shallow and perfectly turquoise. But there was so much of it, for so far around, and she felt his small-boy fear and did not want him to be afraid for her so early in life.

But it wasn't Roland crying. And it wasn't the complacent little waves sighing on their way back through the sand and tiny shells that woke her up. It was Tommy's breathing, a gasping struggle between wet and dry, and other strange noises from other parts of his body, this body that she knew so well. His lips arced downward, but he always slept with that face on, as if he were angry at the world for making him waste precious time in bed. Pieces of him, his hands and feet, were trembling as if they were being disconnected or electrically short-circuited. His chest heaved and sank and stopped.

She rang for Nurse and Lucas and for a moment thought she shouldn't turn on the light because it might wake him up, but then she did and she dared to touch him, his shoulders, the shiny scar bisecting his aching, quiet chest, the soft, fine hair of his brows, and she called his name, Tommy, oh, Tommy, no, Tommy, please, and tried to wake him up so he could see her at least, so he could choose between the darkness and her light, so he would open his eyes at least once more and she could reach through them, reach deep inside and keep him with her but Nurse came running and shoved her aside and did what she could and told her to call Doctor and then he was still and the trying was over and his body was silent and she knew he was gone.

Where did he go? He was still warm in the bed where she had just been sleeping and dreaming beside him. Where was the rest of him now that what was there was just a body? Take me with you, Tommy. Take me, too. She sat holding his hand as she had spent so much time doing. Her lips were stretched tight and wide into her cheeks and if her eyes were not so shocked with sadness and pale red tears, they would have been the same lips of her smile.

You spend your life living, secretly looking for love but not admitting it because that, too, is an import from another place where women don't have to work so hard and they can afford to look beautiful all the time and have other people raise their children. You spend your life secretly looking for love and then you secretly find it and then it's gone. A few weeks they'd had together, after years of precious weekends and holiday time-outs from real life. A few days, really, of sleeping close together every night, warm, some distant part of one body always in touch with someplace parallel on the other's. Only a few hours, actually, if you ran all the words together that they'd ever spoken to each other. A pure nothing of time.

His body was still warm. Of course. It took some time for everything to die, for the cold to replace the heat of a lifetime of living. Seventy years. God was good not to turn the heat off right away. She needed time to let him go. To let her anger cool. They were still young lovers, having just found each other, delighting in the newness of every discovery, the infinite surprise of every shared touch. They hadn't had a chance to get bored. She envied couples who stayed together for a long time, even the unhappy ones. She envied their monotony, their tongue-bitten hostility, that law of nature as inescapable as gravity that made some of them sleep, untouching, with their backs to each other every night. It was the every night she envied, the bedrock togetherness that was stronger than love or hate or indifference.

It was when Doctor came that she had to let Tommy's hand go and then she was back to the stranger of herself.

From every cell of Tina's body her shout reached every corner of the house, filling it with anger and pity, sadness and terror and regret that she was, it was, now and forever too late. Derek was the first at her bedside, then Nicky, then Mrs. English. But it was Mrs. English who cradled Tina in her arms and rocked her until the howling subsided into shuddering waves of sobs.

"Should we come over now, Clarice?" Nicky asked over the phone.

"Oh, no, darling, there's nothing to be done here right now. Wait at least till the sun comes up. Help Mona with Tina. I know she's going to take it bad."

"And who's helping you?"

"I'm an old woman, baby, only God can help me."

Nicky wanted to accept her wisdom as truth but after listening to Clarice cry for a few moments, she knew there was no age to tears. The broken heart of an old woman sounded exactly like her own.

Derek retreated to the doorway and there, for just a moment, he watched the three women, three generations of women crying together. He had seen it all his life, wailing women, unashamed to body-surf through their emotions, to keep each other company as they bathed in tears. As he left them to their private ritual, he realized that he had never seen men that way. They let tears out one by one, one man birthing a single tear as if it were a monstrous infant, wiping away all trace as soon as it came. Feeling the weight of the women's sadness, he sat on the steps alone in the hallway and wondered if he would ever be the kind of man whose natural death would cost anyone such an agony of tears.

CHAPTER TWENTY-FIVE

THE BELLMAN deposited an imposing amount of Gucci luggage on the black and white marble squares in Thomas Thompson's foyer. An imposing amount of woman, striding as if she led a retinue of starched retainers, swept into the entryway.

"Good to see you still holding down the fort, Lucas."

"It's good to see you, too, Mrs. Whitman."

"Mrs. Stallworthy now, Lucas. Well, you can take my things into the guest room. As soon as I catch my breath, I'll call Tina. Be a dear and point me to the bar, will you?"

Clarice entered the living room with a wan hello.

"Yes, well, hello. I'm Rosemary Stallworthy, Mr. Thompson's sister. And you are?"

"Clarice."

"From?"

"St. Martin."

"Of course. I knew it from the accent. Thomas always loved the island people. Would you mind fixing me a drink? Scotch with just a splash of soda, please. Three rocks."

In careful gestures Clarice fixed the drink, opened a fresh tin of unsalted cashews and arranged the engraved crystal, silver and a fan of sheer paper napkins on a rosewood tray. She placed it on the coffee table in front of the brocade sofa where Rosemary Stallworthy sat in straight-backed command at one end with her black mink neatly neglected at the other.

"Thank you ever so much," she said, and smiled curtly.

Then Clarice sat down in an armchair opposite her. Mrs. Stallworthy nearly choked on a nut.

"Certainly you have some other work to do?" she asked, trying to clear her throat. "In the kitchen, perhaps?"

"Oh, no, that's all taken care of."

"Well, in a household this size you must have other chores to attend to."

"Actually, I'm waiting for a call to come from the funeral home any minute."

"But I'm here now. I'll take charge of those things. I can understand if poor Tina is too upset to handle details like that but I think such matters are best left to family. Don't you, Clara?"

"Clarice."

"Don't you, Clarice?"

"Absolutely. That's why I'll be talking with them."

"But just who do you think you are?"

"Tommy's wife."

Thomas N. Thompson's sister looked at Clarice, this shapeless creature in painfully plain gray clothes, seeing for the first time the woman, the large heart-shaped diamond resting in the hollow of her neck and the diamond band she wore on her finger. Rosemary Stallworthy drained her glass and, looking no longer at anyone or anything, called out to Lucas to get her things and fetch her a cab. But when she got to the door her bags were sitting in the foyer where the bellman had left them, and, oddly, Lucas was nowhere in sight.

Nicky wrenched open the French doors and stumbled out onto the balcony off her room. She needed the fresh air. She couldn't drink another drop of wine. She had taken the last of her Valium. The lovely room was choking her, the florals growing right off the fabrics, reaching out for her, entwining themselves around her arms and legs. She couldn't breathe in there. Memories and other things crowded the space, and left no room for her.

Looking across 76th Street, she saw the unmarked car still on surveillance. One of the cops nodded to her and, ashamed, she turned her head away. Leaning against the railing and looking down to Riverside Park, she could see faint signs of spring. The eastern winters were hard. Colorless. White cold she knew. Bright slopes in Colorado. But people bunched inside rows of stone houses with lights burning all day, that was new to her. Cave city. Still, the source. Energy, juice, jams. Serious success. She'd have to find her own place, that's all. And right away, or she would go crazy.

"You OK?" Derek startled her.

"I don't know. So much is happening."

"And the beat goes on."

"Yeah, that's why I wanted to talk to you. I've got to leave here, Derek. I'm suffocating. I gotta get out. Now. Help me. If they see you with me . . ."

"Whoa, slow down. You're not going anywhere and you know it. You're confined to quarters until further notice."

"But I didn't *do* anything, Derek."

"Except try to take Tina's car last night. Set off alarms all over the place, scaring everybody to death. Wake up, Nicky!"

"So you think I'm out of control, too?"

"I wouldn't lend you *my* car."

"You don't even *have* a car."

Derek looked at her for a long ferocious minute. "You're crazy."

"Don't you think I have a right to be? Who's next, Derek? I've got to get away from here before somebody else dies."

"It's not your fault. Mr. Thompson was an old man."

"It doesn't matter, don't you see? They take anybody. Makes it look more natural . . ." Her eyes wandered, unfocused, confused.

"You're losing it, Nicky. And it's almost like you want to. As soon as your father gets back, I'm outta here." He shrugged his shoulders, throwing off her despair and madness.

As he headed back inside, she grabbed his arm. "Don't leave me, Derek." Her voice was tiny and pitiful.

"Why not?"

"Am I really that bad?"

"I'd say you're in pretty bad shape."

"And that makes me not a good person?"

"I didn't say that." He did not say that because he did not mean it. She had a willful, selfish quality that scared him. Sure, she was under pressure, the kind of pressure he hadn't felt even in a war. But she was too close to the edge and as far as he was concerned, she could keep that perch all to herself. He wasn't about to go down with her. Not on a mental trip. That wasn't part of the job.

Her soft voice surprised him as much as her question.

"When I get my own place, would you be my bodyguard?" she asked.

"When you get your own place, you'll want somebody to live in."

"Yeah, like you. Will you come with me?"

"Nicky, I couldn't do that."

"Why not?"

"It wouldn't be right . . . And there're things I need to do, go back to school, start a career. I want to be somebody."

"But if you were with me, I could help you with that. I have to do the same thing."

"No, you don't. You're already rich and you don't even have to work hard at it."

"But I want to be somebody else, too."

"But see, I want to be somebody *first*."

The air was fresh and cool but it was still hard for her to breathe. There were things she wanted to say. They seemed pointless now. No one would understand her.

"So, I'm losing you, too? It's so funny. You know, at times, in Paris especially, I thought you had, you know, feelings for me. That's wild, huh?"

"Not that wild." What could he say? That he'd never known anyone like her before? She was the kind of woman who'd be hearing that for the rest of her life. What else could he say? That being so close to her made him nervous, made him wonder how soft she was and what it would feel like to hold her in his arms? He had nothing to give her but himself and that was still a work in progress. He leaned on the railing next to her and looked down toward the park. "In case I never said it before, thanks for Paris." Then he left.

"You're welcome," said Nicky to no one.

It was the time for high oratory.

The time for high fashion and high drama had coincided, peaked and passed, as the congregation and guests of Abyssinian Baptist Church settled in for the funeral of Thomas N. Thompson.

Some barely stifled their scandalized reactions to Tina Thompson dressed in purple ("Well, at least it's trimmed in black, shows some respect!"), seated in the first pew next to Clarice Thompson ("Since when?!" "Girl, I just found out and you know if I just found out, grapes're still green on the vine!") in an ivory white suit. A few others, knowing Thomas, appreciated his parting joke on them all. It was, after all, April 1. But most people just couldn't believe he was gone. And so quickly. It wasn't like him to do things so quickly.

Over two thousand people packed the amphitheater of the church Thomas Thompson had belonged to for almost fifty years. Family and dignitaries sat in the first pews. Seated next to Tina, her aunt Rosemary Thompson Stallworthy was resplendent in a black wool ottoman suit with dark mink at the collar and cuffs. Next to her, Skippy Saunders kept fidgeting with the fringe of the paisley cashmere shawl around her shoulders. Seated on the other side of her, Kayo Knight asked if she was feeling all right.

"I'm so cold, Kayo, looking at Thomas, knowing how cold he is. It's hard to remember when I didn't know him." Skippy sighed wearily. "My daughter's gone and now my dearest friend. What is there left for me?"

"Come on, now. It's almost over."

"I know that, too."

The mayor had already spoken, the deep bags under his eyes expressing a weary determination to persevere. They had known each other for over thirty years, he said. It was for him a deeply personal loss. Many others had participated in the service: business tycoons reading passages from the Bible, the lodge members, the fraternity brothers, a

Thompson Scholar who had gone on to become a Rhodes Scholar. Leontyne, diva emerita but still a homegirl from Mississippi, sang. And now the last of the three ministers to preside was gathering his forces, gaining momentum, ready to take flight.

When he spoke of this being "a time when Black men constitute an endangered species, attacked by poverty and powerlessness, drugs and despair," Kayo Knight, for one, tried to remember when it had not been this way. He tried hard.

And when the clergyman spoke of this being "a time when Black women are being abused, abandoned and viciously, systematically murdered," Tina Thompson, for one, prayed to keep the demons from her own door.

Then when he spoke of "no mortal being able to judge Heaven's design but how fitting it was that this gentle warrior died in a peaceful sleep," Clarice Thompson lowered her head, and watched her two gloved hands hold on to themselves, alone in the lap of her wedding suit.

Mrs. English sat directly behind Mrs. Stallworthy and between Lucas and Connors. While the minister preached she twisted a damp white handkerchief around her finger. She missed her knitting. Knitting was good for relaxing, for accomplishing something practical while something else more mysterious was going on. Ministers were like that, too, good for tying emotions together and putting them into words so you didn't have to go to all the trouble to think and feel and talk, all at the same time. Actually, at a time like this, you did none of that. You simply sat in space and time and tried to get through it all. You let others, who had not lost what you had, express and gesticulate and commiserate. All you really had to do was sit there. That, by itself, she thought, was difficult enough.

"I think it's perfectly ridiculous."

"Don't be so hardheaded, Nicky," Nadja said, sitting cross-legged on the other bed in Nicky's room. "Over two thousand people there? You down front, a sitting duck for a perfect shot from the balcony? You'd have been exposed to too many dangers, come on. It wasn't a safe place to be."

"For Christ's sake, nobody gets killed in a church."

"And we'd like to keep it that way." Nadja looked through the latest French *Elle*.

"Did you have to book out today?"

"No problem. My client rebooked me for tomorrow."

"What'd you say? Sorry, I have to baby-sit?"

"Will you just come off it? It was no problem. Mrs. English definitely had to be there at the funeral. And you definitely had not to be there."

"Or left alone. Ever again. Is that what everyone's decided? You know, even though we had a fight, Derek is still right here in the house. New York's Finest are right outside the door and . . ."

"And extra precautions never hurt anyone."

"But what's the difference between the church and here? There're going to be gobs of people in both places."

"Here there's the minor detail of a metal detector, need I remind you? Front-door screening for everyone's safety. Anyway, when are they expected back?"

"Between five and six, Mrs. E said. First, they have the reception at the church and then the thousand closest friends will be coming back here. There's a ton of food already in the kitchen. You hungry?"

"I don't know. I don't have much appetite these days."

"Why?"

"I'm just nervous, I guess. So many changes so fast."

"You nervous about getting married?"

"Yeah, that, too. That, a lot."

"Now *you* come off it. You and JJ are the perfect couple."

"And then what happens? It can't stay that way. It's like sticking your neck out and asking for trouble."

"D'you ever talk to JJ about it?"

"Are you kidding? He's so excited looking for a new place and doing this and that. How can I say I'm scared?"

"Easy. Read my lips and repeat after me: I'm scared."

"Yeah, well, I can't wait till you get a boyfriend."

"Me either. Jesus, send me a man, please, Lord!"

"You're so crazy. We'll have to start calling you Nookie instead of Nicky."

"I like that. Needy Nookie. Naked Nookie. Naughty by Nature Nookie."

"Stop it!" Nadja reprimanded her. "How can you joke about something so serious?" But she relented when she saw the tears in Nicky's eyes and the despair on her face. She got up and hugged her, apologized and hugged her again.

Nadja was scared. Nicky was in such a strange mood, vacillating between common sense and hysteria. She hadn't seen Nicky drink anything, but medication was a different matter. JJ had suggested that she spend some time with Nicky before the crowd arrived after the funeral. She was glad she'd come but now she didn't know what to do. All she knew was that she couldn't leave her alone.

There were well-meaning people here, Clarice was certain of that. Who they were was the problem. By the hundreds they extended their condolences to her with damp, invasive cheeks and insistent handshakes, sometimes firm, sometimes flabby, but often with a crystalline curiosity glinting in their eyes. The funeral service was magnificent, exactly the right combination of pomp and popularity Tommy would have loved. So many people knew him and cared about him. It was only natural that they would have questions about who she was and what she was doing in his life all of a sudden. But the bustling crowd at the church reception was too much now. All this putting up a brave front, smiling at strangers sincere and otherwise, thanking them for their show of concern, all that was wearing her down.

And was it God's joke on her to hold Tommy's funeral on April 1, what Americans called April Fools' Day? It was one thing to have to hold your head up high in front of people who didn't know you and were prone to think the worst of you. It was another thing altogether to hold your head up when God the All-knowing Himself made fun of you.

"Tina, I don't mean to be rude, but I'm afraid I have to leave. I just can't . . ."

Tina heard the tiny fissures in her voice, saw the cracks begin to vein the smooth round face. "Don't explain a thing. Kayo, maybe you could find Lucas and Connors to take Clarice home."

"Oh, no," Clarice gathered her strength to protest. "They were his friends, too. They deserve to be here. One of the limousine drivers can take me."

"Absolutely not," Kayo said. "You sit tight and I'll be right back."

In minutes Lucas was clearing a path through the crowd so that Mrs. Thompson, accompanied by Mr. Knight, could exit.

In the familiar security of Tommy's car Clarice started to cry. The buildings of Harlem looked so sad, their jagged, empty windows like the blinded eyes and decayed mouths of the living dead who walked the streets. Life had been present once but now black shadows stood, framed by sturdy brick and stone, stronger and longer-lasting than the black joys that used to laugh there. They looked like she felt.

"I'm sorry," she said, "to disrupt things. Everything hurts so much. I didn't mean for you all to come."

"Shhhh, now. Thomas was one of my oldest friends and one of the truest. It's my responsibility to see that you're all right. And neither Lucas nor Connors would hear of you going anywhere without them. Anywhere."

"I appreciate it. But you know I'll be going home, to St. Martin, as soon as I get the ashes back from the crematory. I'd leave tomorrow but I don't want to go without something of him."

"You'll have to stay for the legal proceedings."

"No, I won't. Before we married I made Tommy promise he would change nothing in his estate. I don't want any of his money or any of the art collection, the properties. Nothing like that. I know it's hard to believe but I had the best of him in his love. I could read it in people's eyes at the reception. How much is she going to get? Who does she think she is? Some island gold digger out to fleece a sick old man. I just hate it."

"Anybody who thought like that, Clarice, would not be considered Thomas' friend or Tina's or mine."

"But it's natural, Kayo. I don't hold it against them personally. It's a natural reaction. I'm just tired of it. I loved Tommy a long time. Whether he knew it for a long time or not, he loved me back. That's all I ever wanted, for us to be together. That's all. When he got sick, suddenly he was adamant about us getting married. I never dared think that far. And I told him more than once that we should wait until he recovered. It was Mona who convinced me . . ."

"Mona?"

"Mrs. English. She's the one who convinced me that it's not always wise to wait. That the heart is tuned to rhythms that the mind and body can't hear. She said that you could wait too late. That the very fact of life gives us the illusion of eternity. It's funny, isn't it? We know we have to die one day and yet as long as we don't, we think this living can go on forever."

"Thomas was always one of those people to me. Even after the surgery I never once stopped to imagine that the world could exist without him in it, without him just about running it. He wasn't the dying kind."

"You see what I mean? I think he felt that way, too. I wonder if we women ever have the luxury of that delusion. I don't think so. Maybe that's why we put so much stock in love, thinking that love will live forever. Beyond time, beyond death." She took his hand, smoothing down the blood vessels that looked so hard but felt so soft. And that was how she thanked him as they both sat, quiet in their thoughts, riding back to Tommy's apartment.

Kayo watched the wreckage of Harlem slide by. It was not all dead. People were still here. Stores and shops were still there. The plastic flags of perpetual grand openings still fluttered along 125th Street. The Schomburg Library, Harlem Hospital and the State Office Building. Strivers' Row, Lenox Terrace and Esplanade. They were here. And where they stood, they stood tall. But they were few and far between, and amassed in between were the ruins of a people. If there was hope it was on its last leg. Thomas hadn't been one of those successes who had to make a painful, guilt-ridden return to the old neighborhood. He'd never left. He'd gone out into the world with a pocket full of roots and a knapsack full of dreams and the combination seemed to prosper wherever he went. He had always been a very lucky man in life. And to have died with his woman's love around him made him truly blessed, Kayo thought, truly and finally and eternally blessed.

"I'm so glad to hear from you, Kayo." Tina's voice radiated relief over the telephone. "How is Clarice?"

"She's resting now. We talked for a long while. So many stories to tell. She's quite a wonderful woman. I wish I had known her longer."

"You sound like she's going somewhere."

"You know what I mean . . . And she is going back home."

"Yes, she's told me. Still, she's part of the family and if home is where the heart is, she's home here, too."

"She loves you for that, Tina."

"Well, that's nothing compared to how I feel about what she did for my father all these years. If I could only get Aunt Rosemary to see that. She had the nerve to say that she was glad Clarice had bowed out, that she would never be found under the same roof with her. Can you imagine?"

"She's upset."

"She's mean."

"Well, we'll deal with her later. How are things going with you?"

"The house is packed, of course. It's sad and very wonderful at the same time. The mayor and his wife stopped in along with every other big shot in town. It feels like half the church is here. But people are being very, very kind."

"I'm glad to hear it. It's a tribute to you as much as to Thomas, you know. How's Nicky doing?"

"I'm not sure. Nadja's been an angel. She spent all day with her here. She said Nicky took a nap but then she woke up crying from a nightmare. Something about a car, dying in a car crash. She's very depressed. Had a fight with Derek. I don't know what about. This thing is snowballing, Kayo, and I'm afraid for her. She got dressed and started to come downstairs but she couldn't make it. She's not talking at all, just crying an awful lot. It's like she's completely swamped by grief. I think it's bringing back her mother's death. Max. Everyone, even her grandfather, JJ said. He was with her for a long while and then her old roommate. Mother Saunders is still with her. She's taken everything the doctor prescribed but I don't know if that's helping or hurting. I'll just be glad when you get here."

"I had no idea . . . Look, I think everything's pretty well situated over here for the time being. Clarice said she's in for the evening. Lucas is here and Connors is on standby. I'll be there as soon as I can."

"Do you want me to send your car back?"

"No need for all that. Connors will bring me or I'll take a cab. But what about you? You still haven't told me how you're feeling."

"I'm OK. I'm tough."

"No, you're not. I don't mean that. I mean, tough is not all you are."

"I'll be glad when you get here, Kayo."

"I'm on my way."

Corky and a couple of the bookers were wrapping up a meeting in the big conference room at MacLean. When the audition tapes finished rewinding on the VCR the TV switched over to the six o'clock news. The popular news anchor was an ex-MacLean girl who'd done well, very well.

The crime-of-the-day passed, followed by the litany of lesser-ranking tragedies. And then footage from Thomas Thompson's funeral that afternoon came on. The camera panned over a huge crowd of well-dressed Black mourners with many prominent personalities among them, including many models who had been featured in Aura ads over the years.

But something made Corky nervous, and nervous to the point of silence. Was it just her or did it look to everyone as though the White people there stood out like aberrations? Like the new minority. Like the yogurt-covered raisins she was munching on would stand out in a bowl full of regular raisins. Something was happening to her and she couldn't put her finger on it.

"Quick, Corky, isn't that Vanessa Seymour?" Robin asked. "I'd recognize Her Blondness anywhere. What would she be doing at Thomas Thompson's funeral?"

What would she, indeed? Corky wondered.

"Mrs. English, you're knocking yourself out, doing entirely too much. Upstairs, I mean out of this kitchen and up to your rooms, now. You've shown us what to do and I'm not totally helpless, you know. Off with you. Now."

Tina proceeded to unbutton the white smock Mrs. English always wore over her clothes in the big ground-floor kitchen.

"You know how much I loved Mr. Thompson, Miss Christina." Two fine wet lines crawled down over her lean mahogany cheeks. "The best way to praise him is to serve him, to serve his people."

"You've done that far beyond the call of love or duty. Please, I will not be comfortable until I know that you are off your feet."

"But it's eight-thirty and there're still so many guests here."

"And they'll all have to go home sooner or later. But you're already home. Off you go. You're officially discharged, honorably discharged, of course. I want you upstairs and I don't want to see you or hear one peep out of you tomorrow. I want you to get some rest. This may be your kitchen but it is still my house. Do you understand me, my dear?"

"Of course, I understand, but there is no way that I can agree, Miss Christina."

"Naturally. Just go." Tina embraced the thin shoulders still rigid with protest and wiped the tears from Mrs. English's face. Hugs were entirely too rare between them, and even now she felt that holding her close was a reversal of roles she had never considered. Who would hold Mrs. English when her time came? She thought she knew the answer, but she could not deal with it right now. Tina kissed her on the cheek. "Thank you and good night."

Mrs. English held her hand for an extra moment, and then turned toward the staircase. "Maybe I'll give Mrs., ah, Clarice a call."

Tina was pleased to hear her say that and in that way, too. "Good idea. Give her my love. Oh, and if Mrs. Stallworthy rings you, you are not to respond. She will just have to fend for herself."

"Miss Christina! That is extremely rude behavior."

"Appropriate for an extremely rude person, don't you think? Good night, now."

Tina turned her attention to the several young men and women, assistants and secretaries from the office, who were replenishing trays of hot and cold hors d'oeuvres, finger sandwiches and tiny dessert pastries. The staff had refused to let her hire outsiders. It was their way of honoring the chairman. In service, just as Mrs. English had said and done. Although Tina did not watch Mrs. English mount the stairs, she heard in the slower tread the weight of her sorrow and fatigue. Everyone bore a loss, but not everyone showed it. Today, even Mrs. English did, and hearing her steps made Tina somehow even sadder than seeing the tracks of her silent tears.

Skippy Saunders stood in the foyer of Tina Thompson's brownstone and watched her son-in-law being frisked by a security guard with a metal detector. Necessary, but what an indignity. Life—and death—had become so complicated.

"Kayo, I was waiting for you to come before I left," she said, turning her cheek up for a kiss. JJ held her sand-colored mink coat ready.

"I'm glad you did, Mother Saunders. I wanted to stay with Clarice for a while and I didn't realize what time it was getting to be."

"You've always been sweet like that. And see, here you are. My timing is still pretty good for an old girl. I know Tina is simply exhausted but she's too polite to tell folks when it's time to go home. Maybe you can pass the word. Looks like some of them intend to sit shiva for seven days right here. You take care now. You too, JJ." She slipped into her coat. "And please take care of my poor baby Nicky."

"How is she?" Kayo asked.

"She's not well. Like she's sort of lost touch. She's in a state of shock. It's hitting her all at once and very hard. Easy to understand. I left her with a friend from the business, a White woman she's done some modeling for. Maybe she can help snap Nicky back to the real world."

"Mother Saunders," asked JJ, "you don't remember her name, do you?"

"No, sweetheart. Just a real tall woman, blonde, long hair."

"Excuse me," said JJ as he kissed her goodbye and turned quickly for the crowded stairs.

"I'm gone anyway. My, he's a handsome young man. Reminds me of some on my side of the family. Well, we're all family, anyway, aren't we, Kayo?"

As he smiled to agree, a car horn sounded from the street. "That'll be one of my boys," she said.

"Come on, I'll walk you down."

"Always the gentleman."

"You're very tired, aren't you, Nicky? So tired. I locked the door so you can have some peace, so people won't be barging in every five minutes to see how you're doing. You can't rest with all these interruptions, can you? How can you rest? People keep bothering you and telling you what to do. Telling you what you need. It doesn't have to be like that. You already know what you want to do, don't you? You don't need other people to tell you. You want to leave, leave all this behind. You want all this to be over, all this pain and misery and mystery and crying.

"I can help you, Nicky. Help you to relax. See how I'm just sitting here with my eyes closed? I'm clearing out my mind. Getting rid of all the things that are hurting me, annoying me, tying me down, making it hard for me to do what I want to do. It's easy. I can see it all in my mind's eye. I can see me being free, flying above all this other stuff, leaving it all behind because I'm above it all, flying away.

"You can do it, too. You don't have to stay here, trapped in all this sadness and confusion. You can be free, too. We can meditate together. Just relax right there where you're sitting and close your eyes. Wait, though, maybe we need a little fresh air. That will help clear our minds. Why don't you open the windows, those tall, lovely windows that open onto your balcony? Oh, that's good. Spring is coming. I can feel it. Can you? I can smell it. Can't you? It's coming. Everything is going to be green and happy again.

"Doesn't that air feel good? Good. Why don't we just sit here. No, let's stand. Don't you like being tall? Isn't it nice up here? Over here. Now let's close our eyes. Yes, that's so good. We can fly away together. Here, give me your hand. Oh, it's so cold. Soon it'll be warm. See? So easy. It's so easy. No runway. You just open up and spread your wings and lift off and look, I'm already flying. Can't you feel me flying? I can feel you. I feel everything you feel. You feel everything I feel. Everything. Don't you feel the air on your face, too? It's cool, but doesn't it feel fresh and good? Come with me. I'll take you. We can go anywhere. Where do you want to go? Back home to California? Oh, yes, that's nice. Nice and green and blue. Or maybe someplace you've never been before. Egypt? Good. We'll fly to Egypt and go to the pyramids and walk along the Nile like we used to. Remember? I can take you there. Don't you want to come?"

A sudden knock shook the door to Nicky's room. "Nick, are you OK? This is JJ."

"She's fine, JJ, she's meditating," a woman's voice answered.

"Why is this door locked? Answer me, Nicky. Are you OK?"

"I'm flying," came the faint reply.

"What did you say?"

"She said, 'I'm fine.' Don't worry, she's resting. She needs peace and quiet now."

JJ turned around and found Derek at his shoulder. "What's going on here, man?"

"I don't know. Miss Seymour . . ."

"Vanessa Seymour? From the agency?"

"Yeah. Well, you know how Nicky was when you talked with her and then a lot of people have been in and out and Miss Seymour said she was going to stay with her and lock the door so Nicky could get some rest without being interrupted."

"How long has she been with her?"

"Not long. Ten minutes, max."

"I don't like it."

"What do you mean?"

"I don't like it. I don't like what can happen."

"What do you *mean*?"

Just then Kayo came panting up the stairs. "Nicky's out on the balcony! She's flipped out. She looks like she's trying to fly!"

"Jesus, Kayo, the door's locked."

"And we can't go busting in there and freak her out," said Derek.

Kayo knocked. "Nicky, sweetheart, open the door for Daddy. I need to talk to you. Nicky, are you all right? I can't hear you."

"I'm flying, Daddy."

"Good, open the door so I can see."

"OK, wait a minute."

"No, Miss Nicky, *you* wait a minute," said Vanessa Seymour in a cold whisper as she grabbed Nicky's wrist. "First, you have to try it on your own, then you can show your daddy."

"I want Daddy to see."

"Of course you do, but not yet, not just yet. Let's try it together first. Now close your eyes. Just a little closer and up, higher. That's good and up, spread your wings, see? Come on now, you can . . ."

In one forceful rush Derek and JJ broke through the door. Kayo yelled, "Stop!"

But it was too late. She was soaring, free, flying, then falling lightly through the night air, cool still with just a touch of spring in it, cool on her face and cool in her long blond hair.

Then when she opened her eyes to the soft, strong arms around her and heard the loud, liquid thump far below, Nicky knew that the sound did not come from her. And she also knew that now, at last, now she could truly rest.